THE
PUFFIN
CHILDREN'S
TREASURY

THE PUFFIN
CHILDREN'S TREASURY

OVER 200 STORIES AND POEMS

SELECTED AND WITH COMMENTARY BY
CLIFTON FADIMAN

WITH ADDITIONAL ILLUSTRATIONS BY
LESLIE MORRILL

FOREWORD BY
NAOMI LEWIS

VIKING KESTREL

To Jono, Anne, and Kim,
as they were when they were small
and as they are now that they are big

I am grateful to the staff of my publisher for suggesting several selections that I might well have overlooked. I am more than grateful to my assistant, Siu Zimmerman, who did all the dirty work and whose judgment and good sense have helped immeasurably to give these volumes whatever virtue they may possess.

VIKING KESTREL

Penguin Books Ltd, Harmondsworth, Middlesex, England
Viking Penguin Inc., 40 West 23rd Street, New York, New York 10010, U.S.A.
Penguin Books Australia Ltd, Ringwood, Victoria, Australia
Penguin Books Canada Ltd, 2801 John Street, Markham, Ontario, Canada L3R 1B4
Penguin Books (N.Z.) Ltd, 182-190 Wairau Road, Auckland 10, New Zealand

First published in the USA by Little, Brown and Company (Inc.), 1984, as
The World Treasury of Children's Literature.
First published in Great Britain by Viking Kestrel, 1985

This selection copyright © Clifton Fadiman, 1984
Copyright information for individual works is given on pages v to viii, which
constitute an extension of this copyright page.
New illustrations copyright © Little, Brown and Company (Inc.), 1984
Jacket illustration copyright © Michael Foreman, 1985

Designed by Robert G. Lowe

British Library Cataloguing in Publication Data available

ISBN 0-670-80505-X

Printed in Spain by Graficas Reunidas S.A.

The editor gratefully acknowledges the following publishers and individuals for permission to reprint the selections indicated:

BOOK ONE

'The Fox and the Crane' from *Russian Fairy Tales*, collected by Aleksandr Afanas'ev, translated by Norbert Guterman. Copyright 1945 by Random House, Inc. Copyright renewed © 1973 by Pantheon Books, Inc. Reprinted with permission of Pantheon Books, a division of Random House, Inc.

'A Cat Came Fiddling out of a Barn', 'Desperate Dan', 'The Man in the Wilderness Asked of Me', and 'There Was a Man of Newington', from *Cakes and Custard* by Brian Alderson. Text copyright © 1974 by Brian Alderson. By permission of William Heinemann Limited.

'Alone' by Dorothy Aldis from *All Together* reprinted by permission of G.P. Putnam's Sons. Copyright 1925-1928, 1934, 1939, 1952; renewed © 1953-56, 1962, 1967 by Dorothy Aldis.

'The Husband Who Was to Mind the House', by P.C. Asbjornsen and Jorgen E. Moe. Reprinted by permission of Macmillan Publishing Company.

The complete text from Elsa Beskow's picture book *Pelles Nya Klader (Pelle's New Suit)* published by Albert Bonnier's Forlag, Stockholm, and by Harper & Row, Publishers, Inc. © Albert Bonnier's Forlag 1981. Reprinted by permission of Bonnier Juveniles International.

Selections from *A Bad Child's Book of Beasts*, by Hilaire Belloc. Reprinted by permission of A.D. Peters Limited and Gerald Duckworth & Co. Limited.

'Song of the Pop Bottlers', from *A Bowl of Bishop* by Morris Bishop. Copyright 1954 by Morris Bishop. A Dial Press book. Reprinted by permission of Doubleday & Company, Inc.

From Quentin Blake and John Yeoman, *The Improbable Book of Records*. Text copyright © 1975, 1976 by Quentin Blake and John Yeoman, illustrations copyright © 1975 by Quentin Blake. Reprinted by permission of Penguin Books Limited.

N.M. Bodecker, translator, *It's Raining Said John Twaining: Danish Nursery Rhymes*. Copyright © 1973 by N.M. Bodecker. A Margaret K. McElderry Book (New York: Atheneum, 1973). Reprinted by permission of Atheneum Publishers.

'Mr. Skinner', and 'Mr. 'Gator', from *Let's Marry Said the Cherry, and Other Nonsense Poems* by N.M. Bodecker. A Margaret McElderry Book (New York: Atheneum, 1974). Copyright © 1974 by N.M. Bodecker. Reprinted by permission of Atheneum Publishers.

'Johnny Crow's Garden' by L. Leslie Brooke (Frederick Warne & Co.). Reprinted by permission of the publishers.

'A New Song to Sing About Jonathan Bing', from *Jonathan Bing and Other Verses* by Beatrice Curtis Brown (published by Oxford University Press). Reprinted by permission of Curtis Brown Limited.

Selected illustrations by Clement Hurd and the complete text of *Goodnight Moon*, written by Margaret Wise Brown. Copyright 1947 by Harper & Row, Publishers, Inc. Renewed © 1965 by Roberta Brown Rauch and Clement Hurd. Reprinted by permission of Harper & Row, Publishers, Inc. and World's Work Limited.

Selected illustrations and entire text from *The Story of Babar* by Jean de Brunhoff, translated by Nellie Rieu. Copyright © Methuen Children's Books. Reprinted by permission of Methuen Children's Books.

The Little House by Virginia Burton. Copyright 1942 by Virginia Lee Burton. Copyright © renewed 1969 by George Demetrios. Reprinted by permission of Houghton Mifflin Company.

Text of the title story from *The Talking Cat and Other Stories of French Canada*, written by Natalie Savage Carlson. Copyright 1952, 1980 by Natalie Savage Carlson. Reprinted by permission of Harper & Row, Publishers, Inc.

Excerpt from *The Children of Odin* by Padraic Colum. Copyright 1920 by Macmillan Publishing Co., Inc. Copyright renewed 1948 by Padraic Colum. Reprinted by permission of Macmillan Publishing Co., Inc.

Excerpts from *D'Aulaires' Book of Greek Myths* by Ingri D'Aulaire and Edgar Parin D'Aulaire. Copyright © 1962 by Ingri and Edgar Parin D'Aulaire. Reprinted by permission of Doubleday & Company, Inc.

Play with Me, written and illustrated by Marie Hall Ets. Copyright 1955 by Marie Hall Ets. Copyright renewed © 1983 by Marie Hall Ets. Reprinted by permission of Viking Penguin, Inc.

Contents

BOOK I

BOOK II

Let's Talk

ONE of my favourite books is E. Nesbit's *The Treasure Seekers*. It's about six children who, noticing that their father is having trouble paying his bills, decide to help out by digging for treasure. The narrator of the story, one of the children, never tells us his name, and part of the fun lies in guessing which one it is. But I have never met a reader who wasn't clever enough to guess it. It's Oswald.

The uncle of Albert, the boy-next-door, is a professional author, so perhaps that gave Oswald the idea of writing the story. Anyway, Oswald has this to say:

> I have often thought that if the people who write books for children knew a little more, it would be better. I shall not tell you anything about us except what I should like to know about, if I was reading the story and you were writing it. Albert's uncle says I ought to have put this in the preface, but I never read prefaces, and it is not much good writing things just for people to skip. I wonder other authors have never thought of this.

I wonder, too. I wondered for some time about writing this talk. Suppose it turned out to be something "just for people to skip"? Then I realized that the world wouldn't end if you *did* skip it. The important thing is to read the stories in this book, or as much of it as you want to. That would satisfy me. Nevertheless — for those still with me — I'd like to explain a few things about the book and also talk for a few minutes about reading in general.

Reading is one of the few things I know much about. I started at four and I've kept at it for over three-quarters of a century with occasional interruptions for eating, sleeping, and a few other matters. Within that vast stretch of years my most enjoyable reading was done between four and fourteen. You yourself are probably between four and fourteen. As far as reading is concerned, you're lucky. That's the best time.

During those ten years I read for reading's sake. I didn't do it to learn anything, though I found later on that I had learnt a lot. I didn't read to prepare myself for a grown-up career, though I found later on that my ability to read helped me to make a living. I didn't read because anybody told me to. I didn't read to get ahead of anyone else, or to improve my marks in school. I read for the same reason we all like to open Christmas gifts. Each book was a surprise package stuffed with things I had no idea ever existed.

I marvelled over the miracle of language. How could a few punctuation marks plus words made out of twenty-six letters be put together so as actually to *make* (inside my head) people, animals, stories, landscapes, streets, towns, and even ideas? Here I was, a rather dull boy looking at an unopened book. Then within a short time the dull boy found he was entertained, amused, saddened, delighted, mystified, scared, dreamy, puzzled, astonished, held in suspense — all depending on what was in those pages. And sometimes he was bored — a perfectly reasonable thing to be and a good mood in which to develop judgement, for we can learn from what we dislike as well as from what we like.

My wish is that this book will give you some of these feelings — though I hope not boredom. It's good to get such feelings at an early age. They're never quite the same for the older reader. The older reader gets some of them, but more thinly, more weakly. He gets others, too, more complicated perhaps. But what he doesn't get in quite the same way is — surprise.

Let me tell you how I put this book together. Mainly I followed one rule: I have included nothing I didn't myself enjoy reading — and rereading. The reason I didn't worry about you or what you might like is simple: you're different from me just as you're different from each and every one of the 4.4 billion people (that's a rough count) attached to the skin of our planet. Not everything in these books will interest all of you, and that's okay. And there's an enormous amount of reading not included that some of you might well prefer. That's okay, too. If your tastes and mine come together on a fair quantity of the contents, that's good enough.

You'll notice that this book is aimed more or less at younger readers — say from four to eight. The next volume will be aimed at older readers — say from nine to thirteen or fourteen. But my aim is very uncertain; I'd never win a medal for marksmanship. There's really no such thing as an eight-year-old reader or a twelve-year-old reader. There isn't even any such thing as an eighty-year-old reader, for if there were I could never have put the set together with as much pleasure as it has given me. Read what, when, and where you like. Think of these books not as "graded" (except very roughly) but rather as a vast country, crowded with varied landscapes, inviting exploration.

Some people like to read *through*. Others like to read *in*. I have known some odd folk who have gone through the entire *Encyclopaedia Britannica*, beginning with Å (which is not an ordinary A but a unit of wavelength) and ending with Zwyny, who was Chopin's first piano teacher. If you would like to read this set that way, go ahead. My own preference would be to skip around and read according to my mood. But of course those *Britannica* readers who did that would probably die without knowing that Å is a unit of wavelength.

If you'll glance over the table of contents you'll see that there's not much system in the arrangement. I do, true enough, start with nursery rhymes and fables because that's how we usually start reading or being read to. But after that — with one small exception — this set is a plum pudding waiting for your thumb.

The exception is this. I've alternated, generally speaking, prose and verse, stories and rhymes. I don't want to fool you, so I'll tell you why I did it. It's to trap those of you who think you don't like verse. If I put all the verse together in one place you might never read it. But if you come upon it accidentally, you won't be prepared to skip it.

Now, about verse. There are splendid exceptions, but in school "poetry" is often taught in a way guaranteed to make some children think they dislike it. I was taught that way — as if verse were a subject like the multiplication table — and it took me a long time to get untaught.

The fact is that verse is just as "natural" a way of communicating as are the sentences you are now reading. It's just a special way of saying things that can't be said as well in any other way, as computer language is such a way. In a sense verse has a language of its own just as football does, or chess. The words aren't necessarily different from ordinary words, but they're put together differently. Also, they affect us differently, as rock affects us in a way classical music doesn't.

Not only is verse a special way of saying certain things (not all things) but it's often the most *efficient* way. It does more *work* on your mind and feelings than ordinary language does. Often ordinary language really cleverly conceals some of the tricks of verse. I can say to you: "Always stop and look around and listen for an approaching truck when you're crossing the street." You'd understand me perfectly well. But if I put up a sign reading, "*Stop! Look! Listen!*" you'd understand even better. It's not poetry but, like poetry, it has rhythm. *Stóp, loók, lísten.* And the *l*'s that begin *look* and *listen* somehow make the words creep into our minds and stay there.

To show how efficient verse can be let's take a simple example. A lot of bees are buzzing around. Clear? Sure, perfectly clear. But suppose you wanted to do more than make that clear statement. Suppose you wanted to say something more interesting than "A lot of bees are buzzing around". Suppose you wanted to put the statement in a form that would really give a *feeling* of how those bees sounded and also wanted to state the fact in a way hard to forget. Here's how one man put it: "And murmuring of innumerable bees". Say the line softly two or three times. Ask yourself why it makes you hear and feel and even see more than "A lot of bees are buzzing around". If you come up with the answers (and they're easy) you'll begin to see why verse can sometimes perform more work than prose can. And this is just as true of "Humpty-Dumpty" as it is of the poetry of William Shakespeare.

So even if you think you don't like verse, I wish you'd give it a try. None of it you'll find here is hard to understand. Most of what I've included is funny but that doesn't mean it's not important. Some of it is plain silly, because at times people enjoy being silly. Once you've enjoyed these light pieces you can, if you wish, go on to discover the entire world of poetry by yourself.

As you work or play your way through the set you'll see that at times I've led off a selection with a few sentences or paragraphs of my own. You may read these little introductions or not, as you please. At times they tell you something about the author's life; at times they express some idea or feeling I had about the piece. When I had nothing to say, I said nothing, which is a rule I wish I had followed during my career as a writer. In general, good writing speaks for itself. But the brief forewords may occasionally tease you into doing more reading of that particular author. That was the idea.

Another thing. Almost all the pieces (and all of the verse) in this book are complete in themselves, with a beginning, a middle, and an end. But in the next volume some are parts of longer stories. It can't be helped. There just wouldn't be room to print in full the novels from which these parts are taken. The idea, of course, is to get you to read the complete novel, available in your library or through your bookshop.

However, some long stories or novels just don't break up into short, understandable episodes. In order that such good books and authors may not be entirely lost, I've added a list of them at the end of this talk. Sometimes, after the author's name I've added what I consider her or his best book. But please remember that this list doesn't include all the interesting storytellers there are. It may fail to include some authors you're particularly fond of. The works of all the writers on the list appear in English even though some of them may not have been written in English originally.

A last word. I suppose this set is for two kinds of children: those who love to read and those who think they don't.

Those who love to read will find their way around without trouble. They'll use the set as a springboard for further exploration of the authors and books represented. They will be wise enough to know that they can't like everything. Also they will be wise enough to know that if something does not hook them at first reading, it may prove enjoyable at a later time or when they're in a different reading mood. They will understand the basic difference between reading and watching most of TV: reading makes the mind and imagination do some interesting work or play, and most of TV simply doesn't. In another of my favourite books, Louise Fitzhugh's *Harriet the Spy*, Harriet sits down to read. "How I love to read, she thought. The whole world gets bigger. . . ." Those who are like Harriet will know that the secret, the magic is in the phrase "the whole world gets bigger".

As for those who think they don't like reading, well, I know they're making a mistake, just as all of us do when we try to judge ourselves. Now is the time to give reading a chance, for if you don't get the habit when you're young, you may never get it. And if you don't get it, you may grow up to be just as dull as most adults are. For they're the ones for whom, as Harriet would say, the world never got bigger.

Some Good Writers Who Don't Appear in These Books

RICHARD ADAMS
Watership Down
JOAN AIKEN
The Wolves of Willoughby Chase
WILLIAM H. ARMSTRONG
Sounder
BERNARD ASHLEY

HANS BAUMANN
NINA BAWDEN
LUDWIG BEMELMANS
Madeline
PAUL BERNA
A Hundred Million Francs
L. M. BOSTON

FRANCES HODGSON BURNETT
HESTER BURTON
BETSY BYARS
JOHN CHRISTOPHER
RICHARD CHURCH
  Five Boys in a Cave
SUSAN COOPER
ROBERT CORMIER
HELEN CRESSWELL
  The Piemakers
PETER DICKINSON
ELEANOR ESTES
  The Moffats
J. MEADE FALKNER
  Moonfleet
PENELOPE FARMER
NICHOLAS FISK
JANE GARDAM
LEON GARFIELD
ALAN GARNER
RUMER GODDEN
MARIA GRIPE
RENÉ GUILLOT
VIRGINIA HAMILTON
CYNTHIA HARNETT
ROBERT A. HEINLEIN
  Farmer in the Sky
RUSSELL HOBAN
  You'll find something by Mr. Hoban in
  the set, but his masterpiece is a long novel
  called *The Mouse and His Child*
ANNE HOLM
  I Am David
TOVE JANSSON
DIANA WYNNE JONES
ERICH KÄSTNER
GENE KEMP
CLIVE KING
DICK KING-SMITH
ERIC KNIGHT
  Lassie-Come-Home
A. LAMORISSE
  The Red Balloon

URSULA K. LE GUIN
MADELEINE L'ENGLE
  A Wrinkle in Time
JOAN LINGARD
PENELOPE LIVELY
GEORGE MACDONALD
JAN MARK
JOHN MASEFIELD
  The Bird of Dawning
ANDRÉ MAUROIS
  Fattypuffs and Thinifers
WILLIAM MAYNE
E. NESBIT
ROBERT C. O'BRIEN
SCOTT O'DELL
MARY O'HARA
  My Friend Flicka
KATHERINE PATERSON
K. M. PEYTON
ANTOINE DE SAINT-EXUPÉRY
  The Little Prince
IAN SERRAILLIER
  The Silver Sword
MARGERY SHARP
  The Rescuers
DODIE SMITH
  The Hundred and One Dalmatians
IVAN SOUTHALL
NOEL STREATFEILD
MILDRED D. TAYLOR
JOHN ROWE TOWNSEND
GEOFFREY TREASE
HENRY TREECE
ALISON UTTLEY
  A Traveler in Time
A. RUTGERS VAN DER LOEFF
  Avalanche!
ROBERT WESTALL
  The Machine Gunners
URSULA MORAY WILLIAMS
PATRICIA WRIGHTSON
ELIZABETH YATES
PAUL ZINDEL

Foreword

THAT formidable fairy whom prudent parents, royals especially, were well advised to invite to their daughter's christening (or else, or else), was apt to bestow such gifts on the infant as beauty, virtue and such. These pretty offerings have now become hard to define, easy to purchase, or of dubious current value. As for the spell against spindle-prick, when did you last see a spindle? But no child of the time was ever presented with what would now be a gift of utmost worth – an enduring passion for reading. I say "now", for in the heyday of fairy-power, books for the young were few, if any at all. What did the little Brontës (time: around the 1820s) have on their shelves? Not a single cheerful children's picture book, you may be sure. But leap to our own time, and what a change! Never in human history, anywhere in the world, has such an endless feast of books awaited the reading child. And (need I remind you), as with roller skating or swimming or playing a musical instrument, the earlier you tumble in the better. Rapport with the printed word comes fast to the very young, and these two books are meant to entice the youngest children into the endless wonders of the word.

Mr. Fadiman has rightly opened with a handsome group of nursery rhymes. These wild and sturdy verses, often heard before an infant has mastered walking and talking, are almost always the first human experience of verbal magic (call it poetry, literature if you like), of time and distance, the gossip of history, the echoes of love and loss and the day's toil, of night and winter, of the comic use of words, of the pattern of human life. Then the pages of these two books move to fairytale, myth and fable; after that it is open country. Among the numerous items I am glad to find are Sendak's *Where the Wild Things Are*, Lobel's story "Letter for Toad", Lindgren's *The Tomten*, "Ramona's Great Day" from Cleary's *Ramona The Pest*, something of Pooh, the Minarik/Sendak *A Kiss for Little Bear*, Alice Ritchie's *Two of Everything*, and plenty of other goodies.

True, the selection is a personal one (as Mr. Fadiman himself points out), and if I mention a few of the splendid books or stories which he has somehow missed, it is only to offer further suggestions which parents or teachers or other such minders might be glad to have. Two of the best long books (long, but in short suspenseful episodes) that I know for the youngest children are Meindert DeJong's *The Wheel on the School* and Paul Biegel's *The King of the Copper Mountains*. Add these to your list. Other essentials, to my mind, are *Tilly's House* by Faith Jacques, *Monty*, and *Clams Can't Sing* by James Stevenson, "Tearwater Tea" from *Owl at Home* by Arnold Lobel, *Dogger* by Shirley Hughes, almost anything for the very young by Dorothy Edwards, and by William Mayne (let's say, *The Patchwork Cat*, with Nicola Bayley's pictures), Craft's and Blegvad's *The Winter Bear*, any of Tony Ross's pictured fairy tales (say, *Puss in Boots*), David McKee's *I Hate My Teddy Bear*, the Ahlbergs' *Burglar Bill*, Ruth Brown's *A Dark, Dark Tale*, Mimi Vang Olsen's *The Fur Children* – where shall I stop?

Certain views and attitudes have, of course, changed since Mr. Fadiman's childhood. Most thoughtful children today detest the idea of lions, tigers, elephants and bears made objects of fun in wretched circuses, to the sickening sound of the ringmaster's cracking whip. As for sentimental tales about bullfights! How did the silly story of Ferdinand get into this book? Many also feel today that the wolf, most misjudged of animals, has been massacred almost to extinction because of its undeserved "baddy" role in folk lore and fairy tale, – *not*, by the way, in Kipling's Jungle Books. Readers-aloud will know which tales to avoid. And there is enough here *without* these sadistic items, to give a child the beginnings of the enduring passion I spoke of at the start. Soon that fortunate child will find that a book will make him or her a welcome guest in the wildest and strangest places in the world, in bygone or future time. It has the power to dissolve the walls of the dullest room in the dullest town. No one can intrude on the reader's country, or have any idea how far away the child with the book has escaped.

Naomi Lewis

THE
PUFFIN
CHILDREN'S
TREASURY

BOOK ONE

NURSERY RHYMES

There are millions of books in the world and no one will ever read them all. There are millions of songs in the world and no one will ever sing them all. But almost all the people in the world when they are very small will read or sing or listen to some of the nursery rhymes in this book or rhymes much like them.

Almost everybody who talks English knows Jack Horner, Jack Sprat, John who went to bed with his trousers on, Johnny Green who put Pussy in the well, Jack a Nory, Jack who fell down and broke his crown, Jack who jumped over the candlestick, and that poor Jack who, if he cries, shall have nothing but mustard. (You see, I've mentioned *only* the Jacks and Johns.)

Sometimes these rhymes are called Mother Goose rhymes, nobody knows exactly why. Nor does anybody know when they began or who made them up. They are told and sung everywhere. In fact, if you read on in this book you'll find rhymes sung by Hungarian children, Danish children, Chinese children — and they're much like the ones I learnt many years ago.

I have never forgotten them. When I began to make up this book I had to reread them all and I found that I felt almost exactly as I did more than seventy-five years ago when I first learnt to read and sing them. I found myself laughing at the three little ghostesses who ate buttered toastesses. I found myself lost in wonder when I read "Over the hills and far away". I found myself getting all dreamy (and I still don't know why) when I read "How many miles to Babylon. . . ." I found my tongue still tripping over "Peter Piper picked a peck of pickled peppers".

With these funny, sad, silly, sensible, odd, crazy little verses I began my own job in life, which turned out to be reading and writing. All the many words I have written will be forgotten, but these nursery rhymes I first read will live forever. Or at any rate as long as there are small children who like to laugh, sing, and dream — and I hope that means forever.

English Nursery Rhymes

A cat came fiddling out of a barn,
With a pair of bagpipes under her arm;
She could sing nothing but fiddle cum fee,
The mouse has married the bumble-bee.
Pipe, cat; dance, mouse,
We'll have a wedding at our good house.

A diller, a dollar,
A ten o'clock scholar,
What makes you come so soon?
You used to come at ten o'clock,
But now you come at noon.

A wise old owl sat in an oak,
The more he heard the less he spoke;
The less he spoke the more he heard.
Why aren't we all like that wise old bird?

Alas! Alas! for Miss Mackay!
    Her knives and forks have run away;
    And when the cups and spoons are going,
    She's sure there is no way of knowing.

As Tommy Snooks and Bessy Brooks
    Were walking out one Sunday,
Says Tommy Snooks to Bessy Brooks,
    Tomorrow will be Monday.

Awake, arise,
    Pull out your eyes,
And hear what time of day;
    And when you have done,
    Pull out your tongue,
And see what you can say.

Baa, baa, black sheep,
   Have you any wool?
Yes, sir, yes, sir,
   Three bags full;
One for the master,
   And one for the dame,
And one for the little boy
   Who lives down the lane.

Barber, barber, shave a pig,
How many hairs will make a wig?
Four and twenty, that's enough.
Give the barber a pinch of snuff.

Betty Botter bought some butter,
But, she said, the butter's bitter;
If I put it in my batter
It will make my batter bitter,
But a bit of better butter
Will make my batter better.
So she bought a bit of butter
Better than her bitter butter,
And she put it in her batter
And the batter was not bitter.
So 'twas better Betty Botter bought a bit
   of better butter.

Come, let's to bed,
Says Sleepy-head;
Tarry a while, says Slow;
Put on the pot,
Says Greedy-Gut,
We'll sup before we go.

Desperate Dan
The dirty old man
Washed his face
In a frying-pan;
Combed his hair
With the leg of a chair;
Desperate Dan
The dirty old man.

Diddle, diddle, dumpling, my son John,
Went to bed with his trousers on;
One shoe off, and one shoe on,
Diddle, diddle, dumpling, my son John.

Ding, dong bell,
Pussy's in the well.
Who put her in?
Little Johnny Green.
Who pulled her out?
Little Tommy Stout.
What a naughty boy was that
To try to drown poor pussy cat,
Who never did him any harm,
And killed the mice in his father's barn.

Doctor Foster went to Gloucester
In a shower of rain;
He stepped in a puddle,
Right up to his middle,
And never went there again.

For want of a nail
  The shoe was lost,
For want of a shoe
  The horse was lost,
For want of a horse
  The rider was lost,
For want of a rider
  The battle was lost,
For want of a battle
  The kingdom was lost,
And all for the want
  Of a horseshoe nail.

Georgie Porgie, pudding and pie,
Kissed the girls and made them cry;
When the boys came out to play,
Georgie Porgie ran away.

Goosey, goosey gander,
    Whither shall I wander?
Upstairs and downstairs
    And in my lady's chamber.
There I met an old man
    Who would not say his prayers,
I took him by the left leg
    And threw him down the stairs.

Hark, hark,
    The dogs do bark,
The beggars are coming to town;
    Some in rags,
    And some in jags,
And one in a velvet gown.

Here am I,
    Little Jumping Joan;
When nobody's with me
    I'm all alone.

Here's Tom Thumb,
　　Little fellow come,
Dance between my fingers,
　　Rum-tum-tum.
Mind your little steps,
　　Mind you never fail
To take a spring and jump
　　Over my thumbnail.

Hey diddle, diddle,
The cat and the fiddle,
The cow jumped over the moon;
The little dog laughed
To see such sport,
And the dish ran away with the spoon.

Hickory, dickory, dock,
The mouse ran up the clock.
　The clock struck one,
　The mouse ran down,
Hickory, dickory, dock.

Higglety, pigglety, pop!
The dog has eaten the mop:
　The pig's in a hurry,
　The cat's in a flurry,
Higglety, pigglety, pop!

Hot cross buns! Hot cross buns!
One a penny, two a penny,
Hot cross buns!
If your daughters do not like them
Give them to your sons;
And if you have not any of these pretty little elves,
You cannot do better than eat them yourselves.

How many miles to Babylon?
Threescore and ten.
Can I get there by candlelight?
Yes, and back again.
If your heels are nimble and light,
You may get there by candlelight.

Humpty Dumpty sat on a wall,
Humpty Dumpty had a great fall;
All the King's horses and all the King's men
Couldn't put Humpty together again.

I had a little castle upon the sea sand,
One half was water, the other was land;
I opened my little castle door, and guess what I found;
I found a fair lady with a cup in her hand;
The cup was golden, filled with wine;
Drink, fair lady, and thou shalt be mine!

I had a little husband,
     No bigger than my thumb;
I put him in a pint pot
     And there I bade him drum.
I gave him some garters
     To garter up his hose,
And a little silk handkerchief
     To wipe his pretty nose.

I had a little nut tree,
     Nothing would it bear
But a silver nutmeg
     And a golden pear;
The King of Spain's daughter
     Came to visit me,
And all for the sake
     Of my little nut tree.
I skipped over water,
     I danced over sea,
And all the birds in the air
     Couldn't catch me.

I see the moon,
     And the moon sees me;
God bless the moon,
     And God bless me.

If all the seas were one sea,
What a *great* sea that would be!
If all the trees were one tree,
What a *great* tree that would be!
And if all the axes were one ax,
What a *great* ax that would be!
And if all the men were one man,
What a *great* man that would be!
And if the *great* man took the *great* ax,
And cut down the *great* tree,
And let it fall into the *great* sea,
What a splish-splash that would be!

If all the world was paper,
    And all the sea was ink,
If all the trees were bread and cheese,
    What should we have to drink?
It's enough to make a man like me
    Scratch his head and think.

If I'd as much money as I could spend,
I never would cry, Old chairs to mend.
Old chairs to mend! Old chairs to mend!
I never would cry, Old chairs to mend.

I'll tell you a story
 About Jack a Nory,
And now my story's begun;
 I'll tell you another
 Of Jack and his brother,
And now my story is done.

Jack and Jill
Went up the hill,
To fetch a pail of water;
Jack fell down,
And broke his crown,
And Jill came tumbling after.

Jack Sprat could eat no fat,
His wife could eat no lean,
And so between them both, you see,
They licked the platter clean.

   Julius Caesar made a law,
     Augustus Caesar signed it:
   That everyone that made a sneeze
     Should run away and find it.

Little Boy Blue,
    Come blow up your horn,
The sheep's in the meadow,
    The cow's in the corn.
Where is the boy
    Who looks after the sheep?
He's under a haystack
    Fast asleep.
Will you wake him?
    No, not I,
For if I do,
    He's sure to cry.

Little Jack Horner
Sat in the corner,
Eating his Christmas pie;
He put in his thumb,
And pulled out a plum,
And said, What a good boy am I!

Little Miss Muffet
Sat on a tuffet,
Eating her curds and whey;
There came a big spider,
Who sat down beside her
And frightened Miss Muffet away.

Little Polly Flinders
Sat among the cinders,
Warming her pretty little toes;
Her mother came and caught her,
And whipped her little daughter
For spoiling her nice new clothes.

Little Tee-wee,
He went to sea,
In an open boat;
And when it was afloat,
The little boat bended.
My story's ended.

Little Tommy Tittlemouse
Lived in a little house;
He caught fishes
In other men's ditches.

Little Tommy Tucker
  Sings for his supper:
What shall we give him?
  White bread and butter.
How shall he cut it
  Without e'er a knife?
How will he be married
  Without e'er a wife?

Mary, Mary, quite contrary,
  How does your garden grow?
With silver bells and cockle shells,
  And pretty maids all in a row.

Monday's child is fair of face,
Tuesday's child is full of grace,
Wednesday's child is full of woe,
Thursday's child has far to go,
Friday's child is loving and giving,
Saturday's child works hard for a living,
And the child that is born on the Sabbath day
Is bonny and blithe, and good and gay.

Oh that I were
  Where I would be,
Then would I be
  Where I am not;
But where I am
  There I must be,
And where I would be
  I cannot.

Old King Cole
  Was a merry old soul,
And a merry old soul was he;
  He called for his pipe,
  And he called for his bowl,
And he called for his fiddlers three.

Old Mother Hubbard
 Went to the cupboard,
To fetch her poor dog a bone;
 But when she got there
 The cupboard was bare,
And so the poor dog had none.

She went to the baker's
 To buy him some bread;
But when she came back
 The poor dog was dead.

She went to the undertaker's
 To buy him a coffin;
But when she came back
 The poor dog was laughing.

She took a clean dish
 To get him some tripe;
But when she came back
 He was smoking a pipe.

She went to the alehouse
 To get him some beer;
But when she came back
 The dog sat in a chair.

She went to the barber's
 To buy him a wig;
But when she came back
 He was dancing a jig.

She went to the seamstress
    To buy him some linen;
But when she came back
    The dog was a-spinning.

The dame made a curtsey,
    The dog made a bow;
The dame said, "Your servant,"
    The dog said, "Bow-wow."

Old woman, old woman,
    Shall we go a-shearing?
Speak a little louder, sir,
    I'm very thick of hearing.
Old woman, old woman,
    Shall I love you dearly?
Thank you very kindly, sir,
    Now I hear you clearly.

One misty, moisty morning,
    When cloudy was the weather,
I chanced to meet an old man,
    Clothéd all in leather.
He began to compliment
    And I began to grin.
How do you do? And how do you do?
    And how do you do again?

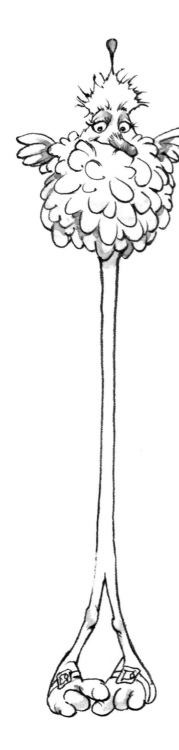

One, two,
Buckle my shoe;

Three, four,
Shut the door;

Five, six,
Pick up sticks;

Seven, eight,
Lay them straight;

Nine, ten,
A good fat hen;

Eleven, twelve,
Who will delve;

Thirteen, fourteen,
Maids a-courting;

Fifteen, sixteen,
Maids a-kissing;

Seventeen, eighteen,
Maids a-waiting;

Nineteen, twenty,
My stomach's empty.

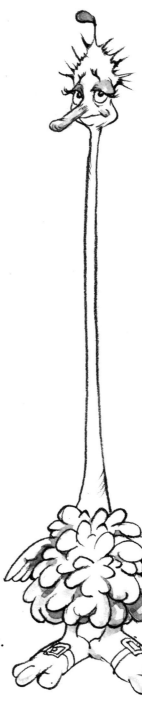

Pease porridge hot,
Pease porridge cold,
Pease porridge in the pot
Nine days old.
Some like it hot,
Some like it cold,
Some like it in the pot
Nine days old.

Peter, Peter, pumpkin eater,
Had a wife and couldn't keep her;
He put her in a pumpkin shell
And there he kept her very well.

Peter Piper picked a peck of pickled peppers;
A peck of pickled peppers Peter Piper picked.
If Peter Piper picked a peck of pickled peppers,
Where's the peck of pickled peppers Peter Piper picked?

Polly put the kettle on,
Polly put the kettle on,
Polly put the kettle on,
  We'll all have tea.

Sukey take it off again,
Sukey take it off again,
Sukey take it off again,
  They've all gone away.

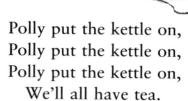

Pussy cat, pussy cat,
  Where have you been?
I've been to London
  To look at the Queen.
Pussy cat, pussy cat,
  What did you there?
I frightened a little mouse
  Under her chair.

Rub-a-dub-dub,
Three men in a tub,
And how do you think they got there?
    The butcher, the baker,
    The candlestick maker,
    They all jumped out of a rotten potato,
'Twas enough to make a man stare.

Sally go round the sun,
Sally go round the moon,
Sally go round the chimney pots
On a Saturday afternoon.

Sammy Smith would drink and eat
    From morning until night;
He filled his mouth so full of meat,
    It was a horrid sight.

Indeed he ate and drank so fast,
    And used to stuff and cram,
The name they called him by at last
    Was Greedy, Greedy Sam.

Simple Simon met a pieman,
    Going to the fair;
Says Simple Simon to the pieman,
    Let me taste your ware.

Says the pieman to Simple Simon,
    Show me first your penny;
Says Simple Simon to the pieman,
    Indeed I have not any.

Simple Simon went a-fishing,
    For to catch a whale;
All the water he had got
    Was in his mother's pail.

Simple Simon went to look
    If plums grew on a thistle;
He pricked his fingers very much,
    Which made poor Simon whistle.

He went for water in a sieve
    But soon it all fell through;
And now poor Simple Simon
    Bids you all adieu.

Sing a song of sixpence,
    A pocket full of rye;
Four and twenty blackbirds
    Baked in a pie;

When the pie was opened
    The birds began to sing;
Wasn't that a dainty dish
    To set before the King?

The King was in his counting house
    Counting out his money;
The Queen was in the parlor
    Eating bread and honey;

The maid was in the garden
    Hanging out the clothes;
There came a little blackbird,
    And snipped off her nose.

Jenny was so mad,
    She didn't know what to do;
She put her finger in her ear,
    And cracked it right in two.

Solomon Grundy,
Born on a Monday,
Christened on Tuesday,
Married on Wednesday,
Took ill on Thursday,
Worse on Friday,
Died on Saturday,
Buried on Sunday.
This is the end
Of Solomon Grundy.

Star light, star bright,
First star I see tonight,
I wish I may, I wish I might,
Have the wish I wish tonight.

The lion and the unicorn
    Were fighting for the crown;
The lion beat the unicorn
    All around the town.

Some gave them white bread,
    And some gave them brown;
Some gave them plum cake
    And drummed them out of town.

The man in the wilderness asked of me,
How many strawberries grew in the sea?
I answered him, as I thought good,
As many red herrings as grew in the wood.

The north wind doth blow,
And we shall have snow,
And what will poor Robin do then?
   Poor thing.
He'll sit in a barn,
And keep himself warm,
And hide his head under his wing,
   Poor thing.

There was a crooked man,
   And he walked a crooked mile,
He found a crooked sixpence
   Against a crooked stile;
He bought a crooked cat,
   Which caught a crooked mouse,
And they all lived together
   In a little crooked house.

There was a man of Newington,
   And he was wond'rous wise,
He jumped into a quickset hedge,
   And scratched out both his eyes:
But when he saw his eyes were out,
   With all his might and main
He jump'd into another hedge,
   And scratch'd 'em in again.

There was an old woman sat spinning,
And that's the first beginning;
She had a calf,
And that's half;
She took it by the tail,
And threw it over the wall,
And that's all.

There was an old woman tossed up in a basket,
   Seventeen times as high as the moon;
Where she was going I couldn't but ask it,
   For in her hand she carried a broom.
   Old woman, old woman, old woman, quoth I,
   Where are you going to up so high?
   To brush the cobwebs off the sky!
   May I go with you? Aye, by-and-by.

There was an old woman who lived in a shoe,
She had so many children she didn't know what to do;
She gave them some broth without any bread;
She whipped them all soundly and put them to bed.

Three little ghostesses,
Sitting on postesses,
Eating buttered toastesses,
Greasing their fistesses,
Up to their wristesses.
Oh, what beastesses
To make such feastesses!

Three wise men of Gotham
Went to sea in a bowl;
If the bowl had been stronger,
My story would have been longer.

To market, to market,
    To buy a fat pig,
Home again, home again,
    Jiggety-jig.
To market, to market,
    To buy a fat hog,
Home again, home again,
    Jiggety-jog.

Tom, he was a piper's son,
He learned to play when he was young,
But all the tunes that he could play
Was "Over the hills and far away."
   Over the hills and a great way off,
   The wind shall blow my topknot off.

Tweedledum and Tweedledee
   Agreed to have a battle,
For Tweedledum said Tweedledee
   Had spoiled his nice new rattle.
Just then flew by a monstrous crow
   As big as a tar barrel,
Which frightened both the heroes so,
   They quite forgot their quarrel.

Two little dogs
   Sat by the fire
Over a fender of coal dust;
   Said one little dog
   To the other little dog,
If you don't talk, why, I must.

What are little boys made of, made of?
What are little boys made of?
  Frogs and snails
  And puppy-dogs' tails,
That's what little boys are made of.

What are little girls made of, made of?
What are little girls made of?
  Sugar and spice
  And all things nice,
That's what little girls are made of.

When Jacky's a good boy,
  He shall have cakes and custard;
But when he does nothing but cry,
  He shall have nothing but mustard.

"Who are you?"
"A dirty old man;
I've always been so
Since the day I began.
Father and Mother
Were dirty before me,
Hot or cold water
Has never come o'er me."

A Hungarian Nursery Rhyme

Translated by Mátyás Sárkozi
and C. Day Lewis

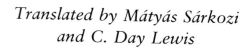

It is raining, it is cold,
Tomtit wonders what to wear.
He has no boots, he has no shoes,
In the mud his feet go bare.

How the wind blew through his skin,
Body shivered, feathers froze!
How can he get home again?
He can hardly move his toes.

Never was such a luckless bird.
Where's his home? What can he do?
He cheeps beneath a holly bush,
He chirps his grief the whole day through.

When you hear a tomtit sing
The song you hear is such a sad one.
If he had a pair of shoes,
He would up and sing a glad one.

Two Danish Nursery Rhymes

Translated by N. M. Bodecker

Two cats were sitting in a tree,
kritte vitte vit bom bom,
a cat called Lew,
a cat called Lee,
kritte vitte vit bom bom.
"Now follow me,"
said Lew to Lee,
kritte vitte vitte vitte vit bom bom,
"for I no longer like this tree,"
kritte vitte vit bom bom!

So Lew and Lee
climbed down the tree,
kritte vitte vit bom bom.
Once down the tree
to Lew said Lee,
kritte vitte vit bom bom,
"Oh, Lew, I rather liked that tree!"
kritte vitte vitte vitte vit bom bom.
So Lew and Lee climbed up the tree,
kritte vitte vit bom bom!

There once was a King
who had three daughters.
The oldest he called
Sip!

The second he called
Sip sippernip!
But the youngest of all he called
Sip sippernip sip sirumsip!

Not far away lived another King
who had three sons.
The oldest was called
Skrat!

The second was called
Skrat skratterat!
But the youngest of all was called
Skrat skratterat skrat skrirumskrat!

Now by and by
the two Kings got together,
the King who had three daughters
and the King who had three sons,
and decided that their children
should marry.
And married they were!

Sip
got
Skrat

and
Sipsippernip got Skratskratterat
and
Sipsippernipsipsirumsip got Skratskratteratskratskrirumskrat.
    As simple as that!

Five Chinese Nursery Rhymes

Translated by Isaac Taylor Headland

Ladybug, ladybug,*
    Fly away, do,
Fly to the mountain,
    And feed upon dew,
Feed upon dew
    And sleep on a rug,
And then run away
    Like a good little bug.

*A ladybug is another name for a ladybird.

Old Mr. Chang,
    I've oft heard it said,
You wear a basket
    upon your head;
You've two pairs of scissors
    to cut your meat,
And two pairs of chopsticks
    with which you eat.

Answer: a crab

On the top of the mount,
    By the road, on a stone —
On a big pile of bricks —
    Sat a bald-headed crone.

On her head were three hairs,
    Which you'll reckon were thin,
In which she was trying
    To wear a jade pin.

She put it in once,
    But once it fell out;
She put it in twice,
    But twice it fell out.

But the old woman said,
    "I know what I'm about,
I'll not pin it in
    And it cannot fall out."

"There's a cow on the mountain,"
    The old saying goes;
On her legs are four feet;
    On her feet are eight toes;
Her tail is behind
    On the end of her back,
And her head is in front
    On the end of her neck.

On the top of a mountain
A hemp stock was growing,
And up it a cricket was climbing.
    I said to him, "Cricket,
    Oh where are you going?"
He answered: "I'm going out dining."

AESOP'S FABLES

Suppose I told you this story: "Jimmy's father offered him a pound to shovel away a heavy fall of snow in front of the house. At first Jimmy was discouraged. But he tackled the job, worked away slowly hour after hour, cleared the snow little by little, and at last earned his pound." Isn't that just about as dull a story as you've ever heard?

Now read the fable below called "The Crow and the Pitcher". Which is better? Which will you remember longer?

Fables go back several thousand years. No one knows who thought them up in the first place. But we do know that a wise, crippled Greek slave named Aesop used to tell them to his master and to anyone else who cared to listen. That was about twenty-five hundred years ago. People have been retelling them, and others like them, ever since.

Most fables are about animals. But are they *really* about animals? Well, yes and no. Take "The Town Mouse and the Country Mouse". When you think about it, wouldn't it make just as much sense if it were about two people, one who liked the country, the other who liked the town? But mice make it more interesting.

These fables weren't written especially for children. They were written for and told to everybody. In olden days — in fact until about three hundred years ago — children and grown-ups weren't thought of as very different from each other. They wore the same kind of clothes and listened to the same stories.

But it's children who have kept these stories alive, just as they have kept Mother Goose rhymes and play-songs alive. They have better memories, maybe, than grown-ups. I also think they've kept fables alive because they seem to like animals more than grown-ups do.

These stories, or stories like them, are found all over the world, in China, in India, in the Far North. "The Fox and the Crane", for example, comes from a book of fairy tales collected by a Russian named Afanas'ev. Fables are really about the way all of us feel and act, no matter where we live, or when we lived.

Lots of times you hear people say "Sour grapes!" or "He's a wolf in sheep's clothing". They've been saying things like that for more than twenty-five hundred years. And most of those sayings come from the Greek slave Aesop and his fables.

Comic strips such as "Peanuts" in a way come from Aesop. They tell a story that makes a point or teaches a lesson. And often they have animals in them. I know Mr. Schulz, who draws and writes "Peanuts". He's handsomer than Aesop was, but he has the same kind of wit and humour and wisdom, too.

The same is true of Dr. Seuss, some of whose work you'll find in these books. He, too, writes fables. I think they're better — they're certainly funnier — than Aesop's. But they also go back to that old Greek slave. Aesop began it. Beginnings are always interesting.

Here are five of Aesop's fables as retold by Joseph Jacobs.

The Crow and the Pitcher

A CROW, half dead with thirst, came upon a Pitcher which had once been full of water; but when the Crow put its beak into the mouth of the Pitcher he found that only very little water was left in it, and that he could not reach far enough down to get at it. He tried, and he tried, but at last had to give up in despair. Then a thought came to him, and he took a pebble and dropped it into the Pitcher. Then he took another pebble and dropped it into the Pitcher. Then he took another pebble and dropped that into the Pitcher. Then he took another pebble and dropped that into the Pitcher. Then he took another pebble and dropped that into the Pitcher. Then he took another pebble and dropped that into the Pitcher. At last, at last, he saw the water mount up near him; and after casting in a few more pebbles he was able to quench his thirst and save his life.

The Town Mouse and the
Country Mouse

NOW you must know that a Town Mouse once upon a time went on a visit to his cousin in the country. He was rough and ready, this cousin, but he loved his town friend and made him heartily welcome. Beans and bacon, cheese and bread were all he had to offer, but he offered them freely. The Town Mouse rather turned up his long nose at this country fare, and said: "I cannot understand, Cousin, how you can put up with such poor food as this, but of course you cannot expect anything better in the country; come you with me and I will show you how to live. When you have been in town a week you will wonder how you could ever have stood a country life."

No sooner said than done: the two mice set off for the town and arrived at the Town Mouse's residence late at night. "You will want some refreshment after our long journey," said the polite Town Mouse, and took his friend into the grand dining room. There they found the remains of a fine feast, and soon the two mice were eating up jellies and cakes and all that was nice. Suddenly they heard growling and barking.

"What is that?" said the Country Mouse.

"It is only the dogs of the house," answered the other.

"Only!" said the Country Mouse. "I do not like that music at my dinner."

Just at that moment the door flew open, in came two huge mastiffs, and the two mice had to scamper down and run off.

"Good-bye, Cousin," said the Country Mouse.

"What! Going so soon?" said the other.

"Yes," he replied; "better beans and bacon in peace than cakes and ale in fear."

Androcles

A SLAVE named Androcles once escaped from his master and fled to the forest. As he was wandering about there he came upon a Lion lying down moaning and groaning. At first he turned to flee, but finding that the Lion did not pursue him, he turned back and went up to him. As he came near, the Lion put out his paw, which was all swollen and bleeding, and Androcles found that a huge thorn had got into it, and was causing all the pain. He pulled out the thorn and bound up the paw of the Lion, who was soon able to rise and lick the hand of Androcles like a dog. Then the Lion took Androcles to his cave, and every day used to bring him meat from which to live.

But shortly afterwards both Androcles and the Lion were captured, and the slave was sentenced to be thrown to the Lion, after the latter had been kept without food for several days. The Emperor and all his Court came to see the spectacle, and Androcles was led out into the middle of the arena. Soon the Lion was let loose from his den, and rushed bounding and roaring towards his victim. But as soon as he came near to Androcles he recognized his friend, and fawned upon him, and licked his hands like a friendly dog. The Emperor, surprised at this, summoned Androcles to him, who told him the whole story. Whereupon the slave was pardoned and freed, and the Lion let loose to his native forest.

The Lion and the Mouse

ONCE when a Lion was asleep a little Mouse began running up and down upon him; this soon wakened the Lion, who placed his huge paw upon him, and opened his big jaws to swallow him. "Pardon, O King," cried the little Mouse; "forgive me this time, I shall never forget it: who knows but what I may be able to do you a turn some of these days?" The Lion was so tickled at the idea of the Mouse being able to help him, that he lifted up his paw and let him go.

Some time after, the Lion was caught in a trap, and the hunters, who desired to carry him alive to the King, tied him to a tree while they went in search of a waggon to carry him on. Just then the little Mouse happened to pass by, and seeing the sad plight in which the Lion was, went up to him and soon gnawed away the ropes that bound the King of the Beasts. "Was I not right?" said the little Mouse.

The Two Fellows and the Bear

TWO Fellows were travelling together through a wood, when a Bear rushed out upon them. One of the travellers happened to be in front, and he seized hold of the branch of a tree, and hid himself among the leaves. The other, seeing no help for it, threw himself flat down upon the ground, with his face in the dust. The Bear, coming up to him, put his muzzle close to his ear, and sniffed and sniffed. But at last with a growl he shook his head and slouched off, for bears will not touch dead meat. Then the Fellow in the tree came down to his comrade, and, laughing, said: "What was it that Master Bruin whispered to you?"

"He told me," said the other, "never trust a friend who deserts you at a pinch."

Here are three more of Aesop's fables, retold by Lloyd W. Daly.

The Farmer's Quarrelsome Sons

A FARMER'S SONS were quarrelsome. When he was unable, after much admonition, to persuade them by what he said to change their ways, he decided that he would have to do it by action and told them to bring him a bundle of sticks. When they had done as he told them, he gave them the sticks all together and told them to break them in two. When they couldn't do it, although they tried with all their might, he undid the bundle and gave them each a single stick. They broke the sticks easily, and their father said, "Well now, boys, it's just the same with you; if you stick together, your enemies won't be able to get you in their clutches, but if you quarrel, you'll be easy to catch."

The Oak and the Reed

AN OAK and a Reed were arguing about their strength. When a strong wind came up, the Reed avoided being uprooted by bending and leaning with the gusts of wind, but the Oak stood firm and was torn up by the roots.

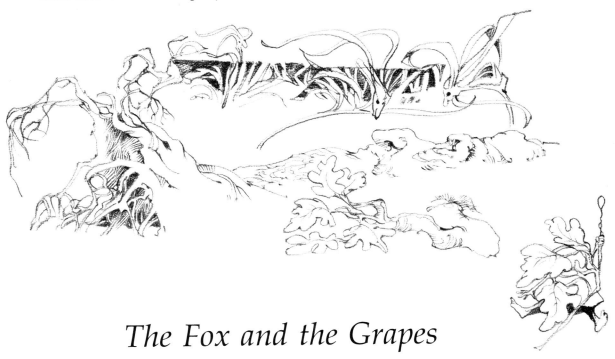

The Fox and the Grapes

A HUNGRY Fox saw some grapes hanging from a vine in a tree and, although he was eager to reach them, was unable to do so. As he went away, he said to himself, "They're sour grapes."

A RUSSIAN FABLE

Here's that Russian fable by Aleksandr Afanas'ev, translated by Norbert Guterman.

The Fox and the Crane

THE FOX and the Crane used to be good friends; they even stood godparents for the same child. The Fox wanted to treat the Crane to dinner and invited him to her house: "Come to see me, gossip! Come, my dear, you'll see how nicely I'll entertain you!" So the Crane came to her house. Meanwhile the Fox had cooked gruel and spread it over a dish. She served it and urged her guest: "Eat, my darling, I cooked it myself." The Crane pecked with his bill, knocked and knocked at the dish, but nothing got into his mouth, while the Fox lapped and lapped the gruel until she had eaten it all. After the gruel was gone, the Fox said: "I'm sorry, dear friend, but that's all I have to offer you." "Thank you, my friend, for what you have given me. You must come to visit me soon."

The next day the Fox came to the Crane's house. The Crane had made a soup and put it in a pitcher with a narrow neck. She placed it on the table and said: "Eat, my friend, that's all I have to offer you." The Fox began to trot around the pitcher; she approached it from one side, then from another, she licked it and smelled it, but all to no avail. Her snout could not get into the pitcher. Meanwhile the Crane sucked and sucked until he had drunk all the soup. "I am sorry, my friend, that's all I have to offer you." The Fox was greatly vexed; for she had thought she would eat for a whole week, and now she had to go home with a long face and an empty stomach. It was tit for tat; and from that moment on the friendship between the Fox and the Crane was over.

ANON.

From time to time in these books we'll come across pieces whose author we don't know. We call that author Anon., short for Anonymous. Here are some verses that I have always liked. I wish I could meet Mr. Anon. (or Mrs. Anon. or Miss Anon.) and thank him (or her) for them.

As I Was Standing in the Street

As I was standing in the street,
  As quiet as could be,
A great big ugly man came up
  And tied his horse to me.

Peas

I eat my peas with honey,
I've done it all my life,
They do taste kind of funny,
But it keeps them on the knife.

The Groaning Board

A buttery, sugary, syrupy waffle —
Gee, but I love it somep'n awful.
Gingercakes dripping with chocolate goo,
Oo! How I love 'em! Oo! *Oo!* Oo!

There Was a Young Lady of Niger

There was a young lady of Niger
Who smiled as she rode on a tiger;
    They returned from the ride
    With the lady inside,
And the smile on the face of the tiger.

Oh! Dear!

Oh! dear! what can the matter be?
Dear! dear! what can the matter be?
Oh! dear! what can the matter be?
Johnny's so long at the fair.

He promised he'd buy me a fairing should please me,
And then for a kiss, oh! he vowed he would tease me,
He promised he'd bring me a bunch of blue ribbons
To tie up my bonny brown hair.

And it's oh! dear! what can the matter be?
Dear! dear! what can the matter be?
Oh! dear! what can the matter be?
Johnny's so long at the fair.

He promised he'd bring me a basket of posies,
A garland of lilies, a garland of roses,
A little straw hat, to set off the blue ribbons
That tie up my bonny brown hair.

And it's oh! dear! what can the matter be?
Dear! dear! what can the matter be?
Oh! dear! what can the matter be?
Johnny's so long at the fair.

52   ANON.

Went to the River

Went to the river, couldn't get across,
Paid five dollars for an old gray hoss.
Hoss wouldn't pull so I traded for a bull.
Bull wouldn't holler so I traded for a dollar.
Dollar wouldn't pass so I threw it on the grass.
Grass wouldn't grow so I traded for a hoe.
Hoe wouldn't dig so I traded for a pig.
Pig wouldn't squeal so I traded for a wheel.
Wheel wouldn't run so I traded for a gun.
Gun wouldn't shoot so I traded for a boot.
Boot wouldn't fit so I thought I'd better quit.
So I quit.

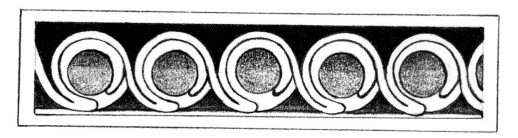

A NORSE MYTH

In their myths of gods and heroes all the world's peoples retain dim memories of their ancient past. The Greek and Norse myths are the ones that have most influenced the imaginations of Western men, women, and especially children.

The Norse myths have been retold by many writers. I like Padraic Colum's retellings, in his *Children of Odin*, as well as any, and I've chosen one episode from it. It's more entertaining than most of the Norse stories. Generally they have a tragic, doom-laden atmosphere, for the Norse Gods knew that eventually the Giants of Jötunheim would destroy them and end their rule.

Thor the Thunderer embodies the strength and courage the old Norsemen admired. Loki, half god, half human, is wily, rather jealous of Thor, and at heart an evil character.

In the story below, they have started from Asgard, home of the Gods, and are journeying to the land of the Giants. They have passed through Midgard, the abode of human beings, where they have impressed into their service the peasant boy Thialfi.

Thor and Loki in the Giants' City

THOR and Loki and the lad Thialfi went across from Midgard into Jötunheim. Because of Miölnir, the great hammer that he carried, Thor felt safe in the Realm of the Giants. And Loki, who trusted in his own cunning, felt safe, too. The lad Thialfi trusted in Thor so much that he had no fear. They were long in making the journey, and while they were travelling Thor and Loki trained Thialfi to be a quick and a strong lad.

One day they came out on a moor. All day they crossed it, and at night it still stretched far before them. A great wind was blowing, night was falling, and they saw no shelter near. In the dusk they saw a shape that looked to be a mountain and they went towards it, hoping to find some shelter in a cave.

Then Loki saw a lower shape that looked as if it might be a shelter. They walked around it, Loki and Thor and the lad Thialfi. It was a house, but a house most oddly shaped. The entrance was a long, wide hall that had no doorway. When they entered this hall they found five long and narrow chambers running off it. "It is an odd place, but it is the best shelter we can get," Loki said. "You and I, Thor, will take the two longest rooms, and the lad Thialfi can take one of the little rooms."

They entered their chambers and they lay down to sleep. But from the mountain outside there came a noise that was like moaning forests and falling cataracts. The chamber where each one slept was shaken by the noise. Neither Thor nor Loki nor the lad Thialfi slept that night.

In the morning they left the five-chambered house and turned their faces towards the mountain. It was not a mountain at all, but a Giant. He was lying on the ground when they saw him, but just then he rolled over and sat up. "Little men, little men," he shouted to them, "have you passed by a glove of mine on your way?" He stood up and looked all around him. "Ho, I see my glove now," he said. Thor and Loki and the lad Thialfi stood still as the Giant came towards them. He leaned over and picked up the five-roomed shelter they had slept in. He put it on his hand. It was really his glove!

Thor gripped his hammer, and Loki and the lad Thialfi stood behind him. But the Giant seemed good-humoured enough. "Where might ye be bound for, little men?" said he.

"To Utgard in Jötunheim," Thor replied boldly.

"Oh, to that place," said the Giant. "Come, then, I shall be with ye so far. You can call me Skyrmir."

"Can you give us breakfast?" said Thor. He spoke crossly, for he did not want it to appear that there was any reason to be afraid of the Giant.

"I can give you breakfast," said Skyrmir, "but I don't want to stop to eat now. We'll sit down as soon as I have an appetite. Come along now. Here is my wallet to carry. It has my provisions in it."

He gave Thor his wallet. Thor put it on his back and put Thialfi sitting upon it. On and on the Giant strode and Thor and Loki were barely able to keep up with him. It was midday before he showed any signs of halting to take breakfast.

They came to an enormous tree. Under it Skyrmir sat down. "I'll sleep before I eat," he said, "but you can open my wallet, my little men, and make your meal out of it." Saying this, he stretched himself out, and in a few minutes Thor and Loki and the lad

Thialfi heard the same sounds as kept them awake the night before, sounds that were like forests moaning and cataracts falling. It was Skyrmir's snoring.

Thor and Loki and the lad Thialfi were too hungry now to be disturbed by these tremendous noises. Thor tried to open the wallet, but he found it was not easy to undo the knots. Then Loki tried to open it. In spite of all Loki's cunning he could not undo the knots. Then Thor took the wallet from him and tried to break the knots by main strength. Not even Thor's strength could break them. He threw the wallet down in his rage.

The snoring of Skyrmir became louder and louder. Thor stood up in his rage. He grasped Miölnir and flung it at the head of the sleeping Giant.

The hammer struck him on the head. But Skyrmir only stirred in his sleep. "Did a leaf fall on my head?" he said.

He turned round on the other side and went to sleep again. The hammer came back to Thor's hand. As soon as Skyrmir snored he flung it again, aiming at the Giant's forehead. It struck there. The Giant opened his eyes. "Has an acorn fallen on my forehead?" he said.

Again he went to sleep. But now Thor, terribly roused, stood over his head with the hammer held in his hands. He struck him on the forehead. It was the greatest blow that Thor had ever dealt.

"A bird is pecking at my forehead — there is no chance to sleep here," said Skyrmir, sitting up. "And you, little men, did you have breakfast yet? Toss over my wallet to me and I shall give you some provision." The lad Thialfi brought him the wallet. Skyrmir opened it, took out his provisions, and gave a share to Thor and Loki and the lad Thialfi. Thor would not take provision from him, but Loki and the lad Thialfi took it and ate. When the meal was finished Skyrmir rose up and said, "Time for us to be going towards Utgard."

As they went on their way Skyrmir talked to Loki. "I always feel very small when I go into Utgard," he said. "You see, I'm such a small and a weak fellow and the folk who live there are so big and powerful. But you and your friends will be welcomed in Utgard. They will be sure to make little pets of you."

And then he left them and they went into Utgard, the City of the Giants. Giants were going up and down in the streets. They were not so huge as Skyrmir would have them believe, Loki noticed.

Utgard was the Asgard of the Giants. But in its buildings there was not a line of the beauty that there was in the palaces of the Gods, Gladsheim and Breidablik or Fensalir. Huge but shapeless the buildings arose, like mountains or icebergs. O beautiful Asgard with the dome above it of the deepest blue! Asgard with the clouds around it heaped up like mountains of diamonds! Asgard with its Rainbow Bridge and its glittering gates! O beautiful Asgard, could it be indeed that these Giants would one day overthrow you?

Thor and Loki with the lad Thialfi went to the palace of the King. The hammer that Thor gripped would, they knew, make them safe even there. They passed between rows of Giant guards and came to the King's seat. "We know you, Thor and Loki," said the Giant King, "and we know that Thor has come to Utgard to try his strength against the Giants. We shall have a contest tomorrow. Today there are sports for our boys. If your young servant should like to try his swiftness against our youths, let him enter the race today."

Now Thialfi was the best runner in Midgard and all the time he had been with them Loki and Thor had trained him in quickness. And so Thialfi was not fearful of racing against the Giants' youths.

The King called on one named Hugi and placed him against Thialfi. The pair started together. Thialfi sped off. Loki and Thor watched the race anxiously, for they thought it would be well for them if they had a triumph over the dwellers in Utgard in the first contest. But they saw Hugi leave Thialfi behind. They saw the Giant youth reach the winning post, circle round it, and come back to the starting place before Thialfi had reached the end of the course.

Thialfi, who did not know how it was that he had been beaten, asked that he be let run the race with Hugi again. The pair started off once more, and this time it did not seem to Thor and Loki that Hugi had left the starting place at all — he was back there almost as soon as the race had started.

They came back from the racing ground to the palace. The Giant King and his friends with Thor and Loki sat down to the supper table. "Tomorrow," said the King, "we shall have our great contest when Asa Thor will show us his power. Have you of Asgard ever heard of one who would enter a contest in eating? We might have a contest in eating at this supper board if we could get one who would match himself with Logi here. He can eat more than anyone in Jötunheim."

"And I," said Loki, "can eat more than any two in Jötunheim. I will match myself against your Logi."

"Good!" said the Giant King. And all the Giants present said, "Good! This will be a sight worth seeing."

Then they put scores of plates along one side of the table, each plate filled with meat. Loki began at one end and Logi began at the other. They started to eat, moving towards each other as each cleared a plate. Plate after plate was emptied, and Thor standing by with the Giants was amazed to see how much Loki ate. But Logi on the other side was leaving plate after plate emptied. At last the two stood together with scores of plates on each side of them. "He has not defeated me," cried Loki. "I have cleared as many plates as your champion, O King of the Giants."

"But you have not cleared them so well," said the King.

"Loki has eaten all the meat that was upon them," said Thor.

"But Logi has eaten the bones with the meat," said the Giant King. "Look and see if it be not so."

Thor went to the plates. Where Loki had eaten, the bones were left on the plates. Where Logi had eaten, nothing was left: bones as well as meat were consumed, and all the plates were left bare.

"We are beaten," said Thor to Loki.

"Tomorrow, Thor," said Loki, "you must show all your strength or the Giants will cease to dread the might of the Dwellers in Asgard."

"Be not afraid," said Thor. "No one in Jötunheim will triumph over me."

The next day Thor and Loki came into the great hall of Utgard. The Giant King was there with a throng of his friends. Thor marched into the hall with Miölnir, his great hammer, in his hands. "Our young men have been drinking out of this horn," said the King, "and they want to know if you, Asa Thor, would drink out of it a morning draft. But I must tell you that they think that no one of the Æsir could empty the horn at one draft."

"Give it to me," said Thor. "There is no horn you can hand me that I cannot empty at a draft."

A great horn, brimmed and flowing, was brought over to him. Handing Miölnir to Loki and bidding him stand so that he might keep the hammer in sight, Thor raised the horn to his mouth. He drank and drank. He felt sure there was not a drop left in the horn as he laid it on the ground. "There," he gasped, "your Giant horn is drained."

The Giants looked within the horn and laughed. "Drained, Asa Thor!" said the Giant King. "Look into the horn again. You have hardly drunk below the brim."

And Thor looked into it and saw that the horn was not half emptied. In a mighty rage he lifted it to his lips again. He drank and drank and drank. Then, satisfied that he had emptied it to the bottom, he left the horn on the ground and walked over to the other side of the hall.

"Thor thinks he has drained the horn," said one of the Giants, lifting it up. "But see, friends, what remains in it."

Thor strode back and looked again into the horn. It was still half filled. He turned round to see that all the Giants were laughing at him.

"Asa Thor, Asa Thor," said the Giant King, "we know not how you are going to deal with us in the next feat, but you certainly are not able to drink against the Giants."

Said Thor: "I can lift up and set down any being in your hall."

As he said this a great iron-coloured cat bounded into the hall and stood before Thor, her back arched and her fur bristling.

"Then lift the cat off the ground," said the Giant King.

Thor strode to the cat, determined to lift her up and fling her amongst the mocking Giants. He put his hands to the cat, but he could not raise her. Up, up went Thor's arms, up, up, as high as they could go. The cat's arched back went up to the roof, but her feet were never taken off the ground. And as he heaved and heaved with all his might he heard the laughter of the Giants all round him.

He turned away, his eyes flaming with anger. "I am not wont to try to lift cats," he said. "Bring me one to wrestle with, and I swear you shall see me overthrow him."

"Here is one for you to wrestle with, Asa Thor," said the King. Thor looked round and saw an old woman hobbling towards him. She was blear-eyed and toothless. "This is Ellie, my ancient nurse," said the Giant King. "She is the one we would have you wrestle with."

"Thor does not wrestle with old women. I will lay my hands on your tallest Giants instead."

"Ellie has come where you are," said the Giant King. "Now it is she who will lay hands upon you."

The old woman hobbled towards Thor, her eyes gleaming under her falling fringes of grey hair. Thor stood, unable to move as the hag came towards him. She laid her hands upon his arms. Her feet began to trip at his. He tried to cast her from him. Then he found that her feet and her hands were as strong against his as bands and stakes of iron.

Then began a wrestling match in earnest between Thor and the ancient crone Ellie. Round and round the hall they wrestled, and Thor was not able to bend the old woman backwards nor sideways. Instead he became less and less able under her terrible grasp. She forced him down, down, and at last he could only save himself from being left prone on the ground by throwing himself down on one knee and holding the hag by the shoulders. She tried to force him down on the ground, but she could not do that. Then she broke from him, hobbled to the door and went out of the hall.

Thor rose up and took the hammer from Loki's hands. Without a word he went out of the hall and along the ways and towards the gate of the Giants' City. He spoke no word to Loki nor to the lad Thialfi, who went with him for the seven weeks that they journeyed through Jötunheim.

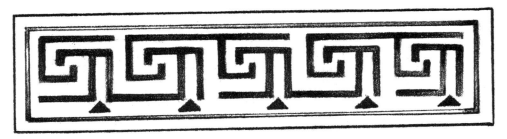

THREE GREEK MYTHS

Here are three of the best-known Greek myths, retold by Ingri and Edgar Parin D'Aulaire. They're from the D'Aulaires' *Book of Greek Myths*, one of many retellings of these ancient stories that the human race refuses to forget.

King Midas

KING MIDAS was a kind but rather stupid man who had always been a friend to the Phrygian satyrs. One morning his servants had found an old satyr sleeping in the king's favourite flower bed. Midas had spared the satyr from punishment and let him go. This old satyr was a follower of Dionysus, and the god had rewarded Midas for his kindness by granting him a wish. Short-sightedly, King Midas wished that everything he touched would turn to gold. His golden touch made him the richest man on earth, but he almost starved to death for even his food and drink turned to gold. And when his little daughter ran to him to hug him, she too turned into gold! Midas had to beg Dionysus to undo his wish and make everything as it had been before.

Now again, King Midas showed poor judgement. The nine Muses all agreed that Apollo was by far the better musician, but Midas voted for the Phrygian satyr. Apollo disdainfully turned his lyre upside down and played just as well as before. He ordered Marsyas to turn his flute and do the same. Not a sound came from Marsyas' flute however hard he blew, and even Midas had to admit that the satyr's flute was inferior to Apollo's lyre. So Marsyas lost the contest and Apollo pulled off his skin and made a drum of it. Then he turned to King Midas and said, "Ears as stupid as yours belong to an ass. Ass's ears you shall have from now on!"

Ever after, King Midas went about with a tall, peaked cap on his head to hide his long ears. His subjects thought he had started a new fashion, and it wasn't long before all the Phrygians wore tall, peaked caps.

The king's barber was the only one who knew what Midas was hiding. He had been forbidden to breathe a word about it and he almost burst from having to keep such an important secret. When he could bear it no longer he ran out to a deserted field, dug a hole in the ground, and whispered into it, "King Midas has ass's ears!" He quickly covered up the hole and thought the secret was safe. But the nearby reeds had heard and as they swayed in the wind they whispered, "Midas has ass's ears, Midas has ass's ears," and soon the secret spread all over the world.

King Midas was so ashamed that he left his throne and hid deep in the woods where no one could see him.

Theseus

THE MUSES sang of Heracles and his labours, and they also sang of the island of Crete, ruled by King Minos, the son of Zeus and Europa. His queen, Pasiphaë, a daughter of the sun-god Helios, had a golden glimmer in her eyes like all the descendants of the sun, and was accustomed to great magnificence. King Minos wanted his queen to live in a palace as splendid as her father's, and he ordered Daedalus, an Athenian architect and inventor of marvellous skill, to build the great palace of Knossus.

The palace rose up storey upon storey, over a forest of columns. Winding stairs and intricate passageways connected the many halls and courtyards. Pictures were painted on the walls of the great halls, fountains splashed in the courtyards, and the bathrooms even had running water. Bulls' horns of the purest gold crowned the roofs, for the Cretans worshipped the bull, since Zeus, in the shape of a bull, had brought Europa to the island. Here the king and the queen and all their court lived in great splendour and happiness until one day Poseidon sent a snow-white bull from the sea. Since the island of Crete was completely surrounded by his domain, the sea, he too wanted to be honoured, and ordered King Minos to sacrifice the bull to him. But Queen Pasiphaë was so taken by the beauty of the white bull that she persuaded the king to let it live. She admired the bull so much that she ordered Daedalus to construct a hollow wooden cow, so she could hide inside it and enjoy the beauty of the bull at close range.

Poseidon was very angry, and for punishment he made the bull mad. It ravaged the whole island, and though the Cretans were great bullfighters, no one could subdue the beast until Heracles had come to capture it for one of his labours.

To punish the king and queen, Poseidon caused Pasiphaë to give birth to a monster, the Minotaur. He was half man, half bull, and ate nothing but human flesh. Such a fearful monster could not go free, and the clever Daedalus constructed for him a labyrinth under the palace. It was a maze of passageways and little rooms from which nobody could ever hope to find his way out. There the Minotaur was shut in, and as long as he was provided with victims to devour, he kept quiet. When he was hungry, he bellowed so loudly that the whole palace shook. King Minos had to wage war with the neighbouring islands so he could supply the Minotaur with the prisoners of war for food. When a son of Minos visited Athens and was accidentally killed, King Minos used this as an excuse to threaten to sack the city unless seven Athenian maidens and seven Athenian youths were sent to Crete to be sacrificed to the Minotaur every nine years.

To save his city, Aegeus, the king of Athens, had to consent, for Minos was much stronger than he. The people of Athens grumbled, for, while King Aegeus was childless and had nothing to lose, they had to see their sons and daughters sacrificed to the cruel Minotaur.

Two times nine years had passed and the king was growing old. For the third time a ship with black sails of mourning was due to depart, when word came to the king that a young hero, Theseus, from Troezen, was making his way to Athens, destroying all the monsters and highwaymen he met on the road. When King Aegeus heard that, his old heart beat faster. Once in his youth he had visited Troezen and had been secretly married to Princess Aethra. He did not bring Aethra back to Athens with him, but before he left, he said to her, "Should you bear me a son and should he grow up strong enough to lift this boulder under which I hide my sword and golden sandals, send him to me, for then he will be the worthy heir to the throne of Athens." King Aegeus in those days was known for his great strength.

Theseus, the young hero, arrived in Athens and went straight to the king's palace. Tall and handsome, he stood before Aegeus with the sandals and the sword, and the king was overjoyed. At last he had a son who was a hero as well. The king happily proclaimed Theseus the rightful heir to the throne of Athens and he became the hero of all Athens when he offered to take the place of one of the victims who were to be sent to Crete. Old King Aegeus begged his son not to go, but Theseus would not change his mind. "I shall make an end of the Minotaur and we shall return safely," he said. "We sail with black sails, but we shall return with white sails as a signal of my success."

The ship sailed to Crete and the fourteen young Athenians were locked in a dungeon to await their doom. But King Minos had a lovely daughter, Ariadne, as fair a maiden as eyes could see. She could not bear the thought that handsome Theseus should be sacrificed to the ugly Minotaur. She went to Daedalus and begged for help to save him. He gave Ariadne a magic ball of thread and told her that at midnight, when the Minotaur was fast asleep, she must take Theseus to the labyrinth. The magic ball of thread would roll ahead of him through the maze and lead him to the monster, and then it was up to Theseus to overpower the beast.

In the dark of the night, Ariadne went to Theseus' prison and whispered that, if he would promise to marry her and carry her away with him, she would help him. Gladly Theseus gave his word, and Ariadne led him to the gate of the labyrinth, tied the end of the thread to the gate so he would find his way back, and gave him the ball. As soon as Theseus put the ball of thread on the ground, it rolled ahead of him through dark corridors, up stairs, down stairs, and around winding passageways. Holding on to the unwinding thread, Theseus followed it wherever it led him, and before long he heard the thunderous snoring of the Minotaur, and there, surrounded by skulls and bleached bones, lay the monster fast asleep.

Theseus sprang at the Minotaur. It roared so loudly that the whole palace of Knossus shook, but the monster was taken by surprise, and so strong was Theseus that, with his bare hands, he killed the cruel Minotaur.

Theseus quickly followed the thread back to Ariadne, who stood watch at the gate. Together they freed the other Athenians and ran to their ship in the harbour. Before they sailed, they bored holes in all of King Minos' ships so he could not pursue them. Ariadne urged them to hurry, for even she could not save them from Talos, the bronze robot who guarded the island. If he should see their ship leaving, he would throw rocks at it and sink it. Should one of them manage to swim ashore, Talos would throw himself into a blazing bonfire until he was red-hot. Then he would burn the survivor to ashes in a fiery embrace. They could already hear his clanking steps, when just in time they hoisted their sail and a brisk wind blew them out to sea. In their rush they forgot to hoist the white sail of victory instead of the black sail of mourning.

Theseus' heart was filled with joy. Not only had he saved the Athenians from the Minotaur, he was also bringing a beautiful bride home to Athens. But in the middle of the night the god Dionysus appeared to him and spoke: "I forbid you to marry Ariadne. I myself have chosen her for my bride. You must set her ashore on the island of Naxos."

Theseus could not oppose an Olympian god. When they came

to Naxos, he ordered everyone to go ashore and rest. There Ariadne fell into a heavy slumber, and while she slept, Theseus led the others back to the ship and they sailed off without her.

Poor Ariadne wept bitterly when she awoke and found herself deserted. Little did she suspect that the handsome stranger who came walking towards her was the god Dionysus and that it was he who had ordered Theseus to abandon her. The god gently dried her tears and gave her a drink from the cup in his hand and right away the sadness left her. She smiled up at the god and he put a crown of sparkling jewels on her head and made her his bride. They lived happily together for many years and their sons became kings of the surrounding islands. Dionysus loved Ariadne greatly, and when she died he put her jewelled crown into the sky as a constellation so she would never be forgotten.

Theseus, in his grief at having lost Ariadne, again forgot to hoist the white sail. When King Aegeus saw the black-sailed ship returning from Crete, he threw himself into the sea in despair.

Theseus inherited his father's throne and he and all of Athens mourned the loss of the old king and in his honour named the sea in which he had drowned the Aegean.

King Minos was beside himself with fury when he discovered that his daughter had fled with the Athenians. He knew that no one but the brilliant Daedalus could have helped Theseus unravel the mystery of the labyrinth, so Daedalus was kept a prisoner in the palace and treated very harshly. Daedalus could not bear to be locked up and let his talents go to waste. Secretly he made two sets of wings, one pair for himself and one pair for his son, Icarus. They were cleverly fashioned of feathers set in beeswax. He showed his son how to use them and warned him not to fly too high or the heat of the sun would melt the wax. Then he led him up to the highest tower, and, flapping their wings, they flew off like two birds. Neither King Minos nor Talos, the robot, could stop their flight.

Young and foolish, Icarus could not resist the temptation to rise ever higher into the sky; the whole world seemed at his feet. He flew too close to the sun and the wax began to melt. The feathers came loose, the wings fell apart, and Icarus plunged into the sea and drowned. Sadly, Daedalus flew on alone and came to the

island of Sicily. His fame had flown ahead of him and the King of Sicily welcomed him warmly, for he too wanted a splendid palace and bathrooms with running water.

As soon as King Minos' ships were mended, he set off in pursuit of Daedalus, the cunning craftsman. He sailed east and he sailed west, and when he came to the Sicilian shore and saw the wondrous palace going up, he had no doubts who was building it. But the King of Sicily hid Daedalus and denied that he had him in his service. Slyly King Minos sent a conch shell up to the palace, with a message that, if anyone could pull a thread through the windings of the conch, he would give him a sack of gold as a reward. The King of Sicily asked Daedalus to solve the problem. Daedalus thought for a while; then he tied a silken thread to an ant, put the ant at one end of the conch shell and a bit of honey at the other end. The ant smelled the honey and found its way through the conch, pulling the thread along with it. When King Minos saw this, he demanded the immediate surrender of Daedalus, for now he had proof that the King of Sicily was hiding him. Nobody but Daedalus could have threaded the conch!

The King of Sicily had to give in. He invited Minos to a feast, promising to surrender Daedalus. As was the custom, King Minos took a bath before the feast. But when he stepped into the fabulous bath that Daedalus had built, boiling water rushed out of the tap and scalded him to death. And Daedalus remained for the rest of his life at the court of the King of Sicily.

After the death of King Minos there was peace between Crete and Athens, and Theseus married Phaedra, Ariadne's younger sister. He became the greatest king Athens ever had, and his fame as a hero spread all over Greece. Another great hero, Pirithoüs, king of the Lapith people in northern Greece, was his inseparable friend. The first time the two heroes had met, they faced each other in combat. But each was so impressed by the other that instead of fighting, they dropped their weapons and swore eternal friendship. Together they performed many great deeds, and when Pirithoüs married a Lapith princess, Theseus, of course, was invited to the wedding feast. The centaurs were invited too, for though wild and lawless they were nonetheless distant relatives. At first they behaved quite mannerly, but as the wine jugs were passed around, they became boisterous and rowdy. Suddenly a young centaur sprang up, grasped the bride by the hair, and galloped away with her. At that, the other centaurs each grasped a screaming girl and took to the hills.

Theseus and Pirithoüs with their men set off in swift pursuit and soon caught up with the centaurs. There was a brutal battle, for the wild centaurs tore up big trees and swung them as clubs. But in Theseus and Pirithoüs they had found their masters. They were chased out of Greece, and the victorious heroes, with the bride and the other Lapith girls, returned to the feast.

Pirithoüs lived happily for a while; then he became a widower and asked his friend Theseus to help him win a new bride. Theseus vowed to help him, but shuddered when he heard that Pirithoüs wanted no one less than Persephone, the queen of the dead. She was unhappy with Hades, he said. Since Theseus had promised to help his friend, and a promise could not be broken, he descended to the underworld with Pirithoüs. They forced their way past Cerberus and entered the gloomy palace. Hades glowered at the two heroes, who had dared to enter his realm, but he listened politely while they stated their errand. "Sit down on that bench," he said, "so we can discuss the matter." Grim Hades smiled as the two friends sat down, for it was a magic bench from which no one could ever rise. There they were to sit forever with ghosts and bats flitting about their heads.

A long time later Heracles came to Hades on an errand, and pitied the two heroes trying vainly to get up from the bench. He took hold of Theseus and tore him loose with a mighty tug. But when he tried to free Pirithoüs there came a loud earthquake. The gods did not allow Heracles to set him free, for he had shown too great irreverence by daring to want a goddess for a wife. Theseus returned to Athens wiser but thinner, for a part of him had remained stuck to the bench. Ever since, the Athenians have had lean thighs.

The Golden Fleece

THE MUSES sang about handsome Jason and his quest for the Golden Fleece.

Jason of Iolcus was as strong and well bred as he was handsome, for he had been raised by the wise centaur Chiron. Jason's father had brought the boy to the centaur and had asked him to bring him up, for he feared that his own brother, Pelias, who had taken from him the throne of Iolcus, might harm his heir. In Chiron's lonely mountain cave young Jason was raised to be a hero, skilled in all manly sports. When he was grown he left his foster father to go to Iolcus and reclaim his father's throne.

Hera, who was paying a visit to earth, saw the handsome youth as he walked down from the mountain. His golden hair hung to his shoulders and his strong body was wrapped in a leopard skin. Hera was taken by his fine looks. She quickly changed herself into an old crone and stood helplessly at the brink of a swollen stream as if she did not dare to wade across. Jason offered politely to carry her and lifted her on his strong shoulders. He started to wade and at first she was very light. But with each step she grew heavier, and when he reached midstream, she was so heavy that his feet sank deep into the mud. He lost one of his sandals, but struggled bravely on, and when he reached the other side, the old crone revealed herself as the goddess Hera.

"Lo," she said. "You are a mortal after my liking. I shall stand by you and help you win back your throne from your uncle Pelias." This was a promise the goddess gladly gave, for she had a grudge against Pelias, who had once forgotten to include her when he sacrificed to the gods.

Jason thanked her and went on his way in high spirits. When he arrived in Iolcus, people crowded around him, wondering who the handsome stranger might be, but when King Pelias saw him, his cheeks paled. An oracle had predicted that a youth with only one sandal would be his undoing. Pelias feigned great friendship when Jason said who he was and why he had come, but underneath he held dark thoughts and planned to do away with his guest. Pelias feasted Jason and flattered him and promised him the throne as soon as he had performed a heroic deed to prove himself worthy of being a king.

"In the kingdom of Colchis, at the shores of the Black Sea," said Pelias, "on a branch in a dark grove, there hangs a golden fleece shining as brightly as the sun. Bring the fleece to me and the throne shall be yours."

The Golden Fleece was once the coat of a flying ram, sent by Zeus to save the life of young Prince Phrixus of Thessaly. The crops had failed and Phrixus' evil stepmother had convinced his father that he must sacrifice his son to save his country from famine. Sadly the king built an altar and put his son on it, but Zeus hated human sacrifice, and as the king lifted his knife, a golden ram swooped down from the skies and flew off with Phrixus on his back. They flew far to the east and landed in the kingdom of Colchis. The king of Colchis understood that Phrixus had been sent by the gods. He gave him his daughter in marriage and sacrificed the ram. Its glittering fleece was hung in a sacred grove and it was the greatest treasure of the country.

King Pelias was certain that Jason would not return alive, for he knew that the warlike king of Colchis would not part with the fleece and that a never-sleeping dragon was guarding it. But Pelias did not know that Jason had Hera's help.

"Give me timber and men to build for me a sturdy ship and I shall sail off at once," said Jason. The king gave him what he asked for and a great ship, the *Argo*, was built. It was the most seaworthy ship ever seen. Athena, herself prodded by Hera, put a piece of sacred oak in its prow. The oak had the power to speak in time of danger and advise Jason what to do.

With a ship like that it was not hard for Jason to gather a crew of heroes. Even Heracles came with his young friend Hylas. Calaïs and Zetes, winged sons of the North Wind, joined, and Orpheus came along to inspire the crew with his music. Soon each of the fifty oars of the ship was manned by a hero who swore to stand by Jason through all dangers.

Before they set sail, the heroes, who called themselves the Argonauts, sacrificed richly to the gods and made sure to forget no one. Poseidon was in a good mood. He called for the West Wind and under full sail the *Argo* sped toward the east. When the wind grew tired and died down, the Argonauts put out their oars and rowed with all their might. Orpheus beat out the time with his lyre and the ship cut through the waves like an arrow. One after the other the heroes grew tired and pulled in their oars. Only Heracles and Jason were left rowing, each trying to outlast the other. Jason finally fainted, but just as he slumped forward, Heracles' huge oar broke in two, so equal glory was won by them both.

The Argonauts landed at a wooded coast so Heracles could cut himself a new oar. While Heracles searched for a suitable tree, his young friend Hylas went to a pool to fill his jar with fresh water. When the nymph of the pool saw the handsome boy bending down, she fell in love with him. She pulled him down with her to the bottom of the pool and Hylas vanished forever without leaving a trace.

Heracles went out of his mind with grief when he could not find his friend. He ran through the woods, calling for Hylas, beating down whatever was in his way. The Argonauts, brave as they were, all feared Heracles when he was struck with folly. They hastily boarded the ship and sailed away without him.

On towards the east the Argonauts sailed until they came to a country ruled by a king who was known for his knowledge and wisdom. They went ashore to ask the way to Colchis, but the king was so weak that he could barely answer their questions. He was so thin that only his skin held his bones together. Whenever food was set before him, three disgusting Harpies, fat birds with women's heads, swooped down and devoured it. What they did not eat they left so foul and filthy that it was not fit to be eaten. No one in his kingdom could keep the Harpies away.

The Argonauts felt sorry for the starving king. They told him to have his table set, and when the Harpies swooped down again, Zetes and Calaïs, the sons of the North Wind, took to their wings. They could fly faster than the Harpies, and when they caught them, they whipped the evil pests so hard that they barely escaped with their lives. The Harpies flew to the south, never to be seen again. At last the famished king could eat in peace. He could not thank the Argonauts enough and told them how to set their course and what dangers they would encounter. No ship had yet been able to reach the shores of Colchis, he said, for the passage to the Black Sea was blocked by two moving rocks. The rocks rolled apart and clashed together, crushing whatever came between them. But if a ship could move as fast as a bird in flight, it might get through. He gave Jason a dove and told him to send the bird ahead of the ship. If the dove came through alive, they had a chance, he said. If not, they had better give up and turn back.

The Argonauts took leave of the king and sailed toward the clashing rocks. From afar they could hear the din and the heroes trembled, but as the rocks rolled apart, Jason released the dove and the bird flew between them like a dart. Only the very tips of its tail feathers were clipped off when the rocks clashed together.

"All men to the oars!" Jason shouted. Orpheus grasped his lyre and played and his music inspired the heroes to row as never before. The *Argo* shot ahead like an arrow when the rocks rolled apart, and only the very end of its stern was crushed as they clashed together. Again the rocks rolled apart and stood firmly anchored. The spell was broken, and from then on ships could safely sail in and out of the Black Sea.

The Black Sea was a dangerous sea to sail upon, and Hera had her hands full, guiding the Argonauts through perils. But with her help Jason brought his ship safely through raging storms, past pirate shores and cannibal islands, and the Argonauts finally arrived in Colchis.

Aeëtes, king of Colchis, a son of Helios, the sun, was a very inhospitable king. In fact he was so inhospitable that he killed all foreigners who came to his country. When he saw the *Argo* landing he was furious, and when Jason led his men to his palace and said that they were all great heroes and had come to offer the king their services in return for the Golden Fleece, he fumed with rage. "Very well," he said to Jason. "Tomorrow, between sunrise and sunset, you must harness my fire-breathing bulls, plough up a field, and sow it with dragon's teeth as Cadmus did at Thebes. If you succeed, the Golden Fleece is yours. But if you fail, I shall cut out the tongues and lop off the hands of you and all your great heroes." King Aeëtes knew well that no man could withstand the searing heat that blew from the bulls' nostrils. What he did not know was that Hera was helping Jason.

Hera knew that the king's daughter, Medea, who stood at her father's side with modestly downcast eyes, was the only one who could save Jason. She was a lovely young sorceress, a priestess of the witch-goddess Hecate, and must be made to fall in love with Jason. So Hera asked Aphrodite to send her little son Eros to shoot one of his arrows of love into Medea's heart. Aphrodite promised Eros a beautiful enamel ball, and he shot an arrow into Medea's heart just as she lifted up her eyes and saw Jason. Her golden eyes gleamed; never had she seen anyone so handsome. She just had to use her magic and save him from her cruel father; there was nothing she would not do to save Jason's life. She went to Hecate's temple and implored the witch-goddess to help her and, guided by the witch-goddess, she concocted a magic salve so powerful that for one day neither iron nor fire could harm the one who was covered with it.

In the dark of the night, Medea sent for Jason. When he came to the temple, she blushingly told him that she loved him so much she would betray her own father to save him. She gave him the magic salve and told him to go up to the fire-breathing bulls without fear. Jason took the young sorceress in his arms and swore by all the gods of Olympus to make her his queen and love her to his dying day. Hera heard him and nodded, very pleased.

When the sun rose in the morning, Jason went straight up to the fire-breathing bulls. They bellowed and belched flames at him, but with Medea's salve he was invulnerable and so strong that he harnessed the bulls and drove them back and forth till the whole field was ploughed. Then he seeded the dragon's teeth, and right away a host of warriors sprang up from the furrows. As Cadmus had done, he threw a rock among them and watched from afar as they killed one another. Before the sun had set, they all lay dead.

Jason had fulfilled his task, but King Aeëtes had no intention of keeping his part of the bargain. He called his men together and ordered them to seize the *Argo* and kill the foreigners at daybreak. In secrecy, Medea went to Jason and told him that he must take the Golden Fleece, now rightfully his, and flee from Colchis before dawn. Under cover of night she led him to the dark grove where the Golden Fleece, shining like the sun, hung on a branch of a tree. Around the trunk of the tree lay coiled the never-sleeping dragon. But Medea chanted incantations and bewitched the dragon. She stared at it with her golden eyes and it fell into a deep magic sleep. Quickly Jason took the Golden Fleece and ran with Medea to the waiting *Argo*, and quietly they slipped out to sea.

At daybreak, when the king's men were to attack the ship, they found it was gone. So were the Golden Fleece and the king's daughter, Medea. Red-faced with fury, Aeëtes set off in pursuit with his great fleet of Colchian warships. He wanted the Golden Fleece back and he wanted to punish his daughter. The fastest of his ships, steered by one of his sons, soon overtook the *Argo*.

The Argonauts thought themselves lost, but again Medea saved them.

She called to her brother, who stood at the helm of his ship, and pretended to be sorry for what she had done. She said she would go home with him if he would meet her alone on a nearby island. At the same time, she whispered to Jason to lie in wait and kill her brother when he came. She knew that her father would have to stop the pursuit to give his son a funeral.

Hera and all the gods looked in horror at Medea, stained with her brother's blood. No mortal could commit a worse crime than to cause the death of his own kin. Zeus in anger threw thunderbolts. Lightning flashed, thunder roared, and the sea foamed. Then the sacred piece of oak in the bow of the *Argo* spoke. "Woe," it said, "woe to you all. Not a one among you will reach Greece unless the great sorceress Circe consents to purify Medea and Jason of their sin."

Tossed about by howling winds and towering waves, the Argonauts sailed in search of Circe's dwelling. At long last, off the coast of Italy, they found her palace. Medea warned the Argonauts not to leave the ship, for Circe was a dangerous sorceress who amused herself by changing men who came to her island into the animal nearest the nature of each man. Some became lions, some rabbits, but most of them were changed into pigs and asses. Medea took Jason by the hand so no harm would befall him, and went ashore.

Circe was Medea's aunt. Like all the descendants of Helios, the sun, she had a golden glint in her eyes, and the moment she saw Medea, she recognized her as her kin. But she was not happy to see her niece, for through her magic she knew what Medea had done. Still she consented to sacrifice to Zeus and ask him to forgive Medea and Jason for their crime. The scented smoke of her burnt offering of sweetmeats and cakes reached Zeus and put him in a good humour. He listened to Circe's words and again smiled down upon Medea and Jason.

They thanked Circe and rushed back to the ship. The Argonauts rejoiced. Now they could set sail for Greece. But still they had to pass through dangerous and bewitched waters. Soon they came to the island of the Sirens. The Sirens were half birds, half women, not loathsome like the Harpies, but enchanting creatures. They sat on a cliff, half hidden by sea spray, and sang so beautifully that all sailors who heard them dived into the sea and tried to swim to them, only to drown or pine to death at the Sirens' feet. When the alluring voices of the Sirens reached the ears of the Argonauts, Orpheus grasped his lyre and sang so loudly and sweetly that all other sounds were drowned out, and not one of the Argonauts jumped overboard.

After a while the *Argo* had to sail through a narrow strait that was guarded by two monsters. On one side lurked the monster Scylla. From her waist up she looked like a woman, but instead of legs, six furious, snarling dogs grew out from her hips, and they tore to pieces whatever came close to them. The monster Charybdis lived on the other side of the strait. She was forever hungry and sucked into her gullet all ships that ventured within her reach.

Helplessly, the *Argo* drifted between the two monsters, and the Argonauts again gave themselves up for lost, when up from the bottom of the sea rose the playful Nereids. They had come at

Hera's bidding and they lifted up the *Argo* and threw it from hand to hand over the dangerous waters until it reached the open sea beyond. Poseidon called for the West Wind and the *Argo* sped homeward under full sail.

A loud cheer rang out from the valiant crew when they sighted the shore of Greece. They had been away for many long years and were homesick. But as the *Argo* neared the port of Iolcus, the ship was hailed by a fisherman, who warned Jason that King Pelias had heard of his safe return and had made plans to kill him. Jason was downcast at his uncle's treachery, but Medea, her eyes flashing, asked to be set ashore alone. Once again she wanted to save his life.

Disguised as an old witch, she entered Iolcus, saying that she had magic herbs to sell that would make old creatures young again. The people crowded around her, wondering from where the witch had come. King Pelias himself came out from his palace and asked her to prove that what she said was true, for he felt he was growing old.

"Bring me the oldest ram in your flock and I will show you the magic of my herbs," said Medea.

An old ram was brought to her and she put it into a cauldron full of water. On top she sprinkled some of her magic herbs, and lo! the water in the cauldron boiled and out of the steam and bubbles sprang a frisky young lamb.

Now King Pelias asked Medea to make him young too. She answered that only his daughters could do that, but she would gladly sell them her magic herbs. But the herbs she gave them had no magic at all, and so King Pelias found his death in the boiling cauldron at his own daughters' hands.

Now the throne of Iolcus was Jason's, but again Medea had committed a terrible crime. She had tricked innocent daughters into killing their own father. The gods turned from her and she changed from a lovely young sorceress into an evil witch. The people of Iolcus refused to accept her for their queen and took another king in Jason's stead. With the loss of his throne, Jason also lost his love for Medea. He forgot that he had sworn to love her till his dying day and that she had committed her crimes for his sake. He asked her to leave so he could marry the Princess of Corinth and inherit her father's kingdom.

Medea, scorned and furious, turned more and more to evil sorcery. To revenge herself on Jason, she sent a magic robe to his new bride. It was a beautiful gown, but the moment the bride put it on she went up in flames and so did the whole palace. Then Medea disappeared into a dark cloud, riding in a carriage drawn by two dragons.

Jason found no more happiness, for when he broke his sacred oath to Medea, he lost Hera's goodwill. His good looks left him and so did his luck and his friends. Lonely and forgotten, he sat one day in the shade of his once glorious ship, the *Argo*, now rotting on the beach of Corinth. Suddenly the sacred piece of oak in the prow broke off, fell on him, and killed him.

The Golden Fleece was hung in Apollo's temple in Delphi, a wonder for all Greeks to behold and a reminder of the great deeds of Jason and the Argonauts.

THE LITTLE HOUSE

STORY AND PICTURES
BY
VIRGINIA LEE BURTON

ONCE upon a time there was a Little House way out in the country. She was a pretty Little House and she was strong and well built. The man who built her so well said, "This Little House shall never be sold for gold or silver and she will live to see our great-great-grandchildren's great-great-grandchildren living in her."

The Little House was very happy as she sat on the hill and watched the countryside around her. She watched the sun rise in the morning and she watched the sun set in the evening. Day followed day, each one a little different from the one before . . . but the Little House stayed just the same.

In the nights she watched the moon grow from a thin new moon to a full moon, then back again to a thin old moon; and when there was no moon she watched the stars. Way off in the distance she could see the lights of the city. The Little House was curious about the city and wondered what it would be like to live there.

Time passed quickly for the Little House as she watched the countryside slowly change with the seasons. In the Spring, when the days grew longer and the sun warmer, she waited for the first robin to return from the South. She watched the grass turn green. She watched the buds on the trees swell and the apple trees burst into blossom. She watched the children playing in the brook.

In the long Summer days she sat in the sun and watched the trees cover themselves with leaves and the white daisies cover the hill. She watched the gardens grow, and she watched the apples turn red and ripen. She watched the children swimming in the pool.

In the Fall, when the days grew shorter and the nights colder, she watched the first frost turn the leaves to bright yellow and orange and red. She watched the harvest gathered and the apples picked. She watched the children going back to school.

In the Winter, when the nights were long and the days short, and the countryside covered with snow, she watched the children coasting and skating.

Year followed year. . . . The apple trees grew old and new ones were planted. The children grew up and went away to the city . . . and now at night the lights of the city seemed brighter and closer.

One day the Little House was surprised to see a horseless carriage coming down the winding country road. . . . Pretty soon there were more of them on the road and fewer carriages pulled by horses. Pretty soon along came some surveyors and surveyed a line in front of the Little House. Pretty soon along came a steam shovel and dug a road through the hill covered with daisies. . . . Then some trucks came and dumped big stones on the road, then some trucks with little stones, then some trucks with tar and sand, and finally a steamroller came and rolled it all smooth, and the road was done.

Now the Little House watched the trucks and automobiles going back and forth to the city. Gasoline stations . . . roadside stands . . . and small houses followed the new road. Everyone and everything moved much faster now than before.

More roads were made, and the countryside was divided into lots. More houses and bigger houses . . . apartment houses and

VIRGINIA LEE BURTON

tenement houses . . . schools . . . stores . . . and garages spread over the land and crowded around the Little House. No one wanted to live in her and take care of her anymore. She couldn't be sold for gold or silver, so she just stayed there and watched.

Now it was not so quiet and peaceful at night. Now the lights of the city were bright and very close, and the streetlights shone all night.

"This must be living in the city," thought the Little House, and didn't know whether she liked it or not. She missed the field of daisies and the apple trees dancing in the moonlight.

Pretty soon there were trolley cars going back and forth in front of the Little House. They went back and forth all day and part of the night. Everyone seemed to be very busy and everyone seemed to be in a hurry.

Pretty soon there was an elevated train going back and forth above the Little House. The air was filled with dust and smoke, and the noise was so loud that it shook the Little House. Now she couldn't tell when Spring came, or Summer or Fall, or Winter. It all seemed about the same.

Pretty soon there was a subway going back and forth underneath the Little House. She couldn't see it, but she could feel and hear it. People were moving faster and faster. No one noticed the Little House anymore. They hurried by without a glance.

Pretty soon they tore down the apartment houses and tenement houses around the Little House and started digging big cellars . . . one on each side. The steam shovels dug down three stories on one side and four stories on the other side. Pretty soon they started building up. . . . They built up twenty-five stories on one side and thirty-five stories on the other.

Now the Little House only saw the sun at noon, and didn't see the moon or stars at night at all because the lights of the city were too bright. She didn't like living in the city. At night she used to dream of the country and the field of daisies and the apple trees dancing in the moonlight.

The Little House was very sad and lonely. Her paint was cracked and dirty. Her windows were broken and her shutters hung crookedly. She looked shabby . . . though she was just as good a house as ever underneath.

Then one fine morning in Spring along came the great-great-granddaughter of the man who built the Little House so well. She saw the shabby Little House, but she didn't hurry by. There was something about the Little House that made her stop and look again.

She said to her husband, "That Little House looks just like the Little House my grandmother lived in when she was a little girl, only *that* Little House was way out in the country on a hill covered with daisies and apple trees growing around."

They found out it was the very same house, so they went to the Movers to see if the Little House could be moved. The Movers looked the Little House all over and said, "Sure, this house is as good as ever. She's built so well we could move her anywhere." So they jacked up the Little House and put her on wheels. Traffic was held up for hours as they slowly moved her out of the city.

At first the Little House was frightened, but after she got used to it she rather liked it. They rolled along the big road, and they rolled along the little roads, until they were way out in the country.

When the Little House saw the green grass and heard the birds singing, she didn't feel sad anymore. They went along and along, but they couldn't seem to find just the right place.

They tried the Little House here, and they tried her there. Finally they saw a little hill in the middle of a field . . . and apple trees growing around.

"There," said the great-great-granddaughter, "that's just the place."

"Yes, it is," said the Little House to herself.

A cellar was dug on top of the hill and slowly they moved the house from the road to the hill.

The windows and shutters were fixed and once again they painted her a lovely shade of pink. As the Little House settled down on her new foundation, she smiled happily. Once again she could watch the sun and moon and stars. Once again she could watch Spring and Summer and Fall and Winter come and go.

Once again she was lived in and taken care of.

Never again would she be curious about the city. . . . Never again would she want to live there. . . . The stars twinkled above her . . . a new moon was coming up . . . it was Spring . . . and all was quiet and peaceful in the country.

JOHNNY CROW'S GARDEN

L·LESLIE BROOKE

Johnny Crow
Would dig and sow
Till he made a little garden.
And the lion
Had a green and yellow tie on
In Johnny Crow's garden.
And the rat
Wore a feather in his hat
But the bear
Had nothing to wear
In Johnny Crow's garden.
So the ape
Took his measure with a tape
In Johnny Crow's garden.

And the pig
Danced a jig
In Johnny Crow's garden.
And the whale
Told a very long tale
In Johnny Crow's garden.
And the fox
Put them all in the stocks
In Johnny Crow's garden.
But Johnny Crow
He let them go
And they all sat down to their dinner in a row
In Johnny Crow's garden.

PLAY WITH ME
STORY AND PICTURES BY
MARIE HALL ETS

The sun was up and there was dew on the grass and I went to the meadow to play.

A grasshopper sat on the leaf of a weed. He was eating it up for his breakfast.

"Grasshopper," I said, "will you play with me?" And I tried to catch him, but he leaped away.

A frog stopped jumping and sat down by the pond. I think he was waiting to catch a mosquito.

"Frog," I said, "will you play with me?" And I tried to catch him, but he leaped away too.

A turtle was sitting on the end of a log. He was just sitting still, getting warm in the sun.

"Turtle," I said, "will you play with me?" But before I could touch him he plopped into the water.

A chipmunk was sitting beneath the oak tree, shelling an acorn with his sharp little teeth.

"Chipmunk," I said, "will you play with me?" But when I ran near him, he ran up the tree.

A blue jay came and sat down on a bough, and jabbered and scolded the way blue jays do.

"Blue Jay," I said, "will you play with me?" But when I held up my hands he flew away.

A rabbit was sitting behind the oak tree. He was wiggling his nose and nibbling a flower.

"Rabbit," I said, "will you play with me?" And I tried to catch him, but he ran to the woods.

A snake came sneaking through the grass, zigzagging and sliding the way snakes do.

"Snake," I said, "will you play with me?" But even the snake ran away, down his hole.

None of them, none of them, would play with me. So I picked a milkweed and blew off its seeds.

Then I went to the pond and sat down on a rock and watched a bug making trails on the water.

And as I still sat there without making a sound (so they wouldn't get scared and run away), out from the bushes where he had been hiding came a baby fawn, and looked at me.

I held my breath and he came nearer. He came so near I could have touched him.

But I didn't move and I didn't speak. And Fawn came up and licked my cheek.

And as I sat there without making a sound, Grasshopper came back and sat down beside me.

Then Frog came back and sat down in the grass. And slowpoke Turtle crawled back to his log.

And Chipmunk came and watched me and chattered. And Blue Jay came back to his bough overhead.

And Rabbit came back and hopped around me. And Snake came out of his hole.

Oh, now I was happy — as happy could be! For all of them — ALL OF THEM — were playing with me.

GELETT BURGESS
The Goops

The Goops they lick their fingers,
    And the Goops they lick their knives;
They spill their broth on the tablecloth —
    Oh, they lead disgusting lives!
The Goops they talk while eating,
    And loud and fast they chew;
And that is why I'm glad that I
    Am not a Goop — are you?

GOODNIGHT MOON

by Margaret Wise Brown
Pictures by Clement Hurd

In the great green room
There was a telephone
And a red balloon
And a picture of
The cow jumping over the moon

And there were three little bears sitting on chairs
And two little kittens
And a pair of mittens
And a little toyhouse
And a young mouse
And a comb and a brush and a bowl full of mush
And a quiet old lady who was whispering "hush"

Goodnight room
Goodnight moon
Goodnight cow jumping over the moon
Goodnight light
And the red balloon

Goodnight bears
Goodnight chairs
Goodnight kittens
And goodnight mittens
Goodnight clocks
And goodnight socks
Goodnight little house
And goodnight mouse

Goodnight comb
And goodnight brush
Goodnight nobody
Goodnight mush
And goodnight to the old lady whispering "hush"
Goodnight stars
Goodnight air
Goodnight noises everywhere

RACHEL FIELD
General Store

Someday I'm going to have a store
With a tinkly bell hung over the door,
With real glass cases and counters wide
And drawers all spilly with things inside.
There'll be a little of everything:
Bolts of calico; balls of string;
Jars of peppermint; tins of tea;
Pots and kettles and crockery;
Seeds in packets; scissors bright;
Kegs of sugar, brown and white;
Sarsaparilla for picnic lunches,
Bananas and rubber boots in bunches.
I'll fix the window and dust each shelf,
And take the money in all myself,
It will be my store and I will say:
"What can I do for you today?"

LITTLE TOOT
on the
GRAND CANAL

by HARDIE GRAMATKY —

LITTLE TOOT loved life on the river. He tooted and towed with the hardworking tugboats. He did figure 8's on the river. And at times the little tugboat went on adventures around old docks and wharves.

He always liked to explore.

One day his father, Big Toot, took him on a real adventure. Together they went to Venice, a land far over the sea. Big Toot is the mightiest tugboat on the ocean, so Little Toot had nothing to fear.

When they got to Venice, Big Toot had work to do in the shipyard. And Little Toot was left all alone. Big round smoke balls welled up out of his smokestack and he tried hard to hold back a tear. Little Toot was afraid.

But not for long. He began to see and hear Venice. It was beautiful! Bells rang. Bands played. It looked like a carnival of fun.

Little Toot bounded across the bay.

Venice, indeed, was a lovely place.

In front was a palace of pink and white marble. It looked like a jewel box open to the sea. Beyond that was a golden cathedral. And a tall bell tower chimed out gay tunes.

Yet with all this gaiety there was a sad note. The sad note came from the singing gondoliers. It was not that the gondoliers were unhappy. Not at all. They had nothing at all to be unhappy about, yet the songs they sang were sad.

But Little Toot was in no mood for sad songs. And especially not today. Today he was out to have fun.

By a stroke of good luck a high tide washed him into the Piazza of San Marco and past the golden cathedral. Great jewelled domes sparkled in the sunlight and frescoes flashed like fire.

So exciting was it that it sparked a spirit of adventure in Little Toot he had never quite known before.

Then even more exciting, out he came into the Grand Canal. Magnificent mansions rose on all sides like palaces of princes and kings. Most magnificent of all was a house on the canal that looked like a birthday cake. Its doorways and windows were trimmed with pink frosting and icing dripped down into the canal. Even its fine-lace balconies were made of spun sugar.

This was gorgeous enough, yet even more to Little Toot's taste was a forest of candystick canes that grew right out of the canal. They were delicious-looking, red and white striped candystick canes . . . the most beautiful thing he had seen in all Venice.

Now Little Toot was really happy.

So happy was he, he could have stayed there forever. He might well have, too, had he not taken a wrong turn. It was the worst turn he could have taken, because it took him down into a darkened canal.

Suddenly before him he saw the Bridge of Sighs.

It was an awful thing for a little tugboat to see. The bridge looked like a monster that had turned into stone. And it grew out of a prison with black barred windows.

Great round smoke balls welled out of Little Toot's smokestack. He was filled with such fear he didn't know which way to turn.

He wanted his father. More than anything else he wanted to go home.

He dashed for the lagoon. But just then the bells of San Marco began to ring. And all the birds flew into the air.

When the birds saw the unhappy little tugboat, they all flew down again. They fluttered their wings around him like worried friends wringing their hands.

No one can be unhappy in Venice. The old saying is true. In no time at all the Bridge of Sighs was forgotten.

Little Toot and the birds became companions from the beginning. They loved to have fun and play games. Soon they were racing down narrow canals and squeezing under all the low bridges.

The day was so beautiful. Bells rang. Bands played. And, as though they had always been waiting for this . . . shopkeepers, waiters, and bootblacks alike . . . everyone joined in the fun.

Even the great bronze horses high on the balcony of San Marco pranced with the joy of the crowd.

But nothing could be done to change the spirit of the singing gondoliers.

Their songs grew sadder than before.

No one took notice of them and all went on with their fun.

In a game of hide-and-seek Little Toot found a friendly looking building with a painting on its front. Its water door was open, so he ducked right in.

But it wasn't the friendly place he had hoped for. Fire poured from a furnace, filling the place with fumes. Hot melting glass boiled over in black cauldrons. It was the shop of the glassblower.

Before the poor little tugboat could find his way out again, he inhaled hot molten glass down into his smokestack.

It burned awfully! Out he came, coughing and choking. He tried to blow smoke balls, but none would come out. Harder, he tried . . . then even harder.

Suddenly, and as if by magic, instead of his big black smoke balls, out came *bubbles of glass.*

It was enough to humiliate anyone: To make matters worse, there were the *carabinieri.* They popped out from behind everything. The carabinieri are the police. They protect Venice from pirates.

There had not been pirates around for years; still the carabinieri were on guard. With nothing better to do for the moment, they decided to put the little tugboat in chains.

Suddenly, the boom of a cannon halted everything. A pirate ship had entered the harbour unnoticed. Already it had anchored right in the lagoon.

Then quickly over the sides came pirates bulging with pistols. Quicker still, they overpowered the carabinieri.

The pirates lost no time in looting. They stole rubies and emeralds from the cathedral and pearls from the pink and white palace. The scoundrels had no shame.

In no time at all their pockets were stuffed with precious jewels and their eyes were filled with greed.

Indeed, they were so greedy they tore the wings off a golden lion.

And what was even worse, they ripped the spun-sugar balcony off the house that looked like a birthday cake.

But when the pirates came to the candystick canes, they had gone just too far. Little Toot set up an awful howl. Those were his favourite red and white striped candystick canes . . . the most valued treasure in all Venice.

Without help from anyone he took on the pirates single-handed. He darted in and out like a mother bird, trying desperately to draw the pirates away from his candystick canes.

It was no use. The hoodlums only laughed at the little tugboat. And to get rid of him they drove him back into the shop of the glassblower.

What a sad day for Venice. All their beautiful treasures were aboard the pirate ship.

Never again would bells ring. Nevermore would the birds fly so happily.

Even the sad singing gondoliers now had reason to be sad.

But Little Toot was not ready to give up. Without anyone noticing, he slipped out of the shop of the glassblower. He coughed and choked as before, and again he was blowing glass bubbles.

This time, though, instead of blowing ordinary glass bubbles, he blew bubbles of richly coloured, beautiful Venetian glass.

So dazzling were the bubbles they sparkled in the sunlight like enormous jewels.

When the pirates saw them they stopped and stared. This was a prize too tempting to resist. And almost too much for their large, greedy eyes.

They dropped everything they had stolen and raced after the great giant pearls.

Like a swarm of bees they pursued the bubbles through all the byways of Venice.

Then, they chased the bubbles through the courtyard of the pink and white palace and up the great marble stairs.

But those foolish pirates! They pushed to be first over the Bridge of Sighs. Then they fought their way wildly into prison.

When iron gates of the dungeon clanged shut behind them, all the bells in Venice began to ring. Bands played. And happy birds flew into the air.

Happiest of all were the gondoliers. Their celebration on the Grand Canal was without equal. And the songs they sang were so joyous, everyone sang along with them.

And the carabinieri joined in with the chorus.

Presents of silver and gold were offered to Little Toot. But politely and with a smile he refused.

If the truth were known, the little tugboat would have been happy with a candystick cane. But then, no one thought even to ask him.

Happily, someone did.

　HARDIE GRAMATKY

DENNIS LEE
Alligator Pie

Alligator pie, alligator pie,
If I don't get some I think I'm gonna die.
Give away the green grass, give away the sky,
But don't give away my alligator pie.

Alligator stew, alligator stew,
If I don't get some I don't know what I'll do.
Give away my furry hat, give away my shoe,
But don't give away my alligator stew.

Alligator soup, alligator soup,
If I don't get some I think I'm gonna droop.
Give away my hockey-stick, give away my hoop,
But don't give away my alligator soup.

P. C. ASBJØRNSEN AND
JØRGEN E. MOE

The Husband Who Was to Mind the House

ONCE on a time there was a man, so surly and cross he never thought his Wife did anything right in the house. So, one evening, in haymaking time, he came home, scolding and swearing, and showing his teeth and making a dust.

"Dear love, don't be so angry; there's a good man," said his Goody; "tomorrow let's change our work. I'll go out with the mowers and mow, and you shall mind the house at home."

Yes, the Husband thought that would do very well.

So, early next morning, his Goody took a scythe over her neck, and went out into the hayfield with the mowers, and began to mow; but the man was to mind house, and do the work at home.

First of all, he wanted to churn the butter; but when he had churned awhile, he got thirsty, and went down to the cellar to tap a barrel of ale. So, just when he had knocked in the bung, and was putting the tap into the cask, he heard overhead the pig come into the kitchen. Then off he ran up the cellar steps, with the tap in his hand, as fast as he could, to look after the pig, lest it should upset the churn; but when he got up, and saw the pig had already knocked the churn over, and stood there, rooting and grunting amongst the cream which was running all over the floor, he got so wild with rage that he quite forgot the ale barrel, and ran at the pig as hard as he could. He caught it, too, just as it ran out of doors, and gave it such a kick, that piggy lay for dead on the spot. Then all at once he remembered he had the tap in his hand; but when he got down to the cellar, every drop of ale had run out of the cask.

Then he went into the dairy and found enough cream left to fill the churn again, and so he began to churn, for butter they must have at dinner. When he had churned a bit, he remembered that their milking cow was still shut up in the byre, and hadn't had a bit to eat or a drop to drink all the morning, though the sun was high. Then all at once he thought 'twas too far to take her down to the meadow, so he'd just get her up on the housetop — for the house, you must know, was thatched with sods, and a fine crop of grass was growing there. Now the house lay close up against a steep down, and he thought if he laid a plank across to the thatch at the back he'd easily get the cow up.

But still he couldn't leave the churn, for there was his little babe crawling about on the floor, and "if I leave it," he thought, "the child is safe to upset it." So he took the churn on his back, and went out with it; but then he thought he'd better first water the cow before he turned her out on the thatch; so he took up a bucket to draw water out of the well; but, as he stooped down at the well's brink, all the cream ran out of the churn over his shoulders, and so down into the well.

Now it was near dinner time, and he hadn't even got the butter yet; so he thought he'd best boil the porridge, and filled the pot with water and hung it over the fire. When he had done that, he thought the cow might perhaps fall off the thatch and break her legs or her neck. So he got up on the house to tie her up. One end of the rope he made fast to the cow's neck and the other he slipped down the chimney, and tied round his own thigh; and he had to make haste, for the water now began to boil in the pot, and he had still to grind the oatmeal.

So he began to grind away; but while he was hard at it, down fell the cow off the housetop after all, and as she fell, she dragged the man up the chimney by the rope. There he stuck fast; and as for the cow, she hung halfway down the wall, swinging between heaven and earth, for she could get neither down nor up.

And now the Goody had waited seven lengths and seven breadths for her Husband to come and call them home to dinner; but never a call they had. At last she thought she'd waited long enough, and went home. But when she got there and saw the cow hanging in such an ugly place, she ran up and cut the rope in two with her scythe. But, as she did this, down came her husband out of the chimney; and so, when his old dame came inside the kitchen, there she found him standing on his head in the porridge pot.

Ruth Krauss
A Hole Is To Dig
A FIRST BOOK OF FIRST DEFINITIONS

PICTURES BY
Maurice Sendak

Mashed potatoes are to give everybody enough
A face is so you can make faces

A face is something to have on the front of your head
Dogs are to kiss people
Hands are to hold
A hand is to hold up when you want your turn

A hole is to dig

The ground is to make a garden
Grass is to cut
Grass is to have on the ground with dirt under it and clover in it
Maybe you could hide things in a hole
A party is to say how-do-you-do and shake hands

A party is to make little children happy
Arms are to hug with
Toes are to wiggle
Ears are to wiggle
Mud is to jump in and slide in and yell doodleedoodleedoo
Anh-h-h-h! Doodleedoodleedoo-oo!

A castle is to build in the sand
A hole is to sit in
A dream is to look at the night and see things
Snow is to roll in

Buttons are to keep people warm
The world is so you have something to stand on
The sun is to tell you when it's every day
When you make your bed you get a star
Little stones are for little children to gather up and put in little
   piles
Oo! A rock is when you trip on it you should have watched where
   you were going
Children are to love
A brother is to help you
A principal is to take out splinters

A mountain is to go to the top
A mountain is to go to the bottom
A lap is so you don't get crumbs on the floor
A moustache is to wear on Halloween
A hat is to wear on a train
Toes are to dance on
Eyebrows are to go over your eyes
A sea shell is to hear the sea
A wave is to wave bye-bye
Big shells are to put little shells in
A hole is to plant a flower
A watch is to hear it tick
Dishes are to do
Cats are so you can have kittens

Mice are to eat your cheese

Noses are to rub
A nose is to blow
A match is to blow
A whistle is to make people jump
Rugs are so you don't get splinters in you
Hunh! Rugs are so dogs have napkins
A floor is so you don't fall in the hole your house is in
A hole is for a mouse to live in
A door is to open
A door is to shut
A hole is to look through
Steps are to sit on
A hole is when you step in it you go down
Hands are to make things
Hands are to eat with
A tablespoon is to eat a table with
A package is to look inside
The sun is so it can be a great day

A book is to look at

CLEMENT MOORE

Almost everybody knows " 'Twas the night before Christmas". We know it so well that it doesn't seem possible that a real person actually sat down one day and wrote the fifty-six lines of the poem.

Clement Moore was an American who lived a long, long time ago. He was born in 1779, during the American War of Independence. He died in 1863, while another great war, the Civil War, was being fought.

One snowy, blowy day, when New York City was more like a collection of busy villages, he was driving home in his sleigh, his horse's harness all a-jingle. The idea of the poem came into his head, perhaps because he was thinking of a fat, red-faced Dutchman who lived in his neighbourhood. This Dutchman may have given him the idea for his Saint Nick, with his round little belly that shook like a jelly, his twinkling eyes, and his stump of a pipe.

As soon as he reached home he wrote the verses down to amuse his six children — Margaret, Charity, Benjamin, Mary, Clement, and Emily. And that's why "A Visit from Saint Nicholas" is still read on Christmas Eve in millions of homes.

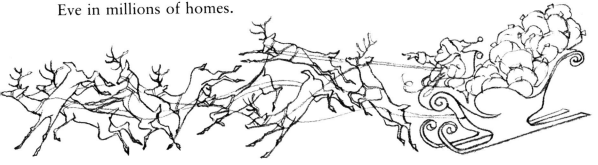

A Visit from Saint Nicholas

'Twas the night before Christmas, when all through the house
Not a creature was stirring, not even a mouse.
The stockings were hung by the chimney with care,
In hopes that Saint Nicholas soon would be there.
The children were nestled all snug in their beds,
While visions of sugarplums danced in their heads;
And mamma in her kerchief, and I in my cap,
Had just settled our brains for a long winter's nap —
When out on the lawn there arose such a clatter
I sprang from my bed to see what was the matter.
Away to the window I flew like a flash,
Tore open the shutter, and threw up the sash.
The moon on the breast of the new-fallen snow
Gave a lustre of midday to objects below;
When what to my wondering eyes should appear
But a miniature sleigh and eight tiny reindeer,
With a little old driver, so lively and quick,
I knew in a moment it must be Saint Nick!
More rapid than eagles his coursers they came,
And he whistled and shouted and called them by name.
"Now, Dasher! now, Dancer! now, Prancer and Vixen!
On, Comet! on, Cupid! on, Donder and Blitzen! —
To the top of the porch, to the top of the wall,
Now, dash away, dash away, dash away all!"
As dry leaves that before the wild hurricane fly,
When they meet with an obstacle mount to the sky,
So, up to the housetop the coursers they flew,
With a sleigh full of toys — and Saint Nicholas, too.

And then, in a twinkling, I heard on the roof
The prancing and pawing of each little hoof.
As I drew in my head and was turning around,
Down the chimney Saint Nicholas came with a bound:
He was dressed all in fur from his head to his foot,
And his clothes were all tarnished with ashes and soot:
A bundle of toys he had flung on his back,
And he looked like a peddler just opening his pack.
His eyes, how they twinkled! his dimples, how merry!
His cheeks were like roses, his nose like a cherry;
His droll little mouth was drawn up like a bow,
And the beard on his chin was as white as the snow.
The stump of a pipe he held tight in his teeth,
And the smoke, it encircled his head like a wreath.
He had a broad face and a little round belly
That shook, when he laughed, like a bowl full of jelly.
He was chubby and plump — a right jolly old elf:
And I laughed when I saw him, in spite of myself;
A wink of his eye, and a twist of his head,
Soon gave me to know I had nothing to dread.
He spoke not a word, but went straight to his work,
And filled all the stockings: then turned with a jerk,
And laying his finger aside of his nose,
And giving a nod, up the chimney he rose.
He sprang to his sleigh, to his team gave a whistle,
And away they all flew like the down of a thistle.
But I heard him exclaim, ere they drove out of sight,
"Happy Christmas to all, and to all a good-night!"

JEAN DE BRUNHOFF

Jean de Brunhoff was a French painter. It was his wife, Cecile, who first thought of Babar the Elephant King. She used to tell bedtime stories about him to her two little sons. They all enjoyed these so much that one of the sons, Laurent, said Babar "was like a member of our family". Soon they coaxed Papa de Brunhoff into making some little "family books" out of Babar's adventures.

These became known over the whole world. At one time one French person out of four (and that's millions) knew about Babar. He's the most famous elephant there ever was.

People who try to find out such things have discovered that, of all animal books, children like books about cats most. But almost as popular, especially among boys, are elephants. Why is this? I don't know.

But I do know why I keep on liking Babar and the Old Lady and Arthur and Celeste. It's because Jean de Brunhoff loved them and somehow the words and pictures make you feel that he did. I like the pictures especially because there's so much to *see* in them. I get a lot for my money.

Jean de Brunhoff was born in 1899 and died at thirty-eight, still a young man. His son Laurent continued with the series but I prefer his father's books.

THE STORY
OF
BABAR
the little elephant

IN THE GREAT FOREST a little elephant was born. His
name was Babar. His mother loved him dearly, and used to
rock him to sleep with her trunk, singing to him softly the while.

Babar grew fast. Soon he was playing with the other baby elephants. He was one of the nicest of them. Look at him digging in the sand with a shell.

One day Babar was having a lovely ride on his mother's back, when a cruel hunter, hiding behind a bush, shot at them.

He killed Babar's mother. The monkey hid himself, the birds flew away, and Babar burst into tears. The hunter ran up to catch poor Babar.

Babar was very frightened and ran away from the hunter. After some days, tired and footsore, he came to a town.

He was amazed, for it was the first time he had ever seen so many houses.

What strange things he saw! Beautiful avenues! Motorcars and motorbuses! But what interested Babar most of all was two gentlemen he met in the street.

He thought to himself: "What lovely clothes they have got! I wish I could have some too! But how can I get them?"

Luckily he was seen by a very rich old lady who understood little elephants, and knew at once that he was longing for a smart suit. She loved making others happy, so she gave him her purse. "Thank you, Madam," said Babar.

Without wasting a moment Babar went into a big shop. He got into the lift. It was such fun going up and down in this jolly little box that he went ten times to the very top and ten times down again to the bottom. He was going up once more when the lift-boy said to him: "Sir, this is not a toy. You must get out now and buy what you want. Look, here is the shop-walker."

Then he bought a shirt, collar and tie, a suit of a delightful green colour, next a lovely bowler hat, and finally shoes and spats.

Babar was so pleased with his purchases, and satisfied with his appearance, that he paid a visit to the photographer.

And here is his photograph.

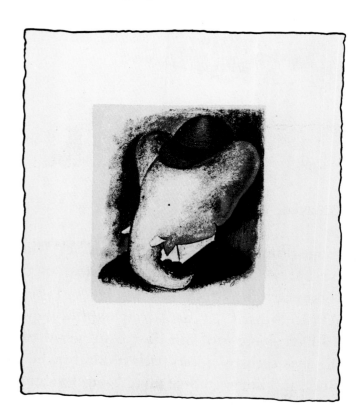

Babar went to dinner with his friend the old lady. She, too, thought he looked very smart in his new suit. After dinner, he was so tired that he went early to sleep.

Babar made his home in the old lady's house. Every morning they did their exercises together, and then Babar had his bath. Every day he drove out in the car that the old lady had bought him. She gave him everything that he wanted.

A learned professor gave him lessons. Babar was attentive, and always gave the right answer. He was a most promising pupil.

In the evenings, after dinner, he told the old lady's friends all about his life in the Great Forest.

And yet Babar was not altogether happy: he could no longer play about in the Great Forest with his little cousins and his friends the monkeys. He often gazed out of the window, dreaming of his childhood, and when he thought of his dear mother he used to cry.

Two years passed by. One day he was out for a walk, when he met two little elephants with no clothes on. "Why, here are Arthur and Celeste, my two little cousins!" he cried in amazement to the old lady.

Babar hugged Arthur and Celeste and took them to buy some lovely clothes.

Next, he took them to a tea-shop, where they had some delicious cakes.

Meanwhile in the Great Forest all the elephants were searching for Arthur and Celeste and their mothers grew more and more anxious. Luckily, an old bird flying over the town had spied them, and hurried back to tell the elephants.

The mothers went to the town to fetch Arthur and Celeste. They were glad when they found them, but they scolded them all the same for having run away.

Babar made up his mind to return to the Great Forest with Arthur and Celeste and their mothers. The old lady helped him to pack.

When everything was ready for the journey Babar kissed his old friend good-bye. If he had not been so sorry to leave her he would have been delighted to go home. He promised to come back to her, and never to forget her.

Off they went! There was no room for the mother elephants in the car. So they ran behind, lifting their trunks so as not to breathe in the dust. The old lady was left alone, sadly thinking: "When shall I see my little Babar again?"

Alas! That very day the King of the elephants had eaten a bad mushroom.

It had poisoned him. He had been very ill, and then had died.

It was a terrible misfortune.

After his funeral the oldest elephants met together to choose a new King.

Just at that moment they heard a noise and turned round. What a wonderful sight they saw! It was Babar arriving in his car, with all the elephants running and shouting: "Here they are! Here they are! They have come back! Hullo, Babar! Hullo, Arthur! Hullo, Celeste! What lovely clothes! What a beautiful car!"

Then Cornelius, the oldest elephant of all, said, in his quavering voice: "My dear friends, we must have a new King. Why not choose Babar? He has come back from the town, where he has

lived among men and learnt much. Let us offer him the crown."
All the elephants thought that Cornelius had spoken wisely, and
they listened eagerly to hear what Babar would say.

"I thank you all," said Babar; "but before accepting the crown I
must tell you that on our journey in the car Celeste and I got
engaged to be married. If I become your King, she will be your
queen."

"Long live Queen Celeste! Long live King Babar!" the elephants
shouted with one voice. And that was how Babar became King.

"Cornelius," said Babar, "you have such good ideas that I shall
make you a general, and when I get my crown I will give you my
hat. In a week's time I am going to marry Celeste. We will give a
grand party to celebrate our marriage and our coronation." And
Babar asked the birds to take invitations to all the animals, and he
told the dromedary to go to the town to buy him some fine
wedding clothes.

The guests began to arrive. The dromedary brought the clothes
just in time for the ceremony.

After the wedding and the coronation everyone danced merrily.

The party was over. Night fell, and the stars came out. The
hearts of King Babar and Queen Celeste were filled with happy
dreams.

Then all the world slept. The guests had gone home, very
pleased and very tired after dancing so much. For many a long day
they will remember that wonderful ball.

Then King Babar and Queen Celeste set out on their honey-
moon, in a glorious yellow balloon, to meet with new adventures.

ELIZABETH MADOX ROBERTS

The People

The ants are walking under the ground,
And the pigeons are flying over the steeple,
And in between are the people.

The Star: A Song

O little one away so far,
You cannot hear me when I sing.

You cannot tell me what you are,
I cannot tell you anything.

ISSUN BOSHI, THE INCHLING

An Old Tale of Japan

retold by Momoko Ishii

translated by Yone Mizuta • illustrated by Fuku Akino

LONG, long ago, in a certain village, there lived an old man and his wife. They were quite old, and they had never had any children of their own. Because of this, they were sad and lonely. Each day they said, "How wonderful it would be if we only had a child." And each day they prayed to the Sun to grant them a child.

At last a baby was born to them. Although he was strong and healthy, the baby was no bigger than a person's thumb. The old man and his wife were at first surprised. Then they saw it as the will of Heaven, and were content. They brought him up with loving care, calling him Issun Boshi, which means "the Inchling".

As time passed, Inchling grew no bigger. He could dance and sing well, but he was just as small as ever. When he was twelve years old, he was still no higher than his father's anklebone. The old man and his wife were disheartened. And the boy was disheartened, too.

One day, the boy asked his parents for permission to go to the Capital. He wished to try his fortune there. His old parents sadly agreed to let him go.

For the journey, Inchling took a lacquered soup bowl to use as a hat, a chopstick for a walking stick, and a needle for a sword, with a bit of straw for its sheath.

His old parents went with him to the edge of the village to see him off. They told him to follow a certain road until he came to a river, then to go up the river to the Capital.

Inchling walked and walked, thinking he would never reach the river. Suddenly he met an ant.

"Please, where is the river that leads to the Capital?" he asked the ant.

"Follow the path of dandelions, then cross the field of horse-tails," replied the ant.

Inchling walked for a long time between the dandelions and across a wide field of horsetails. At last he came to the river.

Setting his soup-bowl hat afloat on the river, and using his chopstick for an oar, he rowed upstream.

When night fell, he tied up his boat in a clump of reeds, curled up, and went to sleep.

Inchling awoke early the next morning, and continued his journey upstream. Around noon, he arrived at the Capital.

"Finally, I am at the Capital!" he thought as he brought his boat to rest at the pier and climbed ashore.

My! What a lot of people there were in the Capital! Legs to the right of him, legs to the left of him.

Taking care not to get trampled on, Inchling turned his steps

toward a place where there were fewer people, and continued walking.

Soon he came to a beautiful mansion.

"There must be some work for me here," he said to himself.

Standing at the foot of the steps, he cried, "May I speak to someone, please."

An old man soon appeared.

"I am here, under your clog!" Inchling said, seeing the old man look this way and that. "Be careful not to step on me."

The man, who was the lord of the mansion, was most surprised as he leaned over and peeked under the clog.

"But what brings you here, my little fellow?" he asked, picking Inchling up in his hand.

When Inchling told his story and asked for work, the old man laughed and said, "But what can such a tiny fellow do?"

Inchling drew out his tiny sword, and — fftt — slew a fly that flew by. Then he jumped up on the old man's fan and performed a charming dance.

When he finished his dance he heard a lot of clapping. It seems the people of the mansion had gathered to watch him dance.

Inchling was at once hired by the lord and went to live in the mansion. Most of his time was spent with the princess, the beautiful daughter of the lord. His job was to act as a paperweight, holding down the sheet when she practiced her writing. Another task was to line up the dice when she played backgammon.

Many years passed in this way, and the princess came to love Inchling very much.

One day, Inchling accompanied the beautiful princess and her companions on a visit to the famous Kiyomizu Temple.

On the way back to the mansion, three demons — one black, one red, and one green — suddenly jumped out from behind a tree. The green demon and the black demon clutched large iron rods. The red demon held a magic mallet in his hand.

Spreading out their arms to block the way, the demons roared that they had come to kidnap the princess.

Inchling quickly ran forward, placing himself between the princess and the demons.

"You will do no such thing," he cried.

With that, he leaped at the black demon and with his tiny sword jabbed at the demon's eyes until the demon was forced to flee. Inchling then turned on the green demon. Jab! jab! jab! went his sword. The green demon soon also turned and fled.

The red demon then rushed at Inchling with an open mouth, ready to eat him. But Inchling quickly slipped behind the demon's teeth and with his sword jabbed and stabbed in every direction.

It was not long before the red demon was crying surrender. Inchling sprang from the demon's mouth, and picked up the magic mallet, which the fleeing demon had left behind.

Handing the magic mallet to the princess, Inchling said, "Wish on the mallet and your wish will come true."

"Oh, no," she answered. "You have won the mallet in a brave fight! You should be the first to wish on it."

"My greatest wish," said Inchling, "is to be as tall as other men."

The princess then took the mallet and said, "Your wish is my wish, too."

In the next instant there stood before the princess a handsome young man.

Filled with joy, the princess and the handsome young man returned to the mansion.

Inchling's brave deed became known throughout the land. He married the beautiful princess. How proud his old parents were! And how happy they were when their son invited them to come and live with him and his beautiful bride.

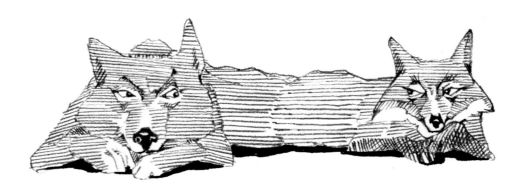

RUTH KRAUSS

No More Woxes: A Short Tall Tale

There was a wolf
and there was a fox and
they ate each other up.
And that made the wox.

Then the wox
ate himself up and
that's why there are
no more woxes.

HI, CAT!

EZRA JACK KEATS

O N HIS WAY to meet Peter, Archie saw someone new on
the block.

"Hi, cat," he said as he walked by.

He looked at his reflection in a store window.

Peter was waiting at the corner.

"Make way for your ol' gran'pa," Archie said in a shaky voice.
He looked Peter up and down. "My, my, Peter, how you've
grown!"

"Why, gran'pa," Peter said, "It's good to see you."

"Hello, my children," Archie croaked.

"Hi, gran'pa!" Susy giggled.

Willie was so happy to see Archie he ran over and licked his face. Archie tasted delicious! Willie licked and licked and licked.
"No respect for old age!"

Archie whispered something to Peter and ran off.
"Stick around, folks," Peter called. "We have a surprise for you."

When Archie got back, he and Peter worked while everyone waited.

"OK!" Peter announced. "Make way for Mister Big Face!"

A big paper bag appeared. Then a tongue stuck out of one of the eyes!

A hand came out of an ear and motioned everyone to move closer. They all obeyed.

Suddenly the bag began to shake.

It shook harder, and harder, and —
MEEOOW!

People started to leave.
"Wait — wait — the show'll go on! See the tallest dog in the world take a walk!" Archie shouted.

"Some show, gran'pa!"

"Some tall dog!"

"Who ate your moustache, gran'pa?"

Everyone walked away, laughing.

Soon no one was left except Archie, Peter, Willie and the torn paper bag.

"It would have been great if it wasn't for that crazy cat," said Peter as they walked home.

"Mmmm," said Archie. "He sure stuck around."

". . . and all I said was 'Hi, cat'," said Archie, finishing his story.

"You're well rid of a cat like that," said his mother.

Archie thought for a while.

"You know what, Ma?" he said. "I think that cat just kinda liked me!"

ROBERT LOUIS STEVENSON

Perhaps some of you have already read Stevenson's *Treasure Island*. It's pretty hard to think of growing up and *not* reading one of the best adventure books ever written.

While working on *Treasure Island*, Stevenson also wrote the first few of the verses that later became *A Child's Garden of Verses*. Others were written later on when he was very ill and could hardly move. Several he wrote in the dark with his left hand.

Stevenson was often in poor health. As a boy in Edinburgh, he passed many long nights of illness and had to live mostly inside his head. His feelings as a child come out in these verses, which, though almost one hundred years old, still talk to us.

They sound like the voice of a friend.

Here are a few of them.

Bed in Summer

In winter I get up at night
And dress by yellow candlelight.
In summer, quite the other way,
I have to go to bed by day.

I have to go to bed and see
The birds still hopping on the tree,
Or hear the grown-up people's feet
Still going past me in the street.

And does it not seem hard to you,
When all the sky is clear and blue,
And I should like so much to play,
To have to go to bed by day?

At the Seaside

When I was down beside the sea
A wooden spade they gave to me
    To dig the sandy shore.

My holes were empty like a cup.
In every hole the sea came up,
    Till it could come no more.

Rain

The rain is raining all around,
It falls on field and tree,
It rains on the umbrellas here
And on the ships at sea.

My Shadow

I have a little shadow that goes in and out with me,
And what can be the use of him is more than I can see.
He is very, very like me from the heels up to the head;
And I see him jump before me, when I jump into my bed.

The funniest thing about him is the way he likes to grow —
Not at all like proper children, which is always very slow;
For he sometimes shoots up taller like an india-rubber ball,
And he sometimes gets so little that there's none of him at all.

He hasn't got a notion of how children ought to play,
And can only make a fool of me in every sort of way.
He stays so close beside me, he's a coward you can see;
I'd think shame to stick to nursie as that shadow sticks to me!

One morning, very early, before the sun was up,
I rose and found the shining dew on every buttercup;
But my lazy little shadow, like an arrant sleepyhead,
Had stayed at home behind me and was fast asleep in bed.

The Swing

How do you like to go up in a swing,
   Up in the air so blue?
Oh, I do think it the pleasantest thing
   Ever a child can do!

Up in the air and over the wall,
   Till I can see so wide,
Rivers and trees and cattle and all
   Over the countryside —

Till I look down on the garden green,
   Down on the roof so brown —
Up in the air I go flying again,
   Up in the air and down!

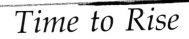

Time to Rise

A birdie with a yellow bill
Hopped upon the windowsill,
Cocked his shining eye and said:
"Ain't you 'shamed, you sleepyhead!"

THE LITTLE ENGINE THAT COULD

RETOLD BY WATTY PIPER

Illustrated by George & Doris Hauman

CHUG, chug, chug. Puff, puff, puff. Ding-dong, ding-dong. The little train rumbled over the tracks. She was a happy little train for she had such a jolly load to carry. Her cars were filled full of good things for boys and girls.

There were toy animals — giraffes with long necks, Teddy bears with almost no necks at all, and even a baby elephant. Then there were dolls — dolls with blue eyes and yellow curls, dolls with brown eyes and brown bobbed heads, and the funniest little toy clown you ever saw. And there were cars full of toy engines, aeroplanes, tops, jackknives, picture puzzles, books, and every kind of thing boys or girls could want.

But that was not all. Some of the cars were filled with all sorts of good things for boys and girls to eat — big golden oranges, red-cheeked apples, bottles of creamy milk for their breakfasts, fresh spinach for their dinners, peppermint drops, and lollipops for after-meal treats.

The little train was carrying all these wonderful things to the

good little boys and girls on the other side of the mountain. She puffed along merrily. Then all of a sudden she stopped with a jerk. She simply could not go another inch. She tried and she tried, but her wheels would not turn.

What were all those good little boys and girls on the other side of the mountain going to do without the wonderful toys to play with and the good food to eat?

"Here comes a shiny new engine," said the funny little clown who jumped out of the train. "Let us ask him to help us."

So all the dolls and toys cried out together:

"Please, Shiny New Engine, won't you please pull our train over the mountain? Our engine has broken down, and the boys and girls on the other side won't have any toys to play with or good food to eat unless you help us."

But the Shiny New Engine snorted: "I pull you? I am a Passenger Engine. I have just carried a fine big train over the mountain, with more cars than you ever dreamed of. My train had sleeping cars, with comfortable berths; a dining car where waiters bring whatever hungry people want to eat; and parlour cars in which people sit in soft armchairs and look out of big plate-glass windows. I pull the likes of you? Indeed not!" And off he steamed to the roundhouse, where engines live when they are not busy.

How sad the little train and all the dolls and toys felt!

Then the little clown called out, "The Passenger Engine is not the only one in the world. Here is another engine coming, a great big strong one. Let us ask him to help us."

The little toy clown waved his flag and the big strong engine came to a stop.

"Please, oh, please, Big Engine," called all the dolls and toys together. "Won't you please pull our train over the mountain? Our engine has broken down, and the good little boys and girls on the other side won't have any toys to play with or good food to eat unless you help us."

But the Big Strong Engine bellowed: "I am a Freight Engine. I have just pulled a big train loaded with big machines over the mountain. These machines print books and newspapers for grownups to read. I am a very important engine indeed. I won't pull the likes of you!" And the Freight Engine puffed off indignantly to the roundhouse.

The little train and all the dolls and toys were very sad.

"Cheer up," cried the little toy clown. "The Freight Engine is

not the only one in the world. Here comes another. He looks very old and tired, but our train is so little, perhaps he can help us."

So the little toy clown waved his flag and the dingy, rusty old engine stopped.

"Please, Kind Engine," cried all the dolls and toys together. "Won't you please pull our train over the mountain? Our engine has broken down, and the boys and girls on the other side won't have any toys to play with or good food to eat unless you help us."

But the Rusty Old Engine sighed: "I am so tired. I must rest my weary wheels. I cannot pull even so little a train as yours over the mountain. I can not. I can not. I can not."

And off he rumbled to the roundhouse chugging, "I can not. I can not. I can not."

Then indeed the little train was very, very sad, and the dolls and toys were ready to cry.

But the little clown called out, "Here is another engine coming, a little blue engine, a very little one, maybe she will help us."

The very little engine came chug, chugging merrily along. When she saw the toy clown's flag, she stopped quickly.

"What is the matter, my friends?" she asked kindly.

"Oh, Little Blue Engine," cried the dolls and toys. "Will you pull us over the mountain? Our engine has broken down and the good boys and girls on the other side won't have any toys to play with or good food to eat, unless you help us. Please, please, help us, Little Blue Engine."

"I'm not very big," said the Little Blue Engine. "They use me only for switching trains in the yard. I have never been over the mountain."

"But we must get over the mountain before the children awake," said all the dolls and toys.

The very little engine looked up and saw the tears in the dolls' eyes. And she thought of the good little boys and girls on the other side of the mountain who would not have any toys or good food unless she helped.

Then she said, "I think I can. I think I can. I think I can." And she hitched herself to the little train.

She tugged and pulled and pulled and tugged and slowly, slowly, slowly they started off.

The toy clown jumped aboard and all the dolls and the toy animals began to smile and cheer.

Puff, puff, chug, chug, went the Little Blue Engine. "I think I can — I think I can — I think I can — I think I can — I think I can — I think I can — I think I can — I think I can — I think I can."

Up, up, up. Faster and faster and faster and faster the little engine climbed, until at last they reached the top of the mountain.

Down in the valley lay the city.

"Hurray, hurray," cried the funny little clown and all the dolls and toys. "The good little boys and girls in the city will be happy because you helped us, kind Little Blue Engine."

And the Little Blue Engine smiled and seemed to say as she puffed steadily down the mountain:

"I thought I could. I thought I could. I thought I could.

I thought I could.

I thought I could.

I thought I could."

DOROTHY ALDIS
Alone

I was alone the other day
And stopped to watch some children play
Beneath a tree.

They ran and ran and ran around
And then fell flat upon the ground.
It looked like fun to me.

I only stood and watched them play,
I didn't know their names. And they
Did not know me.

NATALIE SAVAGE CARLSON

The Talking Cat

ONCE in another time, my friends, a great change came into Tante Odette's life although she was already an old woman who thought she had finished with such nonsense as changing one's habits.

It all happened because of a great change that came over Chouchou. The grey cat was a good companion because he seemed quite content to live on bread crusts and cabbage soup. Tante Odette kept a pot of soup boiling on the back of the stove. She added a little more water and a few more cabbage leaves to it each day. In this way, she always had soup on hand and she never had to throw any of it away.

She baked her own bread in her outdoor oven once a week, on Tuesday. If the bread grew stale by Saturday or Sunday, she softened it in the cabbage soup. So nothing was wasted.

As Tante Odette worked at her loom every evening, Chouchou would lie on the little rug by the stove and steadily stare at her with his big green eyes.

"If only you could talk," Tante Odette would say, "what company you would be for me."

One autumn evening, Tante Odette was busy at her loom. Her stubby fingers flew among the threads like pigeons. Thump, thump went the loom.

Suddenly there was a thump, thump that didn't come from the loom. It came from the door.

The old woman took the lamp from the low table and went to the door. She opened it slowly. The light from the lamp shone on a queer old man who had the unmistakable look of the woods. He wore a bright red sash around his waist and a black crow's feather in his woollen cap. He had a bushy moustache like a homemade broom and a brown crinkled face.

"Pierre Leblanc at your service," said the old man, making a deep bow.

"What do you want?" asked Tante Odette sharply. "I can't stand here all night with the door open. It wastes heat and firewood."

"I seek shelter and work," answered Pierre Leblanc. "I am getting too old to trap for furs or work in the lumber camps. I would like a job on just such a cosy little place as this."

"I don't need any help," snapped Tante Odette. "I am quite able to do everything by myself. And I have my cat."

She was beginning to close the door, but the man put his gnarled hand against it. He was staring at Chouchou.

"A very smart cat he looks to be," he said. "Why don't you ask him if you should take me in? After all, you need pay me nothing but a roof over my head and a little food."

Tante Odette's eyes grew bigger.

"How ridiculous!" she said. "A cat can't talk. I only wish —"

To her great surprise, Chouchou started to talk.

"Oh, indeed I can," he told her, "if the matter is important enough. This Pierre Leblanc looks to me like a very fine man and a good worker. You should take him in."

Tante Odette stood with her mouth open for two minutes before she could make any sound come out of it. At last she said, "Then come in. It is so rare for a cat to be able to talk that I'm sure one should listen to him when he does."

The old man walked close to the stove and stretched his fingers towards it. He looked at the pot of soup bubbling on the back.

Chouchou spoke again.

"Pierre looks hungry," he said. "Offer him some soup — a big, deep bowl of it."

"Oh, dear," sighed Tante Odette, "at this rate, our soup won't last out the week. But if you say so, Chouchou."

Pierre sat at the wooden table and gulped down the soup like a starved wolf. When he had finished, Tante Odette pointed to the loft where he would sleep. Then she took the big grey cat on her lap.

"This is a most amazing thing that you should begin talking after all these years. Whatever came over you?"

But Chouchou had nothing more to say. He covered his nose with the tip of his tail, and there was not another word out of him all night.

Tante Odette decided that the cat's advice had been good. No longer did she have to go to the barn and feed the beasts. And no more skunks crawled into her oven because Pierre saw to it that the door was kept closed. He was indeed a good worker. He seemed quite satisfied with his bed in the loft and his bowls of cabbage soup and chunks of bread.

Only Chouchou seemed to have grown dissatisfied since his arrival.

"Why do you feed Pierre nothing but cabbage soup and bread?" he asked one day. "A workingman needs more food than that. How about some headcheese and pork pie?"

Tante Odette was startled, but Pierre went on drinking his soup.

"But meat is scarce and costs money," she told the cat.

"Pouf!" said the cat. "It is well worth it. Even I am getting a little tired of cabbage soup. A nice pork pie for dinner tomorrow would fill all the empty cracks inside me."

So when Pierre went out to the barn to water the beasts, Tante Odette stealthily lifted the lid of the chest, fished out a torn woollen sock and pulled a few coins out of it. She jumped in surprise when she raised her head and saw Pierre standing in the open doorway watching her.

"I forgot the pail," said Pierre. "I will draw some water from the well while I am about it."

The old woman hastily dropped the lid of the chest and got the pail from behind the stove.

"After Pierre has done his chores," said Chouchou, "he will be glad to go to the store and buy the meat for you."

Tante Odette frowned at the cat.

"But I am the thriftiest shopper in the parish," she said. "I can bring old Henri Dupuis down a few pennies on everything I buy."

"Pierre is a good shopper, too," said Chouchou. "In all Canada, there is not a better judge of meat. Perhaps he will even see something that you would not have thought to buy. Send him to the store."

It turned out that the old man was just as good a shopper as Chouchou had said. He returned from the village with a pinkish piece of pork, a freshly dressed pig's head, a bag of candy, and some tobacco for himself.

"But my money," said Tante Odette. "Did you spend all of it?"

"What is money for but to spend?" asked Chouchou from his rug by the stove. "Can you eat money or smoke it in a pipe?"

"No," said Tante Odette.

"Can you put it over your shoulders to keep you warm?"

"No."

"Would it burn in the stove to cook your food?"

"Oh, no, indeed!"

Chouchou closed his eyes.

"Then what good is money?" he asked. "The sooner one gets rid of it, the better."

Tante Odette's troubled face smoothed.

"I never saw it that way before," she agreed. "Of course, you are right, Chouchou. And you are right, too, Pierre, for choosing such fine food."

But when Pierre went out to get a cabbage from the shed, Tante Odette walked to the chest again and counted her coins.

"I have a small fortune, Chouchou," she said. "Now explain to me again why these coins are no good."

But Chouchou had nothing more to say about the matter.

One Tuesday when Pierre Leblanc was cutting trees in the woods and Tante Odette was baking her loaves of bread in the outdoor oven, a stranger came galloping down the road on a one-eyed horse. He stopped in front of the white fence. He politely dismounted and went over to Tante Odette.

The old woman saw at a glance that he was a man of the woods. His blouse was checked and his cap red. Matching it was the red sash tied around his waist. He looked very much like Pierre Leblanc.

"Can you tell me, madame," he asked, "if a man named Pierre Leblanc works here?"

"Yes, he does," answered Tante Odette, "and a very good worker he is."

The stranger did not look satisfied.

"Of course, Canada is full of Pierre Leblancs," he said. "It is a very common name. Does this Pierre Leblanc wear a red sash like mine?"

"So he does," said Tante Odette.

"On the other hand," said the man, "many Pierre Leblancs wear red sashes. Does he have a moustache like a homemade broom?"

"Yes, indeed," said the woman.

"But there must be many Pierre Leblancs with red sashes and moustaches like brooms," continued the stranger. "This Pierre Leblanc who now works for you, can he throw his voice?"

"Throw his voice!" cried Tante Odette. "What witchcraft is that?"

"Haven't you heard of such a gift?" asked the man. "But of course only a few have it — probably only one Pierre Leblanc in a thousand. This Pierre with you, can he throw his voice behind trees and in boxes and up on the roof so it sounds as if someone else is talking?"

"My faith, no!" cried the woman in horror. "I wouldn't have such a one in my house. He would be better company for the *loup-garou,* that evil one who can change into many shapes."

The man laughed heartily.

"My Pierre Leblanc could catch the *loup-garou* in a wolf trap and lead him around by the chain. He is that clever. That is why I am trying to find him. I want him to go trapping with me in the woods this winter. One says that never have there been so many foxes. I need Pierre, for he is smarter than any fox."

The creak of wheels caused them both to turn around. Pierre Leblanc was driving the ox team in from the woods. He stared at the man standing beside Tante Odette. The man stared back at Pierre. Then both men began bouncing on their feet and whooping in their throats. They hugged each other. They kissed each other on the cheek.

"Good old Pierre!"

"Georges, my friend, where have you kept yourself all summer? How did you find me?"

Tante Odette left them whooping and hugging. She walked into the house with a worried look on her face. She sat down at her loom. Finally she stopped weaving and turned to Chouchou.

"I am a little dizzy, Chouchou," she said. "This *loup-garou* voice has upset me. What do you make of it all?"

Chouchou said nothing.

"Please tell me what to do," pleaded Tante Odette. "Shall we let him stay here? It would be very uncomfortable to have voices coming from the roof and the trees."

Chouchou said nothing.

"Is he maybe in league with the *loup-garou*?"

Chouchou said nothing. Tante Odette angrily threw the shuttle at him.

"Where is your tongue?" she demanded. "Have you no words for me when I need them most?"

But if a cat will not speak, who has got his tongue?

Pierre Leblanc came walking in.

"Such a man!" he roared gleefully. "Only the woods are big enough for him."

"Are you going away with him?" asked the woman, not knowing whether she wanted him to say yes or no. If only Chouchou hadn't been so stubborn.

"That makes a problem," said Pierre. "If I go into the woods this winter, it will be cold and I will work like an ox. But there will be much money in my pocket after the furs are sold. If I stay here, I will be warm and comfortable but —"

He pulled his pockets inside out. Nothing fell from them.

"What is this business about your being able to throw your voice to other places?" asked Tante Odette.

"Did Georges say I could do that?"

Tante Odette nodded.

"Ha! Ha!" laughed Pierre. "What a joker Georges is!"

"But perhaps it is true," insisted the woman.

"If you really want to know," said Pierre, "ask Chouchou. He would not lie. Can I throw my voice, Chouchou?"

Chouchou sank down on his haunches and purred.

"Of course not!" he answered. "Whoever heard of such nonsense?"

Tante Odette sighed in relief. Then she remembered that this did not fix everything.

"Will you go with him?" she asked Pierre. "I have made it very comfortable for you here. And now it is only for supper that we have cabbage soup."

Chouchou spoke up.

"Tante Odette, how can you expect such a good man as Pierre Leblanc to work for only food and shelter? If you would pay him a coin from time to time, he would be quite satisfied to stay."

"But I can't afford that," said the woman.

"Of course you can," insisted Chouchou. "You have a small fortune in the old sock in your chest. Remember what I told you about money?"

"Tell me again," said Tante Odette. "It is hard to hold on to such a thought for long."

"Money is to spend," repeated the cat. "Can it carry hay and water to the beasts? Can it cut down trees for firewood? Can it dig paths through the snow when winter comes?"

"I have caught it again," said Tante Odette. "If you will stay with me, Pierre, I will pay you a coin from time to time."

Pierre smiled and bowed.

"Then I shall be very happy to stay here with you and your wise cat," he decided. "Now I will unload my wood and pile it into a neat stack by the door."

He briskly stamped out. Tante Odette sat down at her loom again.

"We have made a good bargain, haven't we, Chouchou?" She smiled contentedly.

But Chouchou tickled his nose with his tail and said nothing.

That is the way it was, my friends. It would have been a different story if Pierre had not been such a good worker. So remember this: if you must follow the advice of a talking cat, be sure you know who is doing the talking for him.

AGNIA BARTO

Two Sisters Looking at Baby Brother

Translated from the Russian by Avril Pyman

Two sisters looked at Baby Brother.
"How helpless! Look, how weak! How small!
See! He can twitch his brows together
But he cannot smile at all."

Baby Brother woke and sneezed.
"How fast they grow, these little boys,"
The sisters chorused, very pleased.
"That sneeze made quite a grown-up noise."

Curious George

by
H. A. Rey

THIS is George. He lived in Africa. He was very happy. But he had one fault. He was too curious.

One day George saw a man. He had on a large yellow straw hat. The man saw George, too. "What a nice little monkey," he thought. "I would like to take him home with me."

The man put his hat on the ground, and of course George was curious. He came down from the tree to look at the large yellow hat.

The hat had been on the man's head. George thought it would be nice to have it on his own head. He picked it up and put it on.

The hat covered George's head. He couldn't see.

The man picked him up quickly and popped him into a bag. George was caught.

The man with the big yellow hat put George into a little boat, and a sailor rowed them both across the water to a big ship.

George was sad, but he was still a little curious.

On the big ship, things began to happen.

The man took off the bag.

George sat on a little stool, and the man said, "George, I am going to take you to a big Zoo in a big city. You will like it there. Now run along and play, but don't get into trouble."

George promised to be good. But it is easy for little monkeys to forget.

On the deck he found some sea gulls. He wondered how they could fly. He was very curious. Finally he HAD to try. It looked easy. But — oh, what happened!

First this —

and then this!

"WHERE IS GEORGE?" The sailors looked and looked.

At last they saw him struggling in the water, and almost all tired out.

"Man overboard!" the sailors cried as they threw him a life belt. George caught it and held on. At last he was safe on board.

After that, George was more careful to be a good monkey, until at last the long trip was over.

George said good-bye to the kind sailors, and he and the man with the yellow hat walked off the ship onto the shore and on into the city to the man's house.

After a good meal and a good pipe, George felt very tired. He crawled into bed and fell asleep at once.

The next morning the man telephoned the Zoo. George watched him. He was fascinated. Then the man went away.

George was curious. He wanted to telephone, too. One, two, three, four, five, six, seven. What fun!

DING-A-LING-A-LING! GEORGE HAD TELEPHONED
THE FIRE STATION! The firemen rushed to the telephone.
"Hello! Hello!" they said. But there was no answer.

Then they looked for the signal on the big map that showed
where the telephone call had come from. They didn't know it was
GEORGE. They thought it was a real fire.

HURRY! HURRY! HURRY! The firemen jumped onto the fire
engines and onto the hook-and-ladders.

Ding-dong-ding-dong. Everyone out of the way! Hurry! Hurry!
Hurry!

The firemen rushed into the house. They opened the door. NO
FIRE! ONLY a naughty little monkey.

"Oh, catch him, catch him," they cried. George tried to run
away. He almost did, but he got caught in the telephone wire,
and —

a thin fireman caught one arm and a fat fireman caught the other.

"You fooled the Fire Department," they said. "We will have to shut you up where you can't do any more harm."

They took him away and shut him in a prison.

George wanted to get out. He climbed up to the window to try the bars.

Just then the watchman came in. He got on the wooden bed to catch George. But the watchman was too big and heavy. The bed tipped up, the watchman fell over, and, quick as lightning, George ran out through the open door.

He hurried through the building and out onto the roof. And then he was lucky to be a monkey. Out he walked onto the telephone wires. Quickly and quietly over the guard's head, George walked away.

He was free!

Down in the street, outside the prison wall, stood a balloon man. A little girl bought a balloon for her brother. George watched.

He was curious again. He felt he MUST have a bright red balloon. He reached over and tried to help himself, but — instead of one balloon, the whole bunch broke loose. In an instant the wind whisked them all away, and with them went George, holding tight with both hands.

Up, up he sailed, higher and higher. The houses looked like toy houses and the people like dolls.

George was frightened. He held on very tight.

At first the wind blew in great gusts. Then it quieted. Finally it stopped blowing altogether.

George was very tired. Down, down he went — bump, onto the top of a traffic light. Everyone was surprised. The traffic got all mixed up. George didn't know what to do, and then he heard someone call, "GEORGE!"

He looked down and saw his friend, the man with the big yellow hat!

George was very happy. The man was happy, too. George slid down the post, and the man with the big yellow hat put him under his arm. Then he paid the balloon man for all the balloons.

And then George and the man climbed into the car, and at last away they went — to the ZOO!

What a nice place for George to live!

HILAIRE BELLOC

G

G stands for Gnu, whose weapons of Defence
Are long, sharp, curling Horns, and Common Sense.
To these he adds a Name so short and strong,
That even Hardy Boers pronounce it wrong.
How often on a bright Autumnal day
The Pious people of Pretoria say,
"Come, let us hunt the —" Then no more is heard
But Sounds of Strong Men struggling with a word.
Meanwhile, the distant Gnu with grateful eyes
Observes his opportunity, and flies.

MORAL.

Child, if you have a rummy kind of name,
Remember to be thankful for the same.

The Hippopotamus

I shoot the Hippopotamus
    with bullets made of platinum,
Because if I use leaden ones
    his hide is sure to flatten 'em.

The Lion

The Lion, the Lion, he dwells in the waste,
He has a big head and a very small waist;
But his shoulders are stark, and his jaws they are grim,
And a good little child will not play with him.

The Tiger

The Tiger, on the other hand, is kittenish and mild,
He makes a pretty playfellow for any little child;
And mothers of large families (who claim to common sense)
Will find a Tiger well repays the trouble and expense.

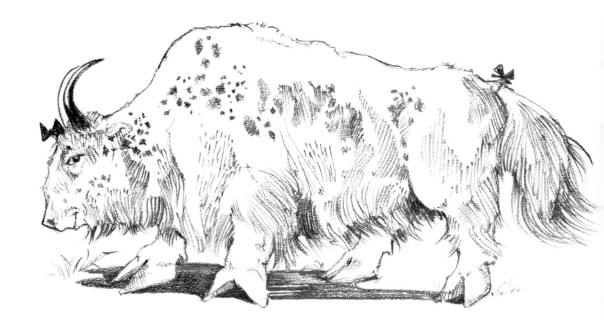

The Yak

As a friend to the children commend me the Yak.
   You will find it exactly the thing:
It will carry and fetch, you can ride on its back,
   Or lead it about with a string.
The Tartar who dwells on the plains of Thibet
   (A desolate region of snow)
Has for centuries made it a nursery pet,
   And surely the Tartar should know!
Then tell your papa where the Yak can be got,
   And if he is awfully rich
He will buy you the creature — or else he will *not*.
   (I cannot be positive which.)

WANDA GA'G

Wanda Ga'g (you say it as if it were *Gog*) grew up in a small town in Minnesota in America. Her parents died when she was only fourteen. She was the eldest of seven children, six of them girls. They were very poor. Wanda tells us they had "ten years of corn mush" and the sisters skipped breakfast for two years so that their hungry younger brother would have enough to eat.

But it was not an unhappy family. The father had been a painter in his spare time and all the children had been brought up to read and draw. Later on Wanda was surprised to find that "to many people drawing was not as important as sleeping and eating".

She had a hard time taking care of her brother and sisters. Once she supported herself by painting lampshades for twenty-five cents an hour. For a while she lived with a family whose two children would beg for stories. These stories became *Millions of Cats, The Funny Thing*, and *Snippy and Snappy* — and Wanda became famous. When her editor first looked at *Millions of Cats*, she hugged herself with joy.

Wanda's life was not long, from 1893 to 1946. But she wrote and drew many books; the best of them, like *The Funny Thing*, almost sing themselves as you read them.

Just before he died her father called her to his bedside, took her hands in his, and said, "What Papa couldn't do, Wanda will have to finish." And she did.

THE FUNNY THING

BY WANDA GÁG

IT WAS a beautiful day in the mountains. The sun was playing hide-and-seek among the fluffy, floating clouds, and the air was soft and warm.

Bobo, the good little man of the mountains, was waiting for the birds and animals to come. To come for what do you suppose? To come for food — because at the door of his mountain cave, Bobo had many good things for them to eat.

He had nut cakes for the fuzzy-tailed squirrels.

He had seed puddings for the pretty fluttering birds.

He had cabbage salads for the long-eared rabbits.

He had tiny cheeses — no bigger than cherries — and these were for the little mice.

Now on this beautiful sunny day, there came a Funny Thing which Bobo had never seen before. It looked something like a dog

and also a little like a giraffe, and from the top of its head to the tip of its curled tail, there was a row of beautiful blue points.

"Good morning," said Bobo. "And what kind of an animal are you?"

"I'm not an animal," said the Funny Thing. "I'm an *aminal*!"

Bobo was about to say that there was no such word as *aminal*, when the Funny Thing looked around fiercely and cried, "And what have you for a hungry *aminal* to eat?"

"Oh," said Bobo, "here are some lovely nut cakes. I also have some fine seed puddings. This cabbage salad is very nice — and I'm sure you'd like these little cheeses."

But the Funny Thing turned away and said, "I never heard of such silly food! No *aminal* would eat those things. Haven't you any dolls today?"

"Dolls!" cried Bobo in surprise.

"Certainly," said the Funny Thing. "And very good they are — dolls."

"To eat?" cried Bobo, opening his eyes very wide at such an idea.

"To eat, of course," said the Funny Thing, smacking his lips. "And very good they are — dolls."

"But it is not kind to eat up little children's dolls," said Bobo. "I should think it would make them very unhappy."

"So it does," said the Funny Thing, smiling pleasantly, "but very good they are — dolls."

"And don't the children cry when you take away their dolls?" asked Bobo.

"Don't they though!" said the Funny Thing with a cheerful grin, "but very good they are — dolls."

Tears rolled down Bobo's face as he thought of the Funny Thing going around eating up dear little children's dolls.

"But perhaps you take only naughty children's dolls," he said, brightening up.

"No, I take them specially from good children," said the Funny Thing gleefully, "and *very* good they are — good children's dolls!"

"Oh, what shall I do?" thought Bobo, as he walked back and forth, back and forth. He was trying to think of a plan to make this naughty *aminal* forget to eat dolls.

At last he had an idea!

So he said to the Funny Thing, "What a lovely tail you have!"

The Funny Thing smiled and wriggled his tail with a pleased motion.

"And those pretty black eyebrows," Bobo continued.

The Funny Thing looked down modestly and smiled even more.

"But most wonderful of all is that row of blue points down your back," said Bobo.

The Funny Thing was so pleased at this that he rolled foolishly on the ground and smiled very hard.

Then Bobo, who was really a wise old man, said to the Funny Thing, "I suppose you are so beautiful because you eat a great many jum-jills?"

The Funny Thing had never heard of them.

"Jum-jills?" he asked eagerly. "What is a jum-jill — is it a kind of doll?"

"Oh no," said Bobo. "Jum-jills are funny little cakes which make blue points more beautiful, and little tails grow into big ones."

Now the Funny Thing was very vain and there was nothing he would rather have had than a very long tail and bigger and more beautiful blue points. So he cried, "Oh please, dear kind man, give me many jum-jills!"

"Very well," said Bobo. "Sit down under this tree and wait for me."

The Funny Thing was all smiles and did as he was told, while Bobo went into his cosy little home, which was like a sort of tunnel under the mountain.

First he had to go through his little bedroom. Next he came to his study and finally he reached the kitchen, where he usually made up the food for the birds and animals.

Now he took a big bowl, into which he put:

> seven nut cakes
> five seed puddings
> two cabbage salads
> and fifteen little cheeses.

He mixed them with a spoon and rolled them into little round balls.

These little balls were jum-jills.

He put them all on a plate and carried them out to the Funny Thing, who was still waiting under the tree.

"Here are your jum-jills," said Bobo, as he handed the plate to the Funny Thing.

The Funny Thing ate one and said, "And very good they are — jum-jills."

Then he ate another and said, "And very good they are — jum-jills."

And so on until he had eaten them all up.

"And *very* good they are — jum-jills," he said with a smack of his lips, after they were all gone.

Then the Funny Thing went home, but the next day he came back for more jum-jills. His tail was already a little longer, his blue points were beginning to grow, and he looked very happy indeed.

Every day the Funny Thing came back for more jum-jills. He came for a long, long time and each day his tail was a little longer.

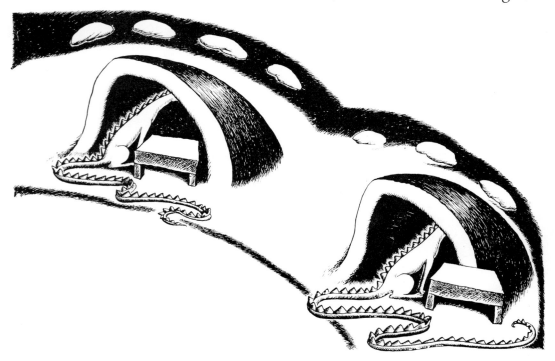

But on the twentieth day his tail had grown so long that he couldn't move about much.

So he chose a nice big mountain and sat on the very top of it. Every day Bobo sent birds to carry jum-jills to the Funny Thing, and as the Funny Thing's tail grew longer and longer, he curled it contentedly around his mountain.

His one joy in life was his beautiful blue-pointed tail, and by and by the only words he ever said were:

"And very good they are — jum-jills!"

So of course he ate no more dolls and we have kind old Bobo to thank for that.

Improbable Records

Compiled by Quentin Blake and John Yeoman
and illustrated by Quentin Blake

The worst child ballet dancers in the world were Miss Treldiana Pelkey and the Honorable Miss Dorothea ffortescue-Wood. At one charity concert they tripped over forty-seven times, and finally fell off the stage altogether, injuring several members of the audience.

A sausage at Saint Cynthia's School in West Drayton has been served for school dinner 8,947 times and returned uneaten on each occasion.

The world's soppiest fairy-story is *Cuddly-Bunnikins and Little Fairy Twinklewand* by Emily Tichweed. Above: Miss Tichweed and her pet rabbit, Cecil.

These examples of the Eskimo art of carving on walrus tusks are believed to be the only ones where the tusks were not removed from the walrus first.

The boy with the most disgusting table manners was Terry Wormold of Shropshire. In parts of Shropshire mothers still tell their children to "stop Wormolding."

The first inflatable swimming aid was the Bickerstaff Brothers' Buoyancy Bathing Suit for Beginners (1865). Its usefulness was often questioned.

Jimmy Fluff, aged eleven, was proclaimed British record holder at the Crystal Palace chicken pox spots competition of 1903, after the judge had declared the other principal contestant guilty of cheating.

One of the finalists in the ballroom-dancing championship of 1962, Mrs. Berenice Stoll of Deptford, sewed a grand total of 16,449 sequins onto her dress. Unfortunately, her husband, Tancred, was unable to lift such a weight from the floor.

The noisiest veteran car still on the road is a 1914 Musgrove Whirlwind belonging to Mr. Alistair Whimbrel of Bath. At its full speed of 27 kilometres per hour it makes 176 distinct noises, including *skreek, grunge, kdoink, blonk-blonk-blonk, flippety-flappety, ptwang,* and *urrgggh.*

A potato bearing a striking resemblance to Queen Victoria was grown by Mr. Norbert Thrimble of Strood. An unconfirmed report has it that the potato, suitably dressed, stood in for Her Majesty at a number of rather boring royal functions.

Mr. Thrimble's Potato   The real Queen Victoria

The largest unfinished statue in the world was a symbolic figure of "Progress" commissioned by Darlington Corporation from R. Figgis-Jones in 1899. Unfortunately funds ran out in 1901 when only the big toe of the left foot had been completed.

The world's most hopeless daily help was Eliza Widdershins of East Penge. In one day alone, in May 1923, she broke a complete Crown Derby tea service while washing up, reduced the weekly wash to shreds, and absentmindedly threw the baby into the dustbin.

Did you know:
— that while at work on these "Improbable Records", the compilers ate 4,978 bacon sandwiches and drank 9,983 mugs of cocoa?
— that while doing the pictures for these "Improbable Records", Quentin Blake 48 times dipped his brush into the mug of cocoa instead of into the paint water?
— that 17 times he drank the paint water instead of the mug of cocoa?

The Letter
Arnold Lobel

TOAD was sitting on his front porch.
Frog came along and said, "What is the matter, Toad? You are looking sad."

"Yes," said Toad. "This is my sad time of day. It is the time when I wait for the mail to come. It always makes me very unhappy."

"Why is that?" asked Frog.

"Because I never get any mail," said Toad.

"Not ever?" asked Frog.

"No, never," said Toad. "No one has ever sent me a letter.

Every day my mailbox is empty. That is why waiting for the mail is a sad time for me."

Frog and Toad sat on the porch, feeling sad together.

Then Frog said, "I have to go home now, Toad. There is something that I must do."

Frog hurried home. He found a pencil and a piece of paper. He wrote on the paper. He put the paper in an envelope. On the envelope he wrote "A LETTER FOR TOAD".

Frog ran out of his house. He saw a snail that he knew.

"Snail," said Frog, "please take this letter to Toad's house and put it in his mailbox."

"Sure," said the snail. "Right away."

Then Frog ran back to Toad's house.

Toad was in bed, taking a nap.

"Toad," said Frog, "I think you should get up and wait for the mail some more."

"No," said Toad, "I am tired of waiting for the mail."

Frog looked out of the window at Toad's mailbox. The snail was not there yet.

"Toad," said Frog, "you never know when someone may send you a letter."

"No, no," said Toad. "I do not think anyone will ever send me a letter."

Frog looked out of the window. The snail was not there yet.

"But, Toad," said Frog, "someone may send you a letter today."

"Don't be silly," said Toad. "No one has ever sent me a letter before, and no one will send me a letter today."

Frog looked out of the window. The snail was still not there.

"Frog, why do you keep looking out of the window?" asked Toad.

"Because now I am waiting for the mail," said Frog.

"But there will not be any," said Toad.

"Oh, yes there will," said Frog, "because I have sent you a letter."

"You have?" said Toad. "What did you write in the letter?"

Frog said, "I wrote 'Dear Toad, I am glad that you are my best friend. Your best friend, Frog.'"

"Oh," said Toad, "that makes a very good letter."

Then Frog and Toad went out onto the front porch to wait for the mail. They sat there, feeling happy together.

Frog and Toad waited a long time.
Four days later the snail got to Toad's house and gave him the letter from Frog. Toad was very pleased to have it.

The Story of
FERDINAND
By Munro Leaf

Illustrated by Robert Lawson

ONCE upon a time in Spain there was a little bull and his
name was Ferdinand.

All the other little bulls he lived with would run and jump and
butt their heads together, but not Ferdinand.

He liked to sit just quietly and smell the flowers.

He had a favourite spot out in the pasture under a cork tree. It was his favourite tree and he would sit in its shade all day and smell the flowers.

Sometimes his mother, who was a cow, would worry about him. She was afraid he would be lonely all by himself.

"Why don't you run and play with the other little bulls and skip and butt your head?" she would say.

But Ferdinand would shake his head. "I like it better here where I can sit just quietly and smell the flowers."

His mother saw that he was not lonely, and because she was an understanding mother, even though she was a cow, she let him just sit there and be happy.

As the years went by Ferdinand grew and grew until he was very big and strong.

All the other bulls who had grown up with him in the same pasture would fight each other all day. They would butt each other and stick each other with their horns. What they wanted most of all was to be picked to fight at the bull fights in Madrid.

But not Ferdinand — he still liked to sit just quietly under the cork tree and smell the flowers.

One day five men came in very funny hats to pick the biggest, fastest, roughest bull to fight in the bull fights in Madrid.

All the other bulls ran around snorting and butting, leaping and jumping so the men would think that they were very very strong and fierce and pick them.

Ferdinand knew that they wouldn't pick him and he didn't care. So he went out to his favourite cork tree to sit down.

He didn't look where he was sitting and instead of sitting on the nice cool grass in the shade he sat on a bumble bee.

Well, if you were a bumble bee and a bull sat on you what would you do? You would sting him. And that is just what this bee did to Ferdinand.

Wow! Did it hurt! Ferdinand jumped up with a snort. He ran

around puffing and snorting, butting and pawing the ground as if he were mad.

The five men saw him and they all shouted with joy. Here was the largest and fiercest bull of all. Just the one for the bull fights in Madrid!

So they took him away for the bull fight day in a cart.

What a day it was! Flags were flying, bands were playing . . . and all the lovely ladies had flowers in their hair.

They had a parade into the bull ring.

First came the Banderilleros with long sharp pins with ribbons on them to stick in the bull and make him angry.

Next came the Picadores who rode skinny horses and they had long spears to stick in the bull and make him angrier.

Then came the Matador, the proudest of all — he thought he was very handsome, and bowed to the ladies. He had a red cape and a sword and was supposed to stick the bull last of all.

Then came the bull, and you know who that was don't you?
—FERDINAND.

They called him Ferdinand the Fierce and all the Banderilleros were afraid of him and the Picadores were afraid of him and the Matador was scared stiff.

Ferdinand ran to the middle of the ring and everyone shouted and clapped because they thought he was going to fight fiercely and butt and snort and stick his horns around.

But not Ferdinand. When he got to the middle of the ring he saw the flowers in all the lovely ladies' hair and he just sat down quietly and smelled.

He wouldn't fight and be fierce no matter what they did. He just sat and smelled. And the Banderilleros were angry and the Picadores were angrier and the Matador was so angry he cried because he couldn't show off with his cape and sword.

So they had to take Ferdinand home.

And for all I know he is sitting there still, under his favourite cork tree, smelling the flowers just quietly.

He is very happy.

ELSA BESKOW
Pelle's New Suit

Translated from the Swedish by Marion Letcher Woodburn

THERE WAS ONCE a little Swedish boy whose name was Pelle. Now, Pelle had a lamb which was all his own and which he took care of all by himself.

The lamb grew and Pelle grew. And the lamb's wool grew longer and longer, but Pelle's coat only grew shorter!

One day Pelle took a pair of shears and cut off all the lamb's wool. Then he took the wool to his grandmother and said: "Granny dear, please card this wool for me!"

"That I will, my dear," said his grandmother, "if you will pull the weeds in my carrot patch for me."

So Pelle pulled the weeds in Granny's carrot patch and Granny carded Pelle's wool.

Then Pelle went to his other grandmother and said: "Grandmother dear, please spin this wool into yarn for me!"

"That will I gladly do, my dear," said his grandmother, "if while I am spinning it you will tend my cows for me."

And so Pelle tended Grandmother's cows and Grandmother spun Pelle's yarn.

Then Pelle went to a neighbour who was a painter and asked him for some paint with which to colour his yarn.

"What a silly little boy you are!" laughed the painter. "My paint is not what you want to colour your wool. But if you will over to the store to get a bottle of turpentine for me, you may buy yourself some dye out of the change from the shilling."

So Pelle rowed over to the store and bought a bottle of turpentine for the painter, and bought for himself a large sack of blue dye out of the change from the shilling.

Then he dyed his wool himself until it was all, all blue.

And then Pelle went to his mother and said: "Mother dear, please weave this yarn into cloth for me."

"That will I gladly do," said his mother, "if you will take care of your little sister for me."

So Pelle took good care of his little sister, and Mother wove the wool into cloth.

Then Pelle went to the tailor: "Dear Mr. Tailor, please make a suit for me out of this cloth."

"Is that what you want, you little rascal?" said the tailor. "Indeed I will, if you will rake my hay and bring in my wood and feed my pigs for me."

So Pelle raked the tailor's hay and fed his pigs.

And then he carried in all the wood. And the tailor had Pelle's suit ready that very Saturday evening.

And on Sunday morning Pelle put on his new suit and went to his lamb and said: "Thank you very much for my new suit, little lamb."

"Ba-a-ah," said the lamb, and it sounded almost as if the lamb were laughing.

LEO LIONNI

Frederick

ALL along the meadow where the cows grazed and the horses
ran, there was an old stone wall.

In that wall, not far from the barn and the granary, a chatty
family of field mice had their home.

But the farmers had moved away, the barn was abandoned, and
the granary stood empty. And since winter was not far off, the
little mice began to gather corn and nuts and wheat and straw.
They all worked day and night.

All — except Frederick.

"Frederick, why don't you work?" they asked.

"I *do* work," said Frederick. "I gather sun rays for the cold dark winter days."

And when they saw Frederick sitting there, staring at the meadow, they said, "And now, Frederick?"

"I gather colours," answered Frederick simply. "For winter is grey."

And once Frederick seemed half asleep. "Are you dreaming, Frederick?" they asked reproachfully.

But Frederick said, "Oh no, I am gathering words. For the winter days are long and many, and we'll run out of things to say."

The winter days came, and when the first snow fell the five little field mice took to their hideout in the stones.

In the beginning there was lots to eat, and the mice told stories of foolish foxes and silly cats. They were a happy family.

But little by little they had nibbled up most of the nuts and berries, the straw was gone, and the corn was only a memory.

It was cold in the wall and no one felt like chatting.

Then they remembered what Frederick had said about sun rays and colours and words.

"What about *your* supplies, Frederick?" they asked.

"Close your eyes," said Frederick, as he climbed on a big stone. "Now I send you the rays of the sun. Do you feel how their golden glow . . ."

And as Frederick spoke of the sun the four little mice began to feel warmer.

Was it Frederick's voice?

Was it magic?

"And how about the colours, Frederick?" they asked anxiously.

"Close your eyes again," Frederick said. And when he told them of the blue periwinkles, the red poppies in the yellow wheat, and the green leaves of the berry bush, they saw the colours as clearly as if they had been painted in their minds.

"And the words, Frederick?"

Frederick cleared his throat, waited a moment, and then, as if from a stage, he said:

"Who scatters snowflakes? Who melts the ice?
Who spoils the weather? Who makes it nice?
Who grows the four-leaf clovers in June?
Who dims the daylight? Who lights the moon?

Four little field mice who live in the sky.
Four little field mice . . . like you and I.

One is the Springmouse who turns on the showers.
Then comes the Summer who paints in the flowers.
The Fallmouse is next with walnuts and wheat.
And Winter is last . . . with little cold feet.

Aren't we lucky the seasons are four?
Think of a year with one less . . . or one more!"

When Frederick had finished, they all applauded. "But Frederick," they said, "you are a poet!"

Frederick blushed, took a bow, and said shyly, "I know it."

A KISS FOR LITTLE BEAR

by ELSE HOLMELUND MINARIK

Pictures by MAURICE SENDAK

"This picture makes me happy," said Little Bear.

"Hello, Hen. This picture is for Grandmother. Will you take it to her, Hen?"

"Yes, I will," said Hen.

Grandmother was happy.

"This kiss is for Little Bear," she said. "Will you take it to him, Hen?"

"I will be glad to," said Hen.

ELSE HOLMELUND MINARIK

Then Hen saw some friends. She stopped to chat.

"Hello, Frog. I have a kiss for Little Bear. It is from his grandmother. Will you take it to him, Frog?"

"OK," said Frog.

But Frog saw a pond. He stopped to swim.

"Hi, Cat. I have a kiss for Little Bear. It is from his grandmother. Take it to him, will you? Cat — hi! Here I am, in the pond. Come and get the kiss."

"Oogh!" said Cat.

But he came and got the kiss.

Cat saw a nice spot to sleep.

"Little Skunk, I have a kiss for Little Bear. It is from his grandmother. Take it to him like a good little skunk."

Little Skunk was glad to do that. But then he saw another little skunk.

She was very pretty. He gave the kiss to her.

And she gave it back.

And he gave it back.

And then Hen came along. "Too much kissing," she said.

"But this is Little Bear's kiss, from his grandmother," said Little Skunk.

"Indeed!" said Hen. "Who has it now?"
Little Skunk had it. Hen got it back.
She ran to Little Bear, and she gave him the kiss.
"It is from your grandmother," she said. "It is for the picture you sent her."
"Take one back to her," said Little Bear.
"No," said Hen. "It gets all mixed up!"

The skunks decided to get married.
They had a lovely wedding.

Everyone came.

And Little Bear was best man.

ROBERT McCLOSKEY

When Mr. McCloskey was living in Boston, in America, he noticed the ducks in the Public Garden and he saw that they had a traffic problem. That's how *Make Way for Ducklings* started.

He used to feed the ducks peanuts and popcorn to watch how they bobbed their heads and tilted their tails. Before he made his final drawings, he lived with some ducks in his New York apartment, sketching them as they wandered around the room and splashed all over the place in the bathtub. He says he had to slow them down somehow, so he fed them red wine. "They loved it and went into slow motion right away." All that work helped to make these drawings and that's one reason they're so real and ducklike.

Mr. McCloskey says it helps if you can more or less think like a duck, too. But he doesn't tell us how he did it.

MAKE WAY FOR DUCKLINGS

By ROBERT McCLOSKEY

MR. AND MRS. MALLARD were looking for a place to live. But every time Mr. Mallard saw what looked like a nice place, Mrs. Mallard said it was no good. There were sure to be foxes in the woods or turtles in the water, and she was not going to raise a family where there might be foxes or turtles. So they flew on and on.

When they got to Boston, they felt too tired to fly any further. There was a nice pond in the Public Garden, with a little island on it. "The very place to spend the night," quacked Mr. Mallard. So down they flapped.

Next morning they fished for their breakfast in the mud at the bottom of the pond. But they didn't find much.

Just as they were getting ready to start on their way, a strange enormous bird came by. It was pushing a boat full of people, and there was a man sitting on its back. "Good morning," quacked Mr. Mallard, being polite. The big bird was too proud to answer. But the people on the boat threw peanuts into the water, so the Mallards followed them all round the pond and got another breakfast, better than the first.

"I like this place," said Mrs. Mallard as they climbed out on the bank and waddled along. "Why don't we build a nest and raise our ducklings right in this pond? There are no foxes and no turtles, and the people feed us peanuts. What could be better?"

"Good," said Mr. Mallard, delighted that at last Mrs. Mallard had found a place that suited her. But —

"Look out!" squawked Mrs. Mallard, all of a dither. "You'll get run over!" And when she got her breath she added: "*This* is no place for babies, with all those horrid things rushing about. We'll have to look somewhere else."

So they flew over Beacon Hill and round the State House, but there was no place there.

They looked in Louisburg Square, but there was no water to swim in.

Then they flew over the Charles River. "This is better," quacked Mr. Mallard. "That island looks like a nice quiet place, and it's only a little way from the Public Garden."

"Yes," said Mrs. Mallard, remembering the peanuts. "That looks like just the right place to hatch ducklings."

So they chose a cosy spot among the bushes near the water and settled down to build their nest. And only just in time, for now they were beginning to moult. All their old wing feathers started to drop out, and they would not be able to fly again until the new ones grew in.

But of course they could swim, and one day they swam over to the park on the riverbank, and there they met a policeman called Michael. Michael fed them peanuts, and after that the Mallards called on Michael every day.

ROBERT MCCLOSKEY

After Mrs. Mallard had laid eight eggs in the nest she couldn't go to visit Michael anymore, because she had to sit on the eggs to keep them warm. She moved off the nest only to get a drink of water, or to have her lunch, or to count the eggs and make sure they were all there.

One day the ducklings hatched out. First came Jack, then Kack, and then Lack, then Mack and Nack and Ouack and Pack and Quack. Mr. and Mrs. Mallard were bursting with pride. It was a great responsibility taking care of so many ducklings, and it kept them very busy.

One day Mr. Mallard decided he'd like to take a trip to see what the rest of the river was like, further on. So off he set. "I'll meet you in a week, in the Public Garden," he quacked over his shoulder. "Take good care of the ducklings."

"Don't you worry," said Mrs. Mallard. "I know all about bringing up children." And she did.

She taught them how to swim and dive.

She taught them to walk in a line, to come when they were called, and to keep a safe distance from bikes and scooters and other things with wheels.

When at last she felt perfectly satisfied with them, she said one morning: "Come along, children. Follow me."

Before you could wink an eyelash Jack, Kack, Lack, Mack, Nack, Ouack, Pack, and Quack fell into line, just as they had been taught. Mrs. Mallard led the way into the water and they swam behind her to the opposite bank.

There they waded ashore and waddled along till they came to the highway.

Mrs. Mallard stepped out to cross the road. "Honk, honk!"

went the horns on the speeding cars. "Qua-a-ack!" went Mrs. Mallard as she tumbled back again. "Quack! Quack! Quack! Quack!" went Jack, Kack, Lack, Mack, Nack, Ouack, Pack, and Quack, just as loud as their little quackers could quack. The cars kept speeding by and honking, and Mrs. Mallard and the ducklings kept right on quack-quack-quacking.

They made such a noise that Michael came running, waving his arms and blowing his whistle.

He planted himself in the centre of the road, raised one hand to stop the traffic, and then beckoned with the other, the way policemen do, for Mrs. Mallard to cross over.

As soon as Mrs. Mallard and the ducklings were safe on the other side and on their way down Mount Vernon Street, Michael rushed back to his police booth.

He called Clancy at headquarters and said: "There's a family of ducks walkin' down the street!"

Clancy said: "Family of *what?*"

"*Ducks!*" yelled Michael. "Send a police car, quick!"

Meanwhile Mrs. Mallard had reached the Corner Book Shop and turned into Charles Street, with Jack, Kack, Lack, Mack, Nack, Ouack, Pack, and Quack all marching in line behind her.

Everyone stared. An old lady from Beacon Hill said: "Isn't it amazing!" and the man who swept the streets said: "Well, now, ain't that nice!" and when Mrs. Mallard heard them she was so proud she tipped her nose in the air and walked along with an extra swing in her waddle.

When they came to the corner of Beacon Street there was the police car with four policemen that Clancy had sent from headquarters. The policemen held back the traffic so Mrs. Mallard and the ducklings could march across the street, right on into the Public Garden.

Inside the gate they all turned round to say thank you to the policemen. The policemen smiled and waved good-bye.

When they reached the pond and swam across to the little island, there was Mr. Mallard waiting for them, just as he had promised.

The ducklings liked the new island so much that they decided to live there. All day long they follow the swan boats and eat peanuts.

And when night falls they swim to their little island and go to sleep.

The VELVETEEN RABBIT
OR
HOW TOYS BECOME REAL

By Margery Williams

Illustration by William Nicholson

THERE WAS ONCE a velveteen rabbit, and in the beginning he was really splendid. He was fat and bunchy, as a rabbit should be; his coat was spotted brown and white, he had real thread whiskers, and his ears were lined with pink sateen. On Christmas morning, when he sat wedged in the top of the Boy's stocking, with a sprig of holly between his paws, the effect was charming.

There were other things in the stocking, nuts and oranges and a toy engine, and chocolate almonds and a clockwork mouse, but the Rabbit was quite the best of all. For at least two hours the Boy loved him, and then Aunts and Uncles came to dinner, and there was a great rustling of tissue paper and unwrapping of parcels, and in the excitement of looking at all the new presents the Velveteen Rabbit was forgotten.

For a long time he lived in the toy cupboard or on the nursery floor, and no one thought very much about him. He was naturally shy, and since he was only made of velveteen, some of the more expensive toys quite snubbed him. The mechanical toys were very superior, and looked down upon everyone else; they were full of modern ideas, and pretended they were real. The model boat, who had lived through two seasons and lost most of his paint, caught the tone from them and never missed an opportunity of referring to his rigging in technical terms. The Rabbit could not claim to be a model of anything, for he didn't know that real rabbits existed; he thought they were all stuffed with sawdust like himself, and he understood that sawdust was quite out-of-date and should never be mentioned in modern circles. Even Timothy, the jointed wooden lion, who was made by the disabled soldiers, and should have had broader views, put on airs and pretended he was connected with Government. Between them all the poor little Rabbit was made to feel himself very insignificant and commonplace, and the only person who was kind to him at all was the Skin Horse.

The Skin Horse had lived longer in the nursery than any of the others. He was so old that his brown coat was bald in patches and showed the seams underneath, and most of the hairs in his tail had been pulled out to string bead necklaces. He was wise, for he had seen a long succession of mechanical toys arrive to boast and swagger, and by-and-by break their mainsprings and pass away, and he knew that they were only toys, and would never turn into anything else. For nursery magic is very strange and wonderful, and only those playthings that are old and wise and experienced like the Skin Horse understand all about it.

"What is REAL?" asked the Rabbit one day, when they were lying side by side near the nursery fender, before Nana came to tidy the room. "Does it mean having things that buzz inside you and a stick-out handle?"

"Real isn't how you are made," said the Skin Horse. "It's a thing that happens to you. When a child loves you for a long, long time, not just to play with, but REALLY loves you, then you become Real."

"Does it hurt?" asked the Rabbit.

"Sometimes," said the Skin Horse, for he was always truthful. "When you are Real you don't mind being hurt."

"Does it happen all at once, like being wound up," he asked, "or bit by bit?"

"It doesn't happen all at once," said the Skin Horse. "You become. It takes a long time. That's why it doesn't often happen to people who break easily, or have sharp edges, or who have to be carefully kept. Generally, by the time you are Real, most of your hair has been loved off, and your eyes drop out and you get loose in the joints and very shabby. But these things don't matter at all, because once you are Real you can't be ugly, except to people who don't understand."

"I suppose *you* are Real?" said the Rabbit. And then he wished he had not said it, for he thought the Skin Horse might be sensitive. But the Skin Horse only smiled.

"The Boy's Uncle made me Real," he said. "That was a great many years ago; but once you are Real you can't become unreal again. It lasts for always."

The Rabbit sighed. He thought it would be a long time before this magic called Real happened to him. He longed to become Real, to know what it felt like; and yet the idea of growing shabby and losing his eyes and whiskers was rather sad. He wished that he could become it without these uncomfortable things happening to him.

There was a person called Nana who ruled the nursery. Sometimes she took no notice of the playthings lying about, and sometimes, for no reason whatever, she went swooping about like a great wind and hustled them away in cupboards. She called this "tidying up", and the playthings all hated it, especially the tin ones. The Rabbit didn't mind it so much, for wherever he was thrown he came down soft.

One evening, when the Boy was going to bed, he couldn't find the china dog that always slept with him. Nana was in a hurry, and it was too much trouble to hunt for china dogs at bedtime, so she simply looked about her, and seeing that the toy cupboard door stood open, she made a swoop.

"Here," she said, "take your old Bunny! He'll do to sleep with you!" And she dragged the Rabbit out by one ear, and put him into the Boy's arms.

That night, and for many nights after, the Velveteen Rabbit slept in the Boy's bed. At first he found it rather uncomfortable, for the Boy hugged him very tight, and sometimes he rolled over on him, and sometimes he pushed him so far under the pillow that the Rabbit could scarcely breathe. And he missed, too, those long moonlight hours in the nursery, when all the house was silent, and his talks with the Skin Horse. But very soon he grew to like it, for the Boy used to talk to him, and made nice tunnels for him under the bedclothes that he said were like the burrows the real rabbits lived in. And they had splendid games together, in whispers, when Nana had gone away to her supper and left the night-light burning on the mantelpiece. And when the Boy dropped off to sleep, the Rabbit would snuggle down close under his little warm chin and dream, with the Boy's hands clasped close round him all night long.

And so time went on, and the little Rabbit was very happy — so happy that he never noticed how his beautiful velveteen fur was getting shabbier and shabbier, and his tail coming unsewn, and all the pink rubbed off his nose where the Boy had kissed him.

Spring came, and they had long days in the garden, for wherever the Boy went the Rabbit went too. He had rides in the wheelbarrow, and picnics on the grass, and lovely fairy huts built for him under the raspberry canes behind the flower border. And once, when the Boy was called away suddenly to go out to tea, the Rabbit was left out on the lawn until long after dusk, and Nana

had to come and look for him with the candle because the Boy couldn't go to sleep unless he was there. He was wet through with the dew and quite earthy from diving into the burrows the Boy had made for him in the flower bed, and Nana grumbled as she rubbed him off with a corner of her apron.

"You must have your old Bunny!" she said. "Fancy all that fuss for a toy!"

The Boy sat up in bed and stretched out his hands.

"Give me my Bunny!" he said. "You mustn't say that. He isn't a toy. He's REAL!"

When the little Rabbit heard that he was happy, for he knew that what the Skin Horse had said was true at last. The nursery magic had happened to him, and he was a toy no longer. He was Real. The Boy himself had said it.

That night he was almost too happy to sleep, and so much love stirred in his little sawdust heart that it almost burst. And into his boot-button eyes, that had long ago lost their polish, there came a look of wisdom and beauty, so that even Nana noticed it next morning when she picked him up, and said, "I declare if that old Bunny hasn't got quite a knowing expression!"

That was a wonderful Summer!

Near the house where they lived there was a wood, and in the long June evenings the Boy liked to go there after tea to play. He took the Velveteen Rabbit with him, and before he wandered off to pick flowers, or play at brigands among the trees, he always made the Rabbit a little nest somewhere among the bracken, where he would be quite cosy, for he was a kindhearted little boy and he liked Bunny to be comfortable. One evening, while the

Rabbit was lying there alone, watching the ants that ran to and fro between his velvet paws in the grass, he saw two strange beings creep out of the tall bracken near him.

They were rabbits like himself, but quite furry and brand-new. They must have been very well made, for their seams didn't show at all, and they changed shape in a queer way when they moved; one minute they were long and thin and the next minute fat and bunchy, instead of always staying the same the way he did. Their feet padded softly on the ground, and they crept quite close to him, twitching their noses, while the Rabbit stared hard to see which side the clockwork stuck out, for he knew that people who jump generally have something to wind them up. But he couldn't see it. They were evidently a new kind of rabbit altogether.

They stared at him, and the little Rabbit stared back. And all the time their noses twitched.

"Why don't you get up and play with us?" one of them asked.

"I don't feel like it," said the Rabbit, for he didn't want to explain that he had no clockwork.

"Ho!" said the furry rabbit. "It's as easy as anything." And he gave a big hop sideways and stood on his hind legs.

"I don't believe you can!" he said.

"I can!" said the little Rabbit. "I can jump higher than anything!" He meant when the Boy threw him, but of course he didn't want to say so.

"Can you hop on your hind legs?" asked the furry rabbit.

That was a dreadful question, for the Velveteen Rabbit had no hind legs at all! The back of him was made all in one piece, like a pincushion. He sat still in the bracken, and hoped that the other rabbits wouldn't notice.

"I don't want to!" he said again.

But the wild rabbits have very sharp eyes. And this one stretched out his neck and looked.

"He hasn't got any hind legs!" he called out. "Fancy a rabbit without any hind legs!" And he began to laugh.

"I have!" cried the little Rabbit. "I have got hind legs! I am sitting on them!"

"Then stretch them out and show me, like this!" said the wild rabbit. And he began to whirl round and dance, till the Rabbit got quite dizzy.

"I don't like dancing," he said. "I'd rather sit still!"

But all the while he was longing to dance, for a funny new tickly feeling ran through him, and he felt he would give anything in the world to be able to jump about the way these rabbits did.

The strange rabbit stopped dancing, and came quite close. He came so close this time that his long whiskers brushed the Velveteen Rabbit's ear, and then he wrinkled his nose suddenly and flattened his ears and jumped backwards.

"He doesn't smell right!" he exclaimed. "He isn't a rabbit at all! He isn't real!"

"I *am* Real!" said the little Rabbit. "I am Real! The Boy said so!" And he nearly began to cry.

Just then there was a sound of footsteps, and the Boy ran past near them, and with a stamp of feet and a flash of white tails the two strange rabbits disappeared.

"Come back and play with me!" called the little Rabbit. "Oh, do come back! I *know* I am Real!"

But there was no answer, only the little ants ran to and fro, and the bracken swayed gently where the two strangers had passed. The Velveteen Rabbit was all alone.

"Oh, dear!" he thought. "Why did they run away like that? Why couldn't they stop and talk to me?"

For a long time he lay very still, watching the bracken, and hoping that they would come back. But they never returned, and presently the sun sank lower and the little white moths fluttered out, and the Boy came and carried him home.

Weeks passed, and the little Rabbit grew very old and shabby, but the Boy loved him just as much. He loved him so hard that he loved all his whiskers off, and the pink lining to his ears turned grey, and his brown spots faded. He even began to lose his shape, and he scarcely looked like a rabbit anymore, except to the Boy. To him he was always beautiful, and that was all that the little Rabbit cared about. He didn't mind how he looked to other people, because the nursery magic had made him Real, and when you are Real shabbiness doesn't matter.

And then, one day, the Boy was ill.

His face grew very flushed, and he talked in his sleep, and his little body was so hot that it burned the Rabbit when he held him close. Strange people came and went in the nursery, and a light burned all night and through it all the little Velveteen Rabbit lay there, hidden from sight under the bedclothes, and he never stirred, for he was afraid that if they found him someone might take him away, and he knew that the Boy needed him.

It was a long weary time, for the Boy was too ill to play, and the little Rabbit found it rather dull with nothing to do all day long. But he snuggled down patiently, and looked forward to the time when the Boy should be well again, and they would go out in the garden amongst the flowers and the butterflies and play splendid games in the raspberry thicket the way they used to. All sorts of delightful things he planned, and while the Boy lay half asleep he crept up close to the pillow and whispered them in his ear. And presently the fever turned, and the Boy got better. He was able to sit up in bed and look at picture books, while the little Rabbit cuddled close at his side. And one day, they let him get up and dress.

It was a bright, sunny morning, and the windows stood wide open. They had carried the Boy out onto the balcony, wrapped in a shawl, and the little Rabbit lay tangled up among the bedclothes, thinking.

The Boy was going to the seaside tomorrow. Everything was arranged, and now it only remained to carry out the doctor's orders. They talked about it all, while the little Rabbit lay under the bedclothes, with just his head peeping out, and listened. The room was to be disinfected, and all the books and toys that the Boy had played with in bed must be burnt.

"Hurray!" thought the little Rabbit. "Tomorrow we shall go to the seaside!" For the Boy had often talked of the seaside, and he wanted very much to see the big waves coming in, and the tiny crabs, and the sand castles.

Just then Nana caught sight of him.

"How about his old Bunny?" she asked.

"*That?*" said the doctor. "Why, it's a mass of scarlet fever germs! — Burn it at once. What? Nonsense! Get him a new one. He mustn't have that anymore!"

And so the little Rabbit was put into a sack with the old picture books and a lot of rubbish, and carried out to the end of the garden behind the fowl-house. That was a fine place to make a bonfire, only the gardener was too busy just then to attend to it. He had the potatoes to dig and the green peas to gather, but next morning he promised to come quite early and burn the whole lot.

That night the Boy slept in a different bedroom, and he had a new bunny to sleep with him. It was a splendid bunny, all white plush with real glass eyes, but the Boy was too excited to care very much about it. For tomorrow he was going to the seaside, and that in itself was such a wonderful thing that he could think of nothing else.

And while the Boy was asleep, dreaming of the seaside, the little Rabbit lay among the old picture books in the corner behind the fowl-house, and he felt very lonely. The sack had been left untied, and so by wriggling a bit he was able to get his head through the opening and look out. He was shivering a little, for he had always been used to sleeping in a proper bed, and by this time his coat had been worn so thin and threadbare from hugging that it was no longer any protection to him. Nearby he could see the thicket of raspberry canes, growing tall and close like a tropical jungle, in whose shadow he had played with the Boy on bygone mornings. He thought of those long sunlit hours in the garden — how happy they were — and a great sadness came over him. He seemed to see them all pass before him, each more beautiful than the other, the fairy huts in the flower bed, the quiet evenings in the wood when he lay in the bracken and the little ants ran over his paws; the wonderful day when he first knew that he was Real. He thought of the Skin Horse, so wise and gentle, and all that he had told him. Of what use was it to be loved and lose one's beauty and become Real if it all ended like this? And a tear, a real tear, trickled down his little shabby velvet nose and fell to the ground.

And then a strange thing happened. For where the tear had fallen a flower grew out of the ground, a mysterious flower, not at all like any that grew in the garden. It had slender green leaves the colour of emeralds, and in the centre of the leaves a blossom like a golden cup. It was so beautiful that the little Rabbit forgot to cry, and just lay there watching it. And presently the blossom opened, and out of it there stepped a fairy.

She was quite the loveliest fairy in the whole world. Her dress was of pearl and dewdrops, and there were flowers round her neck and in her hair, and her face was like the most perfect flower of all. And she came close to the little Rabbit and gathered him up in her arms and kissed him on his velveteen nose that was all damp from crying.

"Little Rabbit," she said, "don't you know who I am?"

The Rabbit looked up at her, and it seemed to him that he had seen her face before, but he couldn't think where.

"I am the nursery magic Fairy," she said. "I take care of all the playthings that the children have loved. When they are old and worn out and the children don't need them anymore, then I come and take them away with me and turn them into Real."

"Wasn't I Real before?" asked the little Rabbit.

"You were Real to the Boy," the Fairy said, "because he loved you. Now you shall be Real to everyone."

And she held the little Rabbit close in her arms and flew with him into the wood.

It was light now, for the moon had risen. All the forest was beautiful, and the fronds of the bracken shone like frosted silver. In the open glade between the tree trunks the wild rabbits danced with their shadows on the velvet grass, but when they saw the Fairy they all stopped dancing and stood round in a ring to stare at her.

"I've brought you a new playfellow," the Fairy said. "You must be very kind to him and teach him all he needs to know in Rabbitland, for he is going to live with you forever and ever!"

And she kissed the little Rabbit again and put him down on the grass.

"Run and play, little Rabbit!" she said.

But the little Rabbit sat quite still for a moment and never moved. For when he saw all the wild rabbits dancing around him he suddenly remembered about his hind legs, and he didn't want them to see that he was made all in one piece. He did not know that when the Fairy kissed him that last time she had changed him altogether. And he might have sat there a long time, too shy to move, if just then something hadn't tickled his nose, and before he thought what he was doing he lifted his hind toe to scratch it.

And he found that he actually had hind legs! Instead of dingy velveteen he had brown fur, soft and shiny, his ears twitched by themselves, and his whiskers were so long that they brushed the grass. He gave one leap and the joy of using those hind legs was so great that he went springing about the turf on them, jumping sideways and whirling round as the others did, and he grew so excited that when at last he did stop to look for the Fairy she had gone.

He was a Real Rabbit at last, at home with the other rabbits.

Autumn passed and Winter, and in the Spring, when the days grew warm and sunny, the Boy went out to play in the wood behind the house. And while he was playing, two rabbits crept out from the bracken and peeped at him. One of them was brown all over, but the other had strange markings under his fur, as though long ago he had been spotted, and the spots still showed through. And about his little soft nose and his round black eyes there was something familiar, so that the Boy thought to himself:

"Why, he looks just like my old Bunny that was lost when I had scarlet fever!"

But he never knew that it really was his own Bunny, come back to look at the child who had first helped him to be Real.

MORRIS BISHOP

Song of the Pop-Bottlers

Pop bottles pop-bottles
  In pop shops;
The pop-bottles Pop bottles
  Poor Pop drops.

When Pop drops pop-bottles,
  pop-bottles plop!
Pop-bottle-tops topple!
  Pop mops slop!

Stop! Pop'll drop bottle!
  Stop, Pop, stop!
When Pop bottles pop-bottles,
  Pop-bottles pop!

Alexander and the Terrible, Horrible, No Good, Very Bad Day

JUDITH VIORST

Illustrated by RAY CRUZ

I WENT TO SLEEP with gum in my mouth and now there's gum in my hair and when I got out of bed this morning I tripped on the skateboard and by mistake I dropped my sweater in the sink while the water was running and I could tell it was going to be a terrible, horrible, no good, very bad day.

At breakfast Anthony found a Corvette Sting Ray car kit in his breakfast cereal box and Nick found a Junior Undercover Agent code ring in his breakfast cereal box but in my breakfast cereal box all I found was breakfast cereal.

I think I'll move to Australia.

In the car pool Mrs. Gibson let Becky have a seat by the window. Audrey and Elliott got seats by the window too. I said I was being scrunched. I said I was being smushed. I said, if I don't get a seat by the window I am going to be carsick. No one even answered.

I could tell it was going to be a terrible, horrible, no good, very bad day.

At school Mrs. Dickens liked Paul's picture of the sailboat better than my picture of the invisible castle.

At singing time she said I sang too loud. At counting time she said I left out sixteen. Who needs sixteen?

I could tell it was going to be a terrible, horrible, no good, very bad day.

I could tell because Paul said I wasn't his best friend anymore. He said that Philip Parker was his best friend and that Albert Moyo was his next best friend and that I was only his third best friend.

I hope you sit on a tack, I said to Paul. I hope the next time you get a double-decker strawberry ice-cream cone the ice cream part falls off the cone part and lands in Australia.

There were two cupcakes in Philip Parker's lunch bag and Albert got a Hershey bar with almonds and Paul's mother gave him a piece of jelly roll that had little coconut sprinkles on the top. Guess whose mother forgot to put in dessert?

It was a terrible, horrible, no good, very bad day.

That's what it was, because after school my mom took us all to the dentist and Dr. Fields found a cavity just in me. Come back next week and I'll fix it, said Dr. Fields.

Next week, I said, I'm going to Australia.

On the way downstairs the elevator door closed on my foot and while we were waiting for my mom to go get the car Anthony made me fall where it was muddy and then when I started crying because of the mud Nick said I was a crybaby and while I was punching Nick for saying crybaby my mom came back with the car and scolded me for being muddy and fighting.

I am having a terrible, horrible, no good, very bad day, I told everybody. No one even answered.

So then we went to the shoestore to buy some sneakers. Anthony chose white ones with blue stripes. Nick chose red ones with white stripes. I chose blue ones with red stripes but then the shoe man said, We're all sold out. They made me buy plain old white ones, but they can't make me wear them.

When we picked up my dad at his office he said I couldn't play with his copying machine, but I forgot. He also said to watch out for the books on his desk, and I was careful as could be except for my elbow. He also said don't fool around with his phone, but I think I called Australia. My dad said please don't pick him up anymore.

It was a terrible, horrible, no good, very bad day.

There were butter beans for dinner and I hate butter beans.

There was kissing on TV and I hate kissing.

My bath was too hot, I got soap in my eyes, my marble went down the drain, and I had to wear my railway-train pyjamas. I hate my railway-train pyjamas.

When I went to bed Nick took back the pillow he said I could keep and the Mickey Mouse night-light burned out and I bit my tongue.

The cat wants to sleep with Anthony, not with me.

It has been a terrible, horrible, no good, very bad day.

My mom says some days are like that.

Even in Australia.

N. M. BODECKER

Mr. Skinner

Orville Skinner
(kite-string spinner)
never stopped
to eat his dinner,
for he found it
too rewarding
and exciting
to go kiting.
Flying kites,
he used to sing:
"I'm a spinner
on a string!"
When they warned him:
"Mister Skinner,
capable
but high-strung spinner,
it may take you
to Brazil,"
Skinner cried:
"I hope it will!"

Mr. 'Gator

Elevator operator
P. Cornelius Alligator,
when his passengers
were many,
never
ever
passed up
any:
when his passengers
were few,
always managed
to make do.
When they told him:
"Mister 'Gator!
quickly
in your elevator
take us
to the nineteenth floor!"
they were never
seen no more.

ENGLISH FAIRY TALES

Of all the fairy tales in this book my favourite is the story "Dick Whittington and His Cat". When you grow up you may find that you, too, remember one fairy tale above all others. It may be "Cinderella" or "Rumpelstiltskin" or "The Three Little Pigs". For me it's the one about the adventures of Dick Whittington.

When I first read it, more than seventy years ago, I almost stopped breathing when the Bells of Bow Church rang out and seemed to say:

> *"Turn again, Whittington,*
> *Thrice Lord Mayor of London."*

It was the bells foretelling Dick's good fortune that stirred my heart. I was perhaps five years old and just beginning to realize that the world was big and life was long and would be full of surprises. The words "London" and "Bow Church", even the name "Dick Whittington", all had a kind of magic about them, something strange and faraway and yet somehow having something to do with me.

I have visited London several times and each time Dick Whittington and the sound of Bow Bells were in the back of my mind. Fairy tales can be very real.

By the way, there was a real Dick Whittington and he did really become Lord Mayor of London three times, in 1397, 1406, and 1419. If you go to London you can sit down on Whittington's Stone, where he first heard the Bow Bells.

The four tales that follow are retold by Joseph Jacobs.

The Story of the Three Bears

ONCE upon a time there were Three Bears, who lived together in a house of their own, in a wood. One of them was a Little, Small, Wee Bear; and one was a Middle-sized Bear; and the other was a Great, Huge Bear. They had each a pot for their porridge, a little pot for the Little, Small, Wee Bear; and a middle-sized pot for the Middle Bear; and a great pot for the Great, Huge Bear. And they had each a chair to sit in, a little chair for the Little, Small, Wee Bear; and a middle-sized chair for the Middle Bear; and a great chair for the Great, Huge Bear. And they had each a bed to sleep in, a little bed for the Little, Small, Wee Bear; and a middle-sized bed for the Middle Bear; and a great bed for the Great, Huge Bear.

One day, after they had made the porridge for their breakfast, and poured it into their porridge-pots, they walked out into the wood while the porridge was cooling, that they might not burn their mouths, by beginning too soon to eat it. And while they were walking, a little old Woman came to the house. She could not have been a good, honest old Woman; for first she looked in at the window, and then she peeped in at the keyhole; and seeing nobody in the house, she lifted the latch. The door was not fastened, because the Bears were good Bears, who did nobody any harm, and never suspected that anybody would harm them. So the little old Woman opened the door, and went in; and well pleased she was when she saw the porridge on the table. If she had been a good little old Woman, she would have waited till the Bears came home, and then, perhaps, they would have asked her to breakfast; for they were good Bears — a little rough or so, as the manner of Bears is, but for all that very good-natured and hospitable. But she was an impudent, bad old Woman, and set about helping herself.

So first she tasted the porridge of the Great, Huge Bear, and that was too hot for her; and she said a bad word about that. And then she tasted the porridge of the Middle Bear, and that was too cold for her; and she said a bad word about that too. And then she went to the porridge of the Little, Small, Wee Bear, and tasted that; and that was neither too hot, nor too cold, but just right; and she liked it so well that she ate it all up: but the naughty old Woman said a bad word about the little porridge-pot, because it did not hold enough for her.

Then the little old Woman sat down in the chair of the Great, Huge Bear, and that was too hard for her. And then she sat down in the chair of the Middle Bear, and that was too soft for her. And then she sat down in the chair of the Little, Small, Wee Bear, and that was neither too hard, nor too soft, but just right. So she seated herself in it, and there she sat till the bottom of the chair came out, and down she came, plump upon the ground. And the naughty old Woman said a wicked word about that too.

Then the little old Woman went upstairs into the bedchamber in which the Three Bears slept. And first she lay down upon the bed of the Great, Huge Bear; but that was too high at the head for her. And next she lay down upon the bed of the Middle Bear; and that was too high at the foot for her. And then she lay down upon the bed of the Little, Small, Wee Bear; and that was neither too high at the head, nor at the foot, but just right. So she covered herself up comfortably, and lay there till she fell fast asleep.

By this time the Three Bears thought their porridge would be cool enough; so they came home to breakfast. Now the little old Woman had left the spoon of the Great, Huge Bear standing in his porridge.

"Somebody has been eating my porridge!" said the Great, Huge Bear, in his great, rough, gruff voice. And when the Middle Bear looked at his, he saw that the spoon was standing in it too. They were wooden spoons; if they had been silver ones, the naughty old Woman would have put them in her pocket.

"Somebody has been eating my porridge!" said the Middle Bear in his middle voice.

Then the Little, Small, Wee Bear looked at his, and there was the spoon in the porridge-pot, but the porridge was all gone.

"Somebody has been eating my porridge, and has eaten it all up!" said the Little, Small, Wee Bear, in his little, small, wee voice.

Upon this the Three Bears, seeing that someone had entered their house, and eaten up the Little, Small, Wee Bear's breakfast, began to look about them. Now the little old Woman had not put the hard cushion straight when she rose from the chair of the Great, Huge Bear.

"Somebody has been sitting in my chair!" said the Great, Huge Bear, in his great, rough, gruff voice.

And the little old Woman had squatted down the soft cushion of the Middle Bear.

"Somebody has been sitting in my chair!" said the Middle Bear, in his middle voice.

And you know what the little old Woman had done to the third chair.

"Somebody has been sitting in my chair and has sat the bottom out of it!" said the Little, Small, Wee Bear, in his little, small, wee voice.

Then the Three Bears thought it necessary that they should make further search; so they went upstairs into their bedchamber. Now the little old Woman had pulled the pillow of the Great, Huge Bear out of its place.

"Somebody has been lying in my bed!" said the Great, Huge Bear, in his great, rough, gruff voice.

And the little old Woman had pulled the bolster of the Middle Bear out of its place.

"Somebody has been lying in my bed!" said the Middle Bear, in his middle voice.

And when the Little, Small, Wee Bear came to look at his bed, there was the bolster in its place; and the pillow in its place upon the bolster; and upon the pillow was the little old Woman's ugly, dirty head — which was not in its place, for she had no business there.

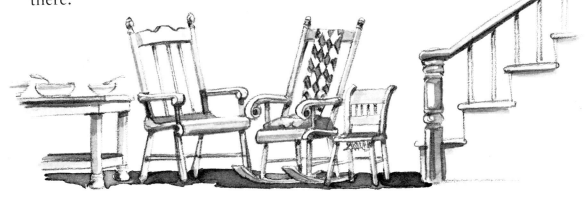

"Somebody has been lying in my bed — and here she is!" said the Little, Small, Wee Bear, in his little, small, wee voice.

The little old Woman had heard in her sleep the great, rough, gruff voice of the Great, Huge Bear; but she was so fast asleep that it was no more to her than the roaring of wind, or the rumbling of thunder. And she had heard the middle voice, of the Middle Bear, but it was only as if she had heard someone speaking in a dream. But when she heard the little, small, wee voice of the Little, Small, Wee Bear, it was so sharp, and so shrill, that it awakened her at once. Up she started and when she saw the Three Bears on one side of the bed, she tumbled herself out at the other, and ran to the window. Now the window was open, because the Bears, like good, tidy Bears, as they were, always opened their bedchamber window when they got up in the morning. Out the little old Woman jumped; and whether she broke her neck in the fall; or ran into the wood and was lost there; or found her way out of the wood, and was taken up by the constable and sent to the House of Correction for a vagrant as she was, I cannot tell. But the Three Bears never saw anything more of her.

The Story of the Three Little Pigs

Once upon a time when pigs spoke rhyme
And monkeys chewed tobacco,
And hens took snuff to make them tough,
And ducks went quack, quack, quack, O!

THERE was an old sow with three little pigs, and as she had not enough to keep them, she sent them out to seek their fortune. The first that went off met a man with a bundle of straw, and said to him:

"Please, man, give me that straw to build me a house."

Which the man did, and the little pig built a house with it. Presently came along a wolf, and knocked at the door, and said:

"Little pig, little pig, let me come in."

To which the pig answered:

"No, no, by the hair of my chiny chin chin."

The wolf then answered to that:

"Then I'll huff, and I'll puff, and I'll blow your house in."

So he huffed, and he puffed, and he blew his house in, and ate up the little pig.

The second little pig met a man with a bundle of furze, and said:

"Please, man, give me that furze to build a house."

Which the man did, and the pig built his house. Then along came the wolf, and said:

"Little pig, little pig, let me come in."

"No, no, by the hair of my chiny chin chin."

"Then I'll puff, and I'll huff, and I'll blow your house in."

So he huffed, and he puffed, and he puffed, and he huffed, and at last he blew the house down, and he ate up the little pig.

The third little pig met a man with a load of bricks, and said: "Please, man, give me those bricks to build a house with."

So the man gave him the bricks, and he built his house with them. So the wolf came, as he did to the other little pigs, and said:

"Little pig, little pig, let me come in."

"No, no, by the hair of my chiny chin chin."

"Then I'll huff, and I'll puff, and I'll blow your house in."

Well, he huffed, and he puffed, and he huffed and he puffed, and he puffed and huffed; but he could *not* get the house down. When he found that he could not, with all his huffing and puffing, blow the house down, he said:

"Little pig, I know where there is a nice field of turnips."

"Where?" said the little pig.

"Oh, in Mr. Smith's home field, and if you will be ready tomorrow morning I will call for you, and we will go together, and get some for dinner."

"Very well," said the little pig, "I will be ready. What time do you mean to go?"

"Oh, at six o'clock."

Well, the little pig got up at five, and got the turnips before the wolf came (which he did about six) and who said:

"Little pig, are you ready?"

The little pig said: "Ready! I have been and come back again, and got a nice potful for dinner."

The wolf felt very angry at this, but thought that he would be up to the little pig somehow or other, so he said:

"Little pig, I know where there is a nice apple tree."

"Where?" said the pig.

"Down at Merry-garden," replied the wolf, "and if you will not deceive me I will come for you, at five o'clock tomorrow, and get some apples."

Well, the little pig bustled up the next morning at four o'clock, and went off for the apples, hoping to get back before the wolf came; but he had farther to go, and had to climb the tree, so that just as he was coming down from it, he saw the wolf coming, which, as you may suppose, frightened him very much. When the wolf came up he said:

"Little pig, what! are you here before me? Are they nice apples?"

"Yes, very," said the little pig. "I will throw you down one."

And he threw it so far, that, while the wolf was gone to pick it up, the little pig jumped down and ran home. The next day the wolf came again, and said to the little pig:

"Little pig, there is a fair at Shanklin this afternoon; will you go?"

"Oh yes," said the pig, "I will go; what time shall you be ready?"

"At three," said the wolf. So the little pig went off before the time as usual, and got to the fair, and bought a butter churn, which he was going home with, when he saw the wolf coming. Then he could not tell what to do. So he got into the churn to hide, and by so doing turned it round, and it rolled down the hill with the pig in it, which frightened the wolf so much that he ran home without going to the fair. He went to the little pig's house, and told him how frightened he had been by a great round thing which came down the hill past him. Then the little pig said:

"Hah, I frightened you, then. I had been to the fair and bought a butter churn, and when I saw you, I got into it, and rolled down the hill."

Then the wolf was very angry indeed, and declared he *would* eat up the little pig, and that he would get down the chimney after him. When the little pig saw what he was about, he hung on the pot full of water, and made up a blazing fire, and, just as the wolf was coming down, took off the cover, and in fell the wolf; so the little pig put on the cover again in an instant, boiled him up, and ate him for supper, and lived happy ever afterwards.

Mr. Miacca

TOMMY GRIMES was sometimes a good boy, and some-times a bad boy; and when he was a bad boy, he was a very bad boy. Now his mother used to say to him: "Tommy, Tommy, be a good boy, and don't go out of the street, or else Mr. Miacca will take you." But still when he was a bad boy he would go out of the street; and one day, sure enough, he had scarcely got round the corner, when Mr. Miacca did catch him and popped him into a bag upside down, and took him off to his house.

When Mr. Miacca got Tommy inside, he pulled him out of the bag and set him down, and felt his arms and legs. "You're rather tough," said he; "but you're all I've got for supper, and you'll not taste bad boiled. But body o' me, I've forgot the herbs, and it's bitter you'll taste without herbs. Sally! Here, I say, Sally!" and he called Mrs. Miacca.

So Mrs. Miacca came out of another room and said: "What d'ye want, my dear?"

"Oh, here's a little boy for supper," said Mr. Miacca, "and I've forgot the herbs. Mind him, will ye, while I go for them."

"All right, my love," said Mrs. Miacca, and off he went.

Then Tommy Grimes said to Mrs. Miacca: "Does Mr. Miacca always have little boys for supper?"

"Mostly, my dear," said Mrs. Miacca, "if little boys are bad enough, and get in his way."

"And don't you have anything else but boy-meat? No pud-ding?" asked Tommy.

"Ah, I loves pudding," said Mrs. Miacca. "But it's not often the likes of me gets pudding."

"Why, my mother is making a pudding this very day," said Tommy Grimes, "and I am sure she'd give you some, if I ask her. Shall I run and get some?"

"Now, that's a thoughtful boy," said Mrs. Miacca, "only don't be long and be sure to be back for supper."

So off Tommy peltered, and right glad he was to get off so cheap; and for many a long day he was as good as good could be, and never went round the corner of the street. But he couldn't always be good; and one day he went round the corner, and as luck would have it, he hadn't scarcely got round it when Mr. Miacca grabbed him up, popped him in his bag, and took him home.

When he got him there, Mr. Miacca dropped him out; and when he saw him, he said: "Ah, you're the youngster that served

me and my missus such a shabby trick, leaving us without any supper. Well, you shan't do it again. I'll watch over you myself. Here, get under the sofa, and I'll set on it and watch the pot boil for you."

So poor Tommy Grimes had to creep under the sofa, and Mr. Miacca sat on it and waited for the pot to boil. And they waited, and they waited, but still the pot didn't boil, till at last Mr. Miacca got tired of waiting, and he said: "Here, you under there, I'm not going to wait any longer; put out your leg, and I'll stop your giving us the slip."

So Tommy put out a leg, and Mr. Miacca got a chopper, and chopped it off, and popped it in the pot.

Suddenly he called out: "Sally, my dear, Sally!" and nobody answered. So he went into the next room to look out for Mrs. Miacca, and while he was there, Tommy crept out from under the sofa and ran out of the door. For it was a leg of the sofa that he had put out.

So Tommy Grimes ran home, and he never went round the corner again till he was old enough to go alone.

Dick Whittington
and His Cat

IN the reign of the famous King Edward III there was a little boy called Dick Whittington, whose father and mother died when he was very young. As poor Dick was not old enough to work, he was very badly off; he got but little for his dinner, and sometimes nothing at all for his breakfast; for the people who lived in the village were very poor indeed, and could not spare him much more than the parings of potatoes, and now and then a hard crust of bread.

Now Dick had heard many, many very strange things about the great city called London; for the country people at that time thought that folks in London were all fine gentlemen and ladies; and that there was singing and music there all day long; and that the streets were all paved with gold.

One day a large waggon and eight horses, all with bells at their heads, drove through the village while Dick was standing by the signpost. He thought that this waggon must be going to the fine town of London; so he took courage, and asked the waggoner to let him walk with him by the side of the waggon. As soon as the waggoner heard that poor Dick had no father or mother, and saw by his ragged clothes that he could not be worse off than he was, he told him he might go if he would, so off they set together.

So Dick got safe to London, and was in such a hurry to see the fine streets paved all over with gold that he did not even stay to thank the kind waggoner, but ran off as fast as his legs would carry him, through many of the streets, thinking every moment to come to those that were paved with gold; for Dick had seen a guinea three times in his own little village, and remembered what a deal of money it brought in change; so he thought he had nothing to do but to take up some little bits of the pavement, and should then have as much money as he could wish for.

Poor Dick ran till he was tired, and had quite forgot his friend the waggoner; but at last, finding it grew dark, and that every way he turned he saw nothing but dirt instead of gold, he sat down in a dark corner and cried himself to sleep.

Little Dick was all night in the streets; and next morning, being very hungry, he got up and walked about, and asked everybody he met to give him a halfpenny to keep him from starving; but nobody stayed to answer him, and only two or three gave him a halfpenny; so that the poor boy was soon quite weak and faint for the want of victuals.

In this distress he asked charity of several people, and one of them said crossly: "Go to work for an idle rogue." "That I will," said Dick, "I will go to work for you, if you will let me." But the man only cursed at him and went on.

At last a good-natured-looking gentleman saw how hungry he looked. "Why don't you go to work, my lad?" said he to Dick. "That I would, but I do not know how to get any," answered Dick. "If you are willing, come along with me," said the gentleman, and took him to a hay field, where Dick worked briskly, and lived merrily till the hay was made.

After this he found himself as badly off as before; and being almost starved again, he laid himself down at the door of Mr. Fitzwarren, a rich merchant. Here he was soon seen by the cook-maid, who was an ill-tempered creature, and happened just then to be very busy dressing dinner for her master and mistress; so she called out to poor Dick: "What business have you there, you lazy rogue? There is nothing else but beggars; if you do not take yourself away, we will see how you will like a sousing of some dishwater; I have some here hot enough to make you jump."

Just at that time Mr. Fitzwarren himself came home to dinner; and when he saw a dirty ragged boy lying at the door, he said to him: "Why do you lie there, my boy? You seem old enough to work; I am afraid you are inclined to be lazy."

"No, indeed, sir," said Dick to him, "that is not the case, for I would work with all my heart, but I do not know anybody, and I believe I am very sick for the want of food."

"Poor fellow, get up; let me see what ails you."

Dick now tried to rise, but was obliged to lie down again, being too weak to stand, for he had not eaten any food for three days, and was no longer able to run about and beg a halfpenny of people in the street. So the kind merchant ordered him to be taken into the house, and have a good dinner given him, and be kept to do what work he was able to do for the cook.

Little Dick would have lived very happily in this good family if it had not been for the ill-natured cook. She used to say: "You are under me, so look sharp; clean the spit and the dripping-pan, make the fires, wind up the jack, and do all the scullery work nimbly, or —" and she would shake the ladle at him. Besides, she was so fond of basting, that when she had no meat to baste, she would baste poor Dick's head and shoulders with a broom, or anything else that happened to fall in her way. At last her ill-usage of him was told to Alice, Mr. Fitzwarren's daughter, who told the cook she should be turned away if she did not treat him better.

The behaviour of the cook was now a little better; but besides this Dick had another hardship to get over. His bed stood in a garret, where there were so many holes in the floor and the walls that every night he was tormented with rats and mice. A gentleman having given Dick a penny for cleaning his shoes, he thought he would buy a cat with it. The next day he saw a girl with a cat, and asked her, "Will you let me have that cat for a penny?" The girl said: "Yes, that I will, master, though she is an excellent mouser."

Dick hid his cat in the garret, and always took care to carry a part of his dinner to her; and in a short time he had no more trouble with the rats and mice, but slept quite sound every night.

Soon after this, his master had a ship ready to sail; and as it was the custom that all his servants should have some chance for good fortune as well as himself, he called them all into the parlour and asked them what they would send out.

They all had something that they were willing to venture except poor Dick, who had neither money nor goods, and therefore could send nothing. For this reason he did not come into the parlour with the rest; but Miss Alice guessed what was the matter, and ordered him to be called in. She then said, "I will lay down some money for him, from my own purse;" but her father told her, "This will not do, for it must be something of his own."

When poor Dick heard this, he said: "I have nothing but a cat which I bought for a penny some time since of a little girl."

"Fetch your cat then, my lad," said Mr. Fitzwarren, "and let her go."

Dick went upstairs and brought down poor puss, with tears in his eyes, and gave her to the captain; "For," he said, "I shall now be kept awake all night by the rats and mice." All the company laughed at Dick's odd venture; and Miss Alice, who felt pity for him, gave him some money to buy another cat.

This, and many other marks of kindness shown him by Miss Alice, made the ill-tempered cook jealous of poor Dick, and she began to use him more cruelly than ever, and always made game of him for sending his cat to sea. She asked him: "Do you think your cat will sell for as much money as would buy a stick to beat you?"

At last poor Dick could not bear this usage any longer, and he thought he would run away from his place; so he packed up his few things, and started very early in the morning, on All Hallows Day, the first of November. He walked as far as Holloway; and there sat down on a stone, which to this day is called "Whittington's Stone", and began to think to himself which road he should take.

While he was thinking what he should do, the Bells of Bow Church, which at that time were only six, began to ring, and their sound seemed to say to him:

> *"Turn again, Whittington,*
> *Thrice Lord Mayor of London."*

"Lord Mayor of London!" said he to himself. "Why, to be sure, I would put up with almost anything now, to be Lord Mayor of London, and ride in a fine coach, when I grow to be a man! Well, I will go back, and think nothing of the cuffing and scolding of the old cook, if I am to be Lord Mayor of London at last."

Dick went back, and was lucky enough to get into the house, and set about his work, before the old cook came downstairs.

We must now follow Miss Puss to the coast of Africa. The ship with the cat on board was a long time at sea; and was at last driven by the winds on a part of the coast of Barbary, where the only people were the Moors, unknown to the English. The people came in great numbers to see the sailors, because they were of different colour to themselves, and treated them civilly; and, when they became better acquainted, were very eager to buy the fine things that the ship was loaded with.

When the captain saw this, he sent patterns of the best things he had to the king of the country; who was so much pleased with them that he sent for the captain to the palace. Here they were placed, as it is the custom of the country, on rich carpets flowered with gold and silver. The king and queen were seated at the upper end of the room; and a number of dishes were brought in for dinner. They had not sat long, when a vast number of rats and mice rushed in, and devoured all the meat in an instant. The captain wondered at this, and asked if these vermin were not unpleasant.

"Oh yes," said they, "very offensive; and the king would give half his treasure to be freed of them, for they not only destroy his dinner, as you see, but they assault him in his chamber, and even in bed, and so that he is obliged to be watched while he is sleeping, for fear of them."

The captain jumped for joy; he remembered poor Whittington and his cat, and told the king he had a creature on board the ship that would dispatch all these vermin immediately. The king jumped so high at the joy which the news gave him that his turban dropped off his head. "Bring this creature to me," said he; "vermin are dreadful in a court, and if she will perform what you say, I will load your ship with gold and jewels in exchange for her."

The captain, who knew his business, took this opportunity to set forth the merits of Miss Puss. He told His Majesty: "It is not very convenient to part with her, as, when she is gone, the rats and mice may destroy the goods in the ship — but to oblige your majesty, I will fetch her."

"Run, run!" said the queen; "I am impatient to see the dear creature."

Away went the captain to the ship, while another dinner was got ready. He put Puss under his arm, and arrived at the palace just in time to see the table full of rats. When the cat saw them, she did not wait for bidding, but jumped out of the captain's arms, and in a few minutes laid almost all the rats and mice dead at her feet. The rest of them in their fright scampered away to their holes.

The king was quite charmed to get rid so easily of such plagues, and the queen desired that the creature who had done them so great a kindness might be brought to her, that she might look at her. Upon which the captain called: "Pussy, pussy, pussy!" and she came to him. He then presented her to the queen, who started back, and was afraid to touch a creature who had made such a havoc among the rats and mice. However, when the captain stroked the cat and called: "Pussy, pussy," the queen also touched her and cried: "Putty, putty," for she had not learned English. He then put her down on the queen's lap, where she purred and played with Her Majesty's hand, and then purred herself to sleep.

The king, having seen the exploits of Miss Puss, and being informed that her kittens would stock the whole country, and keep it free from rats, bargained with the captain for the whole ship's cargo, and then gave him ten times as much for the cat as all the rest amounted to.

The captain then took leave of the royal party, and set sail with a fair wind for England, and after a happy voyage arrived safe in London.

One morning, early, Mr. Fitzwarren had just come to his counting house and seated himself at the desk, to count over the cash, and settle the business for the day, when somebody came tap, tap, at the door. "Who's there?" said Mr. Fitzwarren. "A friend," answered the other; "I come to bring you good news of your ship *Unicorn*." The merchant, bustling up in such a hurry that he forgot his gout, opened the door, and who should he see waiting but the captain and factor, with a cabinet of jewels, and a bill of lading; when he looked at this the merchant lifted up his eyes and thanked Heaven for sending him such a prosperous voyage.

They then told the story of the cat, and showed the rich present that the king and queen had sent for her to poor Dick. As soon as the merchant heard this, he called out to his servants:

> "Go send him in, and tell him of his fame;
> Pray call him Mr. Whittington by name."

Mr. Fitzwarren now showed himself to be a good man; for when some of his servants said so great a treasure was too much for him, he answered: "God forbid I should deprive him of the value of a single penny, it is his own, and he shall have it to a farthing."

He then sent for Dick, who at that time was scouring pots for the cook, and was quite dirty. He would have excused himself from coming into the counting house, saying, "The room is swept, and my shoes are dirty and full of hobnails." But the merchant ordered him to come in.

Mr. Fitzwarren ordered a chair to be set for him, and so he began to think they were making game of him, and at the same time said to them: "Do not play tricks with a poor simple boy, but let me go down again, if you please, to my work."

"Indeed, Mr. Whittington," said the merchant, "we are all quite in earnest with you, and I most heartily rejoice in the news that these gentlemen have brought you; for the captain has sold your cat to the king of Barbary, and brought you in return for her more riches than I possess in the whole world; and I wish you may long enjoy them!"

Mr. Fitzwarren then told the men to open the great treasure

they had brought with them; and said: "Mr. Whittington has nothing to do but to put it in some place of safety."

Poor Dick hardly knew how to behave himself for joy. He begged his master to take what part of it he pleased, since he owed it all to his kindness. "No, no," answered Mr. Fitzwarren, "this is all your own; and I have no doubt but you will use it well."

Dick next asked his mistress, and then Miss Alice, to accept a part of his good fortune; but they would not, and at the same time told him they felt great joy at his good success. But this poor fellow was too kind hearted to keep it all to himself; so he made a present to the captain, the mate, and the rest of Mr. Fitzwarren's servants; and even to the ill-natured old cook.

After this Mr. Fitzwarren advised him to send for a proper tailor and get himself dressed like a gentleman; and told him he was welcome to live in his house till he could provide himself with a better.

When Whittington's face was washed, his hair curled, his hat cocked, and he was dressed in a nice suit of clothes he was as handsome and genteel as any young man who visited at Mr. Fitzwarren's; so that Miss Alice, who had once been so kind to him, and thought of him with pity, now looked upon him as fit to be her sweetheart; and the more so, no doubt, because Whittington was now always thinking what he could do to oblige her, and making her the prettiest presents that could be.

Mr. Fitzwarren soon saw their love for each other, and proposed to join them in marriage; and to this they both readily agreed. A day for the wedding was soon fixed; and they were attended to church by the Lord Mayor, the court of aldermen, the sheriffs, and a great number of the richest merchants in London, whom they afterwards treated with a very rich feast.

History tells us that Mr. Whittington and his lady lived in great splendour, and were very happy. They had several children. He was Sheriff of London, thrice Lord Mayor, and received the honour of knighthood by Henry V.

He entertained this king and his queen at dinner after his conquest of France so grandly that the king said: "Never had prince such a subject"; when Sir Richard heard this, he said: "Never had subject such a prince."

The figure of Sir Richard Whittington with his cat in his arms, carved in stone, was to be seen till the year 1780 over the archway of the old prison of Newgate, which he built for criminals.

BEATRICE CURTIS BROWN

A New Song to Sing about Jonathan Bing

Oh, Jonathan Bing, oh, Bingathan Jon!
Forgets where he's going and thinks he has gone.
He wears his false teeth on the top of his head,
And always stands up when he's sleeping in bed.

Oh, Jonathan Bing has a curious way
Of trying to walk into yesterday.
"If I end with my breakfast and start with my tea,
I *ought* to be able to do it," says he.

Oh, Jonathan Bing is a miser, they say,
For he likes to save trouble and put it away.
"If I never get up in the morning," he said,
"I shall save all the trouble of going to bed!"

"Oh, Jonathan Bing, what a way to behave!
And what do you do with the trouble you save?"
"I wrap it up neatly and send it by post
To my friends and relations who need it the most."

THE
THREE ROBBERS
TOMI UNGERER

ONCE upon a time there were three fierce robbers. They went about hidden under large black capes and tall black hats.
The first had a blunderbuss. The second had a pepper-blower. And the third had a huge red axe.
In the dark of night they walked the roads, searching for victims.

They terrified everyone. Women fainted. Brave men ran. Dogs fled.

To stop carriages, the robbers blew pepper in the horses' eyes. With the axe, they smashed the carriage wheels. And with the blunderbuss, they threatened the passengers and plundered them.

The robbers' hideout was a cave high up in the mountains. There they carried their loot. They had trunks full of gold, jewels, money, watches, wedding rings, and precious stones.

But one bitter, black night the robbers stopped a carriage that had but one passenger, an orphan named Tiffany. She was on her way to live with a wicked aunt. Tiffany was delighted to meet the robbers.

Since there was no treasure but Tiffany, the thieves bundled her in a warm cape and carried her away.

They made up a soft bed for her in a corner of the cave. And there she slept.

The next morning she awoke to find herself surrounded by trunks of glittering riches.

"What is all this for?" she asked.

The robbers choked and spluttered. They had never thought of spending their wealth.

So to use their treasure they gathered up all the lost, unhappy, and abandoned children they could find. They bought a beautiful castle where all of them could live.

Dressed in red caps and capes, the children moved into their new house.

Stories of the castle spread throughout the land. New children came or were brought each day to the doorsteps of the three robbers.

The children grew until they were old enough to marry. Then

they built houses around the castle. A village grew up, full of people dressed in red caps and capes.

These people, in memory of their kind foster fathers, built three tall, high-roofed towers. One for each of the three robbers.

The Bear on the Motorcycle

Reiner Zimnik

Translated from the German by Cornelius Schaeffer

ONCE upon a time there was a fat brown bear. He lived in the Bumblefus circus, a contented, friendly animal. He spent the days lying behind the bars of his cage. When the weather was fine

he was pleased, and he let the sun warm his rough fur; and when it rained he was pleased, too, and watched the raindrops as they fell beyond the bars. And when somebody said to him, "How are you, fat brown bear?" he would rumble in a deep voice: "Hmm. . . . Just no excitement, please. Just quiet, please."

In the evenings, when the big circus tent was filled with people, his keeper would lead him into the great arena, and another circus man would bring out a red motorcycle and start the motor. Then the fat brown bear would sit down on the motorcycle, step on the gas, and ride the motorcycle around in thirteen circles. Every single evening, and on Sunday afternoons, too.

He was the only bear in all the world who could ride a motorcycle; and every evening the people would clap their hands and shout: "Hurray for the fat brown bear, hurray, hurray." And Sunday afternoons, too.

But one day, just as he was going around for the tenth time, a little boy called out, "The bear's stupid; the bear's stupid — all he can do is go around in circles." And even though his mother and his four aunts told him, "Be quiet, it may be nothing special for a person to ride a motorcycle, but for a bear it's a fantastic achievement," the boy kept shouting, "The bear's stupid! The bear's stupid!" And at the end he shouted one more time, very loud, "Circles, just circles."

The bear understood every word, and he was very angry. On the outside nothing showed; but on the inside, underneath his thick fur, he was very excited.

"They think I'm stupid," he growled to himself. "Those children think I'm stupid. Just because I keep riding around in circles, they think I'm stupid. Hmm, I'll show them. I'll show them I'm not stupid."

The next day, when he had finished his thirteenth round, he

THE BEAR ON THE MOTORCYCLE 295

didn't get off the motorcycle. And when the keeper came to take it away, he honked loudly on the horn three times and then, just as fast as he could go, he rode straight out of the circus tent. Even when he was outside the tent, he didn't stop; he rode straight past his cage, out of the circus gate, and still going as fast as he could go, he rode straight into town.

He rode straight down the main street. As he crossed the main intersection, the traffic policeman's whistle fell out of his mouth, he was so surprised. He had seen fire engines and racing cars and trucks with eight wheels, but never a bear on a red motorcycle.

"Unbelievable," he muttered to himself. "Simply unbelievable."

He had hardly recovered when two minutes later, there, running along, came the keeper and the director of the circus and a lot of other people from the circus. Even from far away he could hear them shouting, "Have you seen a bear? A bear on a red motorcycle? Which way did he go?"

"Straight ahead," the policeman said quickly, showing them the way.

So the keeper and the director and the other people from the circus kept running, straight ahead.

And the traffic policeman muttered again, "Unbelievable. Really unbelievable."

In the meantime, the fat brown bear was riding his motorcycle up and down through the town; down main streets and up side streets, sometimes turning right at a corner, sometimes turning left, doing just as he pleased.

Everywhere he went people leaned out of windows, their mouths wide open for the wonder of it all. Those who had no windows on the street rushed into their hallways shouting, "What is it? What's all the noise about?"

And the others answered, "Come here quick! Look at that! A fat brown bear is riding a red motorcycle up and down the streets. Oh, look now! All those circus people are running after him, and they can't catch him. Oh, it's funny; oh, it's so funny!"

Some people on the sidewalks stopped and clapped their hands. Others were scared and ran into doorways or hid behind cars.

But after a while the red motorcycle ran slower and slower. There was beginning to be no more gas in the tank. Finally, the motor went put put put . . . and stopped. The fat brown bear got off, leaned the motorcycle against a lamp post, and sat down at the edge of the sidewalk to wait.

When the keeper and the director and all the other people from the circus came running up, panting and puffing, he waved at them gaily with his bear-paw and growled: "Hmm. . . . Just no excitement, please. Just quiet, please."

He was, you see, a friendly, contented animal, and he didn't really want to run away. He just wanted to show people that he wasn't stupid and that he really could do something besides just ride around in circles under a big tent.

So the circus people calmed down, and they mopped their brows, and then they all went to the inn down the street and ordered root beer because they were thirsty from all that running.

The keeper put the fat brown bear on a leash and, pushing the motorcycle, led the fat brown bear back to the circus.

And from that day on nobody ever shouted, "The bear is stupid!" And the bear, himself, no longer went around in circles. Now every evening he rode figure-eights and zigzags; and when he was in an especially good mood, he rode with no hands and on one wheel.

And when the performance was at an end and he was trotting his way back to his cage, he'd turn around one last time, squint up to the top rows where the children sat and, one paw raised to his bear-brow, he'd rumble, "Just let's see *you* do that!"

BOOK TWO

The House in Sunflower Street

GÜNTER SPANG

Illustrated by FRANZ JOSEF TRIPP

Translated from the German

IN SUNFLOWER STREET there stood an old house; it was number 99. It belonged to Mr. Bumperli, who lived in it.

Mr. Bumperli's father had once lived in the house too. And his grandfather, his great-grandfather, his great-great-grandfather and his great-great-great-grandfather. The house was very old indeed! But it was a good house.

It was very comfortable inside and everyone who had seen it thought it a charming old house.

One day a violent storm raged over the town, with thunder and lightning and torrents of rain. Nearly all the houses in Sunflower Street were badly damaged by it.

So much rain poured into the house next door to Mr. Bumperli that the furniture floated about in the rooms. In the house on the other side the people looked up at the sky from their beds. The wind had torn the roof off!

Only Mr. Bumperli slept soundly, safe and dry in his bed. The old house stood up to the storm and sheltered him.

The old house protected Mr. Bumperli also from fire.

One evening before going to bed he began to smoke one more cigar. But he did not really enjoy it, so he put it into an ashtray and went to bed.

The cigar was still alight however. It fell onto the tablecloth and the tablecloth caught fire. Then the burning tablecloth slipped off the table and set fire to the carpet.

Oh dear! Now the whole house would soon be in flames!

But no! As soon as the old house noticed the smell of burning it turned on the taps in the kitchen. The water gushed out and filled the sink; the sink overflowed, and the water ran over the kitchen floor, out of the kitchen, across the hall and into the living room. It spread over the burning carpet and soon put the fire out.

The old house also protected Mr. Bumperli from burglars. One night when a burglar crept in on tiptoe, the floorboards immediately began to creak and the windows rattled. Every corner of the house rustled and creaked and groaned. The burglar thought it was haunted and ran away as fast as he could.

Mr. Bumperli should have been grateful to the old house for all this. But he was not.

Instead he wished he had a brand new house. And one evening, before going to bed, he drew a plan of one on a piece of paper. It was to have a flat roof, instead of a sloping one, and there were to be no small windows, only very large ones.

Mr. Bumperli wanted so much to have a house like this that he decided to sell his old house. The next morning he hung a large notice on the garden gate; on it were the words: THIS HOUSE TO BE SOLD VERY CHEAP!!

Naturally the old house was sad, because it did not want to have strange people living in it. All at once the chimney became crooked and some tiles crashed down off the roof.

But Mr. Bumperli did not notice. He whistled happily to himself and waited to see whether anyone was coming to buy the house.

At last an elegant old lady came in through the gate. She wanted to look over the house.

Mr. Bumperli showed her all the rooms on the ground floor. Then he took her upstairs.

Suddenly the carpet began to move. It wrinkled up and straightened out again just like a concertina, and Mr. Bumperli and the elegant old lady stumbled against one another and knocked their noses black and blue.

"Well, I never did!" cried the old lady indignantly, crying and rubbing her nose.

Now, of course, she no longer wanted to buy the house.

The next day a young man came to see the house. First of all he caught his hand in the front door. Then, as Mr. Bumperli took him into the sitting room, the polar-bear rug in front of the fire suddenly lifted up its head, opened its jaws wide and roared.

The young man fell down in a faint from shock. Naturally, he no longer wanted to buy the house either.

This annoyed Mr. Bumperli very much. But the old house was very glad.

The following day a married couple came to view the house. They were delighted with it.

"We'll buy it at once," they said, as they stood with Mr. Bumperli in the comfortable old dining room.

No sooner had they said this than the ceiling lowered itself down on them. All three of them had to crouch down and Mr. Bumperli was so startled that he slipped and sprained his left knee.

The man and his wife were not in the least alarmed. When the ceiling had gone up again, they cried: "The house is haunted! How marvellous! We have always wanted to have a crazy old house like this!"

A little later, as they were leaning out of the window and Mr. Bumperli was showing them the beauties of the garden, the old house made another attempt to drive them away. Crash! down came the sun-blind on top of them and they were all three jammed in. Mr. Bumperli and the man and his wife could not free themselves. They had to shout to a boy who was playing in front of the house to go and fetch help.

The boy ran off to call the fire brigade. The fire engine soon came racing along, with its bell ringing wildly. The captain of the firemen ordered the fire-escape ladder to be set up, and Mr. Bumperli and the man and his wife were set free by one of the firemen.

At once the man and his wife were happy again. But not Mr. Bumperli.

"After what has happened, I suppose you will not want to buy the house?" he asked dejectedly.

"Of course we want to buy it!" they said. "We don't mind that the sun-blind is out of order. We can have it mended. We'll come again tomorrow afternoon. And we'll bring you the money then!"

Mr. Bumperli was very pleased. He rubbed his hands together and thought about the new house with the flat roof and large windows that he was going to have built.

"Hurrah!" he shouted. "Hurrah!"

He did not notice how unhappy the old house was. But the old house certainly looked very miserable now. Everything about it seemed to be crooked.

The following afternoon Mr. Bumperli stood at the gate waiting for the man and his wife who were going to buy the old house. Mr. Bumperli had put on his best suit for the occasion, and when he saw the man and his wife coming along, he beamed all over his face.

"Good afternoon!" he said politely, as he opened the gate for them.

But whatever could have happened?

Mr. Bumperli rubbed his eyes. The man and his wife rubbed their eyes too: for the old house had disappeared. There, where it had stood, was a large hole in the ground!

All the neighbours came running and looked at it in amazement.

"How is such a thing possible?" cried Mr. Bumperli, horrified.

"How is it possible?" echoed the man and his wife.

They were both delighted that the old house had played another trick and disappeared. Now they liked it better than ever. But where was the old house?

Mr. Bumperli and the man and his wife went at once to the police station. The police sent thirteen detectives to Sunflower Street. They came riding on thirteen bicycles with thirteen dogs on leashes and they searched the site for suspicious footprints. But the detectives could not discover anything. They, too, had no idea where the old house could be.

Mr. Bumperli and the man and his wife searched all over the town. But they could not find the old house.

And since Mr. Bumperli had to have somewhere to sleep, he took a room in a hotel that night. But he did not sleep well, because the bed was very hard.

Next morning Mr. Bumperli had a notice put in all the newspapers. It looked like this:

ATTENTION
Whoever finds
my old house
will receive
a big reward!
Any information
should be reported
to Mr. Bumperli
at Hotel
Fridolin

But nobody reported. Nobody had seen the old house.

Then Mr. Bumperli and the man and his wife journeyed by train up and down the country. All the time they looked out of the windows, Mr. Bumperli on the left side of the train, and the man and his wife on the right side. But they could not see the old house anywhere.

After that they chartered an aeroplane and flew over fields and meadows, keeping a lookout through their field glasses.

Then at last, one day, they saw the old house. It was standing in a large meadow on the outskirts of a village.

"That's it! That's it!" cried Mr. Bumperli, with tears of joy in his eyes. "I recognize it by the crooked chimney!"

The aeroplane landed in the meadow, and Mr. Bumperli climbed out. He ran off to the post office in the village. From there he telephoned to a building contractor.

The building contractor sent a lot of men; also three powerful cranes and an enormous transport truck. The cranes lifted the old house onto the truck, and the truck carried the old house back into the town.

The three powerful cranes followed behind, and when they arrived at No. 99 Sunflower Street, they put the old house back in its place. And when they saw it standing there again, all the onlookers, and Mr. Bumperli, and the man and his wife who wanted to buy it, shouted: "Hurrah!"

And now what a surprise Mr. Bumperli had when he and the man and his wife went into the house. For while they were all standing in the hall, the portraits of Mr. Bumperli's ancestors which hung on the walls suddenly came to life. They all stepped out of their frames: Mr. Bumperli's father, his grandfather, his great-grandfather, his great-great-grandfather, and his great-great-great-grandfather. Then his mother, his grandmother, his

great-grandmother, his great-great-grandmother, and his great-great-great-grandmother. All those who had once lived in the house stood round Mr. Bumperli and looked at him with frightened faces.

"Surely you do not seriously intend to sell our beautiful old house?" they said. "Wherever should we live?"

And his great-great-great-grandfather, who had had the house built, added: "I forbid you to sell the house. This house belongs to the Bumperlis, and it must always belong to the Bumperlis! And there's an end of it!"

"Of course you can continue to live here!" replied Mr. Bumperli, because naturally he was happy to have all his ancestors around him. "Now that you are alive again, of course I won't sell the house!"

When the man and his wife who wanted to buy the house heard this, they were very angry. They said: "Mr. Bumperli, you are a man who does not know his own mind!"

Mr. Bumperli showed them to the gate without a word.

Then he went back into the house and sat down at the table with his parents, his grandparents, his great-grandparents, his great-great-grandparents and his great-great-great-grandparents and they had a pleasant evening together.

When Mr. Bumperli woke up the next morning, all was quiet in the old house.

Mr. Bumperli looked in all the rooms, but he could not find anybody about. There was no one in the hall either.

Then he looked up at the pictures of his ancestors. All the portraits were in their frames again, as they had always been. And Mr. Bumperli recollected that his parents, his grandparents, his great-grandparents, his great-great-grandparents and his great-

great-great-grandparents had died long ago and were buried in the churchyard.

"I see now that they only came out of their frames to stop me from selling the old house," he said.

And when he found a burglar in the kitchen, trapped between the windowsill and the sun-blind, he was ashamed that he had wanted to sell the house.

He said to himself: "Nowhere else in the world can there be a house like this to take such care of me!" And he felt so ashamed that his ears were red.

Later on Mr. Bumperli released the burglar. He boxed his ears and let him go.

Then he went to his bedroom, took out his plan for the brand-new house, and tore it into tiny pieces. And because he wanted to show the old house he was sorry, he changed into his working suit, climbed up onto the roof, put the chimney straight, and fitted new tiles on the roof where the old ones were missing.

After that he began to whitewash the walls. Mr. Bumperli gave the whole house a new coat of paint inside and out.

He finished it all in a week.

Now the old house looked more beautiful than ever, and was even more quaint. It felt so pleased with its smart appearance that it kept sending funny little clouds of smoke out of the chimney that seemed to write in the sky the words THANK YOU. And Mr. Bumperli rubbed his hands together proudly.

After that, whenever anyone came to ask whether the old house was for sale, he would shake his head and smile. With his finger on his lips he would whisper, "Sh! not so loud! It might become haunted again! Or it might disappear!"

LUCILLE CLIFTON
Sunday Morning Lonely

Daddy's back
is broad and black
and Everett Anderson loves to ride it.

Daddy's side
is black and wide
and Everett Anderson sits beside it.

Daddy's cheek
is black and sleek
and Everett Anderson kisses it.

Daddy's space
is a black empty place
and Everett Anderson misses it.

WILLIAM STEIG
AMOS & BORIS

AMOS, A MOUSE, lived by the ocean. He loved the ocean. He loved the smell of sea air. He loved to hear the surf sounds — the bursting breakers, the backwashes with rolling pebbles.

He thought a lot about the ocean, and he wondered about the faraway places on the other side of the water. One day he started building a boat on the beach. He worked on it in the daytime, while at night he studied navigation.

When the boat was finished, he loaded it with cheese, biscuits, acorns, honey, wheat germ, two barrels of fresh water, a compass, a sextant, a telescope, a saw, a hammer and nails and some wood in case repairs should be necessary, a needle and thread for the mending of torn sails, and various other necessities such as bandages and iodine, a yo-yo and playing cards.

On the sixth of September, with a very calm sea, he waited till the high tide had almost reached his boat; then, using his most savage strength, he just managed to push the boat into the water, climb on board, and set sail.

The *Rodent*, for that was the boat's name, proved to be very well made and very well suited to the sea. And Amos, after one

miserable day of seasickness, proved to be a natural sailor, very well suited to the ship.

He was enjoying his trip immensely. It was beautiful weather. Day and night he moved up and down, up and down, on waves as big as mountains, and he was full of wonder, full of enterprise, and full of love for life.

One night, in a phosphorescent sea, he marvelled at the sight of some whales spouting luminous water; and later, lying on the deck of his boat gazing at the immense, starry sky, the tiny mouse

Amos, a little speck of a living thing in the vast living universe, felt thoroughly akin to it all. Overwhelmed by the beauty and mystery of everything, he rolled over and over and right off the deck of his boat and into the sea.

"Help!" he squeaked as he grabbed desperately at the *Rodent*. But it evaded his grasp and went bowling along under full sail, and he never saw it again.

And there he was! Where? In the middle of the immense ocean, a thousand miles from the nearest shore, with no one else in sight

as far as the eye could see and not even so much as a stick of driftwood to hold on to. "Should I try to swim home?" Amos wondered. "Or should I just try to stay afloat?" He might swim a mile, but never a thousand. He decided to just keep afloat, treading water and hoping that something — who knows what? —

would turn up to save him. But what if a shark, or some big fish, a horse mackerel, turned up? What was he supposed to do to protect himself? He didn't know.

Morning came, as it always does. He was getting terribly tired. He was a very small, very cold, very wet and worried mouse. There was still nothing in sight but the empty sea. Then, as if things weren't bad enough, it began to rain.

At last the rain stopped and the noonday sun gave him a bit of cheer and warmth in the vast loneliness; but his strength was giving out. He began to wonder what it would be like to drown. Would it take very long? Would it feel just awful? Would his soul go to heaven? Would there be other mice there?

As he was asking himself these dreadful questions, a huge head burst through the surface of the water and loomed up over him. It was a whale. "What sort of fish are you?" the whale asked. "You must be one of a kind!"

"I'm not a fish," said Amos. "I'm a mouse, which is a mammal, the highest form of life. I live on land."

"Holy clam and cuttlefish!" said the whale. "I'm a mammal myself, though I live in the sea. Call me Boris," he added.

Amos introduced himself and told Boris how he came to be there in the middle of the ocean. The whale said he would be happy to take Amos to the Ivory Coast of Africa, where he happened to be headed anyway, to attend a meeting of whales from all the seven seas. But Amos said he'd had enough adventure to last him a while. He wanted only to get back home and hoped the whale wouldn't mind going out of his way to take him there.

"Not only would I not mind," said Boris, "I would consider it a privilege. What other whale in all the world ever had the chance to get to know such a strange creature as you! Please climb aboard." And Amos got on Boris's back.

"Are you sure you're a mammal?" Amos asked. "You smell more like a fish." Then Boris the whale went swimming along, with Amos the mouse on his back.

What a relief to be so safe, so secure again! Amos lay down in the sun, and being worn to a frazzle, he was soon asleep.

Then all of a sudden he was in the water again, wide awake, spluttering and splashing about! Boris had forgotten for a moment that he had a passenger on his back and had sounded. When he realized his mistake, he surfaced so quickly that Amos was sent somersaulting, tail over whiskers, high into the air.

Hitting the water hurt. Crazy with rage, Amos screamed and punched at Boris until he remembered he owed his life to the whale and quietly climbed on his back. From then on, whenever Boris wanted to sound, he warned Amos in advance and got his okay, and whenever he sounded, Amos took a swim.

Swimming along, sometimes at great speed, sometimes slowly and leisurely, sometimes resting and exchanging ideas, sometimes stopping to sleep, it took them a week to reach Amos's home shore. During that time, they developed a deep admiration for one another. Boris admired the delicacy, the quivering daintiness, the light touch, the small voice, the gemlike radiance of the mouse. Amos admired the bulk, the grandeur, the power, the purpose, the rich voice, and the abounding friendliness of the whale.

They became the closest possible friends. They told each other about their lives, their ambitions. They shared their deepest secrets with each other. The whale was very curious about life on land and was sorry that he could never experience it. Amos was fascinated by the whale's accounts of what went on deep under the sea. Amos sometimes enjoyed running up and down on the whale's back for exercise. When he was hungry, he ate plankton. The only thing he missed was fresh, unsalty water.

The time came to say good-bye. They were at the shore. "I wish we could be friends forever," said Boris. "We *will* be friends forever, but we can't be together. You must live on land and I must live at sea. I'll never forget you, though."

"And you can be sure I'll never forget *you*," said Amos. "I will always be grateful to you for saving my life and I want you to remember that if you ever need my help I'd be more than glad to give it!" How he could ever possibly help Boris, Amos didn't know, but he knew how willing he was.

The whale couldn't take Amos all the way in to land. They said their last good-bye and Amos dived off Boris's back and swam to the sand.

From the top of a cliff he watched Boris spout twice and disappear.

Boris laughed to himself. "How could that little mouse ever help me? Little as he is, he's all heart. I love him, and I'll miss him terribly."

Boris went to the conference off the Ivory Coast of Africa and then went back to a life of whaling about, while Amos returned to his life of mousing around. And they were both happy.

Many years after the incidents just described, when Amos was no longer a very young mouse, and when Boris was no longer a very young whale, there occurred one of the worst storms of the century, Hurricane Yetta; and it just so happened that Boris the whale was flung ashore by a tidal wave and stranded on the very shore where Amos happened to make his home.

It also just so happened that when the storm had cleared up and Boris was lying high and dry on the sand, losing his moisture in the hot sun and needing desperately to be back in the water, Amos came down to the beach to see how much damage Hurricane Yetta had done. Of course Boris and Amos recognized each other at once. I don't have to tell you how these old friends felt at meeting again in this desperate situation. Amos rushed towards Boris. Boris could only look at Amos.

"Amos, help me," said the mountain of a whale to the mote of a

mouse. "I think I'll die if I don't get back in the water soon." Amos gazed at Boris in an agony of pity. He realized he had to do something very fast and had to think very fast about what it was he had to do. Suddenly he was gone.

"I'm afraid he won't be able to help me," said Boris to himself. "Much as he wants to do something, what can such a little fellow do?"

Just as Amos had once felt, all alone in the middle of the ocean, Boris felt now, lying alone on the shore. He was sure he would die. And just as he was preparing to die, Amos came racing back with two of the biggest elephants he could find.

Without wasting time, these two good-hearted elephants got to pushing with all their might at Boris's huge body until he began turning over, breaded with sand, and rolling down towards the sea. Amos, standing on the head of one of the elephants, yelled instructions, but no one heard him.

In a few minutes Boris was already in water, with waves wash-

ing at him, and he was feeling the wonderful wetness. "You have to be *out* of the sea really to know how good it is to be *in* it," he thought. "That is, if you're a whale." Soon he was able to wiggle and wriggle into deeper water.

He looked back at Amos on the elephant's head. Tears were rolling down the great whale's cheeks. The tiny mouse had tears in his eyes too. "Good-bye, dear friend," squeaked Amos. "Good-bye, dear friend," rumbled Boris, and he disappeared in the waves. They knew they might never meet again. They knew they would never forget each other.

ELIZABETH COATSWORTH
March

A blue day,
a blue jay,
and a good beginning.

One crow,
melting snow —
spring's winning!

As I Was Crossing Boston Common

by NORMA FARBER

pictures by
ARNOLD LOBEL

As I was crossing Boston Common —
not very fast, not very slow —
I met a man with a creature in tow.
Its collar was labelled *Angwantibo*.
I thought it rather uncommon.

As I was crossing Boston Common —
not very fast, not very slow —
Angwantibo passed with a *Boobook* in tow,
Boobook passed with a *Coypu* in tow.

Where in the town were they going to go,
so seldom and uncommon?

As I was crossing Boston Common —
not very fast, not very slow —
Coypu passed with a *Desman* in tow,
Desman had an *Entellus* in tow,
Entellus, in turn, had a *Fennec* in tow,
where Boston folk went to and fro,
scanning the creatures from tip to toe,
and murmuring, "How uncommon!"

As I was crossing Boston Common —
not very fast, not very slow —
Fennec passed me, pulling a *Galliwasp*,
Galliwasp passed, with a *Hoopoe* in tow,
Hoopoe, an *Isabelita* in tow
(in a bowl with a spout — for the overflow).
The fish bowl pulled in tow a *Jacare* —
I snapped a picture, to prove it was so.

And everyone said, "How uncommon!"
"Uncommon!" cried pigeon, squirrel, crow,
and sparrows lined up in a common row.
"Most uncommon!"

As I was crossing Boston Common —
not very fast, not very slow —
Jacare passed me, pulling a *Kiang,*
Kiang was pulling a *Lory* in tow,
Lory was pulling in tow a *Mandrill,*
Mandrill was pulling a *Narwhale* in tow,
in a waggon heaped with ice and snow
(the rope being tied to his horn, in a bow).
Narwhale, riding, pulled an *Okapi.*
Where were they going? I wanted to know.
I looked for a reason, high and low,
for activity so uncommon.

As I slowed down on Boston Common —
not very slow, yet rather slow —
Okapi passed me, pulling a *Pudu,*
Pudu, passing, pulled a *Quirquincho,*
Quirquincho passed me, pulling a *Rhea,*
Rhea passed me, pulling a *Sassaby,*
Sassaby passed me, pulling a *Trogon,*
Trogon had an *Umbrette* in tow.
The line was long, and continued to grow.
A boy cried out, "Bravissimo!"
at the company so uncommon.

As I was dawdling on Boston Common —
slower than ever, slower than slow —
Umbrette came by with a *Vervet* in tow,
Vervet, in turn, was towing a *Wapiti,*
Wapiti pulled in tow a *Xenopus,*
Xenopus pulled on a *Yaguarundi,*
Yaguarundi was leading a *Zibet.*
Zibet — imagine! was leading a *man!* —
the man who'd passed me a while ago!
He himself now looked uncommon.

As I stood still on Boston Common,
they formed a circle, sweet and slow,

with everyone pulling someone in tow —
beginning with A for Angwantibo
in tow to the man, himself in tow —
sweet and slow, sweet and slow,
surprising and uncommon.

And round they went, and round, although
the dusk of Boston began to glow.
The lamps gave light enough to show
the turn of events was uncommon:
sweet and slow, a circular tow,
round as the moon that leaned to blow
its beams upon Boston Common.

Glossary

Angwantibo (an-gwán-ti-boh)   a small West African lemur
Boobook (boó-book)   a small Australian owl
Coypu (kóy-poo)   a South American rodent with webbed hind feet
Desman (dés-man)   a Russian mole-like, water-loving animal
Entellus (en-téll-us)   a long-tailed East Indian monkey
Fennec (fén-nec)   a small African fox with large ears
Galliwasp (gáll-i-wasp)   a harmless lizard of Jamaica
Hoopoe (hoó-poo)   an Old World bird with a handsome crest
Isabelita (iz-a-bel-eé-ta)   a highly coloured West Indian angelfish
Jacare (já-ca-ray)   a tropical American alligator
Kiang (kyáng)   a Tibetan wild ass
Lory (ló-ri)   an Australian parrot that feeds on honey and soft fruit

Mandrill (mán-drill)   a large African baboon

Narwhale (nár-whale)   an Arctic sea mammal with a long, twisted, pointed tusk

Okapi (oh-ká-pi)   a short-necked relative of the giraffe, from Africa

Pudu (poó-doo)   a small, reddish deer with simple spike-like antlers

Quirquincho (kir-keén-choh)   a small, hairy armadillo of South America

Rhea (reé-a)   a South American ostrich with three toes on each foot

Sassaby (sáss-a-bi)   a large, dark South African antelope with curved horns

Trogon (tróh-gon)   a colourful tropical bird whose first and second toes turn backward

Umbrette (um-brét)   an African wading bird

Vervet (vúr-vet)   a long-tailed African monkey

Wapiti (wó-pi-ti)   the noble American elk, high as a horse

Xenopus (xén-oh-pus)   a tongueless African toad

Yaguarundi (yag-war-ún-di)   a greyish unspotted wildcat

Zibet (zí-bet)   an East Indian civet cat

CHARLES PERRAULT

We owe many of the best-known fairy tales to a Frenchman named Charles Perrault. Many, many years ago, to amuse his own children and also the fashionable French court, he retold some almost forgotten folk stories. Among these were "Little Red Riding Hood", "The Sleeping Beauty", "Bluebeard", and "Puss in Boots". An Englishman named Andrew Lang, who spent a large part of his life collecting fairy tales, published "Puss in Boots" in his *Blue Fairy Book,* calling it "The Master Cat". Here it is, one of the best-known stories in the world.

The Master Cat

THERE WAS A MILLER who left no more estate to the three sons he had than his mill, his donkey, and his cat. The division was soon made. Neither scrivener nor attorney was sent for; they would soon have eaten up all the poor patrimony. The eldest had the mill, the second the donkey, and the youngest nothing but the cat. The poor young fellow was quite comfortless at having so poor a lot.

"My brothers," said he, "may get their living handsomely enough by joining their stocks together. But for my part, when I have eaten my cat, and made me a muff of his skin, I must die of hunger."

The cat, who heard all this, said to him with a grave and serious air, "Do not thus afflict yourself, my good master. You need only give me a bag, and have a pair of boots made for me that I may scamper through the brambles. You shall see you have not so bad a portion with me as you imagine."

The cat's master had often seen him play a great many cunning tricks to catch rats and mice; he used to hide himself in the meal, and make as if he were dead; so he did not altogether despair. When the cat had what he asked for, he booted himself very gallantly, and putting his bag about his neck, he held the strings of it in his two forepaws and went into a warren where was a great abundance of rabbits. He put bran and lettuce into his bag and, stretching out at length as if dead, he waited for some young rabbits, not yet acquainted with the deceits of the world, to come and rummage for what he had put into his bag.

Scarce had he lain down but he had what he wanted: a rash and foolish young rabbit jumped into his bag. Monsieur Puss, immediately drawing close the strings, killed him without pity. Proud of his prey, he went with it to the palace, and asked to speak with His Majesty. He was shown into the king's apartment and, making a low reverence, said to him:

"I have brought you, sir, a rabbit from the warren, which my noble lord, the Marquis of Carabas" — for that was the title Puss was pleased to give his master — "has commanded me to present to Your Majesty from him."

"Tell your master," said the king, "that I thank him, and that he gives me a great deal of pleasure."

Another time the cat hid himself among some standing corn, holding his bag open. When a brace of partridges ran into it, he drew the strings and so caught them both. He made a present of these to the king as he had the rabbit. The king, in like manner, received the partridges with great pleasure, and ordered some money to be given to him.

The cat continued thus for two or three months to carry to His Majesty, from time to time, game of his master's taking. One day in particular, when he knew for certain that the king was to take the air along the riverside with his daughter, the most beautiful princess in the world, he said to his master:

"If you will follow my advice your fortune is made. You have nothing to do but wash yourself in the river, where I shall show you, and leave the rest to me."

The Marquis of Carabas did what the cat advised him to do, without knowing why or wherefore. While he was washing, the king passed by, and the cat began to cry out:

"Help! Help! My Lord Marquis of Carabas is going to be drowned."

At this the king put his head out of the coach window, and finding it was the cat who had so often brought him such good game, he commanded his guards to run immediately to the assistance of His Lordship the Marquis of Carabas. While they were drawing him out of the river, the cat came up to the coach and told the king that, while his master was washing, there came by some rogues, who went off with his clothes, though he had cried out, "Thieves! Thieves!" several times, as loud as he could.

This cunning cat had hidden them under a great stone. The king immediately commanded the officers of his wardrobe to run and fetch one of his best suits for the Marquis of Carabas.

The fine clothes set off his good mien, for he was well made and very handsome in his person. The king's daughter took a secret inclination to him, and the Marquis of Carabas had no sooner cast two or three respectful and tender glances upon her than she fell in love with him to distraction. The king would needs have him come into the coach and take the air with them. The cat, quite overjoyed to see his project begin to succeed, marched on before, and meeting with some countrymen, who were mowing a meadow, he said to them:

"Good people, you who are mowing, if you do not tell the king that the meadow you mow belongs to my Lord Marquis of Carabas, you shall be chopped as small as herbs for the pot."

The king did not fail to ask the mowers to whom the meadow belonged.

"To my Lord Marquis of Carabas," they answered all together, for the cat's threat had made them terribly afraid.

"You see, sir," said the marquis, "this is a meadow which never fails to yield a plentiful harvest every year."

The Master Cat, who still went on before, met with some reapers, and said to them, "Good people, you who are reaping, if you do not tell the king that all this corn belongs to the Marquis of Carabas you shall be chopped as small as herbs for the pot."

The king, who passed by a moment after, wished to know to whom all that corn belonged.

"To my Lord Marquis of Carabas," replied the reapers, and the king was very well pleased with it, as well as with the marquis, whom he congratulated thereupon. The Master Cat, who went always before, said the same words to all he met, and the king was astonished at the vast estates of the Marquis of Carabas.

Monsieur Puss came at last to a stately castle, the master of which was an ogre, the richest ever known. All the lands which the king had then gone over belonged to this ogre. The cat, who had taken care to inform himself who this ogre was and what he could do, asked to speak with him, saying he could not pass so near his castle without paying his respects to him.

The ogre received him as civilly as an ogre could and made him sit down.

"I have been assured," said the cat, "that you have the gift of being able to change yourself into any sort of creature. You can, for example, transform yourself into a lion or elephant and the like."

"That is true," answered the ogre briskly, "and to convince you, you shall see me now become a lion."

Puss was so badly terrified at the sight of a lion so near him that he immediately got into the rain gutter, not without abundance of trouble and danger, because of his boots. They were of no use walking upon the tiles. A little while after, when Puss saw that the ogre had resumed his natural form, he came down and owned he had been very much frightened.

"I have been moreover informed," said the cat, "but I know not

how to believe it, that you have also the power to take on the shape
of the smallest animal; for example, to change yourself into a rat
or a mouse; but I must own to you I take this to be impossible."

"Impossible!" cried the ogre. "You shall see that presently."

At the same time he changed himself into a mouse and began to
run about the floor. Puss no sooner perceived this than he fell upon
him and ate him up.

Meanwhile the king, who saw, as he passed, this fine castle of
the ogre's, had a mind to go into it. Puss, who heard the noise of
His Majesty's coach running over the drawbridge, ran out, and
said to the king:

"Your Majesty is welcome to this castle of my Lord Marquis of
Carabas."

"What, my Lord Marquis!" cried the king. "And does this
castle also belong to you? There can be nothing finer than this

court and all the stately buildings which surround it. Let us go in, if you please."

The marquis gave his hand to the princess and followed the king, who went first. They passed into a spacious hall, where they found a magnificent collation, which the ogre had prepared for his friends, who were that very day to visit him, but dared not enter, knowing the king was there. His Majesty was charmed with the good qualities of the Lord Marquis of Carabas, as was his daughter, and seeing the vast estate he possessed, said to him:

"It will be owing to yourself only, my Lord Marquis, if you are not my son-in-law."

The marquis, making several low bows, accepted the honour which his majesty conferred upon him, and forthwith, that very same day, married the princess.

Puss became a great lord, and never ran after mice anymore.

ELEANOR FARJEON

There's a little talk about Eleanor Farjeon on page 475.

The Night Will Never Stay

The night will never stay,
The night will still go by,
Though with a million stars
You pin it to the sky;
Though you bind it with the blowing wind
And buckle it with the moon,
The night will slip away
Like a sorrow or a tune.

ALICE RITCHIE

Two of Everything

MR. AND MRS. HAK–TAK were rather old and rather poor. They had a small house in a village among the mountains and a tiny patch of green land on the mountainside. Here they grew the vegetables which were all they had to live on, and when it was a good season and they did not need to eat up everything as soon as it was grown, Mr. Hak-Tak took what they could spare in a basket to the next village which was a little larger than theirs and sold it for as much as he could get and bought some oil for their lamp, and fresh seeds, and every now and then, but not often, a piece of cotton stuff to make new coats and trousers for himself and his wife. You can imagine they did not often get the chance to eat meat.

Now, one day it happened that when Mr. Hak-Tak was digging in his precious patch, he unearthed a big brass pot. He thought it strange that it should have been there for so long without his having come across it before, and he was disappointed to find that it was empty; still, he thought they would find some use for it, so when he was ready to go back to the house in the evening he decided to take it with him. It was very big and heavy, and in his struggles to get his arms round it and raise it to a good position for carrying, his purse, which he always took with him in his belt, fell to the ground, and, to be quite sure he had it safe, he put it inside the pot and so staggered home with his load.

As soon as he got into the house Mrs. Hak-Tak hurried from the inner room to meet him.

"My dear husband," she said, "whatever have you got there?"

"For a cooking pot it is too big; for a bath a little too small," said Mr. Hak-Tak. "I found it buried in our vegetable patch and so far it has been useful in carrying my purse home for me."

"Alas," said Mrs. Hak-Tak, "something smaller would have done as well to hold any money we have or are likely to have," and she stooped over the pot and looked into its dark inside.

As she stooped, her hairpin — for poor Mrs. Hak-Tak had only one hairpin for all her hair and it was made of carved bone — fell into the pot. She put in her hand to get it out again, and then she gave a loud cry which brought her husband running to her side.

"What is it?" he asked. "Is there a viper in the pot?"

"Oh, my dear husband," she cried. "What can be the meaning of this? I put my hand into the pot to fetch out my hairpin and your purse, and look, I have brought out two hairpins and two purses, both exactly alike."

"Open the purse. Open both purses," said Mr. Hak-Tak. "One of them will certainly be empty."

But not a bit of it. The new purse contained exactly the same number of coins as the old one — for that matter, no one could have said which was the new and which the old — and it meant, of course, that the Hak-Taks had exactly twice as much money in the evening as they had had in the morning.

"And two hairpins instead of one!" cried Mrs. Hak-Tak, forgetting in her excitement to do up her hair which was streaming over her shoulders. "There is something quite unusual about this pot."

"Let us put in the sack of lentils and see what happens," said Mr. Hak-Tak, also becoming excited.

They heaved in the bag of lentils and when they pulled it out again — it was so big it almost filled the pot — they saw another bag of exactly the same size waiting to be pulled out in its turn. So now they had two bags of lentils instead of one.

"Put in the blanket," said Mr. Hak-Tak. "We need another blanket for the cold weather." And, sure enough, when the blanket came out, there lay another behind it.

"Put my wadded coat in," said Mr. Hak-Tak, "and then when the cold weather comes there will be one for you as well as for me. Let us put in everything we have in turn. What a pity we have no meat or tobacco, for it seems that the pot cannot make anything without a pattern."

Then Mrs. Hak-Tak, who was a woman of great intelligence, said, "My dear husband, let us put the purse in again and again and again. If we take two purses out each time we put one in, we shall have enough money by tomorrow evening to buy everything we lack."

"I am afraid we may lose it this time," said Mr. Hak-Tak, but in the end he agreed, and they dropped in the purse and pulled out two, then they added the new money to the old and dropped it in again and pulled out the larger amount twice over. After a while the floor was covered with old leather purses and they decided just to throw the money in by itself. It worked quite as well and saved trouble; every time, twice as much money came out as went in, and every time they added the new coins to the old and threw them all in together. It took them some hours to tire of this game, but at last Mrs. Hak-Tak said, "My dear husband, there is no need for us to work so hard. We shall see to it that the pot does not run away, and we can always make more money as we want it. Let us tie up what we have."

It made a huge bundle in the extra blanket and the Hak-Taks lay and looked at it for a long time before they slept, and talked of all the things they would buy and the improvements they would make in the cottage.

The next morning they rose early and Mr. Hak-Tak filled a wallet with money from the bundle and set off for the big village to buy more things in one morning than he had bought in a whole fifty years.

Mrs. Hak-Tak saw him off and then she tidied up the cottage and put the rice on to boil and had another look at the bundle of money, and made herself a whole set of new hairpins from the pot, and about twenty candles instead of the one which was all they had possessed up to now. After that she slept for a while, having been up so late the night before, but just before the time when her husband should be back, she awoke and went over to the pot. She dropped in a cabbage leaf to make sure it was still working properly, and when she took two leaves out she sat down on the floor and put her arms round it.

"I do not know how you came to us, my dear pot," she said, "but you are the best friend we ever had."

Then she knelt up to look inside it, and at that moment her husband came to the door, and, turning quickly to see all the wonderful things he had bought, she overbalanced and fell into the pot.

Mr. Hak-Tak put down his bundles and ran across and caught her by the ankles and pulled her out, but, oh, mercy, no sooner had he set her carefully on the floor than he saw the kicking legs of another Mrs. Hak-Tak in the pot! What was he to do? Well, he could not leave her there, so he caught her ankles and pulled, and another Mrs. Hak-Tak so exactly like the first that no one would have told one from the other, stood beside them.

"Here's an extraordinary thing," said Mr. Hak-Tak, looking helplessly from one to the other.

"I will not have a second Mrs. Hak-Tak in the house!" screamed the old Mrs. Hak-Tak.

All was confusion. The old Mrs. Hak-Tak shouted and wrung her hands and wept, Mr. Hak-Tak was scarcely calmer, and the new Mrs. Hak-Tak sat down on the floor as if she knew no more than they did what was to happen next.

"One wife is all *I* want," said Mr. Hak-Tak, "but how could I have left her in the pot?"

"Put her back in it again!" cried Mrs. Hak-Tak.

"What? And draw out two more?" said her husband. "If two wives are too many for me, what should I do with three? No! No!" He stepped back quickly as if he was stepping away from the three wives and, missing his footing, lo and behold, he fell into the pot!

Both Mrs. Hak-Taks ran and each caught an ankle and pulled him out and set him on the floor, and there, oh, mercy, was another pair of kicking legs in the pot! Again each caught hold of an ankle and pulled, and soon another Mr. Hak-Tak, so exactly like the first that no one could have told one from the other, stood beside them.

Now the old Mr. Hak-Tak liked the idea of his double no more than Mrs. Hak-Tak had liked the idea of hers. He stormed and raged and scolded his wife for pulling him out of the pot, while the new Mr. Hak-Tak sat down on the floor beside the new Mrs. Hak-Tak and looked as if, like her, he did not know what was going to happen next.

Then the old Mrs. Hak-Tak had a very good idea. "Listen, my

dear husband," she said, "now, do stop scolding and listen, for it is really a good thing that there is a new one of you as well as a new one of me. It means that you and I can go on in our usual way, and these new people, who are ourselves and yet not ourselves, can set up house together next door to us."

And that is what they did. The old Hak-Taks built themselves a fine new house with money from the pot, and they built one just like it next door for the new couple, and they lived together in the

greatest friendliness, because, as Mrs. Hak-Tak said, "The new Mrs. Hak-Tak is really more than a sister to me, and the new Mr. Hak-Tak is really more than a brother to you."

The neighbours were very much surprised, both at the sudden wealth of the Hak-Taks and at the new couple who resembled them so strongly that they must, they thought, be very close relations of whom they had never heard before. They said: "It looks as though the Hak-Taks, when they so unexpectedly became rich, decided to have two of everything, even of themselves, in order to enjoy their money more."

EUGENE FIELD
The Duel

The gingham dog and the calico cat
Side by side on the table sat;
'Twas half-past twelve, and (what do you think!)
Nor one nor t'other had slept a wink!
  The old Dutch clock and the Chinese plate
  Appeared to know as sure as fate
There was going to be a terrible spat.
    (I wasn't there; I simply state
    What was told to me by the Chinese plate!)

The gingham dog went "bow-wow-wow!"
And the calico cat replied "mee-ow!"
The air was littered, an hour or so,
With bits of gingham and calico,
  While the old Dutch clock in the chimney place
  Up with its hands before its face,
For it always dreaded a family row!
    (Now mind: I'm only telling you
    What the old Dutch clock declares is true!)

The Chinese plate looked very blue,
And wailed, "Oh, dear! what shall we do!"
But the gingham dog and the calico cat
Wallowed this way and tumbled that,
   Employing every tooth and claw
   In the awfullest way you ever saw —
And, oh! how the gingham and calico flew!
   (Don't fancy I exaggerate —
   I got my news from the Chinese plate!)

Next morning, where the two had sat
They found no trace of dog or cat;
And some folks think unto this day
That burglars stole that pair away!
   But the truth about the cat and pup
   Is this: they ate each other up!
Now what do you really think of that!
   (The old Dutch clock it told me so,
   And that is how I came to know.)

EDWARD LEAR

A famous Englishman named William Pitt who lived many years ago once said: "Don't tell me of a man's being able to talk sense; everyone can talk sense. Can he talk nonsense?"

Not many of us can talk or write good nonsense. But Edward Lear could. He almost invented nonsense.

He was born long ago, in 1812, in England. He was one of twenty-one children, several of whom died when they were very young. He was brought up among ten sisters, which must be pretty hard for a boy. What was worse, he wasn't very handsome, was often ill, and had bad eyesight. Though he travelled a great deal all over Europe and even India, he lived a lonely life. Perhaps his best friend was his cat, Old Foss, who stayed with him for seventeen years.

Edward Lear spent much of his time painting, drawing, and writing letters. At eighteen he drew all the parrots in the London zoo, not to mention apes, cats, turkey-cocks, turtles, and birds. For a time he taught drawing to Victoria, who was queen of England then. For a time he had a job with the earl of Derby, painting all the animals in the earl's private menagerie. He used to make up nonsense rhymes for his employer's grandchildren, and at last he published a book of them. Some you can read below.

Edward Lear was fat, almost bald, with a jungle of beard and whiskers and a large nose. Wearing enormous spectacles, he looked like a gigantic nearsighted moulting wren. He loved children, and they loved him. Perhaps to show his affection, when he was forty-one years old he cut two new teeth, just like a child.

Once he wrote some sad and funny verses about himself. Here are four lines from them:

His mind is concrete and fastidious,
His nose is remarkably big;
His visage is more or less hideous,
His beard it resembles a wig.

This is all true, even what he says about his mind. Look up *concrete* and *fastidious* in the dictionary.

The Owl and the Pussycat

I

The Owl and the Pussycat went to sea
In a beautiful pea-green boat,
They took some honey, and plenty of money,
Wrapped up in a five-pound note.
The Owl looked up to the stars above,
And sang to a small guitar,
"O lovely Pussy! O Pussy, my love,
What a beautiful Pussy you are,
You are,
You are!
What a beautiful Pussy you are!"

Pussy said to the Owl, "You elegant fowl!
   How charmingly sweet you sing!
O let us be married! too long we have tarried:
   But what shall we do for a ring?"
They sailed away, for a year and a day,
   To the land where the Bong-tree grows
And there in a wood a Piggy-wig stood
     With a ring at the end of his nose,
       His nose,
       His nose,
    With a ring at the end of his nose.

III

"Dear Pig, are you willing to sell for one shilling
   Your ring?" Said the Piggy, "I will."
So they took it away, and were married next day
   By the Turkey who lives on the hill.
They dined on mince, and slices of quince,
   Which they ate with a runcible spoon;
And hand in hand, on the edge of the sand,
     They danced by the light of the moon,
       The moon,
       The moon,
    They danced by the light of the moon.

The Pobble Who Has No Toes

I

The Pobble who has no toes
   Had once as many as we;
When they said, "Someday you may lose them all" —
   He replied, "Fish fiddle de-dee!"
And his Aunt Jobiska made him drink,
Lavender water tinged with pink,
For she said, "The world in general knows
There's nothing so good for a Pobble's toes!"

II

The Pobble who has no toes,
   Swam across the Bristol Channel;
But before he set out he wrapped his nose,
   In a piece of scarlet flannel.
For his Aunt Jobiska said, "No harm
Can come to his toes if his nose is warm;
And it's perfectly known that a Pobble's toes
Are safe — provided he minds his nose."

The Pobble swam fast and well
    And when boats or ships came near him
He tinkledy-binkledy-winkled a bell
    So that all the world could hear him.
And all the Sailors and Admirals cried,
When they saw him nearing the further side —
"He has gone to fish, for his Aunt Jobiska's
Runcible Cat with crimson whiskers!"

IV

But before he touched the shore,
    The shore of the Bristol Channel,
A sea-green Porpoise carried away
    His wrapper of scarlet flannel.
And when he came to observe his feet
Formerly garnished with toes so neat
His face at once became forlorn
On perceiving that all his toes were gone!

V

And nobody ever knew
　　From that dark day to the present,
Whoso had taken the Pobble's toes,
　　In a manner so far from pleasant.
Whether the shrimps or crawfish grey,
Or crafty Mermaids stole them away —
Nobody knew; and nobody knows
How the Pobble was robbed of his twice five toes!

VI

The Pobble who has no toes
　　Was placed in a friendly Bark,
And they rowed him back, and carried him up,
　　To his Aunt Jobiska's Park.
And she made him a feast at his earnest wish
Of eggs and buttercups fried with fish —
And she said, "It's a fact the whole world knows,
That Pobbles are happier without their toes."

Seven Limericks

There was an old man with a beard,
Who said, "It is just as I feared! —
　　Two Owls and a Hen,
　　Four Larks and a Wren,
Have all built their nests in my beard!"

There was an old lady of Chertsey,
Who made a remarkable curtsey;
　　She twirled round and round,
　　Till she sank underground,
Which distressed all the people of Chertsey.

There was a young lady of Norway,
Who casually sat in a doorway;
　　When the door squeezed her flat,
　　She exclaimed, "What of that?"
This courageous young lady of Norway.

There was an old man of the Nile,
Who sharpened his nails with a file;
　　Till he cut off his thumbs,
　　And said calmly, "This comes —
Of sharpening one's nails with a file!"

There was an old man in a barge,
Whose nose was exceedingly large;
　　But in fishing by night,
　　It supported a light,
Which helped that old man in a barge.

There is a young lady, whose nose,
Continually prospers and grows;
　　When it grew out of sight,
　　She exclaimed in a fright,
"Oh! Farewell to the end of my nose!"

There was an old man of Thermopylae,
Who never did anything properly;
　　But they said, "If you choose,
　　To boil eggs in your shoes,
You shall never remain in Thermopylae."

BEATRIX POTTER

When Beatrix Potter was a young lady, almost a hundred years ago, she used to travel with a rabbit hutch and a whole zoo of small animals. On one trip she carried along, just for company, a large family of snails and eleven minnows. Almost all her books — there are twenty-three Peter Rabbit books — are about animals.

The story you can read below is about Peter Rabbit himself. If you read her other books, you'll meet Mrs. Tiggy-Winkle the hedgehog, Mr. Jeremy Fisher the frog, Jemima Puddle-Duck, Nutkin the squirrel, and a whole company of animals.

Even when Beatrix Potter looked at people, animals were on her mind. In her journal (a book in which she put down her thoughts) she wrote: "How amusing Aunt Harriet is. More like a weasel than ever." When Beatrix Potter died in 1943 a great and terrible war was being fought all over Europe and other parts of the world. Among the last words she wrote were these: "The sheep and cattle take no notice."

Even as a child she loved to draw animals, birds, flowers. When she was eighteen she wrote to herself: "I cannot rest, I must draw, however poor the result." But for almost a century the result has been loved by millions of children and grown-ups.

The Tale of Peter Rabbit, the first of her books, started as a letter with pictures, sent to cheer up five-year-old Noel Moore, a friend of hers who was ill at the time. That's how Flopsy, Mopsy, Cotton-tail, and Peter began. Some years later, when she was thirty-five years old, she had the idea of making a little book out of the story and remembered the letter. Luckily for us, Noel had kept it.

Beatrix Potter did have a pet rabbit, named Peter, "an affectionate companion and a quiet friend". So the Peter you can see in the picture opposite was once a real Peter.

When she was forty-seven Beatrix Potter married and became a sheep farmer. In her later years she described herself as "a plain person who believes in saying what she thinks". She became a shrewd, practical dumpling of a woman, dressed in a tweed skirt fastened at the back with a safety pin.

THE TALE OF PETER RABBIT

ONCE upon a time there were four little Rabbits, and their names were — Flopsy, Mopsy, Cotton-tail, and Peter.

They lived with their Mother in a sandbank, underneath the root of a very big fir tree.

"Now, my dears," said old Mrs. Rabbit one morning, "you

may go into the fields or down the lane, but don't go into Mr. McGregor's garden: your Father had an accident there; he was put in a pie by Mrs. McGregor.

"Now run along, and don't get into mischief. I am going out."

Then old Mrs. Rabbit took a basket and her umbrella, and went through the wood to the baker's. She bought a loaf of brown bread and five currant buns.

Flopsy, Mopsy, and Cotton-tail, who were good little bunnies, went down the lane to gather blackberries; but Peter, who was very naughty, ran straight away to Mr. McGregor's garden, and squeezed under the gate!

First he ate some lettuces and some French beans; and then he ate some radishes; and then, feeling rather sick, he went to look for some parsley.

But round the end of a cucumber frame, whom should he meet but Mr. McGregor!

Mr. McGregor was on his hands and knees planting out young cabbages, but he jumped up and ran after Peter, waving a rake and calling out, "Stop, thief!"

Peter was most dreadfully frightened; he rushed all over the garden, for he had forgotten the way back to the gate.

He lost one of his shoes among the cabbages, and the other shoe amongst the potatoes.

After losing them, he ran on four legs and went faster, so that I think he might have got away altogether if he had not unfortunately run into a gooseberry net, and got caught by the large buttons on his jacket. It was a blue jacket with brass buttons, quite new.

Peter gave himself up for lost, and shed big tears; but his sobs were overheard by some friendly sparrows, who flew to him in great excitement, and implored him to exert himself.

Mr. McGregor came up with a sieve, which he intended to pop upon the top of Peter; but Peter wriggled out just in time, leaving his jacket behind him.

And rushed into the tool-shed, and jumped into a can. It would have been a beautiful thing to hide in, if it had not had so much water in it.

Mr. McGregor was quite sure that Peter was somewhere in the tool-shed, perhaps hidden underneath a flower-pot. He began to turn them over carefully, looking under each.

Presently Peter sneezed — "Kertyschoo!" Mr. McGregor was after him in no time, and tried to put his foot upon Peter, who jumped out of a window, upsetting three plants. The window was too small for Mr. McGregor, and he was tired of running after Peter. He went back to his work.

Peter sat down to rest; he was out of breath and trembling with fright, and he had not the least idea which way to go. Also he was very damp with sitting in that can.

After a time he began to wander about, going lippity-lippity — not very fast, and looking all around.

He found a door in a wall; but it was locked, and there was no room for a fat little rabbit to squeeze underneath.

An old mouse was running in and out over the stone doorstep, carrying peas and beans to her family in the wood. Peter asked her the way to the gate, but she had such a large pea in her mouth that she could not answer. She only shook her head at him. Peter began to cry.

Then he tried to find his way straight across the garden, but he became more and more puzzled. Presently, he came to a pond where Mr. McGregor filled his water cans. A white cat was staring at some goldfish; she sat very, very still, but now and then the tip of her tail twitched as if it were alive. Peter thought it best to go away without speaking to her; he had heard about cats from his cousin, little Benjamin Bunny.

He went back towards the tool-shed, but suddenly, quite close to him, he heard the noise of a hoe — sc-r-ritch, scratch, scratch, scritch. Peter scuttered underneath the bushes. But presently, as nothing happened, he came out, and climbed upon a wheelbarrow, and peeped over. The first thing he saw was Mr. McGregor hoeing onions. His back was turned towards Peter, and beyond him was the gate!

Peter got down very quietly off the wheelbarrow, and started running as fast as he could go, along a straight walk behind some black-currant bushes.

Mr. McGregor caught sight of him at the corner, but Peter did not care. He slipped underneath the gate, and was safe at last in the wood outside the garden.

Mr. McGregor hung up the little jacket and the shoes for a scarecrow to frighten the blackbirds.

Peter never stopped running or looked behind him till he got home to the big fir tree.

He was so tired that he flopped down upon the nice soft sand on the floor of the rabbit hole, and shut his eyes. His mother was busy cooking; she wondered what he had done with his clothes. It was the second little jacket and pair of shoes that Peter had lost in a fortnight!

I am sorry to say that Peter was not very well during the evening.

His mother put him to bed, and made some camomile tea; and she gave a dose of it to Peter!

"One table-spoonful to be taken at bed-time."

But Flopsy, Mopsy, and Cotton-tail had bread and milk and blackberries for supper.

Fables Up-to-Date

On page 38 we talked about fables and learnt that they go back a long way. But here are three very up-to-date ones, two by a Russian named Sergei Mikhalkov and one by Arnold Lobel, an American. If Aesop were alive today he might be puzzled by them. They're a little different from the kind he told but much funnier, I think.

SERGEI MIKHALKOV
A Mismatch

A RAM gave his daughter in marriage to, of all things, a Tiger!

The Ox, the Goat, and all the Ram's other friends were frightfully disturbed. "You're out of your mind!" they said to him. "What a terrible fate for your child! Why, he'll tear her to pieces!"

"You don't know my daughter," the Ram said serenely.

Trapped!

AN ELEPHANT was walking along slowly and peacefully, swinging his trunk from side to side. Suddenly he had a feeling he was being followed. He looked back and saw a Rabbit!

"What's the matter with him?" the Elephant wondered. "Has he gone crazy?" He started to walk faster, but the Rabbit speeded up, too.

"What should I do?" he asked himself. "How can I get away from that Rabbit? Anyway, who ever heard of a Rabbit chasing an Elephant?"

But he didn't answer his own question. Instead, he started to run. From time to time he would look back, and each time he saw that the Rabbit was gaining on him!

He ran and ran, till he found himself on the brink of a deep chasm. "I'm lost!" he thought. "I'm done for! I can't jump into that chasm!" So he stopped.

The Rabbit caught up with him.

"What is it?" the Elephant gasped. "What do you want with me?"

"If you please, sir," the Rabbit asked, almost out of breath from running. "Would you . . ." he wheezed and wheedled. "Would you give me your autograph? *Please,* sir!"

THE BAD KANGAROO

Written and
Illustrated
by
ARNOLD LOBEL

THERE WAS a small Kangaroo who was bad in school. He put thumbtacks on the teacher's chair. He threw spitballs across the classroom. He set off firecrackers in the lavatory and spread glue on the doorknobs.

"Your behaviour is impossible!" said the school principal. "I am going to see your parents. I will tell them what a problem you are!"

The principal went to visit Mr. and Mrs. Kangaroo. He sat down in a living-room chair.

"Ouch!" cried the principal. "There is a thumbtack in this chair!"

"Yes, I know," said Mr. Kangaroo. "I enjoy putting thumbtacks in chairs."

A spitball hit the principal on his nose.

"Forgive me," said Mrs. Kangaroo, "but I can never resist throwing those things."

There was a loud booming sound from the bathroom.

"Keep calm," said Mr. Kangaroo to the principal. "The firecrackers that we keep in the medicine chest have just exploded. We love the noise."

The principal rushed for the front door. In an instant he was stuck to the doorknob.

"Pull hard," said Mrs. Kangaroo. "There are little globs of glue on all of our doorknobs."

The principal pulled himself free. He dashed out of the house and ran off down the street.

"Such a nice person," said Mr. Kangaroo. "I wonder why he left so quickly."

"No doubt he had another appointment," said Mrs. Kangaroo. "Never mind, supper is ready."

Mr. and Mrs. Kangaroo and their son enjoyed their evening meal. After the dessert, they all threw spitballs at each other across the dining-room table.

A child's conduct will reflect the ways of his parents.

A. A. MILNE

Try reading these verses aloud. Many have been set to music and you can buy the records in a record shop.

On page 580 there's a little talk about Mr. Milne. You might want to read it before reading these verses.

Buckingham Palace

ILLUSTRATED BY E. H. SHEPARD

They're changing guard at Buckingham Palace —
Christopher Robin went down with Alice.
Alice is marrying one of the guard.
"A soldier's life is terrible hard,"

                Says Alice.

They're changing guard at Buckingham Palace —
Christopher Robin went down with Alice.
We saw a guard in a sentry-box.
"One of the sergeants looks after their socks,"

                Says Alice.

They're changing guard at Buckingham Palace —
Christopher Robin went down with Alice.
We looked for the King, but he never came.
"Well, God take care of him, all the same,"

                Says Alice.

They're changing guard at Buckingham Palace —
Christopher Robin went down with Alice.
They've great big parties inside the grounds.
"I wouldn't be King for a hundred pounds,"
Says Alice.

They're changing guard at Buckingham Palace —
Christopher Robin went down with Alice.
A face looked out, but it wasn't the King's.
"He's much too busy a-signing things,"
Says Alice.

They're changing guard at Buckingham Palace —
Christopher Robin went down with Alice.
"Do you think the King knows all about *me*?"
"Sure to, dear, but it's time for tea,"
Says Alice.

The King's Breakfast

ILLUSTRATED BY E. H. SHEPARD

The King asked
The Queen, and
The Queen asked
The Dairymaid:
"Could we have some butter for
The Royal slice of bread?"
The Queen asked
The Dairymaid,
The Dairymaid
Said, "Certainly,
I'll go and tell
The cow
Now
Before she goes to bed."

The Dairymaid
She curtsied,
And went and told
The Alderney:
"Don't forget the butter for
The Royal slice of bread."
The Alderney
Said sleepily:
"You'd better tell
His Majesty
That many people nowadays
Like marmalade
Instead."

The Dairymaid
Said, "Fancy!"
And went to
Her Majesty.
She curtsied to the Queen, and
She turned a little red:
"Excuse me,
Your Majesty,
For taking of
The liberty,
But marmalade is tasty, if
It's very
Thickly
Spread."

The Queen said
"Oh!"
And went to
His Majesty:
"Talking of the butter for
The Royal slice of bread,
Many people
Think that
Marmalade
Is nicer.
Would you like to try a little
Marmalade
Instead?"

The King said,
"Bother!"
And then he said,
"Oh, deary me!"
The King sobbed, "Oh, deary me!"
And went back to bed.
"Nobody,"
He whimpered,
"Could call me
A fussy man;
I *only* want
A little bit
Of butter for
My bread!"

The Queen said,
"There, there!"

And went to
The Dairymaid.
The Dairymaid
Said, "There, there!"
And went to the shed.
The cow said,
"There, there!
I didn't really
Mean it;
Here's milk for his porringer
And butter for his bread."

The Queen took
The butter
And brought it to
His Majesty;
The King said,
"Butter, eh?"
And bounced out of bed.
"Nobody," he said,
As he kissed her
Tenderly,
"Nobody," he said,
As he slid down
The banisters,
"Nobody,
My darling,
Could call me
A fussy man —
BUT
I do like a little bit of butter to my bread!"

ASTRID LINDGREN

If any mothers, fathers, grandmothers, grandfathers, older sisters or brothers are reading these words, please take note: *The Tomten* is what I call a Readaloudable. It should be read in a very soft voice, and if you can sing or chant the little songs, all the better.

The Tomten is not entirely the work of Astrid Lindgren, but is adapted by her from a poem written by a nineteenth-century Swedish writer named Viktor Rydberg. She has also adapted, from a poem by Karl-Erik Forsslund, another story called *The Tomten and the Fox*. It is just as good as *The Tomten*.

The Tomten

ADAPTED BY ASTRID LINDGREN

FROM A POEM BY VIKTOR RYDBERG

ILLUSTRATED BY HARALD WIBERG

Translated from the Swedish

IT IS the dead of night. The old farm lies fast asleep and every-one inside the house is sleeping too.

The farm is deep in the middle of the forest. Once upon a time someone came here, cut down trees, built a homestead and farmed the land. No one knows who. The stars are shining in the sky tonight, the snow lies white all around, the frost is cruel. On such a night people creep into their small houses, wrap themselves up and bank the fire on the hearth.

Here is a lonely old farm where everyone is sleeping. All but one . . .

The Tomten is awake. He lives in a corner of the hayloft and comes out at night when human beings are asleep. He is an old, old tomten who has seen the snow of many hundreds of winters. No one knows when he came to the farm. No one has ever seen him, but they know he is there. Sometimes when they wake up they see the prints of his feet in the snow. But no one has seen the Tomten.

On small silent feet the Tomten moves about in the moonlight. He peeps into cowshed and stable, storehouse and toolshed. He goes between the buildings making tracks in the snow.

The Tomten goes first to the cowshed. The cows are dreaming that summer is here, and they are grazing in the fields. The Tomten talks to them in tomten language, a silent little language the cows can understand.

> "*Winters come and winters go,*
> *Summers come and summers go,*
> *Soon you can graze in the fields.*"

The moon is shining into the stable. There stands Dobbin, thinking. Perhaps he remembers a clover field, where he trotted around last summer. The Tomten talks to him in tomten language, a silent little language a horse can understand.

"Winters come and winters go,
Summers come and summers go,
Soon you will be in your clover field."

Now all the sheep and lambs are sleeping soundly. But they bleat softly when the Tomten peeps in at the door. He talks to them in tomten language, a silent little language the sheep can understand.

"All my sheep, all my lambs,
The night is cold, but your wool is warm,
And you have aspen leaves to eat."

Then on small silent feet the Tomten goes to the chicken house, and the chickens cluck contentedly when he comes. He talks to them in tomten language, a silent little language chickens can understand.

"Lay me an egg, my jolly chickens, and I will give you corn to eat."

The dog kennel roof is white with snow, and inside is Caro. Every night he waits for the moment when the Tomten will come. The Tomten is his friend, and he talks to Caro in tomten language, a silent little language a dog can understand.

"Caro, my friend, is it cold tonight? Are you cold in your kennel? I'll fetch more straw and then you can sleep."

The house where the people live is silent. They are sleeping through the winter night without knowing that the Tomten is there.

"Winters come and winters go,
I have seen people large and small
But never have they seen me," thinks the Tomten.

He tiptoes across to the children's cot, and stands looking for a long time.

"If they would only wake up, then I could talk to them in tomten language, a silent little language that children can understand. But children sleep at night."

And away goes the Tomten on his little feet. In the morning the children see his tracks, a line of tiny footprints in the snow.

Then the Tomten goes back to his cosy little corner in the hayloft. There, in the hay, the cat is waiting for him, for she wants milk. The Tomten talks to the cat in tomten language, a silent little language a cat can understand.

"Of course you may stay with me, and of course I will give you milk," says the Tomten.

Winter is long and dark and cold, and sometimes the Tomten dreams of summer.

> *"Winters come and winters go,*
> *Summers come and summers go,*
> *Soon the swallows will be here,"* thinks the Tomten.

But the snow still lies in deep drifts around the old farm in the forest. The stars shine in the sky, it is biting cold. On such a night people creep into their small houses and bank the fire on the hearth.

Here is a lonely old farm, where everyone is fast asleep. All but one . . .

Winters come and summers go, year follows year, but as long as people live at the old farm in the forest, every night the Tomten will trip around between the houses on his small silent feet.

DAVID McCORD

Maurice Sendak's "Chicken Soup" (see page 610) was a great favourite of our children when they wanted to read something aloud *very* loud. So was David McCord's "Bananas and Cream", which you'll find below. Of course, it's better if you like bananas.

Mr. McCord, who lives in America, is eighty-six years old and is still writing wonderful verse — for himself, though children like it. Maybe this shows that sometimes very old people and very young people can understand each other pretty well.

When Mr. McCord was five he learnt and sang "The Owl and the Pussycat" by Edward Lear (see page 345). He says this started him off liking poetry. Also he learnt the Morse code when he was seven and maybe that taught him something about rhythm. Morse code is a way of sending messages by dots and dashes or short and long sounds.

I like Mr. McCord because he knows how to play with words almost as if they were toys. In one of his poems he says, "Words have more to them than meaning". They can rhyme, often in an odd way (see "Glow-worm", below). Put together in a certain order, they can make peculiar sounds that please us (see "The Pickety Fence", below). They can do all sorts of tricks, as if they were acrobats. Best of all, some words, arranged just right, can say something to us that each separate word doesn't say at all.

For example, here are six easy words whose meanings you know:

and	*hills*
over	*the*
away	*far*

Now, a nursery rhyme you may have heard mixes up these words so that they come out:

Over the hills and far away.

If you read that line softly, a little drowsily, you suddenly get a kind of feeling you don't have if you read the six words as I've printed them in the column above. Try it.

But if you take the four words *cat, see, the, I,* and put *them* together — *I see the cat* — you don't get the same feeling. Or do you?

Mr. McCord knows all about such things.

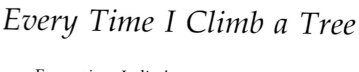

Every Time I Climb a Tree

Every time I climb a tree
Every time I climb a tree
Every time I climb a tree
I scrape a leg
Or skin a knee
And every time I climb a tree
I find some ants
Or dodge a bee
And get the ants
All over me

And every time I climb a tree
Where have you been?
They say to me
But don't they know that I am free
Every time I climb a tree?
I like it best
To spot a nest
That has an egg
Or maybe three

And then I skin
The other leg
But every time I climb a tree
I see a lot of things to see
Swallows rooftops and TV
And all the fields and farms there be
Every time I climb a tree
Though climbing may be good for ants
It isn't awfully good for pants
But still it's pretty good for me
Every time I climb a tree.

Glowworm

Never talk down to a glowworm —
Such as *What do you knowworm?*
How's it down belowworm?
Guess you're quite a slowworm.
No. Just say
　　　　Helloworm!

The Pickety Fence

The pickety fence
The pickety fence
Give it a lick it's
The pickety fence
Give it a lick it's
A clickety fence
Give it a lick it's
A lickety fence
Give it a lick
Give it a lick
Give it a lick
With a rickety stick
Pickety
Pickety
Pickety
Pick

378   DAVID McCORD

Bananas and Cream

Bananas and cream,
Bananas and cream:
All we could say was
Bananas and cream.

We couldn't say fruit,
We wouldn't say cow,
We didn't say sugar —
We don't say it now.

Bananas and cream,
Bananas and cream,
All we could shout was
Bananas and cream.

We didn't say why,
We didn't say how;
We forgot it was fruit,
We forgot the old cow;
We *never* said sugar,
We only said *WOW!*

THE GRIMM BROTHERS

You may already know these stories. Or perhaps they will be new to you. I feel I have *always* known about Cinderella and Little Red Riding Hood. These tales seem to have been part of me, almost from birth. And that's true all over the world. The best-known stories, like "Cinderella", are found in Africa, China, and Japan, just as they are in Europe and America.

Two very learned brothers, Jacob and Wilhelm Grimm, had a good idea many, many years ago. They travelled around the German countryside, going directly to the people for their folktales. One grandmother, a tailor's widow named Katherina Viehmann, knew scores of them, and the brothers took down the stories just as she told them.

They published their first collection in 1812. That seems a long time ago. But probably the stories began to be told many hundreds, perhaps even thousands, of years before that. No one knows who thought of them first, yet someone must have done so.

To me they seem like dreams poor people might have. The poor boy or girl always wins out, the treasure is found, the good food is eaten. But it isn't easy for poor people to get food and money and power by their own efforts. And so they need magic to help them — magic clocks, magic sticks, magic birds, dwarfs, fairies. Fairy tales mix a lot of common sense with a lot of uncommon happenings. They almost always end happily. That's the best part of it.

Here are seven good stories by the good Grimms.

The Shepherd Boy

ONCE there was a shepherd boy whose fame spread far and wide because of the wise answers he gave to every question. The King of the country heard of this, but did not believe it.

He sent for the boy, and he said to him, "If you can give me an answer to three questions which I will ask, I will look on you as my own child, and you shall dwell with me in my royal palace."

The boy said, "What are the three questions?"

The King said, "The first is, how many drops of water are there in the ocean?" The shepherd boy answered, "Lord King, if you will have all the rivers on earth dammed up so that not a single drop runs from them into the sea until I have counted them, I will then tell you how many drops there are in the sea."

The King said, "The next question is, how many stars are there in the sky?" The shepherd boy said, "Give me a great sheet of white paper and a pen." He made so many fine points on it with the pen that they could scarcely be seen, and it was all but impossible to count them. Anyone who looked at them would have lost his sight. Then he said, "There are as many stars in the sky as there are points on the paper; just count them." But no one was able to do it.

The King said, "The third question is, how many seconds of time are there in eternity?"

Then said the shepherd boy, "In Lower Pomerania is the Diamond Mountain, which is two miles and a half high, two miles and a half wide, and two miles and a half in depth; every hundred years a little bird comes and sharpens its beak on it, and when the whole mountain is worn away by this, then the first second of eternity will be over."

The King said, "You have answered the three questions like a wise man, and shall henceforth dwell with me in my royal palace, and I will regard you as my own child."

The Sleeping Beauty

IN TIMES past there lived a King and Queen, who said to each other every day of their lives, "Would that we had a child!" And yet they had none.

It happened one day that when the Queen was bathing, a frog came out of the water, and squatted on the ground, and said to her, "Thy wish shall be fulfilled. Before a year has gone by, you shall bring a daughter into the world."

And as the frog foretold, so it happened. The Queen bore a daughter so beautiful that the King could not contain himself for joy, and he ordained a great feast. Not only did he invite his relations, friends, and acquaintances, but also the wisewomen, that they might be kind and favourable to the child. There were thirteen of them in his kingdom, but as he had only provided twelve golden plates for them to eat from, one of them had not been invited. However, the feast was celebrated with all splendour. As it drew to an end, the wisewomen stood forward to present to the child their wonderful gifts. One bestowed virtue, one beauty, a third riches, and so on: whatever there was in the world to wish for.

And when eleven of them had said their say, in came the uninvited thirteenth, burning to revenge herself. Without greeting or respect, she cried with a loud voice, "In the fifteenth year of her age the Princess shall prick herself with a spindle and shall fall down dead." And without another word she turned away and left the hall.

Everyone was terrified at her speech.

Then the twelfth came forward to bestow her gift. Though she could not do away with the evil prophecy, she could soften it, so she said, "The Princess shall not die, but fall into a deep sleep for a hundred years."

Now the King, desiring to save his child even from this misfortune, gave orders that all the spindles in his kingdom should be burned up.

The maiden grew up, adorned with all the gifts of the wise-women. And she was so lovely, modest, sweet, kind, and clever that no one who saw her could help but love her.

It happened one day, when she was fifteen years old, that the King and Queen rode abroad, and the maiden was left behind alone in the castle. She wandered about into all the nooks and corners, and into all the chambers and parlours, as the fancy took her. At last she came to an old tower. She climbed the narrow winding stair to a little door, with a rusty key sticking out of the lock. She turned the key, and the door opened, and there in the little room sat an old woman with a spindle, diligently spinning her flax.

"Good day, mother," said the Princess. "What are you doing?"

"I am spinning," answered the old woman, nodding her head.

"What thing is that that twists round so briskly?" asked the maiden, and taking the spindle into her hand she began to spin. No sooner had she touched it than the evil prophecy was fulfilled, and she pricked her finger with it. In that very moment she fell back upon the bed that stood there, and lay in a deep sleep. And this sleep fell upon the whole castle. The King and Queen, who had returned and were in the great hall, fell fast asleep, and with them the whole court. The horses in their stalls, and the dogs in the yard, the pigeons on the roof, the flies on the wall, the very fire that flickered on the hearth, became still, and slept like the rest. The meat on the spit ceased roasting, and the cook, who was going to pull the scullion's hair for some mistake he had made, let him go, and fell asleep. The wind ceased, and not a leaf fell from the trees about the castle.

Then around and about that place there grew a hedge of thorns thicker every year, until at last the whole castle was hidden from view, and nothing of it could be seen but the vane on the roof. And a rumour went abroad in all that country of the beautiful sleeping Rosamond, for so was the Princess called. And from time to time many kings' sons came and tried to force their way through the hedge; but it was impossible for them to do so. The thorns held fast together like strong hands, and the young men were caught by them, and not being able to get free, they died a lamentable death.

Many a long year afterwards there came another king's son into that country. He heard an old man tell how there was a castle standing behind the hedge of thorns, and that a beautiful enchanted princess named Rosamond had slept there for a hundred years, and with her the King and Queen, and the whole court. The old man had been told by his grandfather that many kings' sons had tried to pass the thorn hedge, but had been caught and pierced by the thorns, and had died a miserable death. Then said the young man, "Nevertheless, I do not fear to try. I shall win through and see the lovely Rosamond." The good old man tried to dissuade him, but he would not listen to his words.

But now the hundred years were at an end, and the day had come when Rosamond should be awakened. When the Prince drew near the hedge of thorns, it was changed into a hedge of beautiful large flowers, which parted and bent aside to let him pass, and then closed behind him in a thick hedge. He reached the castle yard, and he saw the horses and brindled hunting-dogs lying asleep, and on the roof the pigeons sitting with their heads under their wings. And when he came indoors, he saw the flies asleep on the wall, and the cook in the kitchen with his hand uplifted to strike the scullion, and the kitchenmaid with the black fowl on her lap ready to pluck. He mounted higher, and saw in the hall the whole court lying asleep, and above them, on their thrones, slept the King and Queen. He went farther, and all was so quiet that he could hear his own breathing. At last he came to the tower, and went up the winding stair, and opened the door of the little room where Rosamond lay. And when he saw her looking so lovely in her sleep, he could not turn away his eyes. He stooped and kissed her, and she awakened, and opened her eyes, and looked very kindly on him. She rose, and they went forth together, and the King and the Queen and the whole court woke up, and gazed on one another with great eyes of wonderment. The horses in the yard got up and shook themselves, the hounds sprang up and wagged their tails, the pigeons on the roof drew their heads from under their wings, looked round, and flew into the field, the flies on the wall crept on a little farther, the kitchen fire leaped up and blazed and cooked the meat, the joint on the spit began to roast, the cook gave the scullion such a box on the ear that he roared out, and the maid went on plucking the fowl.

The wedding of the Prince and Rosamond was held in all splendour. And they lived very happily together until their lives' end.

Cinderella

THE WIFE of a rich man fell ill, and when she felt that she was nearing her end, she called her only daughter to her bedside and said, "Dear child, continue to be devout and good. Then God will always help you, and I will look down upon you from heaven and watch over you."

Thereupon she closed her eyes and breathed her last.

The maiden went to her mother's grave every day and wept, and she continued to be devout and good. When the winter came, the snow spread a white covering on the grave. And when the sun of spring had unveiled it again, the husband took another wife. The new wife brought home with her two daughters who were fair and beautiful to look upon, but base and black at heart.

Then began a sad time for the unfortunate stepchild.

"Is this stupid goose to sit with us in the parlour?" they said. "Whoever wants to eat bread must earn it. Go and sit with the kitchenmaid."

They took away her pretty clothes, and made her put on an old grey frock, and gave her wooden clogs.

"Just look at the proud princess! How well she's dressed," they laughed, as they led her to the kitchen.

The girl was obliged to do hard work from morning till night — to get up at daybreak, carry water, light the fire, cook, and wash. Not content with that, the sisters inflicted on her every vexation they could think of. They made fun of her, and tossed the peas and lentils among the ashes, so that she had to sit down and pick them out again. In the evening, when she was worn out with work, she had no bed to go to but had to lie on the hearth among the cinders.

And because she always looked dusty and dirty, they called her Cinderella.

It happened one day that the father had a mind to go to the fair. So he asked both his stepdaughters what he should bring home for them.

"Fine clothes," said one.

"Pearls and jewels," said the other.

"But you, Cinderella," said he, "what will you have?"

"Father, break off for me the first twig which brushes against your hat on your way home."

Well, for his two stepdaughters he brought beautiful clothes, pearls, and jewels. And on his way home, as he was riding through a green thicket, a hazel twig grazed against him and knocked off his hat. He broke off the branch and took it with him.

When he got home he gave his stepdaughters what they had asked for, and to Cinderella he gave the twig from the hazel tree.

Cinderella thanked him, and went to her mother's grave and planted the twig upon it. She wept so much that her tears fell and watered it, and it took root and became a fine tree.

Cinderella went to the grave three times every day. She wept and prayed there. Every time she went a little white bird came and perched upon the tree. And when she uttered a wish, the little bird threw down to her what she had wished for.

Now it happened that the King proclaimed a festival which was to last three days, and to which all the beautiful maidens in the country were invited, in order that his son might choose a bride.

When the two stepdaughters heard that they were also to be present, they were in high spirits.

They called Cinderella and said, "Brush our hair and clean our shoes and fasten our buckles, for we are going to the feast at the King's palace."

Cinderella obeyed but wept, for she also would gladly have gone to the ball with them. And she begged her stepmother to allow her to go.

"You, Cinderella?" she said. "Why, you are covered with dust and dirt. You go to the festival? You have no clothes or shoes, and yet you want to go to the ball."

She went on asking, however, and her stepmother said, "Well, I have thrown a dishful of lentils into the cinders. If you have picked them all out in two hours you shall go."

The girl went through the back door into the garden and cried, "Ye gentle doves, ye turtledoves, and all ye little birds under heaven, come and help me,

"The good into a dish to throw,
The bad into your crops can go."

Then two white doves came in by the kitchen window, followed by the turtledoves. And finally all the little birds under heaven flocked in, chirping and settling down among the ashes. The doves gave a nod with their little heads, peck, peck, peck. The rest began also, peck, peck, peck, and collected all the good beans into the dish. Scarcely an hour had passed before they had finished and all flown out again.

Then the girl brought the dish to her stepmother, and she was delighted to think that now she would be able to go to the feast with them.

But the stepmother said, "No, Cinderella, you have no clothes and cannot dance. You will only be laughed at."

When she began to cry, the stepmother said, "If you can pick out two whole dishes of lentils from the ashes in an hour, you shall go with us." And she thought, "She will never be able to do that."

When her stepmother had thrown the dishes of lentils among

the ashes, the girl went out through the back door and cried, "Ye gentle doves, ye turtledoves, and all ye little birds under heaven, come and help me,

> "*The good into a dish to throw,*
> *The bad into your crops can go.*"

Then two white doves came in by the kitchen window, followed by the turtledoves and all the other little birds under heaven. And in less than an hour the lentils had been picked up, and the birds had all flown away.

The girl carried the dish to her stepmother and was delighted to think that she would now be able to go to the ball.

But she said, "It's still no good. You can't go with us, for you've got no clothes and you can't dance. We should be quite ashamed of you."

Thereupon she turned her back upon her and hurried off with her two proud daughters.

After everyone had left the house, Cinderella went out to her mother's grave under the hazel tree and cried,

> "*Shiver and shake, dear little tree,*
> *Gold and silver shower on me.*"

Then the bird threw down to her a gold and silver robe and a pair of slippers embroidered with silk and silver. With all speed she put on the robe and went to the feast. But her stepsisters and their mother did not recognize her. They supposed that she was some foreign princess, so beautiful did she appear in her golden dress. They never gave a thought to Cinderella, but imagined that she was sitting at home in the dirt, picking the lentils out of the cinders.

The Prince came up to the stranger, took her by the hand, and

danced with her. In fact he would not dance with anyone else and never let go of her hand. If anyone came up to ask her to dance, he said, "This is my partner."

She danced until nightfall and then wanted to go home, but the Prince said, "I will go with you and escort you." He wanted to see to whom the beautiful maiden belonged. But she slipped out of his way and sprang into the pigeon house.

The Prince waited till her father came, and told him that an unknown maiden had vanished into the pigeon house.

The old man thought, "Could it be Cinderella?" And he had an axe brought to him so that he might break down the pigeon house, but there was no one inside.

When they went home, there lay Cinderella in her dirty clothes among the cinders, and a dismal oil lamp was burning in the chimney corner. For Cinderella had quietly jumped out of the pigeon house and had run back to the hazel tree. There she had taken off her beautiful clothes and laid them on the grave, and the bird had taken them away again. Then she had settled herself among the ashes on the hearth in her old grey frock.

On the second day, when the festival was renewed and her parents and stepsisters had started forth again, Cinderella went to the hazel tree and said,

> "Shiver and shake, dear little tree,
> Gold and silver shower on me."

Then the bird threw down a still more gorgeous robe than on the previous day. And when she appeared at the festival in this robe, everyone was astounded by her beauty.

The King's son had waited till she came and at once took her hand. She danced with no one but him. When others came forward and invited her to dance, he said, "This is my partner."

At nightfall she wished to leave; but the Prince went after her, hoping to see where she went. But she sprang out into the garden behind the house. There stood a fine big tree on which the most delicious pears hung. She climbed up among the branches as nimbly as a squirrel, and the Prince could not make out what had become of her.

He waited till her father came and then said to him, "The unknown maiden has slipped away from me again. I think that she has jumped into the pear tree."

The father thought, "Can it be Cinderella?" And he had the axe brought to cut down the tree, but there was no one in it. When they went home and looked into the kitchen, there lay Cinderella among the cinders as usual. For she had jumped down on the other side of the tree, taken back the beautiful clothes to the bird on the hazel tree, and put on her old grey frock.

On the third day, when her parents and sisters had started out, Cinderella went again to her mother's grave and said,

"Shiver and shake, dear little tree,
Gold and silver shower on me."

Then the bird threw down a dress which was so magnificent that no one had ever seen the like before. The slippers were entirely of gold. When she appeared at the festival in this attire, they were all speechless with astonishment. The Prince danced only with her, and if anyone else asked her to dance he said, "This is my partner."

When night fell and she wanted to leave, the Prince was more desirous than ever to accompany her, but she darted away from him so quickly that he could not keep up with her. But this time the Prince had used a stratagem, and had caused the steps to be covered with cobbler's wax. The consequence was that, as the maiden sprang down them, her left slipper remained sticking there. The Prince took it up. It was small and dainty and made entirely of gold.

The next morning he went with it to Cinderella's father and said to him, "No other shall become my wife but she whose foot this golden slipper fits."

The two sisters were delighted at that, for they both had beautiful feet. The eldest went into the room intending to try on the slipper, and her mother stood beside her. But her great toe prevented her from getting it on. Her foot was too long.

Then her mother handed her a knife and said, "Cut off the toe. When you are Queen you won't have to walk anymore."

The girl cut off her toe, forced her foot into the slipper, stifled her pain, and went out to the Prince. He took her up on his horse as his bride and rode away with her.

However, they had to pass the grave on the way, and there on the hazel tree sat the two doves crying,

> "*Prithee, look back, prithee, look back,*
> *There's blood on the track.*
> *The shoe is too small;*
> *At home the true bride is waiting thy call.*"

The Prince looked at her foot and he saw how the blood was streaming from it. So he turned his horse round and carried the false bride back to her home, and said that she was not the right one.

Then the second sister tried on the shoe. She went into the room and succeeded in getting her toes in, but her heel was too big.

Her mother handed her a knife and said, "Cut a bit off your heel. When you are Queen, you won't have to walk anymore."

The maiden cut a bit off her heel, forced her foot into the shoe, stifled her pain, and went out to the Prince. He took her up on his horse as his bride and rode off with her. As they passed the grave, the two doves were sitting on the hazel tree, crying,

> "Prithee, look back, prithee, look back,
> There's blood on the track.
> The shoe is too small;
> At home the true bride is waiting thy call."

He looked down at her foot and saw that it was streaming with blood and that there were dark red spots on her stocking. He turned his horse and brought the false bride back to her home.

"This is not the right one either," he said. "Have you no other daughter?"

"No," said the man. "There is only a daughter of my late wife's, a puny, stunted drudge. She cannot possibly be the bride."

Nonetheless, the Prince said that she must be sent for.

But the mother answered, "Oh no. She is much too dirty. She mustn't be seen on any account."

He was absolutely determined, however, to have his way, and they were obliged to summon Cinderella.

When she had washed her hands and face, she went up and curtsied to the Prince, who handed her the golden slipper. She sat down on a bench, pulled off her wooden clog, and put on the slipper. It fit ever so nicely. And when she stood up and the Prince looked into her face, he recognized the beautiful maiden whom he had danced with and cried, "This is the true bride!"

The stepmother and the two sisters were dismayed and turned white with rage. And he took Cinderella on his horse and rode off with her.

As they rode past the hazel tree the two doves cried,

"Prithee, look back, prithee, look back,
No blood's on the track.
The shoe's not too small;
You carry the true bride home to your hall."

And when the doves had said this they both came flying down and settled on Cinderella's shoulders, one on the right and one on the left, and they remained perched there.

When the wedding was about to take place, the two false sisters came and wanted to curry favour with her and take part in her good fortune. But as the bridal party was going to the church — the elder sister on the right side, the younger sister on the left — the doves picked out one of the eyes of each of them.

Afterwards, when the Prince and Cinderella were coming out of the church, the elder sister was on the left, the younger sister on the right, and the doves picked out the other eye of each of them. So, for their wickedness and their falseness they were punished with blindness for the rest of their days. And Cinderella lived happily with her Prince ever after.

Rumpelstiltskin

THERE WAS ONCE a miller who was very poor, but he had one beautiful daughter. It happened one day that he came to speak with the King, and to give himself consequence, he told him that he had a daughter who could spin gold out of straw.

The King said to the miller, "That is an art that pleases me well. If your daughter is as clever as you say, bring her to my castle tomorrow, that I may put her to the test."

When the girl was brought to him, he led her into a room that was quite full of straw. He gave her a wheel and spindle, and said, "Now set to work, and if by the early morning you have not spun this straw to gold you shall die." And he shut the door himself, and left her there alone.

And so the poor miller's daughter was left there sitting. She could not think what to do for her life, and she had no notion how to set to work to spin gold from straw. Her distress grew so great that she began to weep.

Then all at once the door opened, and in came a little man, who said, "Good evening, miller's daughter; why are you crying?"

"Oh!" answered the girl, "I have got to spin gold out of straw, and I don't understand the business."

Then the little man said, "What will you give me if I spin it for you?"

"My necklace," said the girl.

The little man took the necklace, seated himself before the wheel, and whirr, whirr, whirr! three times round and the bobbin was full. Then he took up another, and whirr, whirr, whirr! three times round, and that was full. And so he went on till the morning, when all the straw had been spun, and all the bobbins were full of gold.

At sunrise came the King, and when he saw the gold he was astonished and very much rejoiced, for he was very avaricious. He had the miller's daughter taken into another room filled with straw, much bigger than the last, and told her that if she valued her life she must spin it all in one night. The girl did not know what to do, so she began to cry. The door opened, and the little man appeared again and said, "What will you give me if I spin all this straw into gold?"

"The ring from my finger," answered the girl.

So the little man took the ring, and began to send the wheel whirring round, and by the next morning all the straw was spun into glistening gold. The King was rejoiced beyond measure at the sight, but as he could never have enough of gold, he had the miller's daughter taken into a still larger room full of straw, and said, "This, too, must be spun in one night, and if you accomplish it you shall be my wife." For he thought, "Although she is but a miller's daughter, I am not likely to find anyone richer in the whole world."

As soon as the girl was left alone, the little man appeared for the third time and said, "What will you give me if I spin the straw for you this time?"

"I have nothing left to give," answered the girl.

"Then you must promise me the first child you have after you are Queen," said the little man.

"But who knows whether that will happen?" thought the girl. But she did not know what else to do in her necessity, so she promised the little man what he desired, upon which he began to

spin, until all the straw was gold. And when in the morning the King came and found all done according to his wish, he caused the wedding to be held at once, and the miller's pretty daughter became a queen.

In a year's time she brought a fine child into the world. She thought no more of the little man; but one day he came suddenly into her room, and said, "Now give me what you promised me."

The Queen was greatly terrified, and offered the little man all the riches of the kingdom if he would only leave the child. But the little man said, "No, I would rather have something living than all the treasures of the world."

The Queen began to lament and to weep, so that the little man had pity upon her.

"I will give you three days," said he, "and if at the end of that time you cannot tell me my name, you must give up the child to me."

The Queen spent the whole night thinking over all the names that she had ever heard, and sent a messenger through the land to ask far and wide for all the names that could be found. And when the little man came next day, she repeated all she knew (beginning with Caspar, Melchior, Balthazar), and went through the whole list. But after each the little man said, "That is not my name."

The second day the Queen sent out to inquire of all the neighbours what their servants were called, and she told the little man all the most unusual and singular names, saying, "Perhaps you are called Roast-ribs, or Sheepshanks, or Spindleshanks?"

But he answered nothing but, "That is not my name."

The third day the messenger came back again and said, "I have not been able to find one single new name; but as I passed through the woods I came to a high hill, and near it was a little house, and before the house burned a fire, and round the fire danced a comical little man, and he hopped on one leg and cried,

"Today do I bake, tomorrow I brew,
The day after that the Queen's child comes in;
And oh! I am glad that nobody knew
That the name I am called is Rumpelstiltskin!"

You cannot think how pleased the Queen was to hear that name, and soon afterwards, when the little man walked in and said, "Now, Mrs. Queen, what is my name?" she said at first, "Are you called Jack?"

"No," he answered.

"Are you called Harry?" she asked again.

"No," answered he.

And then she said, "Then perhaps your name is Rumpelstiltskin!"

"The devil told you that! The devil told you that!" cried the little man, and in his anger he stamped with his right foot so hard that it went into the ground above his knee; then he seized his left foot with both hands in such a fury that he split in two, and that was the end of him.

Rapunzel

ONCE upon a time there lived a man and his wife, who had long wished for a child, but all in vain. And, it so happened that at the back of their house was a little window which overlooked a beautiful garden full of the finest vegetables and flowers. But there was a high wall round it, and no one ventured there, for it belonged to a witch of great power of whom all the world was afraid.

One day when the wife was standing at the window, and looking into the garden, she saw a bed filled with the finest rampion; and it looked so fresh and green that she began to wish for some; and at length she longed for it greatly.* This went on for days, and as she knew she could not get the rampion, she pined away, and grew pale and miserable. The man was uneasy, and he asked, "What is the matter, dear wife?"

"Oh," answered she, "I shall die unless I can have some of that rampion to eat that grows in the garden at the back of our house."

The man, who loved her very much, thought to himself, "Rather than lose my wife I will get the rampion, cost what it will."

So in the twilight he climbed over the wall into the witch's garden, plucked hastily a handful of rampion, and brought it to his wife. She made a salad of it at once; and ate to her heart's content. She liked it so much, and it tasted so good, that the next day she longed for it thrice as much as she had before; if she was to

---

*Rampion is a kind of flower whose root can be used in salads.

have any rest the man must climb over the wall once more. So he went in the twilight again; and as he was climbing back, he saw the witch standing before him, and was terribly frightened, as she cried, with angry eyes, "How dare you climb over into my garden like a thief, and steal my rampion! It shall be the worse for you!"

"Oh," answered he, "be merciful rather than just; I have only done it through necessity. My wife saw your rampion from our window, and became possessed with so great a longing for it that she would have died if she could not have some to eat."

Then the witch said, "If it is all as you say you may have as much rampion as you like, on one condition — the child that will come into the world must be given to me. It shall go well with the child, and I will care for it like a mother."

In his distress the man promised everything, and when the time came and the child was born the witch appeared, and gave the child the name of Rapunzel (which is the same as rampion). Then she took it away with her.

Rapunzel grew to be the most beautiful child in the world. When she was twelve years old the witch shut her up in a tower in the midst of a wood. It had neither steps nor door, only one small window above.

When the witch wished to be let in, she would stand below and cry, "Rapunzel, Rapunzel! Let down thy hair!"

Rapunzel had beautiful long hair that shone like gold. When she heard the voice of the witch she would undo the fastening of the upper window, unbind the plaits of her hair, and let it fall down twenty ells below, and the witch would climb up by it.

They had lived thus a few years when it happened that the King's son came riding through the wood. He came to the tower; and as he drew near he heard a voice singing so sweetly that he stood still and listened. It was Rapunzel. In her loneliness she tried to pass away the time with sweet songs. The King's son wished to go in to her, and sought to find a door in the tower, but there was none. So he rode home, but the song had entered his heart, and every day he went into the wood and listened to it.

Once, as he was standing there under a tree, he saw the witch come up, and he listened while she called out, "O Rapunzel, Rapunzel! Let down thy hair."

Then he saw how Rapunzel let down her long tresses, and how the witch climbed up by them and went in to her, and he said to himself, "Since that is the ladder I will climb it, and seek my fortune." And the next day, as soon as it began to grow dusk, he went to the tower and cried, "O Rapunzel, Rapunzel! Let down thy hair."

And she let down her hair, and the King's son climbed up by it.

Rapunzel was greatly terrified when she saw that a man had come in to her, for she had never seen one before. But the King's son began speaking so kindly to her, telling her how her singing had entered into his heart, so that he could have no peace until he had seen her himself, that Rapunzel forgot her terror. When he asked her to take him for her husband, she saw that he was young and beautiful, and she thought to herself, "I certainly like him much better than old mother Gothel."

She put her hand into his hand, and said, "I would willingly go with thee, but I do not know how I shall get out. Each time thou comest, bring a silken rope, and I will make a ladder. When it is quite ready I will use it to get down out of the tower, and thou shalt take me away on thy horse." They agreed that he should come to her every evening, as the old woman only came in the daytime.

Now the witch knew nothing of all this until one day when Rapunzel said to her unwittingly, "Mother Gothel, how is it that you climb up here so slowly, and the King's son is with me in a moment?"

"O wicked child," cried the witch, "what is this I hear! I thought I had hidden thee from all the world, and now thou hast betrayed me!"

In her anger she seized Rapunzel by her beautiful hair, struck her several times with her left hand, and then grasping a pair of shears in her right — snip, snap — she cut, and the beautiful locks lay on the ground. The witch was so hardhearted that she took Rapunzel and put her in a waste and desert place, where the young girl lived in great woe and misery.

On the evening of the same day on which she took Rapunzel

away she went back to the tower and made fast the severed lock of hair to the window hasp.

The King's son came and cried, "Rapunzel, Rapunzel! Let down thy hair."

The witch let down the hair, and the King's son climbed up. But instead of his dearest Rapunzel he found the witch looking at him with her wicked glittering eyes.

"Aha!" cried she, mocking him, "you came for your darling, but the sweet bird sits no longer in the nest. She sings no more. The cat has got her, and will scratch out your eyes as well! Rapunzel is lost to you; you will see her no more."

The King's son was beside himself with grief, and in his agony he sprang from the tower. He escaped with his life, but the thorns on which he fell put out his eyes. He wandered blindly through the wood, eating nothing but roots and berries, and doing nothing but lamenting and weeping for the loss of his dearest wife.

He wandered for several years in this misery until one day he came to the desert place where Rapunzel lived with her twin children. She had borne him a boy and a girl. At first he heard a voice that he thought he knew, and when he reached the place from which it seemed to come Rapunzel recognized him, and fell on his neck and wept. When her tears touched his eyes they became clear again, and he could see as well as ever.

He took her and the children to his kingdom, where he was received with great joy, and there they lived long and happily.

Red Riding Hood

ONCE upon a time there was a sweet little maiden who was loved by all who knew her. She was especially dear to her grandmother, who did not know how to make enough of the child. Once she gave her a little red velvet cloak. It was so becoming and she liked it so much that she would never wear anything else, and so she got the name Red Riding Hood.

One day her mother said to her, "Come here, Red Riding Hood! Take this cake and bottle of wine to Grandmother. She is weak and ill, and they will do her good. Go quickly, before it gets hot. Don't loiter by the way, or run, or you will fall down and break the bottle, and there will be no wine for Grandmother. When you get there, don't forget to say 'Good morning' prettily, without staring about you."

"I will do just as you tell me," Red Riding Hood promised her mother.

Her grandmother lived away in the wood, a good half hour from the village. When she got to the wood she met a wolf. Red Riding Hood did not know what a wicked animal he was, so she was not a bit afraid of him.

"Good morning, Red Riding Hood," he said.

"Good morning, wolf!" she answered.

"Where do you go so early, Red Riding Hood?"

"To Grandmother's."

"What have you got in your basket?"

"Cake and wine. We baked yesterday, so I'm taking a cake to Grandmother. She wants something to make her well."

"Where does your grandmother live, Red Riding Hood?"

"A good quarter of an hour farther into the wood. Her house stands under three big oak trees, near a hedge of nut trees which you must know," said Red Riding Hood.

The wolf thought, "This tender little creature will be a plump morsel! She will be nicer than the old woman. I must be cunning and snap them both up."

He walked along with Red Riding Hood for a while. Then he said, "Look at the pretty flowers, Red Riding Hood. Why don't you look about you? I don't believe you even hear the birds sing. You are as solemn as if you were going to school. Everything else is so gay out here in the woods."

Red Riding Hood raised her eyes, and when she saw the sunlight dancing through the trees, and all the bright flowers, she thought, "I'm sure Grandmother would be pleased if I took her a bunch of fresh flowers. It is still quite early. I shall have plenty of time to pick them."

So she left the path and wandered off among the trees to pick the flowers. Each time she picked one, she saw another prettier farther on. So she went deeper and deeper into the forest.

In the meantime the wolf went straight off to the grandmother's cottage and knocked at the door.

"Who is there?"

"Red Riding Hood, bringing you a cake and some wine. Open the door!"

"Lift the latch," called out the old woman. "I am too weak to get up."

The wolf lifted the latch and the door sprang open. He went straight in and up to the bed without saying a word, and ate up the poor old woman. Then he put on her nightdress and nightcap, got into bed, and drew the curtains.

Red Riding Hood ran about picking flowers till she could carry no more, and then she remembered her grandmother again. She was astonished when she got to the house to find the door open, and when she entered the room everything seemed so strange.

She felt quite frightened but she did not know why. "Generally I like coming to see Grandmother so much," she thought. "Good morning, Grandmother," she cried. But she received no answer.

Then she went up to the bed and drew the curtain back. There lay her grandmother. She had drawn her cap down over her face and she looked very odd.

"Oh, Grandmother, what big ears you have," said little Red Riding Hood.

"The better to hear you with, my dear."

"Grandmother, what big eyes you have."

"The better to see you with, my dear."

"What big hands you have, Grandmother."

"The better to catch hold of you with, my dear."

"But Grandmother, what big teeth you have."

"The better to eat you up with, my dear."

Hardly had the wolf said this than he made a spring out of bed and swallowed poor little Red Riding Hood. When the wolf had satisfied himself he went back to bed, and was soon snoring loudly.

A huntsman went past the house and thought, "How loudly the old lady is snoring. I must see if there is anything the matter with her."

So he went into the house and up to the bed, where he found the wolf fast asleep. "Do I find you here, you old sinner!" he said. "Long enough have I sought you!"

He raised his gun to shoot, when it occurred to him that perhaps the wolf had eaten up the old lady, and that she might still be saved. So he took a knife and began cutting open the sleeping wolf. At the first cut he saw the little red cloak, and after a few more slashes, the little girl sprang out and cried, "Oh, how frightened I was! It was so dark inside the wolf." Next the old grandmother came out, alive but hardly able to breathe.

Red Riding Hood brought some big stones with which they filled the wolf. When he woke up and tried to spring away, the stones dragged him back, and he fell down dead.

They were all quite happy now. The huntsman skinned the wolf and took the skin home. The grandmother ate the cake and drank the wine which Red Riding Hood had brought, and she soon felt quite strong. Red Riding Hood thought to herself, "I will never again wander off into the forest as long as I live, when my mother forbids it."

Hansel and Gretel

CLOSE to a large forest there lived a woodcutter with his wife and his two children. The boy was called Hansel and the girl Gretel. They were always very poor and had very little to live on. At one time when there was famine in the land, the woodcutter could no longer procure his daily bread.

One night when he lay in bed worrying over his troubles, he sighed and said to his wife, "What is to become of us? How are we to feed our poor children when we have nothing for ourselves?"

"I'll tell you what, husband," answered the woman. "Tomorrow morning we will take the children out quite early into the thickest part of the forest. We will light a fire and give each of them a piece of bread. Then we will go to our work and leave them alone. They won't be able to find their way back, and so we shall be rid of them."

"Nay, wife," said the man, "we won't do that. I could never find it in my heart to leave my children alone in the forest. Wild animals would soon tear them to pieces."

"What a fool you are!" she said. "Then we must all four die of hunger. You may as well plane the boards for our coffins at once."

She gave him no peace till he consented. "But I grieve over the poor children all the same," said the man.

The two children could not go to sleep for hunger either, and they heard what their stepmother said to their father.

Gretel wept bitterly and said, "All is over with us now."

"Be quiet, Gretel," said Hansel. "Don't cry! I will find some way out of it."

When the old people had gone to sleep, he got up, put on his little coat, opened the door, and slipped out. The moon was shining brightly and the white pebbles round the house shone like newly minted coins. Hansel stooped down and put as many in his pockets as they would hold.

Then he went back to Gretel and said, "Take comfort, little sister, and go to sleep. God won't forsake us." And then he went to bed again.

At daybreak, before the sun had risen, the woman came and said, "Get up, you lazybones! We are going into the forest to fetch wood."

Then she gave them each a piece of bread and said, "Here is something for your dinner, but don't eat it before then, for you'll get no more."

Gretel put the bread under her apron, for Hansel had the stones in his pockets, and they all started for the forest. When they had gone a little way, Hansel stopped and looked back at the cottage. He did the same thing again and again.

His father said, "Hansel, what are you stopping to look back at? Take care and put your best foot foremost."

"Oh, Father," said Hansel, "I am looking at my white cat. It is sitting on the roof, wanting to say good-bye to me."

"Little fool, that's no cat! It's the morning sun shining on the chimney," said the mother.

But Hansel had not been looking at the cat. He had dropped a pebble on the ground each time he stopped.

When they reached the middle of the forest, their father said, "Now, children, pick up some wood. I want to make a fire to warm you."

Hansel and Gretel gathered the twigs together and soon made a huge pile. The pile was lit, and when it blazed up the woman said, "Now lie down by the fire and rest yourselves while we go and cut wood. When we have finished we will come back to fetch you."

Hansel and Gretel sat by the fire, and when dinnertime came they each ate their little bit of bread. They thought their father was still quite near because they could hear the sound of an axe. It was no axe, however, but a branch which the man had tied to a dead tree, and the branch blew backwards and forwards against it. They sat there so long a time that they got tired. Their eyes began to close and they were soon fast asleep.

When they woke it was dark night. Gretel began to cry, "How shall we ever get out of the wood?"

But Hansel comforted her and said, "Wait a little while till the moon rises, and then we will find our way."

When the full moon rose, Hansel took his little sister's hand and they walked on, guided by the pebbles, which glittered like newly

coined money. They walked the whole night, and at daybreak they found themselves back at their father's cottage.

They knocked at the door, and when the woman opened it and saw Hansel and Gretel she said, "You bad children, why did you sleep so long in the wood? We thought you did not mean to come back anymore."

But their father was delighted, for it had bothered him deeply to leave them behind alone.

Not long afterwards they were again in great poverty, and the children heard the woman at night in bed say to their father, "We have eaten up everything again but half a loaf, and then we will be at the end of everything. The children must go away! We will take them farther into the forest so that they won't be able to find their way back. There is nothing else to be done."

The man took this to heart and said, "We had better share our last crust with the children."

But the woman would not listen to a word he said. She only scolded and reproached him. Anyone who once says A must also say B, and as the father had given in the first time he had to do so the second. The children were wide awake and heard what was said.

When the old people went to sleep Hansel again got up, meaning to go out and get more pebbles. But the woman had locked the door and he couldn't get out. He consoled his little sister and said, "Don't cry, Gretel. Go to sleep. God will help us."

In the early morning the woman made the children get up. She gave them each a piece of bread, smaller than the last. On the way to the forest Hansel crumbled it up in his pocket, and stopped every now and then to throw a crumb onto the ground.

"Hansel, what are you stopping to look about you for?" asked his father.

"I am looking at my dove which is sitting on the roof and wants to say good-bye to me," answered Hansel.

"Little fool," said the woman, "that is no dove! It is the morning sun shining on the chimney."

Nevertheless, Hansel dropped the crumbs from time to time on the ground. The woman led the children far into the forest, where they had never been before.

Again they made a big fire, and the woman said, "Stay where you are, children, and when you are tired you may go to sleep for a while. We are going farther on to cut wood, and in the evening when we have finished we will come back and fetch you."

At dinnertime Gretel shared her bread with Hansel, for he had crumbled his upon the road. They went to sleep, and the evening passed but no one came to fetch the poor children.

It was quite dark when they woke up, and Hansel cheered his little sister. "Wait a bit, Gretel, till the moon rises, and then we can see the bread crumbs which I scattered to show us the way home."

When the moon rose they started, but they found no bread crumbs, for all the birds in the forest had picked them up and eaten them.

Hansel said to Gretel, "We shall soon find the way." But they could not find it. They walked the whole night and all the next day from morning till night, but they could not get out of the wood.

They were very hungry, for they had nothing to eat but a few berries which they had found. They were so tired that their legs would not carry them any farther, and they lay down under a tree and went to sleep.

When they woke in the morning, it was the third day since they had left their father's cottage. They started to walk again, but they only got deeper and deeper into the wood. If no help came they must perish.

At midday they saw a beautiful snow-white bird sitting on a tree. It sang so beautifully that they stood still to listen to it. When it stopped, it fluttered its wings and flew around them. They followed it till they came to a little cottage and the bird settled down on the roof of it.

When they got quite near, they saw that the little house was made of bread and roofed with cake. The windows were made of transparent sugar.

"Here is something for us," said Hansel. "We will have a good meal. I will have a piece of the roof, Gretel, and you can have a bit of the window. It will be nice and sweet."

Hansel reached up and broke off a piece of the roof to see what it tasted like. Gretel went to the window and nibbled at that. A gentle voice called out from within,

> "Nibbling, nibbling like a mouse,
> Who's nibbling at my little house?"

The children answered,

> "The wind, the wind doth blow
> From heaven to earth below."

And they went on eating without disturbing themselves. Hansel, who found the roof very good, broke off a large piece for himself, and Gretel pushed a whole round pane out of the window and sat down on the ground to enjoy it.

All at once the door opened, and an old, old woman came hobbling out on a crutch. Hansel and Gretel were so frightened that they dropped what they held in their hands.

The old woman only shook her head and said, "Ah, dear children, who brought you here? Come in and stay with me. You will come to no harm."

She took them by the hand and led them into the little house. A nice dinner was set before them: pancakes and sugar, milk, apples, and nuts. After this she showed them two little white beds into which they crept, and they felt as if they were in heaven.

Although the old woman appeared to be so friendly, she was really a wicked old witch who was on the watch for children, and she had built the bread house on purpose to lure them to her. Whenever she could get a child into her clutches she cooked it and ate it, and considered it a grand feast. Witches have red eyes and can't see very far, but they have keen noses like animals and can scent the approach of human beings.

When Hansel and Gretel came near her, she laughed wickedly to herself and said scornfully, "Now that I have them, they shan't escape me."

She got up early in the morning before the children were awake, and when she saw them sleeping, with their beautiful rosy cheeks, she murmured to herself, "They will be dainty morsels."

She seized Hansel with her bony hand and carried him off to a little stable, where she locked him up behind a barred door. He might shriek as loud as he liked, but she took no notice of him.

Then she went to Gretel and shook her till she woke, and cried, "Get up, little lazybones! Fetch some water and cook something nice for your brother. He is in the stable and has to be fattened. When he is nice and fat, I will eat him."

Gretel began to cry bitterly, but it was no use. She had to obey the witch's orders. The best food was cooked for poor Hansel, but Gretel had only the shells of crayfish.

The old woman hobbled to the stable every morning and cried, "Hansel, put your finger out for me to feel how fat you are."

Hansel put out a knucklebone, and the old woman, whose eyes were too dim to see, thought it was his finger. And she was much astonished that he did not get fat.

When four weeks had passed and Hansel still kept thin, she became impatient and could wait no longer.

"Now then, Gretel," she cried, "bustle along and fetch the water. Fat or thin, I will kill Hansel and eat him."

Oh, how his poor little sister grieved! As she carried the water, the tears streamed down her cheeks. "Dear God, help us!" she cried. "If only the wild animals in the forest had eaten us, we should at least have died together."

"You may spare your lamentations! They will do you no good," said the old woman.

Early in the morning Gretel had to go out to fill the kettle with water, and then she had to kindle a fire and hang the kettle over it.

"We will bake first," said the old witch. "I have heated the oven and kneaded the dough."

She pushed poor Gretel towards the oven and said, "Creep in and see if it is properly heated, and then we will put the bread in."

She meant, when Gretel had gone in, to shut the door and roast her, but Gretel saw her intention and said, "I don't know how to get in. How am I to manage it?"

"Stupid goose!" cried the witch. "The opening is big enough. You can see that I could get into it myself."

She hobbled up and stuck her head into the oven. But Gretel gave her a push and sent the witch right in. Then she banged the door and bolted it.

"Oh! oh!" the witch howled horribly. But Gretel ran away and left the wicked witch to perish.

She ran as fast as she could to the stable, and opened the door and cried, "Hansel, we are saved! The old witch is dead."

Hansel sprang out, like a bird from a cage when the door is set open. How delighted they were. They fell upon each other's necks and kissed each other and danced about for joy.

As they had nothing more to fear, they went into the witch's house, and in every corner they found chests full of pearls and precious stones.

"These are better than pebbles," said Hansel, as he filled his pockets.

Gretel said, "I must take something home with me too." And she filled her apron.

"But now we must go," said Hansel. "We must get out of this enchanted wood."

Before they had gone very far, they came to a great piece of water.

"We can't get across it," said Hansel. "I see no stepping-stones and no bridge."

"And there are no boats either," said Gretel, "but there is a duck swimming. It will help us over if we ask it."

So she cried,

> *"Little duck that cries quack, quack,*
> *Here Gretel and here Hansel stand.*
> *Quickly take us on your back,*
> *No path nor bridge is there at hand!"*

The duck came swimming towards them, and Hansel got on its back and told his sister to sit on his knee.

"No," answered Gretel, "it will be too heavy for the duck. It must take us over one after the other."

The good creature did this, and when they had got safely over and walked for a while, the wood seemed to grow more and more familiar to them. At last they saw their father's cottage in the distance. They began to run, and rushed inside, and threw their arms around their father's neck. The man had not had a single happy moment since he deserted his children in the wood, and in the meantime his wife had died.

Gretel shook her apron and scattered the pearls and precious stones all over the floor, and Hansel added handful after handful out of his pockets.

So all their troubles came to an end, and they lived together as happily as could be.

JAMES REEVES

W

The king sent for his wise men all
   To find a rhyme for W;
When they had thought a good long time
But could not think of a single rhyme,
   "I'm sorry," said he, "to trouble you."

MARIA LEACH
The Yellow Ribbon

JOHN loved Jane. They lived next door to each other, and they went to first grade together, and John loved Jane very much. Jane wore a yellow ribbon around her neck every day.

One day John said, "Why do you wear the yellow ribbon?"

"I can't tell," said Jane. But John kept asking, and finally Jane said maybe she'd tell him later.

The next year they were in the second grade. One day John asked again, "Why do you wear the yellow ribbon around your neck?" And Jane said maybe she'd tell him later.

Time went by, and every once in a while John asked Jane why she wore the yellow ribbon, but Jane never told. So time went by.

John and Jane went through high school together. They loved each other very much. On graduation day John asked Jane please to tell him why she always wore the yellow ribbon around her neck. But Jane said there was no point in telling on graduation day, so she didn't tell.

Time went by, and John and Jane became engaged, and finally Jane said maybe she would tell him on their wedding day.

The wedding day came, and John forgot to ask. But the next day John asked Jane why she wore the yellow ribbon. Jane said, "Well, we are happily married, and we love each other, so what difference does it make?" So John let it pass, but he still *did* want to know.

Time went by, and finally on their golden anniversary John asked again. And Jane said, "Since you have waited this long, you can wait a little longer."

Finally Jane was taken very ill, and when she was dying John asked again, between sobs, "*Please* tell me why you wear the yellow ribbon around your neck."

"All right," said Jane, "you can untie it."

So John untied the yellow ribbon, and Jane's head fell off.

ALEXANDER RESNIKOFF

The poem that follows is called "The Diver". On page 449 you'll find another poem with the same title. It's interesting to see how two poets, both writing on the same subject, came up with two such different poems.

The Diver

This time I'll do it! Mommy, look!
I promise I won't be a fool —
I'm going to climb on that diving board
And dive right into the pool!

Look at me, Mom; I'm doing it!
I never have done it before —
I'm climbing those steps to the diving board.
I'll count them: One, two, three, four. . . .

Look, Mom! I'm on the diving board!
This carpet feels terribly rough —
It hurts the tan on the soles of my feet,
But I can take it; I'm tough.

And now I'm jumping up and down
Right by the steps — Mommy, look!
You sure you're looking? Saw me jump?
Now *please,* Mommy, put down that book!

Hey, Mom, I'm going farther now —
It's cold here; I'm starting to shake,
But I go forward, inch by inch —
I hope these boards will not break.

Look at me, Mom! I'm at the end!
I must be a thousand feet high!
Or maybe higher — I'm not sure
I'm looking with only one eye.

I'll say a prayer, I'll take a deep breath,
I'll hold my nose, and I'll plop —
Maybe you should move a little way back —
Those waves might go over the top!

Mom, are you looking? Watch me
I hope that you are prepared —
Look at me, Mommy, here I come
One . . .
Two . . .
Three . . .
. . . .
. . . .
I am scared. . . .

Russell Hoban

A Near Thing for Captain Najork

Illustrated by
Quentin Blake

ONE MORNING after breakfast Tom was fooling around with his chemistry set and he invented anti-sticky.

Then he fooled around with anti-sticky and jam and springs and wheels and connecting-rods and he made a two-seater jam-powered frog.

Tom got into the frog with Aunt Bundlejoy Cosysweet and started it up. The frog hopped over the fence and the next three gardens in one giant hop.

"What makes it go?" asked Aunt Bundlejoy.

"Jam," said Tom. "When the anti-sticky plate hits the sticky it bounces back. The spring keeps it going, the connecting-rods move up and down, the wheels go round and the frog hops."

Tom and Aunt Bundlejoy took the frog out for a spin.

They hopped along the river and they hopped past Aunt Fidget Wonkham-Strong Najork's house.

Captain Najork was in the observatory looking through his telescope at the girls' boarding-school across the river when the frog hopped past.

"Follow that frog!" he shouted to his hired sportsmen as he

leapt into his pedal-powered snake, and away they undulated. Captain Najork had not forgotten the time when Tom had beaten him and his hired sportsmen at womble, muck, and sneedball. "I'd like to try some new games on him," said the Captain. "I'd like to see how good he is at thud, crunch, and Tom-on-the-bottom."

Aunt Fidget Wonkham-Strong Najork came up the observatory stairs singing "Heart of Oak". She had tea and scones for the Captain's elevenses but he was not there.

She looked out of the window and saw that the Captain's snake was gone.

She looked through the telescope and saw the Headmistress of the girls' boarding-school practicing two-handed clean-and-jerks with her barbells. "Aha!" said Aunt Fidget Wonkham-Strong Najork.

She put on her flippers and snorkel, swam the river, and knocked at the girls' boarding-school door.

"Can I help you, madam?" said the commissionaire.

Aunt Fidget Wonkham-Strong Najork knocked him down and went straight to the Headmistress's office.

"Where is the Captain?" she said.

"Of which team?" said the Headmistress. "Hockey, squash, or lacrosse?"

"You know whom I mean," said Aunt Fidget Wonkham-Strong Najork. "Produce him instantly."

"You're dripping on my carpet," said the Headmistress.

"Very well," said Aunt Fidget Wonkham-Strong Najork. "I will arm-wrestle you for Captain Najork. Best out of three."

Meanwhile . . . Tom and Aunt Bundlejoy hopped on in the jam-powered frog.

"We're being followed by a five-seater snake," said Aunt Bundlejoy.

"That must be Captain Najork," said Tom. "Does he want to race?"

"I think he wants to swallow us," said Aunt Bundlejoy. "The snake has got its mouth wide open."

"Bad luck," said Tom. "We're running out of sticky and I've left the jam at home."

"They're bound to have pots of jam at the girls' boarding-school," said Aunt Bundlejoy.

Tom turned the frog around and away they went back up the river with the snake only a few frog-lengths behind.

"You beat us at womble!" shouted the Captain. "You beat us at muck and sneedball! But you won't win this time!"

Tom and Aunt Bundlejoy barely cleared the boarding-school wall with the frog's last hop.

Aunt Bundlejoy knocked on the door.

"Can I help you, madam?" asked the commissionaire.

"Our frog's out of jam," said Aunt Bundlejoy. "Can you lend us a pot?"

"Just a moment, please," said the commissionaire. "I'll have to ask the Headmistress for the keys to the jam locker."

As the commissionaire came into the Headmistress's office he saw the head of Captain Najork's snake at the open window.

"There is a lady at the door who wants a pot of jam and there is a snake at the window, madam," he said.

"I can't be interrupted now," said the Headmistress. "Ask them to wait."

When Aunt Fidget Wonkham-Strong Najork saw the snake she was so cross with the Captain that she flung the Headmistress through the window into the snake's open mouth.

"Oy!" said the Captain. He stepped on the ejector-pedal and the Headmistress shot back through the window and flattened Aunt Fidget Wonkham-Strong Najork. As his wife's feet flew up, Captain Najork recognized her flippers.

"May I have my wife, please?" he said to the commissionaire.

The commissionaire handed Aunt Fidget Wonkham-Strong Najork out to the Captain and he put her on the sofa in the snake's lounge.

"I think we had better go home now," he said to the hired sportsmen, and they undulated back over the wall and away.

Now that she'd seen Captain Najork the Headmistress had taken a fancy to him.

"After them!" she shouted to Tom and Aunt Bundlejoy. "We haven't finished arm-wrestling!"

"We're out of jam," said Tom.

A pot of jam was quickly fetched and they hopped off after the snake.

They caught up with it at the landing stage by Aunt Fidget Wonkham-Strong Najork's house.

As the Captain was helping his wife ashore the Headmistress leapt out of the frog and plucked at Aunt Fidget Wonkham-Strong Najork's sleeve.

"That's quite all right," said Aunt Fidget Wonkham-Strong Najork. "No explanations are necessary. The Captain has convinced me that my suspicions were unfounded."

"Never mind that," said the Headmistress. "You said best out of three and we haven't even finished one."

"Very well then," said Aunt Fidget Wonkham-Strong Najork, and they arm-wrestled for the Captain on the landing stage.

Aunt Fidget Wonkham-Strong Najork won twice in a row and the Headmistress wept bitter tears.

"The Captain would have lent such an air to the establishment!" she said.

"Did you want to play some more games?" said Tom to the Captain.

"He can't," said Aunt Fidget Wonkham-Strong Najork. "He's got to have his lunch and he'll be learning off pages of the Nautical Almanac for the rest of the day."

"Eat your swede-and-mutton slump," said Aunt Fidget Wonkham-Strong Najork to the Captain. "And think how lucky you are to be here. That was a near thing for you today."

"Yes, dear," said the Captain. He ate it.

LAURA E. RICHARDS
Eletelephony

Once there was an elephant,
Who tried to use the telephant —
No! no! I mean an elephone
Who tried to use the telephone —
(Dear me! I am not certain quite
That even now I've got it right.)

Howe'er it was, he got his trunk
Entangled in the telephunk;
The more he tried to get it free,
The louder buzzed the telephee —
(I fear I'd better drop the song
Of elephop and telephong!)

MICHAEL ROSEN
Before I Count Fifteen

If you don't put your shoes on before I count fifteen then we
   won't go to the woods to climb the chestnut one
        But I can't find them
Two
        I can't
They're under the sofa three
        No
        Oh yes
Four five six
        Stop — they've got knots they've got knots
You should untie the laces when you take your shoes off seven
        Will you do one shoe while I do the other then?
Eight but that would be cheating
        Please
All right
        It always . . .
Nine
        It always sticks — I'll use my teeth
Ten
        It won't it won't
        It has — look.

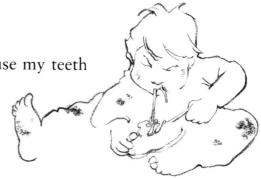

Eleven
         I'm not wearing any socks
Twelve
         Stop counting stop counting. Mum where are my socks
             mum
They're in your shoes. Where you left them.
         I didn't
Thirteen
         Oh they're inside out and upside down and bundled up
Fourteen
         Have you done the knot on the shoe you were . . .
Yes
Put it on the right foot
         But socks don't have right and wrong foot
The shoes silly
Fourteen and a half
         I am I am. Wait.
         Don't go to the woods without me
         Look that's one shoe already
Fourteen and three-quarters
         There
You haven't tied the bows yet
         We could do them on the way there
No we won't fourteen and seven-eighths
         Help me then
         You know I'm not fast at bows
Fourteen and fifteen sixteeeenths
         A single bow is all right isn't it
Fifteen we're off
         See I did it.
         Didn't I?

This Ship

This ship in the dock was at the end of its trip
The man on deck was the captain of the ship
The name of the captain was Old Ben Brown
He played the ukelele with his trousers down.

TED HUGHES

How the Whale Became

NOW GOD had a little back-garden. In this garden he grew carrots, onions, beans, and whatever else he needed for his dinner. It was a fine little garden. The plants were in neat rows, and a tidy fence kept out the animals. God was pleased with it.

One day as he was weeding the carrots, he saw a strange thing between the rows. It was no more than an inch long, and it was black. It was like a black shiny bean. At one end it had a little root going into the ground.

"That's very odd," said God. "I've never seen one of these before. I wonder what it will grow into."

So he left it growing.

Next day as he was gardening, he remembered the little shiny black thing. He went to see how it was getting on. He was surprised. During the night it had doubled its length. It was now two inches long, like a shiny black egg.

Every day God went to look at it, and every day it was bigger. Every morning, in fact, it was just twice as long as it had been the morning before.

When it was six feet long, God said:

"It's getting too big. I must pull it up and cook it."

But he left it a day.

Next day it was twelve feet long and far too big to go into any of God's pans.

God stood scratching his head and looking at it. Already it had crushed most of his carrots out of sight. If it went on growing at this rate, it would soon be pushing his house over.

Suddenly, as he looked at it, it opened an eye and looked at him. God was amazed.

The eye was quite small and round. It was near the thickest end, the farthest from the root. He walked round to the other side, and there was another eye, also looking at him.

"Well!" said God. "And how do you do?"

The round eye blinked, and the smooth glossy skin under it wrinkled slightly, as if the thing were smiling. But there was no mouth, so God wasn't sure.

Next morning God rose early and went out into his garden.

Sure enough, during the night his new black plant with eyes had doubled its length again. It had pushed down part of his fence, so that its head was sticking out into the road, one eye looking up it, and one down. Its side was pressed against the kitchen wall.

God walked round to its front and looked it in the eye.

"You are too big," he said sternly. "Please stop growing before you push my house down."

To his surprise, the plant opened a mouth. A long slit of a mouth, which ran back on either side under the eyes.

"I can't," said the mouth.

God didn't know what to say. At last he said:

"Well then, can you tell me what sort of a thing you are? Do you know?"

"I," said the thing, "am Whale-Wort. You have heard of Egg-Plant, and Buck-Wheat, and Dog-Daisy. Well, I am Whale-Wort."

There was nothing God could do about that.

By next morning, Whale-Wort stretched right across the road, and his side had pushed the kitchen wall into the kitchen. He was now longer and fatter than a bus.

When God saw this, he called the creatures together.

"Here's a strange thing," he said. "Look at it. What are we going to do with it?"

The creatures walked round Whale-Wort, looking at him. His skin was so shiny they could see their faces in it.

"Leave it," suggested Ostrich. "And wait till it dies down."

"But it might go on growing," said God, "until it covers the whole earth. We shall have to live on its back. Think of that."

"I suggest," said Mouse, "that we throw it into the sea."

God thought.

"No," he said at last. "That's too severe. Let's just leave it for a few days."

After three more days, God's house was completely flat, and Whale-Wort was as long as a street.

"Now," said Mouse, "it is too late to throw it into the sea. Whale-Wort is too big to move."

But God fastened long thick ropes round him and called up all the creatures to help haul on the ends.

"Hey!" cried Whale-Wort. "Leave me alone."

"You are going into the sea," cried Mouse. "And it serves you right. Taking up all this space."

"But I'm happy!" cried Whale-Wort again. "I'm happy just lying here. Leave me and let me sleep. I was made just to lie and sleep."

"Into he sea!" cried Mouse.

"No!" cried Whale-Wort.

"Into the sea!" cried all the creatures. And they hauled on the ropes. With a great groan, Whale-Wort's root came out of the ground. He began to thresh and twist, beating down houses and trees with his long root, as the creatures dragged him willy-nilly through the countryside.

At last they got him to the top of a high cliff. With a great shout they rolled him over the edge and into the sea.

"Help! Help!" cried Whale-Wort. "I shall drown! Please let me come back on land where I can sleep."

"Not until you're smaller!" shouted God. "Then you can come back."

"But how am I to get smaller?" wept Whale-Wort, as he rolled to and fro in the sea. "Please show me how to get smaller so that I can live on land."

God bent down from the high cliff and poked Whale-Wort on the top of his head with his finger.

"Ow!" cried Whale-Wort. "What was that for? You've made a hole. The water will come in."

"No it won't," said God. "But some of you will come out. Now just you start blowing some of yourself out through that hole."

Whale-Wort blew, and a high jet of spray shot up out of the hole that God had made.

"Now go on blowing," said God.

Whale-Wort blew and blew. Soon he was quite a bit smaller. As he shrunk, his skin, that had been so tight and glossy, became covered with tiny wrinkles. At last God said to him:

"When you're as small as a cucumber, just give a shout. Then you can come back into my garden. But until then, you shall stay in the sea."

And God walked away with all his creatures, leaving Whale-Wort rolling and blowing in the sea.

Soon Whale-Wort was down to the size of a bus. But blowing was hard work, and by this time he felt like a sleep. He took a deep breath and sank down to the bottom of the sea for a sleep. Above all, he loved to sleep.

When he awoke, he gave a roar of dismay. While he was asleep,

he had grown back to the length of a street and the fatness of a ship with two funnels.

He rose to the surface as fast as he could and began to blow. Soon he was back down to the size of a lorry. But soon, too, he felt like another sleep. He took a deep breath and sank to the bottom.

When he awoke, he was back to the length of a street.

This went on for years. It is still going on.

As fast as Whale-Wort shrinks with blowing, he grows with sleeping. Sometimes, when he is feeling very strong, he gets himself down to the size of a motor-car. But always, before he gets himself down to the size of a cucumber, he remembers how nice it is to sleep. When he wakes, he has grown again.

He longs to come back on land and sleep in the sun, with his root in the earth. But instead of that, he must roll and blow, out on the wild sea. And until he is allowed to come back on land, the creatures call him just Whale.

HUMPHREY HARMAN
Thunder, Elephant and Dorobo

THE PEOPLE of Africa say that if you go to the end of a tree (they mean the top) you find more branches than a man can count, but if you go to the beginning (they mean the bottom) you just find two or three, and that is much easier. Nowadays, they say, we are at the end, and there are so many people and so many things that a man doesn't know where to turn for the clutter the world is in, but that in the beginning things were simpler, and fewer, and a man could see between them. For in the beginning there was only the Earth, and on the Earth were just three important things.

The Earth was much as it is now except that there was nothing on it which had been *made*. Only the things that *grow*. If you go into a corner of a forest very early on a warm misty morning then you might get some idea of what the world was like then. Everything very still and vague round the edges, just growing, quietly.

And in this kind of world were three important things.

First there was Elephant. He was very shiny and black because it was a rather wet world, and he lived in the forest where it is always wet. The mist collected on his cold white tusks and dripped slowly off the tips. Sometimes he trampled slowly through the forest, finding leaves and bark and elephant-grass and wild figs and wild olives to eat, and sometimes he stood, very tall, very secret, just thinking and listening to the deep dignified noises in his stomach.

When he flapped his great ears it was a gesture, no more. There were no flies.

Then there was Thunder. He was much bigger than Elephant. He was black also, but not a shiny black like Elephant. Sometimes there were streaks of white about him, the kind of white that you get on the belly of a fish. And he had no *shape*. Or, rather, one moment he had one shape, and the next another shape. He was always collecting himself in and spreading himself out like a huge jellyfish. And he didn't walk, he rolled along. He was noisy. Sometimes his voice was very far away, and then it was not so much a sound as a shaking, which Elephant could feel coming up from the ground. It made the drops of mist fall off the leaves and patter on his broad back. But sometimes, when Thunder was in his tight shape, his voice cracked high and angrily, and then Elephant would start and snort and wheel away deeper into the forest. Not because he was frightened, but because it hurt his ears.

And last there was Dorobo.

Dorobo is a man, and if you want to see Dorobo you have to go to Africa, because he lives there still. Even then you won't see him very often because he keeps on the edges of places, and most people like to stay in the middle. He lives where the gardens fade out and the forests begin; he lives where the plains stop and the mountains begin, where the grass dries up and the deserts take over. If you want to see him you had better come quickly, because as more and more things are made there is less and less room for Dorobo. He likes to keep himself to himself, and he's almost over the edge.

He is a small man but very stocky. He is the kind of brown that is almost yellow, and he borrows other people's languages to save himself the bother of making up one of his own. He is always looking steadily for small things that are good at hiding, and because of this the skin round his eyes is crinkled. He makes fire by twirling a pointed stick between the palms of his hands, and then he bends his face sideways and just breathes on a pinch of dried leaf powder and it burns. Fire is about the only thing he does make.

He is very simple and wise, and he was wise then too, when the world was beginning, and he shared it with Elephant and Thunder.

Now these three things were young and new in those days, not quite certain of themselves and rather suspicious of the others because they very seldom met. There was so much room.

One day Thunder came to see Elephant, and after he had rumbled and swelled he settled into the shape that soothed him most, and said:

"It's about Dorobo."

Elephant shifted his weight delicately from one foot to the other and said nothing. His ears flapped encouragingly.

"This Dorobo," went on Thunder, "is a strange creature. In fact, so strange that . . . I am leaving the Earth, because I am afraid of him."

Elephant stopped rocking and gurgled with surprise.

"Why?" he asked. "He seems harmless enough to me."

"Listen, Elephant," said Thunder. "When you are sleeping and you get uncomfortable, and need to turn upon your other side, what do you do?"

Elephant pondered this. "I stand up," he said at last. "I stand up, and then I lie down again on my other side."

"Well, Dorobo doesn't," said Thunder. "I know. I've watched him. He rolls over without waking up. It's ugly and very strange, and it makes me uncomfortable. The sky, I think, will be a safer home for me."

And Thunder went there. He went straight up, and he's been

there ever since. Elephant heard his grumbling die away, and he sucked in his cheeks with astonishment. Then he went to find Dorobo.

It took him three days, but he found him at last, asleep beneath a thorn tree with the grass curled beneath him, like the form of a hare. Elephant rolled slowly forward until he stood right over the sleeping man, and Dorobo lay in his gigantic shadow. Elephant watched him and pondered over all that Thunder had said.

Presently Dorobo stirred and shivered in his sleep. Then he sighed and then he rolled over and curled himself tighter. It was precisely as Thunder had described.

Elephant had never noticed it before. It was strange indeed, but not, he thought, dangerous.

Dorobo opened his eyes and stared up at Elephant and smiled.

"You are clever, Elephant," he said. "I didn't hear you come. You move so silently."

Elephant said nothing.

Dorobo sat up and put his arms round his knees.

"I'm glad you came," he went on. "I've been wanting to speak to you. Do you know that Thunder has left us?"

"I had heard that he had gone," replied Elephant.

"Yes," said Dorobo, "I heard him yesterday in the sky. I'm glad and grateful that he's gone, for, to tell you the truth, I was afraid of Thunder. So big, so loud; and you never knew where he might bob up next. Or in what shape. I like things definite."

"He *was* noisy," said Elephant.

"Now you, Elephant, you're quite different. So quiet and kind. Just think, Elephant, now in the whole world there is just you and me, and we shall get on well together because we understand each other."

Then Elephant laughed. He didn't mean to. It rumbled up inside him and took him by surprise. He threw up his trunk and trumpeted. "This ridiculous little creature!"

Then he was ashamed of his bad manners, and he wheeled ponderously and smashed off into the forest, shaking his great head, shaken by enormous bellows of laughter.

"Yes," he shouted back over his shoulder, "we understand . . . ha, ha! . . . understand one another . . . very . . . well!"

He was a good-natured animal, and he didn't want Dorobo to see that he was laughing at him.

But Dorobo had seen, and although the smile stayed on his face, his eyes were very cold and hard and black, like wet pebbles.

Presently he too slipped into the forest, but he walked slowly and looked carefully about him, and after a while he saw the tree he wanted. It was an old white olive tree, a twisted, slow-growing thing, with a very hard tough wood. Dorobo searched that tree, and after a long time he found a branch that was straight enough and he bent and twisted it until it broke off.

Then he skinned it with his teeth and trimmed it and laid it in the shade to dry. Then he found thin, strong vines hanging from tall trees like rope from a mast, and he tore them down and trailed them behind him to the river. There he soaked them and beat them into cords against the river rocks, and plaited them very tightly together. When his cord was long enough he took his wild olive branch, which was dry now, and strung the first bow. And he bent the bow almost double and let it go, and it sang for him. Next he found straight, stiff sticks, and he made a fire and burnt the ends of his sticks a little, and rubbed the charred wood off in the sand. This gave them very hard, sharp points.

Taking his bow and his arrows, he ran to the edge of the desert and found the candelabra tree. The candelabra is a strange tree. It has thick, dull green branches which bear no leaves. And the branches stick up in bunches, a little bent, like the fingers of an old man's hand. And when a branch breaks, and it does very easily, it bleeds a white sticky sap that drips slowly on the sand. You must never shelter beneath a candelabra tree because if the sap drips in your eyes you go blind.

Dorobo broke a branch and dipped his arrows into the thick milky sap, and twisted them like a spoon in syrup. Then he laid each carefully against a stone to dry.

When everything was ready he went in search of Elephant.

Elephant was asleep under a fig tree, but he woke up when he heard Dorobo's footsteps in the undergrowth. There was something in the way Dorobo walked — something secret and unfriendly which Elephant did not like. For the first time in his life he felt afraid. As quickly as he could he got to his feet and made off through the forest. Dorobo grasped his bow and arrows more firmly and began to follow. Elephant trumpeted to the sky for help. But Thunder growled back: "It is useless to ask for help now. I warned you and you did nothing. You can't tell what a man is thinking by what he *says*, you can only tell by what he *does*. It is too late." From that time to this Dorobo has always hunted Elephant, and so have all men that have come after him.

As for Elephant, he has never again laughed at Dorobo, and has kept as far away from him as he can.

IAN SERRAILLIER
Falling Asleep

I can't fall asleep
When Mummy goes to choir. I've said
My prayers, the cat is purring on my bed,
And Daddy's reading downstairs. My head
   Lies pillowed deep,
   But I can't fall asleep,

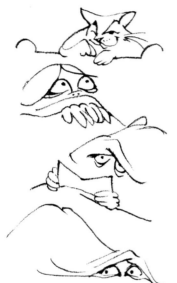

I can't fall asleep
Or settle. Though Mummy has undressed me
And bathed me and bedded me and kissed me,
I wonder — while she's singing — has she missed me?
   Will I never fall asleep?
   The long hours creep,

The long hours creep
So slowly . . . Then at last the front door
Bangs, and I hear her cross the floor.
I call good night and she kisses me once more
   And hugs me. I could weep
   For joy. But I fall asleep.

The Diver

I put on my aqua-lung and plunge,
Exploring, like a ship with a glass keel,
The secrets of the deep. Along my lazy road
On and on I steal —
Over waving bushes which at a touch explode
Into shrimps, then closing rock to the tune of the tide;
Over crabs that vanish in puffs of sand.
Look, a string of pearls bubbling at my side
Breaks in my hand —
Those pearls were my breath! . . . Does that hollow hide
Some old Armada wreck in seaweed furled,
Crusted with barnacles, her cannon rusted,
The great *San Philip?* What bullion in her hold?
Pieces of eight, silver crowns, and bars of solid gold?

I shall never know. Too soon the clasping cold
Fastens on flesh and limb
And pulls me to the surface. Shivering, back I swim
To the beach, the noisy crowds, the ordinary world.

PIERRE GAMARRA
The Bridge on the River Clarinette

Translated from the French by Paulette Henderson

THE INHABITANTS of the little town of Framboisy-sur-Clarinette were worried. The bridge that spanned the River Clarinette was about to collapse. And if the bridge would collapse, the citizens of Framboisy would lose touch with the rest of France. There would be no more trade, no more traffic, no more tourists.

It was therefore necessary to reconstruct the bridge. But Framboisy was poor, and the town council was deeply troubled.

Just the other morning — on Framboisy's large central plaza — Monsieur Leopold, the owner of the Green Swan Inn, greeted Madame Barbette, the grocer. "How are things with you this morning, Madame Barbette?"

"Very bad, Monsieur Leopold. Business is falling off. I did not sell more than one packet of macaroni last week. People just don't have money any more."

Monsieur Leopold sighed. "As for me, I don't have customers either. The tourists don't dare cross the bridge nowadays."

"Did it split last night?"

"Yes, it did; I heard it. It's a disgrace. It could cave in at any moment."

"What's to become of us? What we need is a new bridge."

At that moment Monsieur Leopold and Madame Barbette saw the mayor and the teacher coming out of the town hall.

"Well, well, gentlemen," said Monsieur Leopold, "how are town matters going? Are we going to rebuild the bridge?"

The mayor shook his head with infinite sadness. "The council has examined various bridge plans. But it's an outrageously expensive undertaking. We'll never be able to pay for it."

"Nevertheless, you must make a decision," insisted Madame Barbette, nearly stabbing the mayor with her long, pointed nose. "Without a bridge we're ruined. No one dares to venture across our dilapidated old bridge."

The teacher shaded his eyes and gazed in the direction of the bridge. "Someone is coming!" he called.

"A stranger! Impossible! He wasn't afraid to cross," cried Monsieur Leopold.

"Amazing!" agreed the teacher. "But what an odd sort of person, all dressed in red and black and hopping from side to side. Look at his strange, uncanny smile and the glint in his eyes."

The stranger approached the group and bowed to each of the citizens with great respect. His eyes glowed like deep red rubies. "I am very honoured," he said, "to be visiting the distinguished inhabitants of Framboisy-sur-Clarinette."

"Monsieur is travelling?" the innkeeper asked politely.

"I'm going about the land on business."

"Monsieur is a businessman, then?" queried the teacher.

"Yes, I buy and I sell."

"And what is it that you sell?"

"Anything and everything."

"Anything and everything?"

"Yes, anything at all. Sausages, cars, houses, shirts, bridges. . . ."

The mayor stepped forward. "Did you say bridges? You sell bridges?"

"But of course. Bridges. All sorts of bridges. Big ones, small ones, medium-sized ones. Made of wood, iron, even concrete."

The mayor scratched his head. "It just so happens that, at this time, we are in need of a bridge. A solid bridge with two or three arches."

"Easy!" said the stranger with a soft little laugh.

"And what is the price of a bridge?" demanded Madame Barbette defiantly.

"Nothing at all."

The four inhabitants of Framboisy jumped for joy, but the teacher said, "That can't be true. If you build us a new bridge, certainly you will ask us for something in exchange."

"Almost nothing," said the stranger.

"What would you ask of us?"

"Your words."

To the astonishment of his audience, the stranger explained, "You give me your words, and I will build you a beautiful bridge in five seconds. Note that I am not asking for *all* your words; I will leave you a few for your daily needs — drink, eat, sleep, bread, butter, coffee. . . ."

"I don't understand," murmured the teacher. "What are you going to do with our words?"

"That's *my* business," said the stranger. "Promise that you will give me your words, and I will build you a bridge — a magnificent concrete and steel bridge, guaranteed for ten centuries!"

"It's a bad joke," muttered the mayor. "And furthermore, if you take our words, we shall find it very difficult to converse."

"No, no, no. I will leave you enough to satisfy you. Do you really have to talk so much? I'll leave you the most important words. And you shall have an extraordinary bridge in five seconds."

"So you're a magician, then?" asked the innkeeper.

"I have a very advanced technique at my disposal," the stranger replied modestly.

"We could at least give it a try," said Monsieur Leopold.

"All right," said Madame Barbette. "Let him have our words, and we shall have our bridge."

"I object!" cried the teacher. "We should never give up our words. At any rate, it's a crazy joke. Do you really think that a bridge can be built in five seconds?"

"Let us try, anyway," said the innkeeper.

"You agree, then?" concluded the stranger with a somewhat malicious swiftness. "I leave you a few words — as I said before: bread, milk, eat, drink, sleep, house, chair — and I build you an extraordinary bridge?"

"Agreed," said the mayor, the innkeeper, and the grocer.

The teacher shook his head in refusal. Too late. The stranger was already turning towards the dilapidated bridge, pointing his index finger. And all of a sudden there arose a beautiful three-arched bridge, silhouetted against the sky.

The mayor nudged the innkeeper and said, "Bread, butter, eat, drink."

The innkeeper looked at him and replied, "Drink, sleep, house, chair."

The mayor looked perplexed. "Bread, butter, eat, drink," he repeated.

"Chair, house, sleep, bread," replied the innkeeper.

Madame Barbette wanted to join in the conversation. "Coffee, chair, eat, house," she said in her sharp, shrill voice.

The stranger smiled contentedly.

"It's a disgrace!" the teacher cried out suddenly. "It's a scandal.

The man has robbed you. He has taken your words. You can't understand each other any more."

The stranger eyed the teacher. "You have no right to speak," he said harshly. "I have the mayor's word, and he ruled for the entire community. Keep your silence or I'll destroy the bridge."

"I object!" cried the teacher. "I'm the one who teaches language here. I haven't accepted your contract. You must return the words."

"Drink, bread, eat, milk," babbled the mayor, attempting to participate in the debate.

"Bread, bread, bread, chair, chair, chair," chanted Madame Barbette.

The stranger let out a long sarcastic laugh that echoed through the streets of the small town.

"Never will I return the words!"

The teacher of Framboisy-sur-Clarinette awakened. He had fallen asleep on a chaise longue in his garden. A short distance away, on the edge of the River Clarinette, children were shouting at play. Cars and lorries were travelling across the old bridge. It was a beautiful warm day. It was summertime. The teacher wiped his brow. It had all been a bad dream. The bridge was still solid. People still had their words, a great multitude of words to describe the sky, the earth, children, joy, and the silence of a calm, summer day. Plenty of words, plenty of words.

HANS CHRISTIAN ANDERSEN

I once visited Copenhagen, Denmark's capital and its largest city. There were two places I wanted most to see. The first was the Tivoli pleasure gardens, where everybody goes to eat, to listen to music, to have fun, and just to feel alive and happy. The other place was a rock jutting out into the harbour. On this rock is a statue of the Little Mermaid looking out to sea. She is also to be found in a story of that name, written by Denmark's famous writer of fairy tales, Hans Christian Andersen. I was not surprised to find the Little Mermaid holding fresh flowers in her arms. But I was ashamed I hadn't brought any.

Andersen wrote about himself: "My life is a beautiful fairy tale, rich and happy". This was not entirely true. Andersen throughout his life — he was born in 1805 and died seventy years later — was often ill, fearful, and unhappy. But it was partly true.

He was born in a poor neighbourhood in the town of Odense — you can visit the house today, and thousands of people, especially children, do. His father was a shoemaker whose mind, shortly before he died, was not quite right. His grandfather was really a madman. To feed the family his mother took in washing. Hans himself was awkward, lanky, big-nosed, with a thin, high voice. And yet this ugly duckling (for that famous story, which you can now read, is really about him) grew up to be a kind of swan — one of the most famous and beloved men of his time.

Of certain fairy tales he said: "They become better as they grow older". And this was true of his own life. When he was still a gawky, ugly, poor boy a fortune-teller foretold his future in words that sounded crazy at the time: "He will be a wild, high-flying bird and one day all Odense will be lit up for him." And it came true, even to the fireworks in Odense celebrating his sixty-second birthday.

Not all of his fairy tales, however, end happily. Nor, as I said, was he himself an entirely happy man. He was hungry for fame, and he did become famous. But he was also a nervous man, afraid of accidents, robbery, murder. If you visit the Hans Christian Andersen museum in Odense, you can see a thick rope that he always carried with him on his travels to help him escape from hotel fires. Though he once hoped that Jenny Lind, the great Swedish singer, would become his wife, he never married. His children were born only in his mind.

Everybody wanted to meet the famous teller of tales, but often they found his behaviour odd. He was once a guest in the home of the great novelist Charles Dickens. After he left, Dickens put up a note on the dressing table Andersen had used: "Hans Andersen stayed in this room for five weeks which seemed to the family AGES!"

A strange genius was Hans Christian Andersen. Perhaps inside himself he was always lonely. That may be why in his stories he makes imaginary friends out of darning needles, toys, flowers, animals, china ornaments, snowmen. They all come alive. In his tales not only people but the whole world talks, moves, dances, makes jokes, suffers, rejoices.

Once, talking to a musician friend, he told him how to compose the funeral march that would one day be played at his funeral. He said, "Most of the people who walk after me will be children. So make the beat keep time with little steps."

Here are two of his best stories, translated from the Danish.

The Emperor's New Clothes

MANY years ago there was an emperor who was so excessively fond of new clothes that he spent all his money on them. He cared nothing about his soldiers, nor for the theatre, nor for driving in the woods except for the sake of showing off his new clothes. He had a costume for every hour in the day. Instead of saying as one does about any other king or emperor, "He is in his council chamber," the people here always said, "The Emperor is in his dressing room."

Life was very gay in the great town where he lived. Hosts of strangers came to visit it every day, and among them one day were two swindlers. They gave themselves out as weavers and said that they knew how to weave the most beautiful fabrics imaginable. Not only were the colours and patterns unusually fine, but the clothes that were made of this cloth had the peculiar quality of becoming invisible to every person who was not fit for the office he held, or who was impossibly dull.

"Those must be splendid clothes," thought the Emperor. "By wearing them I should be able to discover which men in my kingdom are unfitted for their posts. I shall distinguish the wise men from the fools. Yes, I certainly must order some of that stuff to be woven for me."

The Emperor paid the two swindlers a lot of money in advance, so that they might begin their work at once.

They did put up two looms and pretended to weave, but they had nothing whatever upon their shuttles. At the outset they asked for a quantity of the finest silk and the purest gold thread, all of which they put into their own bags while they worked away at the empty looms far into the night.

"I should like to know how those weavers are getting on with their cloth," thought the Emperor, but he felt a little queer when he reflected that anyone who was stupid or unfit for his post would not be able to see it. He certainly thought that he need have no fears for himself, but still he thought he would send somebody else first to see how it was getting on. Everybody in the town knew what wonderful power the stuff possessed, and everyone was anxious to see how stupid his neighbour was.

"I will send my faithful old minister to the weavers," thought the Emperor. "He will be best able to see how the stuff looks, for he is a clever man and no one fulfills his duties better than he does."

So the good old minister went into the room where the two swindlers sat working at the empty loom.

"Heaven help us," thought the old minister, opening his eyes very wide. "Why, I can't see a thing!" But he took care not to say so.

Both the swindlers begged him to be good enough to step a little nearer, and asked if he did not think it a good pattern and beautiful colouring. They pointed to the empty loom. The poor old minister stared as hard as he could, but he could not see anything, for of course there was nothing to see.

"Good heavens," thought he. "Is it possible that I am a fool? I have never thought so, and nobody must know it. Am I not fit for my post? It will never do to say that I cannot see the stuff."

"Well, sir, you don't say anything about the stuff," said the one who was pretending to weave.

"Oh, it is beautiful — quite charming," said the minister, looking through his spectacles. "Such a pattern and such colours! I will certainly tell the Emperor that the stuff pleases me very much."

"We are delighted to hear you say so," said the swindlers, and then they named all the colours and described the peculiar pattern. The old minister paid great attention to what they said, so as to be able to repeat it when he got home to the Emperor.

Then the swindlers went on to demand more money, more silk, and more gold, to be able to proceed with the weaving. But they put it all into their own pockets. Not a single strand was ever put into the loom, but they went on as before, weaving at the empty loom.

The Emperor soon sent another faithful official to see how the stuff was getting on and if it would soon be ready. The same thing happened to him as to the minister. He looked and looked, but as there was only the empty loom, he could see nothing at all.

"Is not this a beautiful piece of stuff?" said both the swindlers, showing and explaining the beautiful pattern and colours which were not there to be seen.

"I know I am no fool," thought the man, "so it must be that I am unfit for my good post. It is very strange, though. However, one must not let it appear." So he praised the stuff he did not see, and assured them of his delight in the beautiful colours and the originality of the design.

"It is absolutely charming," he said to the Emperor. Everybody in the town was talking about this splendid stuff.

Now the Emperor thought he would like to see it while it was still on the loom. So, accompanied by a number of selected courtiers, among whom were the two faithful officials who had already seen the imaginary stuff, he went to visit the crafty impostors, who were working away as hard as ever they could at the empty loom.

"It is magnificent," said both the honest officials. "Only see, Your Majesty, what a design! What colours!" And they pointed to the empty loom, for they each thought no doubt the others could see the stuff.

"What?" thought the Emperor. "I see nothing at all. This is terrible! Am I a fool? Am I not fit to be Emperor? Why, nothing worse could happen to me!"

"Oh, it is beautiful," said the Emperor. "It has my highest approval." And he nodded his satisfaction as he gazed at the empty loom. Nothing would induce him to say that he could not see anything.

The whole suite gazed and gazed, but saw nothing more than all the others. However, they all exclaimed with His Majesty, "It is very beautiful." And they advised him to wear a suit made of this wonderful cloth on the occasion of a great procession which was just about to take place. "Magnificent! Gorgeous! Excellent!" went from mouth to mouth. They were all equally delighted with it. The Emperor gave each of the rogues an order of knighthood to be worn in their buttonholes and the title of "Gentleman Weaver".

The swindlers sat up the whole night before the day on which the procession was to take place, burning sixteen candles, so that people might see how anxious they were to get the Emperor's new clothes ready. They pretended to take the stuff off the loom. They cut it out in the air with a huge pair of scissors, and they stitched away with needles without any thread in them.

At last they said, "Now the Emperor's new clothes are ready."

The Emperor with his grandest courtiers went to them himself, and both swindlers raised one arm in the air, as if they were holding something. They said, "See, these are the trousers. This is the coat. Here is the mantle," and so on. "It is as light as a spider's web. One might think one had nothing on, but that is the very beauty of it."

"Yes," said all the courtiers, but they could not see anything, for there was nothing to see.

"Will Your Imperial Majesty be graciously pleased to take off your clothes?" said the impostors. "Then we may put on the new ones, along here before the great mirror."

The Emperor took off all his clothes, and the impostors pretended to give him one article of dress after the other of the new ones which they had pretended to make. They pretended to fasten something around his waist and to tie on something. This was the train, and the Emperor turned round and round in front of the mirror.

"How well His Majesty looks in the new clothes! How becoming they are!" cried all the people round. "What a design, and what colours! They are most gorgeous robes."

"The canopy is waiting outside which is to be carried over Your Majesty in the procession," said the master of the ceremonies.

"Well, I am quite ready," said the Emperor. "Don't the clothes fit well?" Then he turned round again in front of the mirror, so that he should seem to be looking at his grand things.

The chamberlains who were to carry the train stooped and pretended to lift it from the ground with both hands, and they walked along with their hands in the air. They dared not let it appear that they could not see anything.

Then the Emperor walked along in the procession under the gorgeous canopy, and everybody in the streets and at the windows exclaimed, "How beautiful the Emperor's new clothes are! What a splendid train! And they fit to perfection!" Nobody would let it appear that he could see nothing, for then he would not be fit for his post, or else he was a fool.

None of the Emperor's clothes had been so successful before.

"But he has got nothing on," said a little child.

"Oh, listen to the innocent," said its father. And one person whispered to the other what the child had said. "He has nothing on — a child says he has nothing on!"

"But he has nothing on!" at last cried all the people.

The Emperor writhed, for he knew it was true. But he thought, "The procession must go on now." So he held himself stiffer than ever, and the chamberlains held up the invisible train.

The Ugly Duckling

THE COUNTRY was very lovely just then — it was summer. The wheat was golden and the oats still green. The hay was stacked in the rich low meadows, where the stork marched about on his long red legs, chattering in Egyptian, the language his mother had taught him.

Round about field and meadow lay great woods, in the midst of which were deep lakes. Yes, the country certainly was lovely. In the sunniest spot stood an old mansion surrounded by a deep moat, and great dock leaves grew from the walls of the house right down to the water's edge. Some of them were so tall that a small child could stand upright under them. In among the leaves it was as secluded as in the depths of a forest, and there a duck was sitting on her nest. Her little ducklings were just about to be hatched, but she was quite tired of sitting, for it had lasted such a long time. Moreover, she had very few visitors, as the other ducks liked swimming about in the moat better than waddling up to sit under the dock leaves and gossip with her.

At last one egg after another began to crack. "Cheep, cheep!" they said. All the chicks had come to life and were poking their heads out.

"Quack, quack!" said the duck, and then they all quacked their hardest and looked about them on all sides among the green leaves. Their mother allowed them to look as much as they liked, for green is good for the eyes.

"How big the world is, to be sure!" said all the young ones. They certainly now had ever so much more room to move about than when they were inside their eggshells.

"Do you imagine this is the whole world?" said the mother. "It stretches a long way on the other side of the garden, right into the parson's field, though I have never been as far as that. I suppose you are all here now?" She got up and looked about. "No, I declare I have not got you all yet! The biggest egg is still there. How long is this going to take?" she said, and settled herself on the nest again.

"Well, how are you getting on?" said an old duck who had come to pay her a visit.

"This one egg is taking such a long time!" answered the sitting duck. "The shell will not crack. But now you must look at the others. They are the finest ducklings I have ever seen. They are all exactly like their father, the rascal! — yet he never comes to see me."

"Let me look at the egg which won't crack," said the old duck. "You may be sure that it is a turkey's egg! I was cheated like that once and I had no end of trouble and worry with the creatures, for I may tell you that they are afraid of the water. I simply could not get them into it. I quacked and snapped at them, but it all did no good. Let me see the egg! Yes, it is a turkey's egg. You just leave it alone, and teach the other children to swim."

"I will sit on it a little longer. I have sat so long already that I may as well go on till the Midsummer Fair comes round."

"Please yourself," said the old duck, and away she went.

At last the big egg cracked. "Cheep, cheep!" said the young one and tumbled out. How big and ugly he was! The duck looked at him.

"That is a monstrous big duckling," she said. "None of the others looked like that. Can he be a turkey chick? Well, we shall soon find that out. Into the water he shall go, if I have to kick him in myself."

Next day was gloriously fine, and the sun shone on all the green dock leaves. The mother duck with her whole family went down to the moat.

Splash! into the water she sprang. "Quack, quack," she said, and one duckling plumped in after the other. The water dashed over their heads, but they came up again and floated beautifully. Their legs went of themselves, and they were all there. Even the big ugly grey one swam about with them.

"No, that is no turkey," she said. "See how beautifully he uses his legs and how erect he holds himself. He is my own chick, after all, and not bad looking when you come to look at him properly. Quack, quack! Now come with me and I will take you out into the world and introduce you to the duckyard. But keep close to me all the time so that no one will tread upon you. And beware of the cat!"

Then they went into the duckyard. There was a fearful uproar going on, for two broods were fighting for the head of an eel, and in the end the cat captured it.

"That's how things go in this world," said the mother duck, and she licked her bill, because she had wanted the eel's head herself.

"Now use your legs," said she. "Mind you quack properly, and bend your necks to the old duck over there. She is the grandest of us all. She has Spanish blood in her veins and that accounts for her size. And do you see? She has a red rag round her leg. That is a wonderfully fine thing, and the most extraordinary mark of distinction any duck can have. It shows clearly that she is not to be parted with, and that she is worthy of recognition by both beasts and men! Quack, now! Don't turn your toes in! A well-brought-up duckling keeps his legs wide apart just like father and mother. That's it. Now bend your necks and say quack!"

They did as they were bid, but the other ducks round about

looked at them and said, quite loud, "Just look there! Now we are to have that tribe, just as if there were not enough of us already. And, oh dear, how ugly that duckling is! We won't stand him." And a duck flew at him at once and bit him in the neck.

"Let him be," said the mother. "He is doing no harm."

"Very likely not," said the biter. "But he is so ungainly and queer that he must be whacked."

"Those are handsome children mother has," said the old duck with the rag round her leg. "They are all good-looking except this one, but he is not a good specimen. It's a pity you can't make him over again."

"That can't be done, your grace," said the mother duck. "He is not handsome, but he is a thoroughly good creature, and he swims as beautifully as any of the others. I think I might venture even to add that I think he will improve as he goes on, or perhaps in time he may grow smaller. He was too long in the egg, and so he has not come out with a very good figure." And then she patted his neck and stroked him down. "Besides, he is a drake," said she. "So it does not matter so much. I believe he will be very strong, and I don't doubt but he will make his way in the world."

"The other ducklings are very pretty," said the old duck. "Now make yourselves quite at home, and if you find the head of an eel you may bring it to me."

After that they felt quite at home. But the poor duckling who had been the last to come out of the shell, and who was so ugly, was bitten, pushed about, and made fun of by both the ducks and the hens. "He is too big," they all said. And the turkey cock, who was born with his spurs on and therefore thought himself quite an emperor, puffed himself up like a vessel in full sail, made for him, and gobbled and gobbled till he became quite red in the face. The poor duckling was at his wit's end, and did not know which way to turn. He was in despair because he was so ugly and the butt of the whole duckyard.

So the first day passed, and afterwards matters grew worse and worse. The poor duckling was chased and hustled by all of them. Even his brothers and sisters ill-used him. They were always saying, "If only the cat would get hold of you, you hideous object!" Even his mother said, "I wish to goodness you were miles away." The ducks bit him, the hens pecked him, and the girl who fed them kicked him aside.

Then he ran off and flew right over the hedge, where the little birds flew up into the air in a fright.

"That is because I am so ugly," thought the poor duckling, shutting his eyes, but he ran on all the same. Then he came to a great marsh where the wild ducks lived. He was so tired and miserable that he stayed there the whole night. In the morning the wild ducks flew up to inspect their new comrade.

"What sort of a creature are you?" they inquired, as the duckling turned from side to side and greeted them as well as he could. "You are frightfully ugly," said the wild ducks, "but that does not matter to us, so long as you do not marry into our family." Poor fellow! He had not thought of marriage. All he wanted was permission to lie among the rushes and to drink a little of the marsh water.

He stayed there two whole days. Then two wild geese came, or rather two wild ganders. They were not long out of the shell and therefore rather pert.

"I say, comrade," they said, "you are so ugly that we have taken quite a fancy to you! Will you join us and be a bird of passage? There is another marsh close by, and there are some charming wild geese there. All are sweet young ladies who can say quack! You are ugly enough to make your fortune among them." Just at that moment, bang! bang! was heard up above, and both the wild geese fell dead among the reeds, and the water turned bloodred. Bang! bang! went the guns, and flocks of wild geese flew from the rushes and the shot peppered among them again.

There was a grand shooting party, and the sportsmen lay hidden round the marsh. Some even sat on the branches of the trees which overhung the water. The blue smoke rose like clouds among the dark trees and swept over the pool.

The retrieving dogs wandered about in the swamp — splash! splash! The rushes and reeds bent beneath their tread on all sides. It was terribly alarming to the poor duckling. He twisted his head around to get it under his wing, and just at that moment a frightful big dog appeared close beside him. His tongue hung right out of his mouth and his eyes glared wickedly. He opened his great chasm of a mouth close to the duckling, showed his sharp teeth, and — splash! — went on without touching him.

"Oh, thank Heaven!" sighed the duckling. "I am so ugly that even the dog won't bite me!"

Then he lay quite still while the shots whistled among the bushes, and bang after bang rent the air. It became quiet only late in the day, but even then the poor duckling did not dare to get up. He waited several hours more before he looked about, and then he hurried away from the marsh as fast as he could. He ran across fields and meadows, and there was such a wind that he had hard work to make his way.

Towards night he reached a poor little cottage. It was such a miserable hovel that it could not make up its mind which way even to fall, and so it remained standing. The wind whistled so fiercely around the duckling that he had to sit on his tail to resist it, and it blew harder and ever harder. Then he saw that the door had fallen off one hinge and hung so crookedly that he could creep into the house through the crack, and so he made his way into the room.

An old woman lived here with her cat and her hen. The cat, whom she called "Sonnie", would arch his back, purr, and give off electric sparks if you stroked his fur the wrong way. The hen had quite tiny short legs, and so she was called "Chickie-low-legs". She laid good eggs, and the old woman was as fond of her as if she had been her own child.

In the morning the strange duckling was discovered immediately, and the cat began to purr and the hen to cluck.

"What on earth is that?" said the old woman, looking round, but her sight was not good and she thought the duckling was a fat duck which had escaped. "This is a wonderful find!" said she. "Now I shall have duck's eggs — if only it is not a drake. We must wait and see about that."

So she took the duckling on trial for three weeks, but no eggs made their appearance. The cat was master of this house and the hen its mistress. They always said, "We and the world," for they thought that they represented the half of the world, and that quite the better half.

The duckling thought there might be two opinions on the subject, but the cat would not hear of it.

"Can you lay eggs?" she asked.

"No."

"Have the goodness to hold your tongue then!"

And the cat said, "Can you arch your back, purr, or give off sparks?"

"No."

"Then you had better keep your opinions to yourself when people of sense are speaking!"

The duckling sat in the corner nursing his ill humour. Then he began to think of the fresh air and the sunshine and an uncontrollable longing seized him to float on the water. At last he could not help telling the hen about it.

"What on earth possesses you?" she asked. "You have nothing to do. That is why you get these freaks into your head. Lay some eggs or take to purring, and you will get over it."

"But it is so delicious to float on the water," said the duckling. "It is so delicious to feel it rushing over your head when you dive to the bottom."

"That would be a fine amusement!" said the hen. "I think you have gone mad. Ask the cat about it. He is the wisest creature I know. Ask him if he is fond of floating on the water or diving under it. I say nothing about myself. Ask our mistress herself, the old woman. There is no one in the world cleverer than she is. Do you suppose she has any desire to float on the water or to duck underneath it?"

"You do not understand me," said the duckling.

"Well, if we don't understand you, who should? I suppose you don't consider yourself cleverer than the cat or the old woman, not to mention me! Don't make a fool of yourself, child, and thank your stars for all the good we have done you. Have you not lived in this warm room, and in such society that you might have learnt something? But you are an idiot, and there is no pleasure in associating with you. You may believe me: I mean you well. I tell you home truths, and there is no surer way than that of knowing who are one's friends. You just set about laying some eggs, or learn to purr, or to emit sparks."

"I think I will go out into the wide world," said the duckling.

"Oh, do so by all means," said the hen.

So away went the duckling. He floated on the water and ducked underneath it, but he was looked at askance and was slighted by every living creature for his ugliness. Now autumn came. The leaves in the woods turned yellow and brown. The wind took hold of them, and they danced about. The sky looked very cold and the clouds hung heavy with snow and hail. A raven stood on the fence and croaked "Caw, caw!" from sheer cold. It made one shiver only to think of it. The poor duckling certainly was in a bad case!

One evening, the sun was just setting in wintry splendour when a flock of beautiful large birds appeared out of the bushes. The duckling had never seen anything so beautiful. They were dazzlingly white with long waving necks. They were swans, and uttering a peculiar cry they spread out their magnificent broad wings and flew away from the cold regions to warmer lands and open seas. They mounted so high, so very high, and the ugly little duckling became strangely uneasy. He circled round and round in the water like a wheel, craning his neck up into the air after them. Then he uttered a shriek so piercing and so strange that he was quite frightened by it himself. Oh, he could not forget those beautiful birds, those happy birds. And as soon as they were out of sight, he ducked right down to the bottom, and when he came up again he was quite beside himself. He did not know what the birds were, or whither they flew, but all the same he was more drawn towards them than he had ever been by any creatures before. He did not envy them in the least. How could it occur to him even to wish to be such a marvel of beauty? He would have been thankful if only the ducks would have tolerated him among them — the poor ugly creature.

The winter was so bitterly cold that the duckling was obliged to swim about in the water to keep it from freezing over, but every night the hole in which he swam got smaller and smaller. Then it froze so hard that the surface ice cracked, and the duckling had to use his legs all the time so that the ice should not freeze around him. At last he was so weary that he could move no more, and he was frozen fast into the ice.

Early in the morning a peasant came along and saw him. He went out onto the ice and hammered a hole in it with his heavy wooden shoe, and carried the duckling home to his wife. There he soon revived. The children wanted to play with him, but the duckling thought they were going to ill-use him, and rushed in his fright into the milk pan, and the milk spurted out all over the room. The woman shrieked and threw up her hands. Then he flew into the butter cask, and down into the meal tub and out again. Just imagine what he looked like by this time! The woman screamed and tried to hit him with the tongs. The children tumbled over one another in trying to catch him, and they screamed with laughter. By good luck the door stood open, and the duckling flew out among the bushes and the newly fallen snow. And he lay there thoroughly exhausted.

But it would be too sad to mention all the privation and misery he had to go through during the hard winter. When the sun began to shine warmly again, the duckling was in the marsh, lying among the rushes. The larks were singing and the beautiful spring had come.

Then all at once he raised his wings and they flapped with much greater strength than before and bore him off vigorously. Before he knew where he was, he found himself in a large garden where the apple trees were in full blossom and the air was scented with lilacs, the long branches of which overhung the indented shores of the lake. Oh, the spring freshness was delicious!

Just in front of him he saw three beautiful white swans advancing towards him from a thicket. With rustling feathers they swam

lightly over the water. The duckling recognized the majestic birds, and he was overcome by a strange melancholy.

"I will fly to them, the royal birds, and they will hack me to pieces because I, who am so ugly, venture to approach them. But it won't matter! Better be killed by them than be snapped at by the ducks, pecked by the hens, spurned by the henwife, or suffer so much misery in the winter."

So he flew into the water and swam towards the stately swans. They saw him and darted towards him with ruffled feathers.

"Kill me!" said the poor creature, and he bowed his head towards the water and awaited his death. But what did he see reflected in the transparent water?

He saw below him his own image, but he was no longer a

clumsy dark grey bird, ugly and ungainly. He was himself a swan! It does not matter in the least having been born in a duckyard, if only you come out of a swan's egg!

He felt quite glad of all the misery and tribulation he had gone through, for he was the better able to appreciate his good fortune now and all the beauty which greeted him. The big swans swam round and round him and stroked him with their bills.

Some little children came into the garden with corn and pieces of bread which they threw into the water, and the smallest one cried out, "There is a new one!" The other children shouted with joy, "Yes, a new one has come." And they clapped their hands and danced about, running after their father and mother. They threw the bread into the water, and one and all said, "The new one is the prettiest of them all. He is so young and handsome." And the old swans bent their heads and did homage before him.

He felt quite shy, and hid his head under his wing. He did not know what to think. He was very happy, but not at all proud, for a good heart never becomes proud. He thought of how he had been pursued and scorned, and now he heard them all say that he was the most beautiful of all beautiful birds. The lilacs bent their boughs right down into the water before him, and the bright sun was warm and cheering. He rustled his feathers and raised his slender neck aloft, saying with exultation in his heart, "I never dreamt of so much happiness when I was the Ugly Duckling!"

ELEANOR FARJEON

When Eleanor Farjeon died in 1965 she had written just about as many books as the years she had lived, which were eighty-four. She started to type her stories when she was seven. And — she never went to school, not for one day! But in her father's library there were 8,000 books — that's about 800 feet of books, or almost one-sixth of a mile. They educated her. So did the hundreds of artists, writers, playwrights, and musicians who flowed through her lively home.

She came of an unusual family. Her grandmother, born Dinah Levy, was one of *twenty-six* sisters! Seems impossible, doesn't it? Her mother was the daughter of a famous American actor, Joe Jefferson, who for years played Rip Van Winkle on the stage. Her father was a novelist who knew everybody in the London world of his day. She had three remarkable brothers. I like what one of them, Harry, once said: "I am not a boy. I am a Being."

From age five till she was in her late twenties, Eleanor and Harry played a make-believe game called TAR. The word was made up from the first letters of the two main characters Tessie And Ralph.

Eleanor Farjeon was plain, nearsighted, bookish. She tells us that in her childhood she couldn't remember ever being without a headache or getting one night of restful sleep. Yet she somehow, her friends say, seemed to dance through life, always busy, always entertaining people with numberless cups of tea, always writing stories, plays, verses, nursery rhymes, jokes.

Her best story, I think, is "Elsie Piddock Skips in Her Sleep", but it's just too long to print in this book. I hope you'll come across it if you read her many volumes of fairy tales, folktales, and verse. Some of you may find her a little old-fashioned. But then some of you may like old-fashioned writers. There's room for all kinds of readers and writers.

Can Men Be Such Fools as All That?

I WAS nurse to the little Duke of Chinon, who lived in the great grim castle on the hill above the town where the Ragpicker's Son lived. The little Duke, of course, had everything that the poor boy hadn't: fine clothes to wear, white bread and chicken to eat, and a pedigree spaniel called Hubert for a playfellow.

Except for all these differences, the two boys were as like as two peas; when I took the little Duke walking by the river, and we happened to meet the Ragpicker's Son, you could not have told one from the other, if one hadn't worn satin and the other rags, while one had a dirty face and hands and the other was as clean as a new pin. Everybody remarked on it.

The little Duke used to look longingly at the poor boy, though, for he was allowed to splash about in the water of the river as he pleased; and the water of the Loire is more beautiful to splash about in than any water in France, for it is as clear as honey, and has the brightest gold sand-bed you can imagine; and when you get out of the town, it runs between sandy shores, where green willows grow, and flowers of all sorts. But it was against my orders to let the little Duke play in the water, and I had to obey them, though I was sorry for him; for I knew what boys like.

One day as we were out walking, the Duke's spaniel, Hubert, ran up to the Ragpicker's Son's mongrel, Jacques, and they touched noses and made friends. And the Duke and the poor boy smiled at each other and said, "Hullo!" After that, when we met, the boys always nodded, or winked, or made some sign of friendship; and one day the Ragpicker's Son jerked his thumb at the river, as much as to say, "Come in and play with me!"

The Duke looked at me, and I shook my head, so the Duke shook his. But he was cross with me for the rest of the day.

The next day I missed him, and there was a great hullabaloo all over the castle. I and his guardian and all his attendants went down to the town to find him, and asked everybody we met if they had seen him; and presently we met the Ragpicker, who said, "Yes, I saw him an hour ago, going along the riverbank with my son." And we all ran along the bank, the Ragpicker too, and most of the townsfolk behind us.

A mile along the bank, there they were, the two boys, standing in the middle of the river as bare as when they were born, splashing about and screaming with laughter, and on the shore lay a little heap of clothes, rags and fine linen all thrown down anyhow together. We were all very angry with the boys, and called and shouted to them to come out of the water; and they shouted back that they wouldn't. At last the Ragpicker waded in and fetched them out by the scruffs of their necks. And there they stood before us, naked and grinning and full of fun, and just as the Duke's guardian was going to scold his charge, and the Ragpicker to scold his son, they suddenly found themselves in a pickle! For without their clothes, washed clean by the river, they were so exactly alike, that we didn't know which was which. And the boys saw that we didn't and grinned more than ever.

"Now then, my boy!" said the Ragpicker to one of them. But the boy he spoke to did not answer, for he knew if he talked it would give the game away.

And the Duke's guardian said to the other boy, "Come, monseigneur!" But that boy too shook his head and kept mum.

Then I had a bright idea, and said to the boys, "Put on your clothes!" for I thought that would settle it. But the two boys picked up the clothes as they came: one of them put on the ragged shirt and the satin coat, and the other put on the fine shirt and the ragged coat. So we were no better off than before.

Then the Ragpicker and the Duke's guardian lost their tempers, and raised their sticks and gave each of the boys three strokes, thinking that might help; but all it did was to make them squeal, and when a boy squeals it doesn't matter if he's a Duke or a beggar, the sound is just the same.

"This is dreadful," said the Duke's guardian; "for all we know, we shall get the boys mixed forever, and I shall take the Ragpicker's Son back to the castle, and the Duke will grow up as the Ragpicker's Son. Is there no way of telling which is which? Can we all be such fools as that?"

Just as we were scratching our heads and cudgelling our brains, and wondering what on earth to do next, there came a sound of yelps and barks; and out of the willows ran Jacques and Hubert, who had been off on their own, playing together. They came racing towards us joyously, and straight as a die Jacques jumped up and licked the face of the boy in the satin coat, while Hubert licked the boy in the ragged jacket.

So then there was no doubt about it. We made the boys change their coats, and the Ragpicker marched his son home to bed, and the guardian did the same with the Duke. And that night the Duke and the poor boy had exactly the same supper to go to sleep on; in other words, nothing and plenty of it.

But how had the dogs known in the twink of an eye what we hadn't known at all? Can men be such fools as all that?

---

478   ELEANOR FARJEON

MICHAEL BOND

Mr. and Mrs. Brown met the bear Paddington at a railway station in London, brought him home to keep their children company, and found that their lives would never be the same. The chapter that follows is from Mr. Bond's book *A Bear Called Paddington*.

Paddington Goes Underground

PADDINGTON was very surprised when he woke up the next morning and found himself in bed. He decided it was a nice feeling as he stretched himself and pulled the sheets up round his head with a paw. He reached out with his feet and found a cool spot for his toes. One advantage of being a very small bear in a large bed was that there was so much room.

After a few minutes he poked his head out cautiously and sniffed. There was a lovely smell of something coming under the door. It seemed to be getting nearer and nearer. There were footsteps too, coming up the stairs. As they stopped by his door there was a knock and Mrs. Bird's voice called out, "Are you awake, young Paddington?"

"Only just," called out Paddington, rubbing his eyes.

The door opened. "You've had a good sleep," said Mrs. Bird as she placed a tray on the bed and drew the curtains. "And you're a very privileged person to have breakfast in bed on a *weekday!*"

Paddington eyed the tray hungrily. There was half a grapefruit in a bowl, a plate of bacon and eggs, some toast, and a whole pot of marmalade, not to mention a large cup of tea. "Is all that for me?" he exclaimed.

"If you don't want it I can soon take it away again," said Mrs. Bird.

"Oh, I do," said Paddington, hurriedly. "It's just that I've never seen so much breakfast before."

"Well, you'd better hurry up with it." Mrs. Bird turned in the doorway and looked back. "Because you're going on a shopping expedition this morning with Mrs. Brown and Judy. And all I can say is, thank goodness I'm not going too!" She closed the door.

"Now I wonder what she means by that?" said Paddington. But he didn't worry about it for very long. There was far too much to do. It was the first time he had ever had breakfast in bed and he soon found it wasn't quite so easy as it looked. First of all he had trouble with the grapefruit. Every time he pressed it with his spoon a long stream of juice shot up and hit him in the eye, which was very painful. And all the time he was worried because the bacon and eggs were getting cold. Then there was the question of the marmalade. He wanted to leave room for the marmalade.

In the end he decided it would be much nicer if he mixed everything up on the one plate and sat on the tray to eat it.

"Oh, Paddington," said Judy when she entered the room a few

minutes later and found him perched on the tray, "whatever are you doing now? Do hurry up. We're waiting for you downstairs."

Paddington looked up, an expression of bliss on his face; that part of his face which could be seen behind eggy whiskers and toast crumbs. He tried to say something but all he could manage was a muffled grunting noise which sounded like IMJUSTCOMING all rolled into one.

"Really!" Judy took out her handkerchief and wiped his face. "You're the stickiest bear imaginable. And if you don't hurry up all the nice things will be gone. Mummy's going to buy you a complete new outfit from Barkridges — I heard her say so. Now, comb your fur quickly and come on down."

As she closed the door Paddington looked at the remains of his breakfast. Most of it was gone but there was a large piece of bacon left which it seemed a pity to waste. He decided to put it into his suitcase in case he got hungry later on.

He hurried into the bathroom and rubbed his face over with some warm water. Then he combed his whiskers carefully and a few moments later, not looking perhaps as clean as he had done the evening before, but quite smart, he arrived downstairs.

"I hope you're not wearing that hat," said Mrs. Brown, as she looked down at him.

"Oh, do let him, Mummy," cried Judy. "It's so . . . so unusual."

"It's unusual all right," said Mrs. Brown. "I don't know that I've ever seen anything quite like it before. It's such a funny shape. I don't know what you'd call it."

"It's a bush hat," said Paddington, proudly. "And it saved my life."

"Saved your life?" repeated Mrs. Brown. "Don't be silly. How could a hat save your life?"

Paddington was about to tell her of his adventure in the bath the evening before when he received a nudge from Judy. She shook her head. "Er . . . it's a long story," he said, lamely.

"Then you'd better save it for another time," said Mrs. Brown. "Now come along, both of you."

Paddington picked up his suitcase and followed Mrs. Brown and Judy to the front door. By the door Mrs. Brown paused and sniffed.

"That's very strange," she said. "There seems to be a smell of bacon everywhere this morning. Can *you* smell it, Paddington?"

Paddington started. He put the suitcase guiltily behind himself and sniffed. He had several expressions which he kept for emergencies. There was his thoughtful expression, when he stared into space and rested his chin on a paw. Then there was his innocent one which wasn't really an expression at all. He decided to use this one.

"It's very strong," he said, truthfully, for he was a truthful bear. And then he added, perhaps not quite so truthfully, "I wonder where it's coming from?"

"If I were you," whispered Judy, as they walked along the road towards the tube station, "I should be more careful in future when you pack your suitcase!"

Paddington looked down. A large piece of bacon stuck out of the side of his case and was trailing on the pavement.

"Shoo!" cried Mrs. Brown as a grubby-looking dog came bounding across the road. Paddington waved his suitcase. "Go away, dog," he said, sternly. The dog licked its lips and Paddington glanced anxiously over his shoulder as he hurried on, keeping close behind Mrs. Brown and Judy.

"Oh dear," said Mrs. Brown. "I have a funny feeling about

today. As if *things* are going to happen. Do you ever have that feeling, Paddington?"

Paddington considered for a moment. "Sometimes," he said vaguely as they entered the station.

At first Paddington was a little bit disappointed in the Underground. He liked the noise and the bustle and the smell of warm air which greeted him as they went inside. But he didn't think much of the ticket.

He examined carefully the piece of green cardboard which he held in his paw. "It doesn't seem much to get for fourpence," he said. After all the lovely whirring and clanking noises the ticket machine had made it did seem disappointing. He'd expected much more for fourpence.

"But Paddington," Mrs. Brown sighed, "you only have a ticket so that you can ride on the train. They won't let you on otherwise." She looked and sounded rather flustered. Secretly she was beginning to wish they had waited until later in the day, when it wasn't quite so crowded. There was also the peculiar business of the dogs. Not one, but six dogs of various shapes and sizes had followed them right inside. She had a funny feeling it had something to do with Paddington, but the only time she caught his eye it had such an innocent expression she felt quite upset with herself for having such thoughts.

"I suppose," she said to Paddington, as they stepped on the escalator, "we ought really to carry you. It says you're supposed to carry dogs but it doesn't say anything about bears."

Paddington didn't answer. He was following behind in a dream. Being a very short bear he couldn't easily see over the side, but when he did his eyes nearly popped out with excitement. There were people everywhere. He'd never seen so many. There were people rushing down one side and there were more people rushing up the other. Everyone seemed in a terrible hurry. As he stepped off the escalator he found himself carried away between a man with an umbrella and a lady with a large shopping bag. By the time he managed to push his way free both Mrs. Brown and Judy had completely disappeared.

It was then that he saw a most surprising notice. He blinked at it several times to make sure but each time he opened his eyes it said the same thing: FOLLOW THE AMBER LIGHT TO PADDINGTON.

Paddington decided the Underground was quite the most exciting thing that had ever happened to him. He turned and trotted down the corridor, following the amber lights, until he met another crowd of people who were queueing for the "up" escalator.

"'Ere, 'ere," said the man at the top, as he examined Paddington's ticket. "What's all this? You haven't been anywhere yet?"

"I know," said Paddington, unhappily. "I think I must have made a mistake at the bottom."

The man sniffed suspiciously and called across to an inspector. "There's a young bear 'ere, smelling of bacon. Says he made a mistake at the bottom."

The inspector put his thumbs under his waistcoat. "Escalators is for the benefit and convenience of passengers," he said, sternly. "Not for the likes of young bears to play on. Especially in the rush hour."

"Yes, sir," said Paddington, raising his hat. "But we don't have esca . . . esca . . ."

". . . lators," said the inspector, helpfully.

". . . lators," said Paddington, "in Darkest Peru. I've never been on one before, so it's rather difficult."

"Darkest Peru?" said the inspector, looking most impressed. "Oh, well in that case" — he lifted up the chain which divided the "up" and "down" escalators — "you'd better get back down. But don't let me catch you up to any tricks again."

"Thank you very much," said Paddington gratefully, as he ducked under the chain. "It's very kind of you, I'm sure." He turned to wave good-bye, but before he could raise his hat he found himself being whisked into the depths of the Underground again.

Halfway down he was gazing with interest at the brightly coloured posters on the wall when the man standing behind poked him with his umbrella. "There's someone calling you," he said.

Paddington looked round and was just in time to see Mrs. Brown and Judy pass by on their way up. They waved frantically at him and Mrs. Brown called out "Stop!" several times.

Paddington turned and tried to run up the escalator, but it was going very fast, and with his short legs it was as much as he could do even to stand still. He had his head down and he didn't notice a fat man with a briefcase who was running in the opposite direction until it was too late.

There was a roar of rage from the fat man and he toppled over and grabbed at several other people. Then Paddington felt himself falling. He went bump, bump, bump all the way down before he shot off the end and finally skidded to a stop by the wall.

When he looked round everything seemed very confused. A number of people were gathered round the fat man, who was sitting on the floor rubbing his head. Away in the distance he could see Mrs. Brown and Judy trying to push their way down the "up" escalator. It was while he was watching their efforts that he saw another notice. It was in a brass case at the bottom of the escalator and it said, in big red letters: TO STOP THE ESCALATOR IN CASES OF EMERGENCY PUSH THE BUTTON.

It also said in much smaller letters, "Penalty for Improper

Use — £5." But in his hurry Paddington did not notice this. In any case it seemed to him very much of an emergency. He swung his suitcase through the air and hit the button as hard as he could.

If there had been confusion while the escalator was moving, there was even more when it stopped. Paddington watched with surprise as everyone started running about in different directions shouting at each other. One man even began calling out "Fire!" and somewhere in the distance a bell began to ring.

He was just thinking what a lot of excitement pressing one small button could cause when a heavy hand descended on his shoulder.

"That's him!" someone shouted, pointing an accusing finger. "Saw him do it with me own eyes. As large as life!"

"Hit it with his suitcase," shouted another voice. "Ought not to be allowed!" While from the back of the crowd someone else suggested sending for the police.

Paddington began to feel frightened. He turned and looked up at the owner of the hand.

"Oh," said a stern voice. "It's *you* again. I might have known." The inspector took out a notebook. "Name, please."

"Er . . . Paddington," said Paddington.

"I said what's your name, not where do you want to go," repeated the inspector.

"That's right," said Paddington. "That *is* my name."

"*Paddington!*" said the inspector, unbelievingly. "It can't be. That's the name of a station. I've never heard of a bear called Paddington before."

"It's very unusual," said Paddington. "But it's Paddington Brown, and I live at number thirty-two Windsor Gardens. And I've lost Mrs. Brown and Judy."

"Oh!" The inspector wrote something in his book. "Can I see your ticket?"

"Er . . . I had it," said Paddington. "But I don't seem to anymore."

The inspector began writing again. "Playing on the escalator. Travelling without a ticket. *Stopping* the escalator. All serious offences they are." He looked up. "What have you got to say to that, young feller me lad?"

"Well . . . er . . ." Paddington shifted uneasily and looked down at his paws.

"Have you tried looking inside your hat?" asked the inspector, not unkindly. "People often put their tickets in there."

Paddington jumped with relief. "I knew I had it somewhere," he said, thankfully, as he handed it to the inspector.

The inspector handed it back again quickly. The inside of Paddington's hat was rather sticky.

"I've never known anyone take so long not to get anywhere," he said, looking hard at Paddington. "Do you often travel on the Underground?"

"It's the first time," said Paddington.

"And the last if I have anything to do with it," said Mrs. Brown as she pushed her way through the crowd.

"Is this your bear, Madam?" asked the inspector. "Because if it is, I have to inform you that he's in serious trouble." He began to read from his notebook. "As far as I can see he's broken two important regulations — probably more. I shall have to give him into custody."

"Oh dear." Mrs. Brown clutched at Judy for support. "Do you *have* to? He's only small and it's his first time out in London. I'm sure he won't do it again."

"Ignorance of the law is no excuse," said the inspector, ominously. "Not in court! Persons are expected to abide by the regulations. It says so."

"In court!" Mrs. Brown passed a hand nervously over her forehead. The word *court* always upset her. She had visions of Paddington being taken away in handcuffs and being cross-examined and all sorts of awful things.

Judy took hold of Paddington's paw and squeezed it reassuringly. Paddington looked up gratefully. He wasn't at all sure what they were talking about, but none of it sounded very nice.

"Did you say *persons* are expected to abide by the regulations?" Judy asked, firmly.

"That's right," began the inspector. "And I have my duty to do the same as everyone else."

"But it doesn't say anything about bears?" asked Judy, innocently.

"Well." The inspector scratched his head. "Not in so many words." He looked down at Judy, then at Paddington, and then all around. The escalator had started up again and the crowd of sightseers had disappeared.

"It's all highly irregular," he said. "But . . ."

"Oh, thank you," said Judy. "I think you're the kindest man I've ever met! Don't *you* think so, Paddington?" Paddington nodded his head vigorously and the inspector blushed.

"I shall always travel on this Underground in future," said Paddington, politely. "I'm sure it's the nicest in all London."

The inspector opened his mouth and seemed about to say something, but he closed it again.

"Come along, children," said Mrs. Brown, hastily. "If we don't hurry up we shall never get our shopping done."

From somewhere up above came the sound of some dogs barking. The inspector sighed. "I can't understand it," he said. "This used to be such a well-run, respectable station. Now look at it!"

He stared after the retreating figures of Mrs. Brown and Judy with Paddington bringing up the rear and then he rubbed his eyes. "That's funny," he said, more to himself. "I must be seeing things. I could have sworn that bear had some bacon sticking out of his case!" He shrugged his shoulders. There were more important things to worry about. Judging by the noise coming from the top of the escalator there was some sort of dogfight going on. It needed investigating.

BEVERLY CLEARY

Beverly Cleary's husband once said to her, "Why don't you write a book?" She answered, "Because we never have any sharp pencils." Next day Mr. Cleary brought home a pencil sharpener.

Without that pencil sharpener we might never have had all the Cleary books about Henry Huggins and his dog Ribsy, about Beezus and her kid sister Ramona, about Ellen Tebbits and her woollen underwear.

When Mrs. Cleary was eight she wondered why she couldn't find more books that would make her laugh. When she grew up, she wrote lots of them, which is a good thing, because really funny stories are rare. As one of her young fans told her, "I'm glad somebody can still write funny stories."

Ramona is my favourite Cleary character. She isn't well behaved or charming but she's real. In this story she's only five, but I understand she's popular even with college students. I still laugh every time I read about Miss Binney and "Sit here for the present".

In chapter one of *Ramona the Pest,* Ramona is looking forward to kindergarten and her first day at school. On the way there with her mother they meet Mrs. Kemp with her son Howie, also on the way to school. Ramona doesn't like Howie much. At last they reach school and Ramona leads her mother into the kindergarten.

Ramona's Great Day

ONCE inside she stayed close to her. Everything was so strange, and there was so much to see: the little tables and chairs; the row of cupboards, each with a different picture on the door; the play stove; and the wooden blocks big enough to stand on.

The teacher, who was new to Glenwood School, turned out to be so young and pretty she could not have been a grown-up very long. It was rumoured she had never taught school before. "Hello, Ramona. My name is Miss Binney," she said, speaking each syllable distinctly as she pinned Ramona's name to her dress. "I am so glad you have come to kindergarten." Then she took Ramona by the hand and led her to one of the little tables and chairs. "Sit here for the present," she said with a smile.

A present! thought Ramona, and knew at once she was going to like Miss Binney.

"Good-bye, Ramona," said Mrs. Quimby. "Be a good girl."

As she watched her mother walk out the door, Ramona decided school was going to be even better than she had hoped. Nobody had told her she was going to get a present the very first day. What kind of present could it be, she wondered, trying to remember if Beezus had ever been given a present by her teacher.

Ramona listened carefully while Miss Binney showed Howie to a table, but all her teacher said was, "Howie, I would like you to sit here." Well! thought Ramona. Not everyone is going to get a present so Miss Binney must like me best. Ramona watched and listened as the other boys and girls arrived, but Miss Binney did not tell anyone else he was going to get a present if he sat in a certain chair. Ramona wondered if her present would be wrapped in fancy paper and tied with a ribbon like a birthday present. She hoped so.

As Ramona sat waiting for her present she watched the other children being introduced to Miss Binney by their mothers. She found two members of the morning kindergarten especially interesting. One was a boy named Davy, who was small, thin, and eager. He was the only boy in the class in short pants, and Ramona liked him at once. She liked him so much she decided she would like to kiss him.

The other interesting person was a big girl named Susan. Susan's hair looked like the hair on the girls in the pictures of the old-fashioned stories Beezus liked to read. It was reddish-brown and hung in curls like springs that touched her shoulders and bounced as she walked. Ramona had never seen such curls before. All the curly-haired girls she knew wore their hair short. Ramona put her hand to her own short straight hair, which was an ordinary brown, and longed to touch that bright springy hair. She longed to stretch one of those curls and watch it spring back. *Boing!* thought Ramona, making a mental noise like a spring on a television cartoon and wishing for thick, springy *boing-boing* hair like Susan's.

Howie interrupted Ramona's admiration of Susan's hair. "How soon do you think we get to go out and play?" he asked.

"Maybe after Miss Binney gives me the present," Ramona answered. "She said she was going to give me one."

"How come she's going to give you a present?" Howie wanted to know. "She didn't say anything about giving me a present."

"Maybe she likes me best," said Ramona.

This news did not make Howie happy. He turned to the next boy, and said, "*She's* going to get a present."

Ramona wondered how long she would have to sit there to get the present. If only Miss Binney understood how hard waiting was for her! When the last child had been welcomed and the last tearful mother had departed, Miss Binney gave a little talk about the rules of the kindergarten and showed the class the door that led to the bathroom. Next she assigned each person a little cupboard. Ramona's cupboard had a picture of a yellow duck on the door, and Howie's had a green frog. Miss Binney explained that their hooks in the cloakroom were marked with the same pictures. Then she asked the class to follow her quietly into the cloakroom to find their hooks.

Difficult though waiting was for her, Ramona did not budge. Miss Binney had not told her to get up and go into the cloakroom for her present. She had told her to sit for the present, and Ramona was going to sit until she got it. She would sit as if she were glued to the chair.

Howie scowled at Ramona as he returned from the cloakroom, and said to another boy, "The teacher is going to give *her* a present."

Naturally the boy wanted to know why. "I don't know," admitted Ramona. "She told me that if I sat here I would get a present. I guess she likes me best."

By the time Miss Binney returned from the cloakroom, word had spread around the classroom that Ramona was going to get a present.

Next Miss Binney taught the class the words of a puzzling song about "the dawnzer lee light", which Ramona did not understand because she did not know what a dawnzer was. "Oh, say, can you see by the dawnzer lee light," sang Miss Binney, and Ramona decided that a dawnzer was another word for a lamp.

When Miss Binney had gone over the song several times, she

asked the class to stand and sing it with her. Ramona did not budge. Neither did Howie and some of the others, and Ramona knew they were hoping for a present, too. Copycats, she thought.

"Stand up straight like good Americans," said Miss Binney so firmly that Howie and the others reluctantly stood up.

Ramona decided she would have to be a good American sitting down.

"Ramona," said Miss Binney, "aren't you going to stand with the rest of us?"

Ramona thought quickly. Maybe the question was some kind of test, like a test in a fairy tale. Maybe Miss Binney was testing her to see if she could get her out of her seat. If she failed the test, she would not get the present.

"I can't," said Ramona.

Miss Binney looked puzzled, but she did not insist that Ramona stand while she led the class through the dawnzer song. Ramona sang along with the others and hoped that her present came next, but when the song ended, Miss Binney made no mention of the present. Instead she picked up a book. Ramona decided that at last the time had come to learn to read.

Miss Binney stood in front of her class and began to read aloud from *Mike Mulligan and His Steam Shovel*, a book that was a favourite of Ramona's because, unlike so many books for her age, it was neither quiet and sleepy nor sweet and pretty. Ramona, pretending she was glued to her chair, enjoyed hearing the story again and listened quietly with the rest of the kindergarten to the story of Mike Mulligan's old-fashioned steam shovel, which proved its worth by digging the basement for the new town hall of Poppersville in a single day beginning at dawn and ending as the sun went down.

As Ramona listened a question came into her mind, a question that had often puzzled her about the books that were read to her. Somehow books always left out one of the most important things anyone would want to know. Now that Ramona was in school, and school was a place for learning, perhaps Miss Binney could answer the question. Ramona waited quietly until her teacher had finished the story, and then she raised her hand the way Miss Binney had told the class they should raise their hands when they wanted to speak in school.

Joey, who did not remember to raise his hand, spoke out. "That's a good book."

Miss Binney smiled at Ramona, and said, "I like the way Ramona remembers to raise her hand when she has something to say. Yes, Ramona?"

Ramona's hopes soared. Her teacher had smiled at her. "Miss Binney, I want to know — how did Mike Mulligan go to the bathroom when he was digging the basement of the town hall?"

Miss Binney's smile seemed to last longer than smiles usually last. Ramona glanced uneasily around and saw that others were waiting with interest for the answer. Everybody wanted to know how Mike Mulligan went to the bathroom.

"Well —" said Miss Binney at last. "I don't really know, Ramona. The book doesn't tell us."

"I always wanted to know, too," said Howie, without raising his hand, and others murmured in agreement. The whole class, it seemed, had been wondering how Mike Mulligan went to the bathroom.

"Maybe he stopped the steam shovel and climbed out of the hole he was digging and went to a service station," suggested a boy named Eric.

"He couldn't. The book says he had to work as fast as he could all day," Howie pointed out. "It doesn't say he stopped."

Miss Binney faced the twenty-nine earnest members of the kindergarten, all of whom wanted to know how Mike Mulligan went to the bathroom.

"Boys and girls," she began, and spoke in her clear, distinct way. "The reason the book does not tell us how Mike Mulligan went to the bathroom is that it is not an important part of the story. The story is about digging the basement of the town hall, and that is what the book tells us."

Miss Binney spoke as if this explanation ended the matter, but the kindergarten was not convinced. Ramona knew and the rest of the class knew that knowing how to go to the bathroom *was* important. They were surprised that Miss Binney did not understand, because she had showed them the bathroom the very first thing. Ramona could see there were some things she was not going to learn in school, and along with the rest of the class she stared reproachfully at Miss Binney.

The teacher looked embarrassed, as if she knew she had disappointed her kindergarten. She recovered quickly, closed the book, and told the class that if they would walk quietly out to the playground she would teach them a game called Grey Duck.

Ramona did not budge. She watched the rest of the class leave the room and admired Susan's *boing-boing* curls as they bounced about her shoulders, but she did not stir from her seat. Only Miss Binney could unstick the imaginary glue that held her there.

"Don't you want to learn to play Grey Duck, Ramona?" Miss Binney asked.

Ramona nodded. "Yes, but I can't."

"Why not?" asked Miss Binney.

"I can't leave my seat," said Ramona. When Miss Binney looked blank, she added, "Because of the present."

"What present?" Miss Binney seemed so genuinely puzzled that

Ramona became uneasy. The teacher sat down in the little chair next to Ramona's, and said, "Tell me why you can't play Grey Duck."

Ramona squirmed, worn out with waiting. She had an uneasy feeling that something had gone wrong someplace. "I want to play Grey Duck, but you —" She stopped, feeling that she might be about to say the wrong thing.

"But I what?" asked Miss Binney.

"Well . . . uh . . . you said if I sat here I would get a present," said Ramona at last, "but you didn't say how long I had to sit here."

If Miss Binney had looked puzzled before, she now looked baffled. "Ramona, I don't understand —" she began.

"Yes, you did," said Ramona, nodding. "You told me to sit here for the present, and I have been sitting here ever since school started and you haven't given me a present."

Miss Binney's face turned red and she looked so embarrassed that Ramona felt completely confused. Teachers were not supposed to look that way.

Miss Binney spoke gently. "Ramona, I'm afraid we've had a misunderstanding."

Ramona was blunt. "You mean I don't get a present?"

"I'm afraid not," admitted Miss Binney. "You see 'for the present' means for now. I meant that I wanted you to sit here for now, because later I may have the children sit at different desks."

"Oh." Ramona was so disappointed she had nothing to say. Words were so puzzling. *Present* should mean a present just as *attack* should mean to stick tacks in people.

By now all the children were crowding around the door to see what had happened to their teacher. "I'm so sorry," said Miss

Binney. "It's all my fault. I should have used different words."

"That's all right," said Ramona, ashamed to have the class see that she was not going to get a present after all.

"All right, class," said Miss Binney briskly. "Let's go outside and play Grey Duck. You, too, Ramona."

Grey Duck turned out to be an easy game, and Ramona's spirits recovered quickly from her disappointment. The class formed a circle, and the person who was "it" tagged someone who had to chase him around the circle. If "it" was caught before he got back to the empty space in the circle, he had to go into the centre of the circle, which was called the mush pot, and the person who caught him became "it".

Ramona tried to stand next to the girl with the springy curls, but instead she found herself beside Howie. "I thought you were going to get a present," gloated Howie.

Ramona merely scowled and made a face at Howie, who was "it", but quickly landed in the mush pot because his new jeans were so stiff they slowed him down. "Look at Howie in the mush pot!" crowed Ramona.

Howie looked as if he were about to cry, which Ramona thought was silly of him. Only a baby would cry in the mush pot. Me, me, somebody tag me, thought Ramona, jumping up and down. She longed for a turn to run around the circle. Susan was jumping up and down, too, and her curls bobbed enticingly.

At last Ramona felt a tap on her shoulder. Her turn had come to run around the circle! She ran as fast as she could to catch up with the sneakers pounding on the asphalt ahead of her. The *boing-boing* curls were on the other side of the circle. Ramona was coming closer to them. She put out her hand. She took hold of a curl, a thick, springy curl —

"*Yow!*" screamed the owner of the curls.

Startled, Ramona let go. She was so surprised by the scream that she forgot to watch Susan's curl spring back.

Susan clutched her curls with one hand and pointed at Ramona with the other. "That girl pulled my hair! That girl pulled my hair! Ow-ow-ow." Ramona felt that Susan did not have to be so touchy. She had not meant to hurt her. She only wanted to touch that beautiful, springy hair that was so different from her own straight brown hair.

"Ow-ow-ow!" shrieked Susan, the centre of everyone's attention.

"Baby," said Ramona.

"Ramona," said Miss Binney, "in our kindergarten we do not pull hair."

"Susan doesn't have to be such a baby," said Ramona.

"You may go sit on the bench outside the door while the rest of us play our game," Miss Binney told Ramona.

Ramona did not want to sit on any bench. She wanted to play Grey Duck with the rest of the class. "No," said Ramona, preparing to make a great big noisy fuss. "I won't."

Susan stopped shrieking. A terrible silence fell over the playground. Everyone stared at Ramona in such a way that she almost felt as if she were beginning to shrink. Nothing like this had ever happened to her before.

"Ramona," said Miss Binney quietly. "Go sit on the bench."

Without another word Ramona walked across the playground and sat down on the bench by the door of the kindergarten. The game of Grey Duck continued without her, but the class had not forgotten her. Howie grinned in her direction. Susan continued to look injured. Some laughed and pointed at Ramona. Others, particularly Davy, looked worried, as if they had not known such a terrible punishment could be given in kindergarten.

Ramona swung her feet and pretended to be watching some workmen who were building a new market across the street. In spite of the misunderstanding about the present, she wanted so much to be loved by her pretty new teacher. Tears came into Ramona's eyes, but she would not cry. Nobody was going to call Ramona Quimby a crybaby. Never.

Next door to the kindergarten two little girls, about two and four years old, peered solemnly through the fence at Ramona. "See that girl," said the older girl to her little sister. "She's sitting there because she's been bad." The two-year-old looked awed to be in the presence of such wickedness. Ramona stared at the ground, she felt so ashamed.

When the game ended, the class filed past Ramona into the kindergarten. "You may come in now, Ramona," said Miss Binney pleasantly.

Ramona slid off the bench and followed the others. Even though she was not loved, she was forgiven, and that helped. She hoped that learning to read and write came next.

Inside Miss Binney announced that the time had come to rest. This news was another disappointment to Ramona, who felt that anyone who went to kindergarten was too old to rest. Miss Binney gave each child a mat on which there was a picture that matched the picture on his cupboard door and told him where to spread his mat on the floor. When all twenty-nine children were lying down they did not rest. They popped up to see what others were doing. They wiggled. They whispered. They coughed. They asked, "How much longer do we have to rest?"

"Sh-h," said Miss Binney in a soft, quiet, sleepy voice. "The person who rests most quietly will get to be the wake-up fairy."

"What's the wake-up fairy?" demanded Howie, bobbing up.

"Sh-h," whispered Miss Binney. "The wake-up fairy tiptoes

around and wakes up the class with a magic wand. Whoever is the fairy wakes up the quietest resters first."

Ramona made up her mind that she would get to be the wake-up fairy, and then Miss Binney would know she was not so bad after all. She lay flat on her back with her hands tight to her sides. The mat was thin and the floor was hard, but Ramona did not wiggle. She was sure she must be the best rester in the class, because she could hear others squirming around on their mats. Just to show Miss Binney she really and truly was resting she gave one little snore, not a loud snore but a delicate snore, to prove what a good rester she was.

A scatter of giggles rose from the class, followed by several snores, less delicate than Ramona's. They led to more and more, less and less delicate snores until everyone was snoring except the few who did not know how to snore. They were giggling.

Miss Binney clapped her hands and spoke in a voice that was no longer soft, quiet, and sleepy. "All right, boys and girls!" she said. "This is enough! We do not snore or giggle during rest time."

"Ramona started it," said Howie.

Ramona sat up and scowled at Howie. "Tattletale," she said in a voice of scorn. Across Howie she saw that Susan was lying quietly with her beautiful curls spread out on her mat and her eyes screwed tight shut.

"Well, you did," said Howie.

"Children!" Miss Binney's voice was sharp. "We must rest so that we will not be tired when our mothers come to take us home."

"Is your mother coming to take you home?" Howie asked Miss Binney. Ramona had been wondering the same thing.

"That's enough, Howie!" Miss Binney spoke the way mothers sometimes speak just before dinnertime. In a moment she was back to her soft, sleepy voice. "I like the way Susan is resting so quietly," she said. "Susan, you may be the wake-up fairy and tap the boys and girls with this wand to wake them up."

The magic wand turned out to be nothing but an everyday yardstick. Ramona lay quietly, but her efforts were of no use. Susan with her curls bouncing about her shoulders tapped Ramona last. It's not fair, Ramona thought. She was not the worst rester in the class. Howie was much worse.

The rest of the morning went quickly. The class was allowed to explore the paints and the toys, and those who wanted to were allowed to draw with their new crayons. They did not, however, learn to read and write, but Ramona cheered up when Miss Binney explained that anyone who had anything to share with the class could bring it to school the next day for Show and Tell. Ramona was glad when the bell finally rang and she saw her mother waiting for her outside the fence. Mrs. Kemp and Willa Jean were waiting for Howie, too, and the five started home together.

Right away Howie said, "Ramona got benched, and she's the worst rester in the class."

After all that had happened that morning, Ramona found this too much. "Why don't you shut up?" she yelled at Howie just before she hit him.

Mrs. Quimby seized Ramona by the hand and dragged her away from Howie. "Now Ramona," she said, and her voice was firm, "this is no way to behave on your first day of school."

"Poor little girl," said Mrs. Kemp. "She's worn out."

Nothing infuriated Ramona more than having a grown-up say, as if she could not hear, that she was worn out. "I'm *not* worn out!" she shrieked.

"She got plenty of rest while she was benched," said Howie.

"Now Howie, you stay out of this," said Mrs. Kemp. Then to

change the subject, she asked her son, "How do you like kinder-garten?"

"Oh — I guess it's all right," said Howie without enthusiasm. "They don't have any dirt to dig in or tricycles to ride."

"And what about you, Ramona?" asked Mrs. Quimby. "Did you like kindergarten?"

Ramona considered. Kindergarten had not turned out as she had expected. Still, even though she had not been given a present and Miss Binney did not love her, she had liked being with boys and girls her own age. She liked singing the song about the dawnzer and having her own little cupboard. "I didn't like it as much as I thought I would," she answered honestly, "but maybe it will get better when we have Show and Tell."

THE HAPPY LION

by Louise Fatio

pictures by Roger Duvoisin

THERE was once a very happy lion.

Early every morning, François, the keeper's son, stopped on his way to school to say, "*Bonjour*, Happy Lion."

In the afternoons, Monsieur Dupont, the schoolmaster, stopped on his way home to say, "*Bonjour*, Happy Lion."

In the evenings, Madame Pinson, who knitted all day on the bench by the bandstand, never left without saying, "*Au revoir*, Happy Lion."

On summer Sundays, the town band filed into the bandstand to play waltzes and polkas. And the happy lion closed his eyes to listen. He loved music. Everyone was his friend and came to say "*Bonjour*" and offer meat and other titbits.

He *was* a happy lion.

One morning, the happy lion found that his keeper had forgotten to close the door of his house.

"Hmm," he said, "I don't like that. Anyone may walk in.

"Oh, well," he added on second thought, "maybe I will walk out myself and see my friends in town. It will be nice to return their visits."

So the happy lion walked out into the park and said, "*Bonjour,* my friends" to the busy sparrows.

"*Bonjour,* Happy Lion," answered the busy sparrows.

And he said, "*Bonjour,* my friend" to the quick red squirrel who sat on his tail and bit into a walnut.

"*Bonjour,* Happy Lion," said the red squirrel, hardly looking up.

Then the happy lion went into the cobblestone street, where he met Monsieur Dupont just around the corner.

"*Bonjour*," he said, nodding in his polite lion way.

"Hoooooooooohhh . . ." answered Monsieur Dupont, and fainted onto the pavement.

"What a silly way to say *bonjour*," said the happy lion, and he padded along on his big soft paws.

"*Bonjour*, Mesdames," the happy lion said farther down the street when he saw three ladies he had known at the zoo.

"Huuuuuuuuuuuuuuhhhhhh . . ." cried the three ladies, and ran away as if an ogre were after them.

"I can't think," said the happy lion, "what makes them do that. They are always so polite at the zoo."

"*Bonjour*, Madame." The happy lion nodded again when he caught up with Madame Pinson near the greengrocer's.

"Oo la la . . . !" cried Madame Pinson, and threw her shopping bag full of vegetables into the lion's face.

"A-a-a-a-chooooooo," sneezed the lion. "People in this town are foolish, as I begin to see."

Now the lion began to hear the joyous sounds of a military march. He turned around the next corner, and there was the town band, marching down the street between two lines of people. Ratatatum ratata ratatatum ratatata boom boom.

Before the lion could even nod and say, "*Bonjour*," the music became screams and yells.

What a hubbub!

Musicians and spectators tumbled into one another in their flight toward doorways and pavement cafés.

Soon the street was empty and silent.

The lion sat down and meditated.

"I suppose," he said, "this must be the way people behave when they are not at the zoo."

Then he got up and went on with his stroll in search of a friend who would not faint, or scream, or run away. But the only people he saw were pointing at him excitedly from the highest windows and balconies.

Now what was this new noise the lion heard? "Toootoooooot . . . hoootoooootooooot . . ." went that noise. "Hooooot tooooooo TOOOOOOOOOHHHOOOOT . . ." and it grew more and more noisy.

"It may be the wind," said the lion. "Unless it is the monkeys from the zoo, all of them taking a stroll."

All of a sudden a big red fire engine burst out of a side street, and came to a stop not too, too far from the lion. Then a big van came backing up on the other side of him with its back door wide open.

The lion just sat down very quietly, for he did not want to miss what was going to happen.

The firemen got off the fire engine and advanced very, very slowly toward the lion, pulling their big fire hose along.

Very slowly they came closer . . . and closer . . . and the fire hose crawled on like a long snake, longer and longer . . .

SUDDENLY, behind the lion, a little voice cried, "*Bonjour,* Happy Lion."

It was François, the keeper's son, on his way home from school! He had seen the lion and had come running to him. The happy lion was so VERY HAPPY to meet a friend who did not run and who said "*Bonjour*" that he forgot all about the firemen.

And he never found out what they were going to do, because François put his hand on the lion's great mane and said, "Let's walk back to the park together."

"Yes, let's," purred the happy lion.

So François and the happy lion walked back to the zoo. The firemen followed behind in the fire engine, and the people on the balconies and in the high windows shouted at last, "BONJOUR, HAPPY LION!"

From then on the happy lion got the best titbits the town saved for him. But if you opened his door he would not wish to go out visiting again. He was happier to sit in his rock garden while on the other side of the moat Monsieur Dupont, Madame Pinson, and all his old friends came again like polite and sensible people to say "*Bonjour*, Happy Lion."

But he was happiest when he saw François walk through the park every afternoon on his way home from school. Then he swished his tail for joy, for François remained always his dearest friend.

Mr. Gumpy's Motor Car
John Burningham

Mr. GUMPY was going for a ride in his car.
He drove out of the gate and down the lane.

"May we come too?" said the children.

"May we?" said the rabbit, the cat, the dog, the pig, the sheep, the chickens, the calf, and the goat.

"All right," said Mr. Gumpy. "But it will be a squash."

And they all piled in.

"It's a lovely day," said Mr. Gumpy. "Let's take the old cart-track across the fields."

For a while they drove along happily. The sun shone, the engine chugged, and everyone was enjoying the ride.

"I don't like the look of those clouds. I think it's going to rain," said Mr. Gumpy.

Very soon the dark clouds were right overhead. Mr. Gumpy stopped the car. He jumped out, put up the top, and down came the rain.

The road grew muddier and muddier, and the wheels began to spin. Mr. Gumpy looked at the hill ahead.

"Some of you will have to get out and push," he said.

"Not me," said the goat. "I'm too old."
"Not me," said the calf. "I'm too young."
"Not us," said the chickens. "We can't push."
"Not me," said the sheep. "I might catch cold."
"Not me," said the pig. "I've a bone in my trotter."
"Not me," said the dog. "But I'll drive if you like."
"Not me," said the cat. "It would ruin my fur."
"Not me," said the rabbit. "I'm not very well."
"Not me," said the girl. "He's stronger."
"Not me," said the boy. "She's bigger."
The wheels churned. . . .
The car sank deeper into the mud.
"Now we're really stuck," said Mr. Gumpy.
They all got out and pushed.

They pushed and shoved and heaved and strained and gasped and slipped and slithered and squelched.

Slowly the car began to move. . . .

"Don't stop!" cried Mr. Gumpy. "Keep it up! We're nearly there."

Everyone gave a mighty heave — the tyres gripped. . . .

The car edged its way to the top of the hill. They looked up and saw that the sun was shining.

"We'll drive home across the bridge," said Mr. Gumpy. "There'll be time for a swim."

"Goodbye," said Mr. Gumpy. "Come for a drive another day."

The story that follows starts with the best of all words: "Once upon a time". That means Marjorie Flack is telling us about a China very different from that of today. The Chinese no longer wear pigtails, for instance. But life on the Yangtze River perhaps hasn't changed much.

THE STORY ABOUT
PING

BY

MARJORIE FLACK
AND
KURT WIESE

ONCE upon a time there was a beautiful young duck named Ping. Ping lived with his mother and his father and two sisters and three brothers and eleven aunts and seven uncles and forty-two cousins.

Their home was a boat with two wise eyes on the Yangtze river.

Each morning as the sun rose from the east, Ping and his mother and his father and sisters and brothers and aunts and uncles and his forty-two cousins all marched, one by one, down a little bridge to the shore of the Yangtze river.

All day they would hunt for snails and little fishes and other pleasant things to eat. But in the evening as the sun set in the west, "La-la-la-la-lei!" would call the Master of the boat.

Quickly Ping and all his many family would come scurrying, quickly they would march, one by one, up over the little bridge and onto the wise-eyed boat which was their home on the Yangtze river.

Ping was always careful, very very careful not to be last, because the last duck to cross over the bridge always got a spank on the back.

But one afternoon as the shadows grew long, Ping did not hear the call because at that moment Ping was wrong side up trying to catch a little fish.

By the time Ping was right side up his mother and his father and his aunts were already marching, one by one, up over the bridge. By the time Ping neared the shore, his uncles and his cousins were marching over, and by the time Ping reached the shore the last of his forty-two cousins had crossed the bridge!

Ping knew he would be the last, the very last duck if he crossed the bridge. Ping did not want to be spanked. So he hid.

Ping hid behind the grasses, and as the dark came and the pale

moon shone in the sky Ping watched the wise-eyed boat slowly sail away down the Yangtze river.

All night long Ping slept near the grasses on the bank of the river with his head tucked under his wing, and when the sun rose up from the east Ping found he was all alone on the Yangtze river.

There was no father or mother, no sisters or brothers, no aunts or uncles, and no forty-two cousins to go fishing with Ping, so Ping started out to find them, swimming down the yellow waters of the Yangtze river.

As the sun rose higher in the sky, boats came. Big boats and little boats, fishing boats and beggars' boats, house boats and raft boats, and all these boats had eyes to see with, but nowhere could Ping see the wise-eyed boat which was his home.

Then came a boat full of strange dark fishing birds. Ping saw them diving for fish for their Master. As each bird brought a fish to his Master he would give it a little piece of fish for pay.

Closer and closer swooped the fishing birds near Ping. Now Ping could see shining rings around their necks, rings of metal made so tight the birds could never swallow the big fish they were catching.

Swoop, splash, splash, the ringed birds were dashing here and there all about Ping, so down he ducked and swam under the yellow water of the Yangtze river.

When Ping came up to the top of the water far away from the fishing birds, he found little crumbs floating, tender little rice cake crumbs which made a path to a house boat.

As Ping ate these crumbs, he came nearer and nearer to the house boat, then —

SPLASH!

There in the water was a Boy! A little Boy with a barrel on his

back which was tied to a rope from the boat just as all boat boys on the Yangtze river are tied to their boats. In the Boy's hand was a rice cake.

"Oh-owwwwoooo!" cried the little Boy, and up dashed Ping and snatched at the rice cake.

Quickly the Boy grabbed Ping and held him tight.

"Quack-quack-quack-quack!" cried Ping.

"OH! — Ohh-ooo!" yelled the little Boy.

Ping and the Boy made such a splashing and such a noise that the Boy's father came running and the Boy's mother came running and the Boy's sister and brother came running and they all looked over the edge of the boat at Ping and the Boy splashing in the water of the Yangtze river.

Then the Boy's father and mother pulled at the rope which was tied to the barrel on the little Boy's back. They pulled and they pulled and up came Ping and the Boy onto the house boat.

"Ah, a duck dinner has come to us!" said the Boy's father.

"I will cook him with rice at sunset tonight," said the Boy's mother.

"NO-NO! My nice duck is too beautiful to eat," cried the Boy.

But down came a basket all over Ping and he could see no more of the Boy or the boat or the sky or the beautiful yellow water of the Yangtze river.

All day long Ping could see only the thin lines of sun which shone through the cracks in the basket, and Ping was very sad.

After a long while Ping heard the sound of oars and felt the jerk, jerk, jerk of the boat as it was rowed down the Yangtze river.

Soon the lines of sunshine which came through the cracks of the basket turned rose colour, and Ping knew the sun was setting in the west. Ping heard footsteps coming near to him.

The basket was quickly lifted, and the little Boy's hands were holding Ping.

Quickly, quietly, the Boy dropped Ping over the side of the boat and Ping slipped into the water, the beautiful yellow water of the Yangtze river.

Then Ping heard this call, "La-la-la-la-lei!"

Ping looked and there near the bank of the river was the wise-eyed boat which was Ping's home, and Ping saw his mother and his father and his aunts, all marching, one by one, up over the little bridge.

Swiftly Ping turned and swam, paddling toward the shore. Now Ping could see his uncles marching, one by one.

Paddle, paddle, Ping hurried toward the shore. Ping saw his cousins marching, one by one.

Paddle, paddle, Ping neared the shore, but —

As Ping reached the shore the last of Ping's forty-two cousins marched over the bridge and Ping knew that he was LATE again!

But up marched Ping, up over the little bridge and SPANK came the cane on Ping's back!

Then at last Ping was back with his mother and his father and two sisters and three brothers and eleven aunts and seven uncles and forty-two cousins. Home again on the wise-eyed boat on the Yangtze river.

DR. SEUSS

That isn't his real name and he isn't really a doctor. His real name is Theodor Seuss Geisel and the "Seuss" was also his mother's maiden name. Sometimes he writes under the name of LeSieg. You can probably work out how a man named Geisel could also call himself LeSieg.

Dr. Seuss writes his funny stories and dreams up his strange animals in a big, converted watchtower on the highest hill in La Jolla, California. In front of this tower is a wooden gate with a sign: "Beware of the cats". But he and his wife don't have any cats. Figure that one out. He doesn't have any children either, although millions of children love his books. He likes to say to grown-ups, "You make 'em — I amuse 'em."

He has written books about some pretty crazy creatures, such as Tufted Mazurkas, the Bippo-no-Bungus from Hippo-no-Hungus, and Mop-Noodled Finches, and the Grinch who, when he sees anyone else having fun, gets so mad he bites himself.

But Dr. Seuss is quite a sensible fellow. As he says, "If I draw a character with two heads, I always make sure that he has two toothbrushes." Which is as it should be.

On the other hand an eight-year-old once sent him a letter saying: "Dear Dr. Seuss, you sure thunk up a lot of funny books. You sure thunk up a million funny animals . . . who thunk you up, Dr. Seuss?"

Of all his many books my personal favourite is *On Beyond Zebra!* In it I found out that there are lots of letters *after* Z — such as Yuzz, Wum, Humpf, and Fuddle.

One of his very best is also the first one he wrote, and here it is.

AND TO THINK THAT I SAW IT ON MULBERRY STREET

When I leave home to walk to school,
Dad always says to me,
"Marco, keep your eyelids up
And see what you can see."

But when I tell him where I've been
And what I think I've seen,
He looks at me and sternly says,
"Your eyesight's much too keen.
Stop telling such outlandish tales.
Stop turning minnows into whales."

Now what can I say
When I get home today?

All the long way to school
And all the way back,
I've looked and I've looked
And I've kept careful track,
But all that I've noticed,
Except my own feet,
Was a horse and a waggon
On Mulberry Street.

That's nothing to tell of,
That won't do, of course . . .
Just a broken-down waggon
That's drawn by a horse.

That *can't* be my story. That's only a *start*.
I'll say that a ZEBRA was pulling that cart!
And that is a story that no one can beat,
When I say that I saw it on Mulberry Street.

Yes, the zebra is fine,
But I think it's a shame,
Such a marvellous beast
With a cart that's so tame.

The story would really be better to hear
If the driver I saw were a charioteer.
A gold and blue chariot's *something* to meet,
Rumbling like thunder down Mulberry Street!

No, it won't do at all . . .
A zebra's too small.

A reindeer is better;
He's fast and he's fleet,
And he'd look mighty smart
On old Mulberry Street.

Hold on a minute!
There's something wrong!

A reindeer hates the way it feels
To pull a thing that runs on wheels.

He'd be much happier, instead,
If he could pull a fancy sled.

Hmmmm . . . A reindeer and a sleigh . . .

Say — *any*one could think of *that,*
Jack or Fred or Joe or Nat —
Say, even Jane could think of *that.*

But it isn't too late to make one little change.
A sleigh and an ELEPHANT! *There's* something strange!

I'll pick one with plenty of power and size,
A blue one with plenty of fun in his eyes.
And then, just to give him a little more tone,
Have a Rajah, with rubies, perched high on a throne.

Say! That makes a story that *no one* can beat,
When I say that I saw it on Mulberry Street.

But now I don't know . . .
It still doesn't seem right.
An elephant pulling a thing that's so light
Would whip it around in the air like a kite.
But he'd look simply grand
With a great big brass band!

A band that's so good should have someone to hear it,
But it's going so fast that it's hard to keep near it.
I'll put on a trailer! I know they won't mind
If a man sits and listens while hitched on behind.

But now is it fair? Is it fair what I've done?
I'll bet those wagons weigh more than a ton.
That's really too heavy a load for *one* beast;
I'll give him some helpers. He needs two, at least.

But now what worries me is this . . .
Mulberry Street runs into Bliss,
Unless there's something I can fix up,
There'll be an *awful* traffic mix-up!

It takes Police to do the trick,
To guide them through where traffic's thick —
It takes Police to do the trick.

They'll never crash now. They'll race at top speed
With Sergeant Mulvaney, himself, in the lead.

The Mayor is there
And he thinks it is grand,
And he raises his hat
As they dash by the stand.

The Mayor is there
And the Aldermen too,
All waving big banners
Of red, white and blue.

And that is a story that NO ONE can beat
When I say that I saw it on Mulberry Street!

With a roar of its motor an airplane appears
And dumps out confetti while everyone cheers.

And that makes a story that's really not bad!
But it still could be better. Suppose that I add . . .

A Chinese man
Who eats with sticks . . .
A big Magician
Doing tricks . . .
A ten-foot beard
That needs a comb . . .
No time for more,
I'm almost home.

I swung 'round the corner
And dashed through the gate,
I ran up the steps
And I felt simply GREAT!

FOR I HAD A STORY
THAT *NO ONE* COULD BEAT!
AND TO THINK THAT I SAW IT
ON MULBERRY STREET!

But Dad said quite calmly,
"Just draw up your stool
And tell me the sights
On the way home from school."

There was so much to tell, I JUST COULDN'T BEGIN!
Dad looked at me sharply and pulled at his chin.
He frowned at me sternly from there in his seat,
"Was there nothing to look at . . . no people to greet?
Did *nothing* excite you or make your heart beat?"

"Nothing," I said, growing red as a beet,
"But a plain horse and waggon on Mulberry Street."

AILEEN FISHER
Noses

I looked in the mirror
and looked at my nose:
it's the funniest thing,
the way it grows
stuck right out where all of it shows
with two little holes where the breathing goes.

I looked in the mirror
and saw in there
the end of my chin
and the start of my hair
and between there isn't much space to spare
with my nose, like a handle, sticking there.

If ever you want
to giggle and shout
and can't think of what
to do it about,
just look in the mirror and then, no doubt,
you'll see how funny YOUR nose sticks out!

PAUL BIEGEL
The Naughty Shoes

Translated from the Dutch by Celia Amidon

HAVE YOU ever crawled into bed at night with your shoes on? Of course not! You take them off and put them under your chair or under your bed. Grown-ups do the same thing. So just imagine how many thousands of pairs of shoes stand under beds and chairs during the long, dark night, while their owners lie under the covers asleep.

Do the shoes also sleep? Heavens no! Shoes never get tired. Listen to this:

One night my father's left shoe said to my father's right shoe, "I am sick and tired of taking Father places; all day long I have to go where he wants to go — this way and that way, up way and down way, in way and out way! Now I am going by myself, and I am going the *other* way!"

"I am going with you," said my father's right shoe.

So off they went through the open window, out into the dark street. It sounded like a man walking in the street, but it was only an empty pair of shoes, going the other way.

"Coming along?" they called through the open window to the neighbours' shoes. And the shoes of the neighbours — husband and wife — joined my father's shoes; their neighbours' shoes came along too, and the shoes of the neighbours of the neighbours, all down the block.

It became quite a parade. Clickety-click went the high heels; boom-boom went the heavy boots; schwee-schwee went the rubbers. Shoes, shoes, and more shoes — old pairs, new pairs, worn-out pairs; shiny shoes, unpolished shoes, scuffed shoes; brown ones, black ones, big ones, small ones. They walked, they ran, they skipped — always the other way, for this was the Free Shoe Parade and their owners' feet were all at home under the covers.

"Left belongs to right!" called the shoes. "Hold on to each other by the laces!"

But Grandma's left shoe lost track of Grandma's right shoe. And the shoes without laces couldn't hold on to each other at all.

"Where are you? Where are you?" voices called in the dark.

"I'm here! I'm here!" came the answers from here and there and everywhere.

But which belonged to which? There was too much confusion for the right shoes to find their lefts and for the left shoes to find their rights.

"Never mind," someone shouted. "Every shoe for himself from now on. We don't need to be paired off."

And off they went again. Single left shoes and unmatched right shoes. Hoppety-hop. The very dainty and the very shiny shoes waded through all the mud puddles, what fun! But the old, scuffed shoes, the dirty and unkempt ones, walked primly with neat little steps and avoided the puddles. The shoes of old people hopped, skipped, and jumped. The children's shoes took slow, dignified steps. Shoes without feet cramped inside them. Shoes who were their own masters. They all had a glorious time, a wonderful, marvellous time!

But the fun had to come to an end. The sun came up and shooed away the darkness.

"We have to go home! We have to get back before our people get out of bed!" shouted the shoes, and the jolly parade changed into a scramble of confusion and panic.

Most of the shoes had lost their way and did not know how to get home. As the sun rose higher in the sky, they stampeded through the streets, clickety-click, boom-boom, schwee-schwee, scuff-scuff. Boots stomped over slippers. Shoes tripped over their untied laces. Toe-caps banged against toe-caps, and heels stepped on toes.

The sun climbed higher and higher.

"Hurry, hurry!" shouted the shoes. "We'll be late! Quick, get inside!"

Most of the shoes climbed inside the first open window they saw and settled under the first bed they could find. Two left men's shoes under Grandma's bed. Wading boots under the bed of two-year-old Caroline. And when my father got up, he found under his bed a lady's pump, a blue sneaker, a left slipper, and a right boy's shoe.

"What in the world . . ." said my father.

"What in the world . . ." said all the people in town when they got out of bed. And that morning a parade of limping people went to work and to school, for they were all wearing the wrong shoes. Either too big or too small. Either two right shoes or two left ones — click-scuff, boom-schwee, schwee-click. Grandma went around in stocking feet, and Caroline went barefoot.

Everyone asked, "Who has my shoes? Who's wearing my shoes?" And everyone examined everyone else's feet. Now and then someone shouted, "Ah! There's my brown right shoe!" Or, "Yoo-hoo, you have my red sandal!" And so, slowly but surely, everyone got his own shoes back again.

It took longer for my father, though, than for anyone else. Because his left shoe had climbed a tree, and it was not until three days later that the wind finally blew it down.

MARCEL AYMÉ

If you read all through these books you'll find I've included a lot about animals. There's a reason. When I was small I lived in the town. We had no pets. I never felt on good terms with animals. Then I married someone who had been brought up with animals. She understood them, loved them, and taught our children to love them, too.

Sometimes they carried affection pretty far. One Christmas her uncle gave our seven-year-old daughter a peculiarly wrapped present. She opened it, cried out, "Just what I wanted, Uncle Jim! *A human tapeworm!*"

Well, sometimes I feel guilty about having neglected animals when I was young. And perhaps I've put a lot of stories and verses about animals into these books to make it up to them, to show that I think they're important.

"The Elephant" comes from a book of stories about farm animals called *The Wonderful Farm*. The author tells us that "it is a quite ordinary sort of farm, with its yard and stables and cowsheds and duckpond, such as you may find anywhere". But it's not really ordinary, he adds, because "the things that happen on it are just the sort of things one would like to have happen, but which so seldom do". As you will see when you read "The Elephant".

What I like about Marcel Aymé's stories is that strange things happen, but the animals to whom they happen are real as can be. Take the cow, for instance, looking at the kitchen cupboard, and especially at the

cheese and the bowl of milk. She murmurs, "I see. . . . *Now* I understand." And suddenly we seem to be inside that cow's mind. For a
second we're a cow.

Marcel Aymé was born in 1902 in a town called Joigny in Burgundy,
France. Orphaned at the age of two, he was reared by his grandparents
and then his aunt. In the small villages in which he grew up he learnt
more from the rivers, woods, and farms than he did at school.

Later on he became a famous author of books and plays for grown-
ups. But for me these farm stories about two little girls and the remarkable animals they had for friends are his best work.

Among French children the stories are great favourites. But not many
other children know them. After reading "The Elephant" you will
know at least one, and may want to read more.

The Elephant

Translated from the French by Norman Denny

ILLUSTRATED BY MAURICE SENDAK

FATHER and Mother were dressed in their Sunday clothes.
Before going out they said to the two little girls:

"We aren't taking you to see Uncle Alfred because it's raining
too hard. You can spend the time doing your lessons."

"I've done mine," said Marinette. "I did them last night."

"So did I," said Delphine.

"Well, then, you must just play nicely together, and above all,
don't let anyone inside the house."

Father and Mother went off, and the little girls gazed after them
for a long time with their noses to the windowpane. The rain was

falling so hard that they scarcely minded not going to see Uncle Alfred. They were just thinking of playing a game of lotto when they saw the turkey go running across the yard. He took shelter under the shed, shook his wet feathers and wiped his large neck on his fluffy waistcoat.

"It's bad weather for turkeys," said Delphine, "and for the other animals too. It's a good thing it never lasts long. Supposing it rained for forty days and forty nights!"

"There's no reason why it should," said Marinette. "Why *should* it rain for forty days and forty nights?"

"Of course not. Only I was just thinking that instead of playing lotto, we might play at Noah's Ark."

Marinette thought this a very good idea, and she also thought that the kitchen would make a splendid Ark. And there were plenty of animals. The little girls went to the stable and farmyard, and easily persuaded the ox, the cow, the horse, the sheep, the cock, and the hen to follow them into the kitchen. Most of the animals were delighted to play at Noah's Ark; but there were one or two grumblers, such as the turkey and the pig, who said they didn't want to be bothered. Marinette said solemnly:

"It's the Flood! It's going to rain for forty days and forty nights. If you don't want to come into the Ark, so much the worse for you. The waters will cover the earth, and you'll be drowned!"

The grumblers did not need to be told twice, and rushed to get inside the kitchen. There was no need to say anything to frighten the hens. They all wanted to play, and Delphine, after choosing one of them, had to send the rest away.

"You see, we can only have one hen, or the game wouldn't be right."

In less than a quarter of an hour, one of all the different kinds of animals on the farm was in the kitchen. They were afraid the ox

wouldn't be able to get in at the door, because of his big horns; but he managed quite easily by turning his head sideways, and so did the cow. The Ark was so full that the hen and the cock, and the hen-turkey and the cock-turkey and the cat, all had to sit on the table. But there was no jostling, and the animals all did what they were told. Besides, they were all a little scared at finding themselves in the kitchen, where none of them had been before, except the cat and perhaps the hen. The horse, who happened to be near the clock, stared first at the face and then at the pendulum, and got so worried that he kept on pricking his ears. The cow was very interested in the things she could see through the glass doors of the cupboard. In particular, she could scarcely take her eyes off a cheese and a bowl of milk, and she murmured several times: "I see. . . . *Now* I understand!"

Just for a moment the animals got truly frightened. Even the ones who knew they were only playing began to wonder if it was really a game. Delphine, who was sitting on the window ledge, which was the captain's bridge, looked out and said in a grave voice:

"The rain continues! The waters are rising! I can't see the garden any more, and the wind's getting stronger and stronger! . . . Starboard the helm!"

Marinette, who was the steersman, moved the damper of the stove to the right, and the stove smoked a little.

"It's still raining! The water has reached the lowest branches of the apple tree. . . . Look out for rocks! Port the helm!"

Marinette moved the damper to the left, and the stove stopped smoking.

"The rain continues! . . . Now I can only see the very tops of the highest trees, and the waters are still rising. . . . Now they have disappeared, and I can't see anything at all!"

Then there was the sound of a great sob. It was the pig, who could not contain his grief at leaving the farm.

"Silence on board!" cried Delphine. "I won't have any panic! You must all behave like the cat. Look at the way he's purring!"

It was quite true. The cat was purring as though nothing were happening, because he knew that the Flood was only a game.

"If only it doesn't go on too long!" said the pig, with a groan.

"We must expect it to go on for a little more than a year," said Marinette. "But we've got plenty of stores, and no one will go hungry. There's nothing to worry about."

The poor pig subsided, and lay sobbing quietly to himself. He was thinking that perhaps the voyage would be longer than the little girls expected, so that one day the food would run out; and because he was very fat, he was afraid of being eaten. While he lay there shivering, a little white hen, all hunched up in the rain, had climbed onto the ledge outside the window. She tapped with her beak on the windowpane, and said to Delphine:

"Please, I want to play too."

"But, little white hen, you can see for yourself that we can't let you. We've already got a hen."

"And anyway the Ark's full up," said Marinette, who had drawn near.

The white hen looked so disappointed that the little girls were sorry for her. Marinette said to Delphine:

"All the same, we haven't got an elephant. The white hen could be the elephant."

"That's true. The Ark ought to have an elephant."

Delphine opened the window, took the little white hen in her hands, and told her that she was to be the elephant.

"I'd love to," said the white hen. "But what's an elephant like? I've never seen one."

The little girls tried to explain to her what an elephant was like, but they couldn't get her to understand. Then Delphine remembered a book with coloured pictures that Uncle Alfred had given them. It was in the next room, which was Father and Mother's bedroom. Leaving Marinette in command of the Ark, Delphine took the white hen into the bedroom. She showed the hen the picture of an elephant, and did some more explaining. The white hen studied the picture very earnestly and carefully, because she so much wanted to be an elephant.

"I'll leave you here for a minute," said Delphine. "I must go back to the Ark. While you're waiting for me to come and fetch you, you can think about what you have to do."

The little white hen tried so hard to be an elephant that she really turned into one, which was more than she had dared to hope for. It happened so quickly that at first she did not realize that she had changed. She thought she was still just a little hen, perched up very high, near the ceiling. But then she found that she had a trunk and ivory tusks, and four huge feet, and a thick, rough skin in which there were still a few white feathers. She was rather surprised, but very pleased. The thing that pleased her most was to have such enormous ears, because she had scarcely had any at all before. "The pig always thinks so much of his ears," she said to herself. "Perhaps he won't be so proud when he sees these."

In the kitchen the little girls had quite forgotten about the white hen, who was becoming such a splendid elephant. After announcing that the wind had dropped and that the Ark was now sailing on calm water, they were getting ready to inspect the animals under their care. Marinette got a notebook to write down anything they wanted, and Delphine said:

"Friends and shipmates, we are now in our forty-fifth day at sea . . ."

"Well, that's a blessing!" murmured the pig. "The time has passed quicker than I expected."

"Silence, pig! . . . As you see, friends and shipmates, you have no reason to be sorry that you came with us in the Ark. Now that the worst is over, we can be sure of sighting land in about ten months. But I can now tell you that, up to the last few days, our lives were often in great danger, and it is thanks to the steersman that we have survived."

The animals all thanked the steersman warmly.

Marinette blushed with pleasure, and said, pointing to her sister, "It's thanks to the captain, too. You mustn't forget the captain."

"Of course not!" said the animals. "Quite right! If it weren't for the captain . . ."

"Thank you very much," said Delphine. "I can't tell you what a help it is to know that you trust me. And you must go on trusting me. Our voyage is far from being over, although the greatest dangers are past. But I was going to ask you if there is anything you want. Let us start with the cat. Cat, is there anything you would like?"

"Yes, there is," said the cat. "I should very much like a saucer of milk."

"Write that down — a saucer of milk for the cat . . ."

While Marinette was writing this in her notebook, the elephant softly opened the door a little way with his trunk, and peeped into the Ark. He was very pleased by what he saw, and very anxious to join in the game. Delphine and Marinette had their backs to him, and at that moment no one was· looking his way. He thought happily how astonished the little girls would be when they saw him. In a short time the examination of the passengers was nearly ended; and as they came to the cow, who was still staring at the contents of the cupboard, the elephant opened the door wide and said in an enormous voice, which even he did not recognize:

"Here I am!"

The little girls could not believe their eyes. Delphine was dumb with astonishment, and Marinette dropped her notebook. They began to wonder if the Ark were really a game, and could almost believe that the Flood was real.

"Yes, it's me," the elephant said. "Aren't I a lovely elephant?"

Delphine held herself back from running to the window, because after all she was the captain, and she must not show that she was frightened. She bent toward Marinette, and whispered to her to go see if the garden had really disappeared under the water. Marinette went to the window and murmured when she came back:

"No, everything's still there. There's only a few puddles in the yard."

Meanwhile the animals were beginning to grow scared at the sight of the elephant, which was something they had never seen before. The pig began to cry out in a manner that threatened to spread panic among his companions. Delphine said sternly:

"If the pig does not stop at once I shall have him thrown overboard! . . . That's better! . . . I must now explain that I had forgotten to tell you about the elephant who has come on this voyage with us. Will everyone please move closer together to make room for him in the Ark."

Alarmed by the sternness of the captain, the pig had ceased his cries at once. All the animals huddled together, so as to leave as much room as possible for their new shipmate. But when the elephant tried to enter the kitchen he found that the door was not high enough, or wide enough, to let him through. It needed to be at least half as large again.

"I'm afraid to push," he said, "because I might bring the wall with me. You see, I'm rather strong . . . in fact, I'm terribly strong!"

"No, no!" cried the little girls. "You mustn't push. You'll just have to play in the other room."

They had not thought about the door being too small, and this was a new complication to worry them. If the elephant had been able to get out, Father and Mother would certainly have been surprised at finding him wandering round the house, because there was no such animal in the village; but at least they would not have had any reason to think that the little girls had anything to do with it. Perhaps the next day Mother would have found that a white hen was missing, and that would have been all. But if they found an elephant in their bedroom, they would be certain to ask questions; and then Delphine and Marinette would have to confess that they had asked the animals into the kitchen to play Noah's Ark.

"After they specially told us we weren't to let anyone inside the house!" sighed Marinette.

"Perhaps the elephant will turn back into a white hen," murmured Delphine. "After all, she only did it for the game. When we've stopped playing Noah's Ark there won't be any reason for her to go on being an elephant."

"Well, that's true. We'd better hurry up."

Marinette took the helm again, and Delphine went back to the captain's bridge.

"The voyage continues!"

"Good!" said the elephant. "Now I can play!"

"We have been at sea for ninety days," said Delphine. "There's nothing to report."

"It seems a bit smoky," said the pig.

Marinette was so flustered by the elephant that she had moved the damper on the stove without noticing.

"The hundred-and-seventy-second day at sea!" announced the captain. "Still nothing to report."

Most of the animals were quite pleased that the time should be passing so quickly; but the elephant could not help feeling that the voyage was a bit dull, and he said so, adding in a sulky voice:

"This is all very nice, but what am *I* supposed to do?"

"You're being the elephant," replied Marinette, "and you're waiting for the water to go down. I don't see that you've anything to complain of."

"Oh, well — if I'm only waiting . . ."

"Two-hundred-and-thirty-seventh day at sea! The wind's blowing, and it looks as though the water was beginning to subside. . . . Yes, it's going down!"

The pig was so delighted to hear this news that he rolled over on the floor, uttering grunts of joy.

"Be quiet, pig, or I'll tell the elephant to eat you!" said Delphine.

"Yes, do!" said the elephant. "I'd love to eat him!" He winked at Marinette, and added: "I think this is a very nice game!"

"Three-hundred-and-sixty-fifth day at sea! I can see the garden again. Everybody get ready to march out quietly. The Flood is over."

Marinette went to open the door giving onto the yard. The pig was so terrified of being eaten by the elephant that he nearly knocked her over as he rushed out. He found that the ground was not yet dry, and hurried through the rain to his sty. The other animals left the kitchen without hustling, and went back to their places in the stable and the farmyard. Soon only the elephant was left with the two little girls, but he did not seem to be in any hurry to go. Delphine went up to him and said, clapping her hands:

"Now then, little white hen, the game's over! You must go back to the hen-roost."

"Little white hen . . . little white hen . . ." said Marinette softly, offering a handful of corn.

But in spite of all their pleading, the elephant was determined never to be a little white hen again.

"It isn't that I want to be unfriendly," he said, "but I think it's much more fun being an elephant."

Father and Mother came home towards the end of the afternoon, very pleased to have seen Uncle Alfred. Their coats were soaked, and the rain had even got into their boots.

"What dreadful weather!" they said as they opened the door. "It's a good thing we didn't take you with us."

"And how's Uncle Alfred?" asked the two little girls, who were both rather pink.

"We'll tell you all about him in a minute. But first let us go into the bedroom and take our things off."

Father and Mother were moving towards the door of the bedroom as they spoke. They were halfway across the kitchen, and the little girls were trembling with fear. Their hearts were beating so hard that they had to press their hands against them.

"Your coats are very wet," said Delphine, in a small, gasping voice. "Perhaps it would be better to take them off here. I'll put them to dry in front of the stove."

"Why, yes," said Father and Mother. "That's a good idea. We didn't think of that."

They took off their coats, with the water streaming out of them, and spread them out in front of the stove.

"I *do* want to know how Uncle Alfred is," sighed Marinette. "Has he still got rheumatism in his leg?"

"His rheumatism isn't so bad. But just give us time to change out of our Sunday clothes, and you shall hear all about him."

Father and Mother again went towards the door of the bedroom; but when they were within two paces of it Delphine put herself in front of them and said, "Don't you think you'd better take your boots off before you change your clothes? You'll leave mud all over the floor of the bedroom."

"Why, of course; that's a good idea! We didn't think of it," said Father and Mother.

They came back to the stove and took off their boots, but it was done in a minute. Marinette tried to mention Uncle Alfred again, but she spoke so low that they did not hear her. Once again they moved towards the bedroom, and the little girls were so terrified that their cheeks froze, and their noses, and even their ears. Father and Mother were just turning the doorknob when they heard the sound of a sob behind them. It was Marinette, who could no longer keep from crying, because she was so frightened, and so sorry as well.

"But why are you crying?" asked Father and Mother. "Aren't you feeling well? Has the cat scratched you? There, there! — tell us why you're crying."

"It's because of the ele—— because of the ele——," stammered Marinette, but her sobs prevented her from going on.

"It's because she can see you've got your feet wet," said Delphine quickly. "So naturally she's afraid you'll catch cold. She expected you to sit down in front of the stove to dry your stockings. Look — she's even put the chairs ready."

Father and Mother stroked Marinette's fair hair, and said how nice it was to have such a good little girl, but that she need not be afraid of their catching cold. And they promised to come and warm their feet as soon as they had changed their clothes.

"Perhaps it would be better to warm your feet first," persisted Delphine. "It's so easy to catch cold."

"Bless you, this isn't the first time we've got our feet wet! We've had water in our boots before now without catching cold."

"Well, but it would make Marinette feel happier — particularly as she's rather worried about Uncle Alfred's health."

"But Uncle Alfred's very well! He has never been better. There's no reason at all to worry. In five minutes you shall hear all about him. We'll tell you everything."

Delphine could think of nothing more to say. With a smile for Marinette, Father and Mother turned again towards the bedroom; but the cat, who was hidden under the stove, put his tail in the ash pan and waved it about so furiously that as they passed near him a cloud of fine ash rose up to their noses and made them sneeze several times.

"You see!" cried the little girls. "You *have* caught cold! You mustn't waste a minute. You must warm your feet at once. Come and sit down quickly!"

Looking a little foolish, Father and Mother admitted that Marinette was right, and sat down in the chairs. Resting their feet on the hob, they watched their stockings steam and kept yawning as they did so. After their long walk in the rain and on the muddy roads they were so tired that they seemed to be on the verge of

548   MARCEL AYMÉ

falling asleep. The little girls hardly dared to breathe. But suddenly they started up. There was a sound like that of a very heavy footstep, and the crockery rattled in the cupboard.

"What was that? There's something walking about the house! Why, it sounded like —"

"It's nothing," said Delphine. "It's only the cat chasing mice in the attic. He made just the same noise this afternoon."

"But it can't be! You must be mistaken. How could the cat possibly make the cupboard shake? You must be wrong."

"No; he told me himself, a little while ago."

"He did? Well, I'd never have thought the cat could make a noise like that! Still, if he told you himself . . ."

The cat made himself as small as possible under the stove. The noise had stopped at once, but Father and Mother no longer felt sleepy, and while they waited for their stockings to get quite dry they began to tell about their visit to Uncle Alfred.

"Your uncle was waiting for us on the doorstep. Seeing how bad the weather was, he had not expected you to come. But he was very sorry you weren't with us, and he told us to tell you . . . why, there it is again! Even the walls are shaking!"

"Did Uncle Alfred give you a message for us?"

"Yes; he said . . . but really you can't say that was the cat! It felt as though the whole house was coming down!"

The cat made himself smaller than ever under the stove, but he had not thought that the tip of his tail was sticking out, and he was too late in noticing it. Father and Mother caught sight of it just as he was trying to tuck it in between his paws.

"There!" they said. "Now you can't possibly say it was the cat! There he is, under the stove!"

They made a movement to get up from their chairs and go and look for the cause of those enormous footsteps that made the whole house tremble. But then the cat came out of his hiding place, stretched his four legs as though he had just woken up, and said in an angry voice:

"It's really too bad that one can't sleep peacefully anymore! I don't know what's come over the horse since this morning. He keeps on kicking the stable walls and the sides of his stall. I didn't think I'd hear the noise down here in the kitchen, but it's even worse than it is in the hayloft. I can't think what's happened to put him in such a state."

"He must be ill, or else he's cross about something," said Father and Mother. "We'll go and see presently."

While they were talking about the horse the cat looked at the little girls and shook his head, as though to say that all this was no use, and they might as well give up. After all, what good could it do? It would not prevent Father and Mother from going into the bedroom in the end; and whether they went there five minutes earlier, or five minutes later, would make no difference. The little girls almost agreed with the cat, but they thought that just the same five minutes later was better than five minutes earlier. Delphine coughed to clear her throat, and said:

"You were just saying that Uncle Alfred gave you a message for us . . ."

"Ah, yes, Uncle Alfred. . . . Of course he quite understood that it was no weather for children to be out in. It was raining hard, you know, particularly when we arrived — it was a real flood! . . . Still, I don't think it's going to last. In fact, I think it's beginning to stop — don't you?"

Father and Mother looked out of the window, and uttered a cry of astonishment as they saw the horse walking about in the yard.

"Why there he is! He has kicked so hard that he's managed to get loose, and he's come out for a breath of air! Well, so much the better. He'll be feeling calmer in a little while, and at least we won't hear him making noises in the stable."

But at that same moment they heard the footsteps again, and now they were heavier than ever. The floor creaked, and the house shuddered from top to bottom, the table bounced on two legs, and Father and Mother felt themselves shake in their chairs.

"It can't be the horse," they cried, "because he's still in the yard! Isn't that so, cat? It can't be the horse!"

"Of course not," said the cat. "Of course it can't. It must be the oxen getting impatient in their stalls."

"What's that? Why, whoever heard of oxen getting impatient when they're resting!"

"Well, perhaps it's the sheep quarrelling with the cow."

"The sheep quarrelling with the cow? But . . . that doesn't sound right either. H'm. . . . There's something queer about all this!"

The little girls began to tremble so hard that their golden heads shook, and this made Father and Mother think that they were denying that they had been disobedient. They scolded them all the same, and perhaps they were still a little suspicious.

"All right. . . . But if you *had* let anyone inside the house — if you *had*! . . . Well, I wouldn't like to say what would happen to you!"

Father and Mother were frowning in a terrible manner, and Delphine and Marinette dared not look at them. Even the cat was frightened and did not know which way to look.

"There's one thing certain," said Father and Mother; "those footsteps were quite close. They certainly didn't come from the stable. It was more like someone walking in the next room — yes, in the bedroom! . . . Well, we can soon see!"

Their stockings were now quite dry. Without taking their

eyes off the bedroom door they rose from their chairs. As they approached it Delphine and Marinette, who were holding hands, drew closer together. The cat rubbed his coat against their legs to show he was still their friend, and to try and cheer them up, but all the same it was dreadful. They thought their hearts would burst. Father and Mother listened mistrustfully, with their ears to the door. At last they turned the doorknob, the door opened with a squeak, and then there was a moment of silence. Delphine and Marinette, trembling in every limb, looked towards the bedroom. They saw a little white hen creep cautiously between the legs of Father and Mother, and scuttle silently across the kitchen to take refuge under the clock.

LINDA ALLEN
Mrs. Simkin's Bathtub

"ARE YOU aware," said Mr. Simkin to Mrs. Simkin one morning, "that the bathtub's halfway down the stairs?"

"How very inconvenient," said Mrs. Simkin, going to have a look. "How long has it been there?"

"I have no idea," said Mr. Simkin. "It was in the bathroom when I went to bed last night, and now it's here, so it must have moved when we were asleep."

"Well, we shall just have to make the best of it," said Mrs. Simkin. "Will you bathe first, or shall I?"

"I will," said Mr. Simkin bravely.

He stepped into the bathtub. It wobbled a bit at first, but it soon settled down. Mrs. Simkin fetched soap and towels, shampoo and bath salts, and arranged them nicely on the stairs. "There," she said, "it doesn't look too bad now, and if I polish the taps and scrub the feet, it should look quite smart. I'm sure none of the neighbours has a bathtub on the stairs."

Mr. Simkin said she was probably right.

After a day or two they hardly noticed that the bathtub was there at all. It didn't really inconvenience them to squeeze past it when they went upstairs, and the landing smelled so pleasantly of bath salts that Mrs. Simkin began to feel quite happy about it.

She invited the lady next door to have a look, but the lady next door said that she didn't approve of these modern ideas.

One morning Mr. Simkin went to have his bath. "My dear!" he cried. "Come and see! The bathtub's gone!"

"Gone!" cried Mrs. Simkin, leaping out of bed. "Gone where?"

"I don't know," said Mr. Simkin, "but it isn't on the stairs."

"Perhaps it's back in the bathroom," said Mrs. Simkin.

They went to look, but it wasn't there.

"We shall have to buy another one," said Mr. Simkin as they went down to breakfast.

The bathtub was in the kitchen.

"You know, my dear," said Mr. Simkin a few minutes later, "this is a much better place for a bathtub than halfway down the stairs. I quite like having breakfast in the bath."

"Yes," agreed Mrs. Simkin, "I quite like it here, too. The bath towels match the saucepans."

"That's a very good point," said Mr. Simkin.

One day Mr. and Mrs. Simkin went downstairs to find that the bathtub had moved again. It was in the living room, sitting smugly before the fire.

"Oh, I don't think I like it there," said Mrs. Simkin, "but I don't suppose it will stay there very long. Once a bathtub has started to roam, it never knows when to stop."

She was quite right. The next day they found it in the cellar, with spiders in it.

One day they couldn't find the bathtub anywhere.

"What shall I do?" cried Mrs. Simkin. "It's my birthday, and I did so want to use that lovely bubble bath you gave me."

"So did I," said Mr. Simkin.

The lady next door came round. "Happy birthday," she said. "Did you know that your bathtub was on the front lawn?"

They all went to have a look.

There was a horse drinking out of it.

"Go away," said Mrs. Simkin. "How dare you drink my bath water, you greedy creature?"

She stepped into the bathtub. The lady next door said she didn't know what the world was coming to, and she went home and locked herself indoors.

As the bubbles floated down the street, lots of people came to see what was going on. They were very interested.

They leant on the fence and watched.

They asked if they could come again.

One day when there was rather a chilly wind about, they found the bathtub in the greenhouse. Everyone was very disappointed.

"My dear," said Mr. Simkin a few days later, "do you happen to know where the bathtub is today?"

"No," said Mrs. Simkin, "but today's Tuesday. It's quite often in the garage on Tuesdays."

"It isn't there today," said Mr. Simkin. "I've looked everywhere."

"I do hope it hasn't gone next door," sighed Mrs. Simkin. "The lady next door has no sympathy at all."

Mr. Simkin went round to inquire.

The lady next door said she was of the opinion that people ought to be able to control their bathtubs.

Mr. Simkin went home.

Mr. Robinson from across the street rang up. "I know it's none of my business," he said, "but I thought you'd like to know that your bathtub is on the roof of your house."

Mr. Simkin went up to take his bath. All the people cheered.

The bathtub seemed to like being up there, because that's where it stayed.

The people in the street had a meeting in Mr. Simkin's greenhouse. They decided to have their bathtubs on the roofs of their houses, too.

All except the lady next door.

She preferred to take a shower.

RICHARD AND
FLORENCE ATWATER

Mr. Popper's Penguins is the Atwaters' only book but it is the kind that will be read for decades to come.

It all happened this way. Mr. Popper was a house painter who wanted to be an explorer. He couldn't be one, but he could write letters to famous explorers, and he did. One day, in response to one of his letters, a penguin arrived, which the Poppers named Captain Cook. Captain Cook, after causing quite a little trouble in the Popper household, began to get droopy. So the Poppers got a lady penguin, called Greta, from the aquarium, and soon there were ten more little penguins. To make money the Poppers trained the twelve penguins as a vaudeville troupe. The chapters that follow tell us what happened.

Mr. Greenbaum and Popper's Performing Penguins

ILLUSTRATED BY
ROBERT LAWSON

"LOOK HERE," said Mr. Popper at breakfast one morning. "It says here in the *Morning Chronicle* that Mr. Greenbaum, the owner of the Palace Theatre, is in town. He's got a string of theatres all over the country; so I guess we had better go down and see him."

That evening — it was Saturday, the twenty-ninth of January — the Popper family and their twelve trained penguins, two of them carrying flags in their beaks, left the house to find the Palace Theatre.

The penguins were now so well trained that Mr. Popper decided that it was not necessary to keep them on leashes. Indeed, they walked to the bus very nicely in the following line of march: Mr. Popper, Greta, Captain Cook, Columbus, Victoria, Mrs. Popper, Nelson, Jenny, Magellan, Adelina, Bill Popper, Janie Popper, Scott, Isabella, Ferdinand, Louisa.

The bus stopped at the corner, and before the astonished driver could protest, they had all climbed on and the bus was on its way.

"Do I pay half-fare for the birds, or do they go free?" asked Mr. Popper.

"Janie goes half-fare, but I'm ten," said Bill.

"Hush," said Mrs. Popper as she and the children found their seats. The penguins followed in an orderly fashion.

"Say, mister," said the driver, "where do you think you're going with that exhibit?"

"Downtown," said Mr. Popper. "Here, let's call it fifty cents, and let it go at that."

"To tell the truth, I lost count when they went past me," said the driver.

"It's a trained penguin act," explained Mr. Popper.

"Are they really birds?" asked the driver.

"Oh yes," said Mr. Popper. "I'm just taking them down to the Palace to interview Mr. Greenbaum, the big theatre owner."

"Well, if I hear any complaints, off they go at the next corner," said the driver.

"Fair enough," said Mr. Popper, who wanted to ask for transfers in that case, but decided to let well enough alone.

The penguins were behaving very well. They were sitting quietly two in a seat, while the other passengers looked on.

"Sorry," said Mr. Popper, addressing everyone in the bus, "but I'll have to open all the windows. These are Antarctic penguins and they're used to having it a lot colder than this."

It took Mr. Popper quite a while to open the windows, which were stuck fast. When he had succeeded, there were plenty of remarks from the other passengers. Many of them began to complain to the driver, who told Mr. Popper to take his birds off the bus. He had to repeat this several times. Finally he refused to take the bus any farther until Mr. Popper got off. By this time, however, the bus had got so far downtown that none of them minded having to get out into the street.

Only a block ahead of them shone the lights of the Palace Theatre.

"Hello," said the theatre manager, as the Poppers and the penguins trooped past him. "Sure, Mr. Greenbaum's here in my office. You know I've heard about these birds of yours, but I didn't really believe it. Mr. Greenbaum, meet the Popper Penguins. I'll be leaving you. I've got to go backstage."

The penguins, now standing politely in two rows of six each, looked curiously at Mr. Greenbaum. Their twenty-four white-circled eyes were very solemn.

"All you people crowding around the door, go back where you belong," said Mr. Greenbaum. "This is a private conference." Then he got up to shut the door.

The Poppers sat down while Mr. Greenbaum walked up and down the double row of penguins, looking them over.

"It looks like an act," he said.

"Oh, it's an act, all right," said Mr. Popper. "It's Popper's Performing Penguins, First Time on any Stage, Direct from the South Pole." He and Mrs. Popper had thought up this name for the act.

"Couldn't we call them Popper's Pink-toed Penguins?" asked Mr. Greenbaum.

Mr. Popper thought for a moment. "No," he said, "I'm afraid we couldn't. That sounds too much like chorus girls or ballet dancers, and these birds are pretty serious. I don't think they'd like it."

"All right," said Mr. Greenbaum. "Show me the act."

"There's music to it," said Janie. "Mamma plays the piano."

"Is that true, madam?" asked Mr. Greenbaum.

"Yes, sir," answered Mrs. Popper.

"Well, there's a piano behind you," said Mr. Greenbaum. "You may begin, madam. I want to see this act. If it's any good, you people have come to the right place. I've got theatres from coast to coast. But first let's see your penguins perform. Ready, madam?"

"We'd better move the furniture first," said Bill.

At that moment they were interrupted by the manager, who came in with a groan.

"What's the matter?" asked Mr. Greenbaum.

"The Marvellous Marcos, who close the programme, haven't turned up, and the audience are demanding their money back."

"What are you going to do?" asked Mr. Greenbaum.

"Give it to them, I suppose. And here it is Saturday night, the biggest night of the week. I hate to think of losing all that money."

"I have an idea," said Mrs. Popper. "Maybe you won't have to lose it. As long as it's the end of the programme, why don't we just have the penguins rehearse in there on a real stage? We'd have more room, and I think the audience would enjoy it."

"All right," said the manager. "Let's try it."

So the penguins had their first rehearsal on a real stage.

The manager stepped out on the stage. "Ladies and gentlemen," he said, raising his hand, "with your kind indulgence we are going to try out a little novelty number tonight. Owing to unforeseen circumstances, the Marvellous Marcos are unable to appear. We are going to let you see a rehearsal of the Popper Performing Penguins, instead. I thank you."

In a dignified way the Poppers and the penguins walked out on the stage, and Mrs. Popper sat down at the piano.

"Aren't you going to take off your gloves to play?" asked the manager.

"Oh, no," said Mrs. Popper. "I'm so used to playing with them that I'll keep them on, if you don't mind."

Then she started Schubert's "Military March". The penguins began to drill very nicely, wheeling and changing their formations with great precision, until Mrs. Popper stopped playing in the middle of the piece.

The audience clapped vigorously.

"There's more to it," explained Mrs. Popper, half to the manager and half to the audience, "where they form in a hollow square and march in that formation. It's so late we'll skip that tonight and jump to the second part."

"You're sure you don't want to take your gloves off, madam?" asked the manager.

Mrs. Popper smilingly shook her head and began the "Merry Widow Waltz".

Ten of the penguins now formed in a semicircle as Nelson and Columbus in their midst put on a wild sparring contest. Their round black heads leaned far back so that they could watch each other with both round white eyes.

"*Gork*," said Nelson, punching Columbus in the stomach with his right flipper, and then trying to push him over with his left flipper.

"*Gaw*," said Columbus, going into a clinch and hanging his head over Nelson's shoulder as he tried to punch him in the back.

"Hey! No fair!" said the manager. Columbus and Nelson broke loose as the other ten penguins, looking on, applauded with their flippers.

Columbus now sparred politely with Nelson until Nelson hit him on the eye, whereupon Columbus retreated with a loud "*Ork*". The other penguins began to clap, and the audience joined

them. As Mrs. Popper finished the Waltz, both Nelson and Columbus stopped fighting, put down their flippers, and stood still,
facing each other.

"Which bird won? Who's ahead?" shouted the audience.

"*Gook!*" said all the ten penguins in the semicircle.

This must have meant "Look!" for Nelson turned to look at
them, and Columbus immediately punched him in the stomach
with one flipper and knocked him down with the other. Nelson lay
there, with his eyes closed. Columbus then counted ten over the
prostrate Nelson, and again the ten other penguins applauded.

"That's part of the act," explained Janie. "The other penguins
all like Columbus to win, and so they all say '*Gook!*' at the end.
That always makes Nelson look away, so Columbus can sock him
good."

Nelson now rose to his feet, and all the penguins formed in a
row, and bowed to the manager.

"Thank you," said the manager, bowing back.

"Now comes part three," said Mr. Popper.

"Oh, Papa," said Mrs. Popper. "You forgot to bring the two
painting stepladders and the board!"

"That's all right," said the manager. "I'll get the stagehands to
bring some."

In no time at all a pair of ladders and a board were brought in
and Mr. Popper and the children showed them how the ladders
had to be set up with the board resting on top. Then Mrs. Popper
began playing the pretty descriptive piece "By the Brook".

At this point in the act the penguins always forgot their disci-
pline and got dreadfully excited. They would all begin shoving at
once to see which could be the first to climb the ladders. However,
the children had always told Mr. Popper that the act was all the

funnier for all this pushing and scrambling, and Mr. Popper supposed it was.

So now with a great deal of squawking the penguins fought and climbed the ladders and ran across the board in complete confusion, often knocking each other entirely off to the floor below, and then hurrying to toboggan down the other ladder and knock off any penguins who were trying to climb up there.

This part of the act was very wild and noisy in spite of Mrs. Popper's delicate music. The manager and the audience were all holding their sides, laughing.

At last Mrs. Popper got to the end of the music and took off her gloves.

"You'll have to get those ladders off the stage, or I'll never get these birds under control," said Mr. Popper. "The curtain is supposed to fall at this point."

So the manager gave the signal for the curtain to go down, and the audience stood up and cheered.

When the ladders had been taken away, the manager had twelve ice-cream cones brought in for the penguins. Then Janie and Bill began to cry, so the manager ordered several more, and everybody had one.

Mr. Greenbaum was the first to congratulate the Poppers.

"I don't mind telling you, Mr. Popper, that I think you've got something absolutely unique in those birds. Your act is a sensation. And the way you helped out my friend the manager, here, shows that you're real troupers — the kind we need in the show business. I'd like to predict that your penguins will soon be packing the biggest theatres from Oregon to Maine.

"And now to come to terms, Mr. Popper," he continued. "How about a ten-week contract at five thousand dollars a week?"

"Is that all right, Mamma?" asked Mr. Popper.

"Yes, that's very satisfactory," answered Mrs. Popper.

"Well, then," said Mr. Greenbaum, "just sign these papers. And be ready to open next Thursday in Seattle."

"And thanks again," said the manager. "Would you mind putting on your gloves again for just a minute, Mrs. Popper? I'd like you to start playing that 'Military March' again and let the penguins parade for a minute. I want to get my ushers in here to look at those birds. It would be a lesson to them."

MITSUMASA ANNO

I wish this book were like an accordion. Then I could stretch it out and put in some of Mitsumasa Anno's other artwork, done in ink and watercolour.

There's one called *Anno's Alphabet Book,* and I think it's the best alphabet book in the world. If you look closely at "A is for anvil" you'll also discover an acanthus, an anemone, an ant, an aster, and an army of other "As".

Then there's *Anno's Animals.* At first it looks like a lot of pictures of trees and woodland. But look again. What seems like two pages of tree trunks really hides pictures of an owl, a crane, a seal, a goat, a kid, a parrot — and even faces of people.

Some other books of his I love are *Topsy-Turvies,* a book of "impossible pictures"; *Anno's Journey,* which doesn't have a word in it, but taught me more than most long books do; and *Dr. Anno's Magical Midnight Circus.* Perhaps you can find some of these in the library.

The King's Flower is a kind of fable, though it's not about animals, as Aesop's are. It tells us what a lot of grown-ups, especially those who govern large countries, don't seem to understand. Bigger isn't always better.

Mr. Anno was born in 1926 in Tsuwana, a small Japanese town. He began as a schoolteacher, then he became a very fine artist. But he's really a magician. Once someone, looking at his pictures, said to him, "You amuse yourself by fooling people." True, but he also delights them and makes them laugh. In *The King's Flower* what makes me laugh most is the picture showing how the dentist took out the King's tooth.

The King's Flower

THERE was once a King who had to have everything bigger and better than anyone else. He lived in a very big castle and he wore such a very big crown that it was actually rather uncomfortable. He slept in an enormous bed, so high he had to use a ladder to get in and out of it. The King's toothbrush was so big it took two men just to carry it.

When the big clock chimed in the kitchen the noise was quite deafening. It was the signal to start preparing the King's big breakfast.

The King's knife and fork were so big that they had to be hung from the ceiling with ropes and pulleys and he found it very difficult to use them. Soon, of course, the King was hungry.

The food he liked best of all was chocolate, so he sent his servants out to fetch some. They brought him the biggest bar of chocolate ever seen, too big even to get through the castle gate. So the King had to go outside to nibble a bit from the end of it.

"How delicious," he said. "This is the biggest and best chocolate bar ever. Just right for a man of my importance." And he ate some more, and some more, until . . .

"Help! Call the dentist. My tooth hurts most dreadfully," cried the King.

"Only the biggest of everything for the King," remembered the dentist. So he ordered the blacksmiths to make a gigantic pair of pincers to pull out the royal tooth.

The King was just a little uneasy when he saw the huge pincers and again when the dentist tied him down in his chair. But everyone pushed or pulled and at last out came the tiny bad tooth and the King's enormous toothache was over.

The next day the King ordered his servants to take the pincers away.

"Turn them into a birdcage or something," he commanded, for that is what their shape reminded him of.

It was a beautifully big birdcage but the spaces between the bars were so wide that the birds he put inside the cage flew out again.

"What a disappointment," said the King.

One day not long after, however, a great eagle flew over the castle trying to catch some of the little birds. Swiftly they flew back into the new cage and were quite safe, for the eagle could not get through the bars. The King was very pleased.

"I knew biggest was best," he said.

Then the King had another idea and he commanded his servants to build the biggest flowerpot ever made and to fill it with tons of earth. A single tulip bulb was planted in the middle.

"In such a big flowerpot, this one tulip cannot fail to be the biggest and best in all the world," said the King.

While he waited for the tulip to grow, the King ordered that the hole from where the earth had been taken should be made into a pond for fishing. But the first fishing rod that was brought to him was much too small.

"I must have a bigger line," he ordered. "I want to catch the biggest fish in all the world."

The servants knew that the King would not let them rest until he had caught the biggest fish, so they brought in a whale and attached it to the hook. The King was very pleased with his catch but the fish was too heavy for him to lift out of the water and he had to let it go.

Every morning the King climbed up into the big flowerpot to see if the tulip was growing, but there was no sign of it. The King's gardener comforted him.

"The biggest and best flower in all the world is bound to take longer to grow than an ordinary flower," he said.

At last, one spring day, when the King peered over the edge of the pot, there it was! A red tulip blossomed serenely in the middle of the enormous flowerpot. The King looked at it for a long time. It was not big. It was small — but it was very beautiful.

"Perhaps biggest is not best after all," said the King, wondering at the work of nature. "Not even I could make the biggest flower in all the world. And perhaps that is just as well."

Anno's Afterword

One day, when I was looking at a gas storage tank, I wondered what it would be like if there was a coffee cup as large as one of these big containers. I imagined myself climbing up a tall ladder and creeping along the edge on my hands and knees, lapping up the coffee, and I felt almost dizzy. It gives me endless pleasure just imagining huge things — a pencil as large as a telegraph pole, a playground slide as high as a mountain, and a shoe so enormous that I could lie down in it. But could there ever be a tulip as large as an umbrella? The Egyptian kings built the great tombs, the Pyramids, but even the most powerful human beings cannot produce life. We must be content, and recognize that each flower, each worm, is something natural and indispensable.

JOSEF ČAPEK

Puss and Pup

Translated from the Czech

ONCE upon a time Puss and Pup kept house together. They had their own little cottage in the wood. Here they lived together and tried to do everything just like real grown-up people. But somehow they couldn't always manage this. You see, they had small clumsy paws, without any fingers like people have, only little soft pads with claws on them. So they couldn't do everything just like real grown-ups. And they didn't go to school, because school is not meant for animals.

Of course it isn't. School is only for children.

Their home was not always as tidy as it might have been. Some things they did well, and others not so well. And sometimes there was rather a mess.

One day they noticed that the cottage floor was very dirty.

"I say, Pup," said Puss, "our floor's horribly dirty. Don't you think so?"

"Yes, I do. It really is rather dirty," said Pup. "Just look how grubby it's made my paws."

"They're filthy," said Puss. "Ugh, you ought to be ashamed of yourself! We must scrub the floor. People don't have dirty floors. They scrub them."

"All right," replied Pup. "But how are we going to do it?"

"Oh, it's easy," said Puss. "You go and fetch some water, and I'll see to the rest."

Pup took a pail and went for water. Meanwhile Puss took a piece of soap out of her bag and put it on the table. Then she went off to the box room for something; I expect she kept a piece of smoked mouse there.

While she was away Pup came back with the water and saw something lying on the table. He unwrapped it. It was pink.

"Ha, ha! This looks good," said Pup to himself. And because it made him feel hungry, he pushed the whole piece into his mouth and started chewing it.

But it didn't taste so good. Soon Puss came in and heard Pup making all sorts of funny spluttering noises. She saw that Pup's mouth was full of foam and his eyes were streaming with tears.

"Goodness me!" cried Puss. "Whatever's happened to you, Pup? You must be ill. There's foam dripping from your mouth. Whatever's the matter?"

"Well," said Pup, "I found something lying on the table. I thought it might be some cheese, or a piece of cake, so I ate it. But it stings horribly and makes my mouth all full of foam."

"What a silly you are!" scolded Puss. "That was soap! Soap's for washing with, not eating."

"Oh," said Pup. "So that's why it hurts so much. Ow, ow, it stings, ow, it stings!"

"Have a good drink of water," suggested Puss; "that'll stop it smarting."

Pup drank away until he had finished up all the water. It had stopped smarting by now, but there was still plenty of foam. So he went and wiped his muzzle on the grass outside. Then he had to go and fetch some more water because he had drunk it all and there was none left. Luckily Puss had five pence, and she went off to buy some more soap.

"I won't eat that again," said Pup, when Puss returned with the soap. "But, Puss, how are we going to manage without a scrubbing brush?"

"I've already thought about that," said Puss. "You've got a rough, bristly coat, just like a brush. We can scrub the floor with you."

"Right ho!" said Pup. And Puss took the soap and the pail of water, and knelt down on the floor. Then she scrubbed the whole floor with Pup.

"We ought to rub it over with something dry," said Puss.

"I'll tell you what," said Pup. "I'm sopping wet, but you're dry, and your fur is nice and soft. It'll make a lovely floor-cloth. I'll dry the floor with you."

So he took hold of Puss and dried the whole floor with her.

The floor was now washed and dried, but Puss and Pup were all wet and terribly dirty from having been used to wash the floor.

"Well, we do look a sight!" they both said, looking at each other. "We've got the floor clean all right, but now look at us! We can't possibly stay like this. Everybody will laugh. We'll have to be sent to the wash."

"Let's wash each other, the way they do at the laundry," said Pup. "You wash me, and when I'm done, I'll wash you."

They filled the tub of water and took a scrubbing-board. Pup got into the tub and Puss washed him. She rubbed him so much on the scrubbing-board that Pup begged her not to press so hard, as his legs were getting all tangled up.

When Pup was finished, Puss got into the tub and Pup scrubbed and squeezed her so much that she begged him not to press her so hard on the scrubbing-board in case he made a hole in her fur.

Then they wrung each other out.

"Now we'll hang ourselves out to dry," said Puss. So they put out the clothesline.

"First you hang me up on the line, and when I'm up, I'll get down and hang you up," Puss told Pup.

So Pup took hold of Puss and hung her up, just like washing. They didn't need any pegs, because they could hold on to the line with their claws. Once Puss was on the line, she jumped down and hung up Pup.

By now the two of them were hanging nicely and the sun was shining brightly.

"The sun's shining on us," cried Pup. "We'll soon be dry."

No sooner had he said this than it began to rain.

"Oh, dear, it's raining!" shouted Puss and Pup. "The washing will get wet. Let's take it down!"

They jumped down quickly and ran to the cottage for shelter.

"Is it still raining?" asked Puss.

"It's stopped," said Pup, and sure enough the sun was out again.

"Let's hang the washing out again, then," said Puss.

So they hung themselves on the line a second time. First Pup put Puss up, and as soon as she was hanging up she jumped down and put up Pup. So they both hung on the line, just like washing, and were very pleased at the way the sun shone and made such a good drying day.

But then it began to rain again.

"It's raining! Our washing will get wet!" cried Puss and Pup. And they ran for shelter. Soon the sun came out again, and again they hung each other up on the clothesline. Then it started raining, and off they scampered. Then the sun came out again and they hung themselves up again, and so it went on till the evening. By that time they were both quite dry.

"Our washing's dry," they said. "Let's put it in the basket."

So they clambered into the basket. But then they felt so sleepy that they both fell asleep. And they slept in the basket right through until the next morning.

THE STUPIDS STEP OUT

Story by
HARRY ALLARD
Pictures by
JAMES MARSHALL

ONE DAY Stanley Q. Stupid had an idea.
This was unusual.
"Calling all Stupids!" Stanley shouted.
Mrs. Stupid, Buster Stupid, Petunia Stupid, and the Stupids'
wonderful dog Kitty all crawled out from under the rug.
"The Stupids are stepping out today," said Stanley.

The Stupids were delighted.

"Let's go upstairs and get ready," said Mrs. Stupid.

The two Stupid children climbed onto the banister.

"Up we go!" squealed Petunia.

They did not move. They wondered why.

"Bath time!" said Mrs. Stupid.

"Everyone into the tub," ordered Mr. Stupid.

"But where's the water?" asked Petunia.

"Don't be stupid," said Stanley. "If we fill up the tub, our clothes will get wet."

"Listen to your father," said Mrs. Stupid.

"Mother," said Buster, "your new hat is meowing."

"Of course it is, Buster," said Mrs. Stupid. "I'm wearing the cat."

"Don't forget the stockings I knitted for you," said Mrs. Stupid to her husband.

"I have them on, dear," said Mr. Stupid.

While they were walking, Stanley Stupid saw something amusing.

"Look at those funny-looking people in the window," he said to his family.

"Yes, they are certainly stupid-looking," said Mrs. Stupid. "Don't stare at them, children. It's impolite."

"I'm hungry," Petunia whined.

"So am I," said her father. "How about a delicious mashed potato sundae?"

"Um, um," exclaimed Buster, smacking his lips. "Mashed potatoes and butterscotch syrup."

When the Stupids had gobbled up the last of their mashed potato sundaes, they went home.

"Time to get ready for bed," said Mrs. Stupid.

When the Stupids were all tucked into bed, Mrs. Stupid gave her husband a kiss on the cheek.

"Thank you for the lovely day, dear," she said. "It certainly has been fun."

A. A. MILNE

When I was a student in college, one of my teachers taught us Philosophy. Philosophy is about terribly serious matters, such as the meaning and aim of life.

Well, one morning Professor Irwin Edman (that was his name) surprised the class by saying, "Gentlemen, today we will not talk about Philosophy. Instead, I will read from a book that has just come out, called *Winnie-the-Pooh*." And he did. He read so well that he made us roar with laughter. It was certainly the funniest Philosophy class that ever was or ever will be.

Mr. Milne wrote two books about Pooh. The first was called *Winnie-the-Pooh*, and from it I have taken the story you're going to read. The second, called *The House at Pooh Corner*, is just as good as the first one.

The stories are about animals, but they're really toys (except for Rabbit and Owl, who are made up). These toys once actually belonged to Mr. and Mrs. Milne's little boy Christopher Robin. On his first birthday he got a teddy bear, and he and the bear (called Winnie-the-Pooh) were exactly the same size. Piglet was only 3½ inches long.

Mrs. Milne had the idea of bringing the toys to life and Mr. Milne took on the job of telling Christopher Robin at bedtime the stories that later became the two books. When the first one came out, Christopher Robin was six years old.

And that's how they started: Pooh (A Bear of Very Little Brain) and the gloomy Eeyore and Kanga and little Roo and all the rest of them.

Mr. Milne also wrote a lot of verses for Christopher Robin and about him. Some of them are on pages 364–369 of this book.

Eeyore Has a Birthday and Gets Two Presents

ILLUSTRATED BY E. H. SHEPARD

EYORE, the old grey Donkey, stood by the side of the stream, and looked at himself in the water.

"Pathetic," he said. "That's what it is. Pathetic."

He turned and walked slowly down the stream for twenty yards, splashed across it, and walked slowly back on the other side. Then he looked at himself in the water again.

"As I thought," he said. "No better from *this* side. But nobody minds. Nobody cares. Pathetic, that's what it is."

There was a crackling noise in the bracken behind him, and out came Pooh.

"Good morning, Eeyore," said Pooh.

"Good morning, Pooh Bear," said Eeyore gloomily. "If it *is* a good morning," he said. "Which I doubt," said he.

"Why, what's the matter?"

"Nothing, Pooh Bear, nothing. We can't all, and some of us don't. That's all there is to it."

"Can't all *what?*" said Pooh, rubbing his nose.

"Gaiety. Song-and-dance. Here we go round the mulberry bush."

"Oh!" said Pooh. He thought for a long time, and then asked, "What mulberry bush is that?"

"Bon-hommy," went on Eeyore gloomily. "French word meaning bonhommy," he explained. "I'm not complaining, but There It Is."

Pooh sat down on a large stone, and tried to think this out. It sounded to him like a riddle, and he was never much good at riddles, being a Bear of Very Little Brain. So he sang *Cottleston Pie* instead:

> *Cottleston, Cottleston, Cottleston Pie,*
> *A fly can't bird, but a bird can fly.*
> *Ask me a riddle and I reply:*
> *"Cottleston, Cottleston, Cottleston Pie."*

That was the first verse. When he had finished it, Eeyore didn't actually say that he didn't like it, so Pooh very kindly sang the second verse to him:

> *Cottleston, Cottleston, Cottleston Pie,*
> *A fish can't whistle and neither can I.*
> *Ask me a riddle and I reply:*
> "Cottleston, Cottleston, Cottleston Pie."

Eeyore still said nothing at all, so Pooh hummed the third verse quietly to himself:

> *Cottleston, Cottleston, Cottleston Pie,*
> *Why does a chicken, I don't know why.*
> *Ask me a riddle and I reply:*
> "Cottleston, Cottleston, Cottleston Pie."

"That's right," said Eeyore. "Sing. Umty-tiddly, umty-too. Here we go gathering Nuts in May. Enjoy yourself."

"I am," said Pooh.

"Some can," said Eeyore.

"Why, what's the matter?"

"*Is* anything the matter?"

"You seem so sad, Eeyore."

"Sad? Why should I be sad? It's my birthday. The happiest day of the year."

"Your birthday?" said Pooh in great surprise.

"Of course it is. Can't you see? Look at all the presents I have had." He waved a foot from side to side. "Look at the birthday cake. Candles and pink sugar."

Pooh looked — first to the right and then to the left.

"Presents?" said Pooh. "Birthday cake?" said Pooh. "*Where?*"

"Can't you see them?"

"No," said Pooh.

"Neither can I," said Eeyore. "Joke," he explained. "Ha ha!" Pooh scratched his head, being a little puzzled by all this.

"But is it really your birthday?" he asked.

"It is."

"Oh! Well, Many happy returns of the day, Eeyore."

"And many happy returns to you, Pooh Bear."

"But it isn't *my* birthday."

"No, it's mine."

"But you said 'Many happy returns' —"

"Well, why not? You don't always want to be miserable on my birthday, do you?"

"Oh, I see," said Pooh.

"It's bad enough," said Eeyore, almost breaking down, "being miserable myself, what with no presents and no cake and no candles, and no proper notice taken of me at all, but if everybody else is going to be miserable too —"

This was too much for Pooh. "Stay there!" he called to Eeyore, as he turned and hurried back home as quick as he could; for he felt that he must get poor Eeyore a present of *some* sort at once, and he could always think of a proper one afterwards.

Outside his house he found Piglet, jumping up and down trying to reach the knocker.

"Hallo, Piglet," he said.

"Hallo, Pooh," said Piglet.

"What are *you* trying to do?"

"I was trying to reach the knocker," said Piglet. "I just came round —"

"Let me do it for you," said Pooh kindly. So he reached up and knocked at the door. "I have just seen Eeyore," he began, "and poor Eeyore is in a Very Sad Condition, because it's his birthday, and nobody has taken any notice of it, and he's very Gloomy — you know what Eeyore is — and there he was, and—What a long time whoever lives here is answering this door." And he knocked again.

"But Pooh," said Piglet, "it's your own house!"

"Oh!" said Pooh. "So it is," he said. "Well, let's go in."

So in they went. The first thing Pooh did was to go to the cupboard to see if he had quite a small jar of honey left; and he had, so he took it down.

"I'm giving this to Eeyore," he explained, "as a present. What are *you* going to give?"

"Couldn't I give it too?" said Piglet. "From both of us?"

"No," said Pooh. "That would *not* be a good plan."

"All right, then, I'll give him a balloon. I've got one left from my party. I'll go and get it now, shall I?"

"That, Piglet, is a *very* good idea. It is just what Eeyore wants to cheer him up. Nobody can be uncheered with a balloon."

So off Piglet trotted; and in the other direction went Pooh, with his jar of honey.

It was a warm day, and he had a long way to go. He hadn't gone more than halfway when a sort of funny feeling began to creep all over him. It began at the tip of his nose and trickled all through him and out at the soles of his feet. It was just as if somebody inside him were saying, "Now then, Pooh, time for a little something."

"Dear, dear," said Pooh. "I didn't know it was as late as that." So he sat down and took the top off his jar of honey. "Lucky I brought this with me," he thought. "Many a bear going out on a warm day like this would never have thought of bringing a little something with him." And he began to eat.

"Now let me see," he thought, as he took his last lick of the inside of the jar, "where was I going? Ah, yes, Eeyore." He got up slowly.

And then, suddenly, he remembered. He had eaten Eeyore's birthday present!

"*Bother!*" said Pooh. "What *shall* I do? I *must* give him *something.*"

For a little while he couldn't think of anything. Then he thought: "Well, it's a very nice pot, even if there's no honey in it, and if I washed it clean, and got somebody to write 'A Happy Birthday' on it, Eeyore could keep things in it, which might be Useful." So, as he was just passing the Hundred Acre Wood, he went inside to call on Owl, who lived there.

"Good morning, Owl," he said.

"Good morning, Pooh," said Owl.

"Many happy returns of Eeyore's birthday," said Pooh.

"Oh, is that what it is?"

"What are you giving him, Owl?"

"What are *you* giving him, Pooh?"

"I'm giving him a Useful Pot to Keep Things In, and I wanted to ask you —"

"Is this it?" said Owl, taking it out of Pooh's paw.

"Yes, and I wanted to ask you —"

"Somebody has been keeping honey in it," said Owl.

"You can keep *anything* in it," said Pooh earnestly. "It's Very Useful like that. And I wanted to ask you —"

"You ought to write 'A Happy Birthday' on it."

"*That* was what I wanted to ask you," said Pooh. "Because my spelling is Wobbly. It's good spelling but it Wobbles, and the letters get in the wrong places. Would *you* write 'A Happy Birthday' on it for me?"

"It's a nice pot," said Owl, looking at it all round. "Couldn't I give it too? From both of us?"

"No," said Pooh. "That would *not* be a good plan. Now I'll just wash it first, and then you can write on it."

Well, he washed the pot out, and dried it, while Owl licked the end of his pencil, and wondered how to spell "birthday".

"Can you read, Pooh?" he asked, a little anxiously. "There's a notice about knocking and ringing outside my door, which Christopher Robin wrote. Could you read it?"

"Christopher Robin told me what it said, and *then* I could."

"Well, I'll tell you what *this* says, and then you'll be able to."

So Owl wrote . . . and this is what he wrote:

HIPY PAPY BTHUTHDTH THUTHDA BTHUTHDY.

Pooh looked on admiringly.

"I'm just saying 'A Happy Birthday'," said Owl carelessly.

"It's a nice long one," said Pooh, very much impressed by it.

"Well, *actually,* of course, I'm saying 'A Very Happy Birthday with love from Pooh.' Naturally it takes a good deal of pencil to say a long thing like that."

"Oh, I see," said Pooh.

While all this was happening, Piglet had gone back to his own house to get Eeyore's balloon. He held it very tightly against himself, so that it shouldn't blow away, and he ran as fast as he could so as to get to Eeyore before Pooh did; for he thought that he would like to be the first one to give a present, just as if he had thought of it without being told by anybody. And running along, and thinking how pleased Eeyore would be, he didn't look where

he was going . . . and suddenly he put his foot in a rabbit hole, and fell down flat on his face.

BANG!!!???***!!!

Piglet lay there, wondering what had happened. At first he thought that the whole world had blown up; and then he thought that perhaps only the Forest part of it had; and then he thought that perhaps only *he* had, and he was now alone on the moon or somewhere, and would never see Christopher Robin or Pooh or Eeyore again. And then he thought, "Well, even if I'm on the moon, I needn't be face downwards all the time," so he got cautiously up and looked about him.

He was still in the Forest!

"Well, that's funny," he thought. "I wonder what that bang was. I couldn't have made such a noise just falling down. And where's my balloon? And what's that small piece of damp rag doing?"

It was the balloon!

"Oh, dear!" said Piglet. "Oh, dear, oh, dearie, dearie, dear! Well, it's too late now. I can't go back, and I haven't another balloon, and perhaps Eeyore doesn't *like* balloons so *very* much."

So he trotted on, rather sadly now, and down he came to the side of the stream where Eeyore was, and called out to him.

"Good morning, Eeyore," shouted Piglet.

"Good morning, Little Piglet," said Eeyore. "If it *is* a good morning," he said. "Which I doubt," said he. "Not that it matters," he said.

"Many happy returns of the day," said Piglet, having now got closer.

Eeyore stopped looking at himself in the stream, and turned to stare at Piglet.

"Just say that again," he said.

"Many hap——"

"Wait a moment."

Balancing on three legs, he began to bring his fourth leg very cautiously up to his ear. "I did this yesterday," he explained, as he fell down for the third time. "It's quite easy. It's so as I can hear better. . . . There, that's done it! Now then, what were you saying?" He pushed his ear forward with his hoof.

"Many happy returns of the day," said Piglet again.

"Meaning me?"

"Of course, Eeyore."

"My birthday?"

"Yes."

"Me having a real birthday?"

"Yes, Eeyore, and I've brought you a present."

Eeyore took down his right hoof from his right ear, turned round, and with great difficulty put up his left hoof.

"I must have that in the other ear," he said. "Now then."

"A present," said Piglet very loudly.

"Meaning me again?"

"Yes."

"My birthday still?"

"Of course, Eeyore."

"Me going on having a real birthday?"

"Yes, Eeyore, and I brought you a balloon."

"*Balloon?*" said Eeyore. "You did say balloon? One of those big coloured things you blow up? Gaiety, song-and-dance, here we are and there we are?"

"Yes, but I'm afraid — I'm very sorry, Eeyore — but when I was running along to bring it you, I fell down."

"Dear, dear, how unlucky! You ran too fast, I expect. You didn't hurt yourself, Little Piglet?"

"No, but I — I — oh, Eeyore, I burst the balloon!"

There was a very long silence.

"My balloon?" said Eeyore at last.

Piglet nodded.

"My birthday balloon?"

"Yes, Eeyore," said Piglet, sniffing a little. "Here it is. With — with many happy returns of the day." And he gave Eeyore the small piece of damp rag.

"Is this it?" said Eeyore, a little surprised.

Piglet nodded.

"My present?"

Piglet nodded again.

"The balloon?"

"Yes."

"Thank you, Piglet," said Eeyore. "You don't mind my asking," he went on, "but what colour was this balloon when it — when it *was* a balloon?"

"Red."

"I just wondered. . . . Red," he murmured to himself. "My favourite colour. . . . How big was it?"

"About as big as me."

"I just wondered. . . . About as big as Piglet," he said to himself sadly. "My favourite size. Well, well."

Piglet felt very miserable, and didn't know what to say. He was still opening his mouth to begin something, and then deciding that it wasn't any good saying *that*, when he heard a shout from the other side of the river, and there was Pooh.

"Many happy returns of the day," called out Pooh, forgetting that he had said it already.

"Thank you, Pooh, I'm having them," said Eeyore gloomily.

"I've brought you a little present," said Pooh excitedly.

"I've had it," said Eeyore.

Pooh had now splashed across the stream to Eeyore, and Piglet was sitting a little way off, his head in his paws, snuffling to himself.

"It's a Useful Pot," said Pooh. "Here it is. And it's got 'A Very Happy Birthday with love from Pooh' written on it. That's what all that writing is. And it's for putting things in. There!"

When Eeyore saw the pot, he became quite excited.

"Why!" he said. "I believe my Balloon will just go into that Pot!"

"Oh, no, Eeyore," said Pooh. "Balloons are much too big to go into Pots. What you do with a balloon is, you hold the balloon —"

"Not mine," said Eeyore proudly. "Look, Piglet!" And as Piglet looked sorrowfully round, Eeyore picked the balloon up with his teeth, and placed it carefully in the pot; picked it out and put it on the ground; and then picked it up again and put it carefully back.

"So it does!" said Pooh. "It goes in!"

"So it does!" said Piglet. "And it comes out!"

"Doesn't it?" said Eeyore. "It goes in and out like anything."

"I'm very glad," said Pooh happily, "that I thought of giving you a Useful Pot to put things in."

"I'm very glad," said Piglet happily, "that I thought of giving you Something to put in a Useful Pot."

But Eeyore wasn't listening. He was taking the balloon out, and putting it back again, as happy as could be. . . .

"And didn't *I* give him anything?" asked Christopher Robin sadly.

"Of course you did," I said. "You gave him — don't you remember — a little — a little —"

"I gave him a box of paints to paint things with."

"That was it."

"Why didn't I give it to him in the morning?"

"You were so busy getting his party ready for him. He had a cake with icing on the top, and three candles, and his name in pink sugar, and —"

"Yes, *I* remember," said Christopher Robin.

SPIKE MILLIGAN
My Sister Laura

My sister Laura's bigger than me
And lifts me up quite easily.
I can't lift her, I've tried and tried;
She must have something heavy inside.

JOSÉ MARIA SANCHEZ-SILVA

Our family once knew a boy — let's call him Timmy. When he was about eight he had to go to a new school. Now Timmy was very much attached to a small stuffed bear that he'd had since he was three. He wanted very much to take the bear to school with him on the first day but he was ashamed to do so because he thought the other boys and girls would laugh at him. But his mother said, "Take it anyway." So he did. And when he and his mother reached school on opening day they found that about half of all the other children also had stuffed animals with them. Timmy felt better.

When we are very young we need friends who aren't necessarily people and to whom we can say anything — pets, toys, even an object. When I was four I carried everywhere I went a handsome steel "shooter" for playing marbles. Without my shooter I would have felt lonely. With it I didn't.

The Spanish writer Sanchez-Silva has written a book called *The Boy and the Whale*. The title says everything: it's about a boy who had a pet whale that could change its size. Here is the first chapter, which is enough to get you into the story. The rest of it tells about other adventures that the boy and the whale had together. And it ends when the boy grows too old for the whale and has to say good-bye to her.

The Boy and the Whale

Translated from the Spanish by Michael Heron

THE BOY was a boy like most other boys. He lived in Madrid with his family, and he had a Grandmother, a Father, a Mother, a Sister and a Whale.

His Grandmother was old and wise. She had very good hearing, so good that sometimes she could even hear what the Boy was thinking.

The Boy rarely saw his Father, because his Father was still asleep when he got up. Later, when the Boy came home from school for lunch, his Father was still at the office, and when he came home in the afternoon his Father had gone back to the office. When his Father came home at last, tired out, the Boy had gone to bed.

His Mother was a special person; she was someone with whom he was always safe, especially when he was frightened or hurt. The Boy loved her very much when she was there, but sometimes he would forget her and when he realized it, he used to run and find her and give her a kiss.

"What an affectionate child he is!" said his Grandmother.

The Boy's Sister was hardly anything at all, she was so small. When she was born and they had shown her to him, all red and covered with down, the Boy thought, "I'd rather have my Whale."

Indeed, the Whale was not quite as ordinary as the rest of the family. There was something rather mysterious about her. She was like all other whales, as whales go, except for one detail — she could make herself large or small as the Boy wanted. At her biggest she weighed a million tons and was almost a mile long; at her smallest she fitted into his pocket. But if he wanted she could also be the size of a dog, a horse or an elephant.

The Whale was the Boy's very own. He could not remember how long he had had her; she had always been with him. Perhaps she had been born at the same time as he was?

One of the Boy's favourite places for playing with his Whale was under the table in the sewing room. But he kept her with him all the time and at night he left her in a glass of water on his bedside table. It was very simple. When the Boy went to bed he opened his hand above the glass and said, "Good night, Whale."

When he got up in the morning he closed his hand above the glass and said, "Time to get up, Whale."

On some nights he was so sleepy that he didn't have time to leave his Whale in the water and he went to sleep with her clasped in his hand. When this happened he had nice dreams.

The Boy had never been very interested in toys, but when he did play with them his Whale played, too. The Boy wasn't very old, but for several years now he had been seen, both at home and in the street, trailing a piece of string. And *he* knew perfectly well that at the other end of the string was — the Whale.

Sometimes when he said his prayers he prayed for his Whale as well. It was so wonderful to have a Whale!

While the Boy's Sister was still a baby the Whale and he used to play with her very gently, although once she fell out of the Boy's arms and if it hadn't been for the Whale, who got underneath at once and caught her, heaven only knows what would have happened.

Later, between them, they made her laugh. You should have

seen the funny positions the Whale could get into. She could stand on her tail, she could stand on her head and she could walk along on her tail and both fins, looking like a lobster. That made his Sister laugh most of all because of the clumsy hops the Whale had to make. And little by little the Boy and his Whale showed her how to walk, on those rare occasions when there was no one else in the house except the Grandmother, who kept dropping off to sleep. Then the Boy and his Whale used to play with the Sister, but very, very quietly.

If the Sister laughed they could go on, but when she stopped it was better to run away quickly, because a flood of tears, like a storm, was very close.

And when the storm came the Grandmother would wake up and wonder what was the matter.

"What's wrong with my darling? She was sleeping so peacefully and I was sitting here watching her all the time. Let's see, let's see."

And she changed the baby's napkin, but that didn't help. She shook up the pillow in the cot, but that didn't help either. And in desperation she had to pick her up.

A few years later, quite suddenly, the Boy realized that his Sister was no longer a baby and he tried to share his games with her. For a long time he had been finding it hard to keep the Whale a secret, and finally his willpower gave way and he told her. She pulled a very odd face.

"Where is she?" she asked.

"Well, no one can see her," said the Boy.

"What's her name?"

The Boy remembered that his Whale didn't have a name. She was simply called the Whale. But perhaps that was not fair, he thought, so he said the first name that came into his head.

"She's called Josefina."

That seemed to impress his Sister. It was quite different if the Whale was called Josefina.

The Boy told himself that he would only call the Whale Josefina when he was talking to his Sister; on his own he would go on calling her just the Whale.

But he had forgotten what chatterboxes little girls are. On Sunday at lunchtime, in front of everybody, she pointed at him with her spoon and shouted, "He's got a whale!"

His Father thought she was talking about some sort of insect and asked in alarm, "Where?"

His Grandmother chuckled and when his Father realized that no one could carry a whale around he merely said: "What nonsense!" And he took a sip of soda water.

Meanwhile the Boy flashed a look at his Sister which said, "You'd better watch out."

But he had forgotten that the Whale might have an opinion about her new name. When lunch was over and he was searching for his Sister to carry out his threat, he joined the Whale under the table in the sewing room and this is what he heard: "Do you know something? I quite like the name Josefina."

Although she didn't say much the Whale did talk on important occasions. The first time the Boy heard her was when he wondered out loud if whales could jump.

"Yes, we can jump," said the Whale.

"Do you speak Spanish?" asked the Boy after a long pause.

And the Whale, who was as old and wise as the Boy's Grandmother, replied very good-temperedly, "No."

From that day the Whale used to tell him stories, although they were always shorter than the Boy would have liked. In the very first story she tried to explain something about how whales lived.

While the Boy was busy talking to the Whale under the table, his

Sister came into the sewing room and settled down to play with her dolls. The Boy got up very quietly, jumped out at her, and smacked her for telling tales. Then he pulled her hair for luck. The little girl screamed and yelled, and the Grandmother appeared quickly to make peace. His Sister was carried out in her Grandmother's arms, but quite suddenly she jumped down, ran back to the sewing room and, crimson with rage, shouted from the door, "Josefina isn't real, Josefina isn't real!"

"Don't take any notice," said the Whale.

The Boy was still very small when he learned that whales really live in the sea, but the Boy had never been to the seaside. Although the Whale explained it all very carefully, he could hardly believe that the sea had more water in it than a thousand million bathrooms with the bathtubs overflowing.

The Boy had never seen the sea because he lived in Madrid (in the middle of Spain) and his family also had a house in Torrelodones, a place nearby which is cool in summer. But the Whale took him to the sea one night.

In the sea the Whale made herself enormous without being asked, and the Boy rode on her back, which was as firm and comfortable as a mattress. After that they went to sea when he wanted to be alone with the Whale, because what the Boy liked best of all in the world was to be an island. With the Boy perched on top, the two of them, surrounded by the water in the darkness, used to talk, play and think, without anyone bothering them. Except his Grandmother, who sometimes spied his head among the waves and said, "Suppertime," or "Time to go to bed."

If it was raining heavily the Boy climbed into the Whale's mouth. Then, on the high seas, with the Whale her real size, the boy could shelter safely. He thought — and it was perfectly true — that her mouth was as big as, if not bigger than, the living room at home. It would even have held the two pianos (his and his Grandmother's) which had to be left outside in the passage.

His Mother and Father knew nothing about the Whale. Once, and once only, the Boy had told his Mother, "Mummy, I've got a whale in my glass."

But luckily for him he said it when he was ill in bed and his Mother called his Grandmother saying, "Fetch the thermometer, quickly!"

It was a different matter with his Grandmother. I've already told you that the Boy's Grandmother sometimes heard his thoughts. She also heard everything that was said in the house and the house next door, and in the house at Torrelodones and the house next door to that as well. He had no need to tell her that he had a whale.

Almost before he knew how to read, his Grandmother had given him a book about animals with pictures and photographs of whales showing their fins looking like ears. The Boy was fascinated by it and often used to ask her, "Grandmother, tell me more about whales."

First of all she told him that they spouted up great jets of water.

"Steam," corrected the Whale when the Boy told her what he knew.

And it was this remark which was to blame for what happened next day in the shower. The bathroom was another of the Boy's favourite places for playing with the Whale, for it is a place you can have to yourself for a while. Once he had ordered her to make herself big in there and he had had to squash himself against the wall to let her grow. Suddenly he was frightened and had to shout quickly, "Make yourself small!"

But worse was to come, for on this day he did not dare to ask her to make herself big, and he decided to play by himself. He climbed up on two chairs and arranged them so that he could swivel the shower head upwards; then he turned on the water. It did not much look like a whale blowing, but it made a mess of the bathroom and cost him a smacking from his Father and a day without his favourite pudding.

It was not that his Grandmother knew such a lot about whales, but she did her very best because she really loved her grandson.

"Did Grandfather know much more about whales than you?" asked the Boy.

"Well, not really. What your Grandfather was really interested in was partridges."

And so his poor Grandmother racked her brains to find things to tell him about whales and, between what she remembered from her childhood and what she found out secretly from her friends and relations, she always had some piece of information. She also had a whole collection of whale stories to tell him.

One story was about Saint Brendan and the island which later turned out to be a whale. This story made a great impression on the Boy. But the first story was the one about the prophet Jonah who was carried off by a whale to take a message from God to the city of Nineveh. He liked that one, too.

The story of Sinbad the Sailor, which she also told him, was rather like the one about the island of Saint Brendan but he did not like it as much. He liked some of her other stories though.

One afternoon his Grandmother asked, "You're very fond of whales, aren't you?"

The Boy's eyes shone and he said very slowly, "Yes, I've got one."

"Have you?"

The light died out of his eyes. "But you can't see her." His Grandmother understood perfectly: she was at the age when people understand.

"Of course I can't," she said, "because I'm grown up."

The Boy looked doubtful.

"Yes. That's the only reason," and she sighed. "If only I could turn myself into a little girl again!"

"What would happen?"

"I'd be able to see her."

"And what would you do?"

"I would ask her to take good care of you."

"Can I tell her that?"

"Yes. And give her my kind regards."

At that moment the Whale said, "Wish her the same from me."

But his Grandmother did not hear and the Boy had fallen asleep.

It was very hot that summer and the family had to stay in Madrid. The Boy made an awful fuss about his afternoon rest and his Grandmother told him stories to help him to go to sleep. One day when she had told him the last story and thought that he was asleep, she crept out of the room very carefully and shut the door.

But the Boy was not asleep. It was terribly hot and the Whale said with a yawn, "I do wish we were in Torrelodones!"

MAURICE SENDAK

I like everything printed in these books. But perhaps you won't, or you'll like some things much more than you do others. So don't pay too much attention to me when I say that I think Maurice Sendak's picture books are the best now being made in the whole world.

When *Where the Wild Things Are* first came out one grown-up said, "Boys and girls may have to shield their parents from this book. Parents are very easily scared." He meant that as a joke, I guess. But not entirely.

At any rate millions of children seem to have liked *Where the Wild Things Are*. One eight-year-old boy wrote Mr. Sendak a letter. It said: "How much does it cost to get to where the wild things are? If it is not too expensive my sister and I want to spend the summer there. Please answer soon."[*]

If you like *Where the Wild Things Are*, try to get some other Sendak books. I like especially *In the Night Kitchen* and *Outside Over There*. Also, there's a teeny package called *The Nutshell Library*, made up of four very small books. Right after *Where the Wild Things Are* you'll find something from *The Nutshell Library* called "Chicken Soup with Rice."

Our two children, when they were small, used to sing, shout, roar, scream, and yell "Chicken Soup" hour after hour. When this happened their mother and I used to wish Mr. Sendak had never been born.

But now I'm glad he was.

He lives in the country in the state of Connecticut and spends a lot of time with three very large dogs. He draws and paints to classical music on his record player but he does his writing in a silent room, with earplugs in his ears. It took him a year and a half to write the 185 words that make up his latest book, *Outside Over There*. But they are very good words.

Here's *Where the Wild Things Are*.

[*]Quoted in Selma Lanes, *The Art of Maurice Sendak* (New York: Harry N. Abrams, 1980), page 107.

WHERE THE WILD THINGS ARE
STORY AND PICTURES BY MAURICE SENDAK

THE NIGHT Max wore his wolf suit and made mischief of one kind and another his mother called him "WILD THING!" and Max said "I'LL EAT YOU UP!"

so he was sent to bed without eating anything.

That very night in Max's room a forest grew and grew — and
grew until his ceiling hung with vines and the walls became the

world all around and an ocean tumbled by with a private boat for Max and he sailed off through night and day and in and out of weeks and almost over a year to where the wild things are.

And when he came to the place where the wild things are they roared their terrible roars and gnashed their terrible teeth and rolled their terrible eyes and showed their terrible claws till Max

said "BE STILL!" and tamed them with the magic trick of staring into all their yellow eyes without blinking once and they were frightened and called him the most wild thing of all and made him king of all wild things.

"And now," cried Max, "let the wild rumpus start!"

"Now stop!" Max said and sent the wild things off to bed without their supper. And Max the king of all wild things was lonely and wanted to be where someone loved him best of all.

Then all around from far away across the world he smelled good things to eat so he gave up being king of where the wild things are.

But the wild things cried, "Oh please don't go — we'll eat you up — we love you so!"

And Max said, "No!"

The wild things roared their terrible roars and gnashed their terrible teeth and rolled their terrible eyes and showed their terrible claws but Max stepped into his private boat and waved good-bye and sailed back over a year and in and out of weeks and through a day and into the night of his very own room where he found his supper waiting for him and it was still hot.

CHICKEN SOUP WITH RICE

JANUARY

In January it's so nice
while slipping on the sliding ice
to sip hot chicken soup with rice.
Sipping once sipping twice
sipping chicken soup with rice.

FEBRUARY

In February it will be
my snowman's anniversary
with cake for him and soup for me!
Happy once happy twice
happy chicken soup with rice.

MARCH

In March the wind blows down the door
and spills my soup upon the floor.
It laps it up and roars for more.
Blowing once blowing twice
blowing chicken soup with rice.

APRIL

In April I will go away
to far off Spain or old Bombay
and dream about hot soup all day.
Oh my oh once oh my oh twice
oh my oh chicken soup with rice.

MAY

In May I truly think it best
to be a robin lightly dressed
concocting soup inside my nest.
Mix it once mix it twice
mix that chicken soup with rice.

JUNE

In June I saw a charming group
of roses all begin to droop.
I pepped them up with chicken soup!
Sprinkle once sprinkle twice
sprinkle chicken soup with rice.

JULY

In July I'll take a peep
into the cool and fishy deep
where chicken soup is selling cheap.
Selling once selling twice
selling chicken soup with rice.

AUGUST

In August it will be so hot
I will become a cooking pot
cooking soup of course. Why not?
Cooking once cooking twice
cooking chicken soup with rice.

SEPTEMBER

In September for a while
I will ride a crocodile
down the chicken soupy Nile.
Paddle once paddle twice
paddle chicken soup with rice.

OCTOBER

In October I'll be host
to witches, goblins, and a ghost.
I'll serve them chicken soup on toast.
Whoopy once whoopy twice
whoopy chicken soup with rice.

NOVEMBER

In November's gusty gale
I will flop my flippy tail
and spout hot soup. I'll be a whale!
Spouting once spouting twice
spouting chicken soup with rice.

DECEMBER

In December I will be
a baubled bangled Christmas tree
with soup bowls draped all over me.
Merry once merry twice
merry chicken soup with rice.

Index of Titles

Index of Contributors

Page numbers in *italics* indicate illustrations

Index of First Lines

A birdie with a yellow bill, 157
A blue day, 321
A buttery, sugary, syrupy waffle, 51
A cat came fiddling out of a barn, 4
A diller, a dollar, 4
A wise old owl sat in an oak, 5
Alas! Alas! for Miss Mackay!, 5
Alligator pie, alligator pie, 119
As a friend to the children commend me
    the Yak, 190
As I was crossing Boston Common, 322
As I was standing in the street, 50
As Tommy Snooks and Bessy Brooks, 5
Awake, arise, 5

Baa, baa, black sheep, 6
Bananas and cream, 379
Barber, barber, shave a pig, 6
Betty Botter bought some butter, 6

Come, let's to bed, 7

Daddy's back, 311
Desperate Dan, 7
Diddle, diddle, dumpling, my son John, 7
Ding, dong bell, 8
Doctor Foster went to Gloucester, 8

Elevator operator, 264
Every time I climb a tree, 376

For want of a nail, 8

G stands for Gnu, whose weapons
    of Defense, 188
Georgie Porgie, pudding and pie, 9
Goosey, goosey gander, 9

Hark, hark, 9
Here am I, 9
Here's Tom Thumb, 10
Hey diddle, diddle, 10
Hickory, dickory, dock, 10
Higglety, pigglety, pop!, 10
Hot cross buns! Hot cross buns!, 11
How do you like to go up in a swing, 157
How many miles to Babylon?, 11
Humpty Dumpty sat on a wall, 11

I always eat peas with honey, 51
I can't fall asleep, 448
I had a little castle upon the sea sand, 11
I had a little husband, 12
I had a little nut tree, 12
I have a little shadow that goes in and out
    with me, 156
I looked in the mirror, 531
I put on my aqua-lung and plunge, 449
I see the moon, 12
I shoot the Hippopotamus, 189
I was alone the other day, 167
If all the seas were one sea, 13
If all the world was paper, 13
If I'd as much money as I could spend, 13
If you don't put your shoes on before
    I count fifteen then we, 434